CHRISTOPHER HINZ

All my best to
Stuart, a fine writer
and editor.
CHRIS HINZ

SPARTAN X

www.christopherhinz.com

First Print Edition: November 2012

Cover and formatting: Streetlight Graphics

ACKNOWLEDGMENTS

I wish to thank Stuart Moore for applying his keen editorial eye to the manuscript, Glendon Haddix of *Streetlight Graphics* for designing the evocative cover and Etan Ilfeld for his continuing support of my many projects.

I also wish to acknowledge those dedicated fans of the *Paratwa Saga* who were forced to wait far too long for a new novel. May this story reward your patience.

ALSO BY CHRISTOPHER HINZ:

LIEGE-KILLER (Book One of the Paratwa Saga)

ASH OCK (Book Two of the Paratwa Saga)

THE PARATWA (Book Three of the Paratwa Saga)

ANACHRONISMS

Coming soon:

QUIVER X

BINARY (graphic novel)

There is nothing so minute, or inconsiderable, that I would not rather know it than not.

-Samuel Johnson

1

KAYLA ACKERMAN RADIATED BLISS.

NASA wasn't fond of high-energy emotions in this environment. The Agency wanted spacewalkers to maintain an even keel lest they be distracted from the dangers of floating in the void.

Kayla couldn't help how she felt. Here she was, a 39-year-old black woman who had fought her way out of a Los Angeles ghetto to become a geophysicist in orbit, part of the greatest scientific co-op in human history. The International Space Station, a jumble of modules, trusses and solar-panel arrays, was a monument to technological achievement.

Her view of the magnificent Earth 200 miles below was icing on the euphoria cake.

Belgian astronomer Henri Renier floated a few feet away, his thick EVA suit aimed down at the cloudless Northeast.

"Looks like a beautiful morning in New York," he said. "Tourists will be lunching outdoors in Central Park."

"Not for long," Kayla countered, proceeding with her final task of the spacewalk by retrieving a canister of exotic metamaterials from the starboard payload platform. "See that storm brewing over the North Atlantic? Your tourists will be munching on soggy cheeseburgers and waterlogged fries."

"Three months in orbit has made you cynical."

"Three months without a happy meal will do that," she said, eyes twinkling with laughter.

"Kayla, Henri – stop all activity."

Years of training dictated instant obedience to the voice of mission commander and U.S. Air Force pilot Paco Ortiz. He was overseeing their spacewalk from Destiny module, one of the science labs.

"We're stationary," Kayla said, attaching the canister to her utility belt and gripping a rung on the starboard truss. Henri, a few meters away, performed a similar move.

"Unidentified radar blip," Paco said. "In our orbit, a few hundred meters aft. Closure speed just under 20 kilometers per hour."

Paco hesitated, as if receiving more data. When he came back on the line, his voice betrayed tension.

"Houston confirms the object's on a collision course. Impact is projected to be on the rear underside of the starboard array."

Kayla and Henri exchanged wary looks. They were near those solar panels, which blossomed out into the void like symmetrical flowers.

"Time to impact?" she asked.

"Less than a minute. Not enough time to safely move the station or get the two of you inside."

"How big?"

"Two meters in length, roughly cylindrical. Looks like it's tumbling out of control."

Kayla realized they were fortunate the object was in their own orbit, approaching from behind. If something that large slammed into them from the wrong direction, possibly with a closure speed of six of seven miles per second, the results could be devastating.

She had a ton of questions. Foremost was the fact they'd received no alerts.

"SSN didn't spot this until now?"

"Apparently not. Suddenly showed up on everybody's screens."

The Space Surveillance Network tracked thousands of Earth-orbit objects, most of them debris left over from five-plus decades of human exploration. Any object slated to cross the station's orbit should have elicited advance warning.

"Doesn't make sense it could have gotten so close without detection."

"Answer that one, Kayla, and some Space Command general will buy you a month of happy meals."

"Here it comes," Henri said, pointing aft.

Their mysterious visitor had a non-reflective surface a dingy shade of orange, except for one end that was rounded and white. Gently spinning along two axes, the object tumbled relentlessly toward the station.

"Twenty seconds to impact," Paco said. "We have it on video. But I still can't quite make out what it is—"

"A spacesuit," Kayla said, trying to contain her surprise.

The suit's arms hung down against the torso. The legs were pinched together, making the suit appear to be standing at attention. The surface was scarred and the visor so heavily etched it was impossible to see through.

"Looks ancient," Henri said. "More like one of those old high-altitude pressure suits than a contemporary EVA garment."

"Early astronauts wore something like this," Paco agreed. "The Mercury program in the early 1960s used modified versions of Navy jet aircraft gear. Very flimsy stuff."

"But those were silver," Kayla said. "This one's pretty faded, but that orange hue suggests U.S.S.R. I'm guessing it's from the early Soviet space effort."

"Ten seconds to impact," Paco said. "Five... four... three... two..."

The spacesuit intersected the underside of the

array, cracking a small section of solar panels. Glass shards tumbled into the darkness. The suit glanced off the array and assumed a new trajectory. Although the collision had scrubbed its speed, the spacesuit was headed right for them.

Before Kayla could even think to move, the crook of the suit's left arm snagged the shaft of a telecom dish three meters away. Caught on that hook, the suit rotated around the dish like a lazy Susan. Friction finally brought it to a halt with the sandblasted visor pointed directly at them.

"Don't see that every day," she muttered, momentarily at a loss for a more cerebral response. "Anyone else think this is all too weird to be coincidental?"

The suit's mysterious appearance, its slow approach in their own orbit, the way it had caught the telecom dish so close to them... statistically, the odds of those events happening in tandem had to be millions to one.

"Definitely Soviet," Henri said, pointing to faded Cyrillic lettering above the opaque visor. "C-C-C-P. Designation for the old Union of Soviet Socialist Republics."

Now that Kayla was so close to it, she noticed another oddity. "That scarring, I think it's mostly burn marks. Looks like the suit was caught in some sort of fire."

"Does it have an occupant?" Paco asked.

A chill went through Kayla. She hadn't even considered the possibility. A dead cosmonaut in orbit for decades wouldn't be a pretty sight.

"Visor is too scarred," Henri said. "Can't make out if there's a face."

"We need to bring it inside for a closer look," Kayla said, realizing as she uttered the words that her feeling of bliss was a fading memory.

2

CORBET TOMMS HAD A HATE-LOVE relationship with his latest job, which was to sit in Dr. Jarek's office and talk about the most disturbing aspects of his disturbed life.

The office, in an upscale Georgetown row home restored to the splendor of its Colonial-era roots, mimicked a shrink's domain. The brass sign out front reinforced the charade, suggesting that Dr. Abelicus Jarek, Ph.D; PsyD, indeed practiced some form of traditional psychiatry.

Earthy colors dominated the office. Mahogany shelves housed hundreds of reference books. Framed diplomas proclaimed Jarek's psychiatric skills, as well as his expertise in fields ranging from neurology to biomedical engineering. Windows facing the back of the house provided a pleasant view of the old Chesapeake and Ohio canal that flowed where a back alley would be in less auspicious neighborhoods.

Corbet hated coming here several times a week and answering Jarek's probing questions. He hated taking tests to gauge his unusual proficiencies and he hated peeing in a bottle as part of Jarek's random drug testing policy. But most of all, he hated that the Doc believed his special ability was something good, a blessing, a gift.

It was none of those things.

Considering that he was 24 years old and not gainfully employed, however, there was one aspect of the job Corbet loved. For agreeing to be here, he was mailed a generous semimonthly check.

Dr. Jarek hunched forward in his leather armchair and opened today's *Washington Post* to display a page seven headline. The portly doctor, dressed in a rumpled sports jacket and floppy pants, was pushing sixty. But his hands were smooth and delicate, like those of a younger man. He tapped a slender forefinger against the edge of the newspaper, pointing to the story that had snared his attention:

Seven Die in I-395 Smashup.

"I must admit, Corbet, I'm quite impressed. The crash was horrific, the bodies burned beyond recognition. The names of the victims haven't been released. But a Corvette and a minivan were indeed the vehicles involved."

"Told ya."

"Yes you did. And the crash certainly seems like an authentic event."

"I can think of seven corpses who'd agree."

Skepticism crept into Jarek's tone. "However, in my research I've come across numerous charlatans. Some of their tricks are quite sophisticated."

Corbet slouched into the sofa, trying to ignore the insinuation.

"Granted, in your case, deception is highly unlikely. But for the record, I must ask where you were at 9:40 last night when this accident occurred?"

"My apartment. In bed."

"Alone?"

Corbet chuckled. Jarek knew him well enough by now to know what that meant.

"Just one young lady this time?"

"Just one. I was tired." He grinned.

"Does she have a name?"

"Trish."

"Trish what?"

"No idea. We hooked up at The Icicle."

"Is that a nightclub?"

"It's not the Salvation Army."

"I'd like to interview her."

"Not your type, Doc."

"To confirm you were nowhere near the crash site."

"Forget it."

Corbet didn't want to be perceived as being difficult, which might put those paychecks at risk. But interviewing his sex partners crossed the line.

He sat up, smoothed wily strands of brown hair from his brow. "Let me see if I got this straight. Three days ago, I experience a vision. I witness this crash in all its gory detail. I sit here and describe the whole thing to you, correct?"

Jarek nodded.

"Now, do you really think it's even possible I'm faking? That I went out on Interstate 395 last night and somehow caused the driver of a speeding Corvette to lose control, clear the guard rail, and do a head-on into a minivan?"

Jarek shrugged. "As I said, deception is unlikely."

"I'd say impossible."

"Improbable. Very little is impossible."

Corbet settled back into the cushions, adopted a bored expression to signify what he thought of the entire line of questioning. Reading his mood, Jarek folded the newspaper and set it on the coffee table between them.

"All right, why don't we move on. Tell me more about your latest vision. You said it involved a strange creature?"

"Dog-face."

"Not an attractive countenance, I gather."

"One ugly son of a bitch. Freddy Krueger on a bad hair day."

"Freddy Krueger?"

"*Nightmare on Elm Street.* Horror movie?"

Jarek's face remained blank. Corbet figured he didn't get out much.

"Where and when did this vision occur?"

"My apartment. This morning."

Corbet started at the beginning. Jarek didn't just want to hear about a vision, he wanted details of what had preceded and followed it.

"I woke up about 7:30. That's when it happened. And I got to tell you, Doc, it was the weirdest goddamn vision I've ever had."

3

CORBET HAD CLIMBED FROM BED without disturbing Trish, who was swaddled in the sheets like an Egyptian mummy. Donning jeans and a tank top, he'd headed for his apartment's pint-sized kitchen to grind a blend of dark-roast beans for the Cuisinart.

While the coffee brewed, he parted the curtains to check the weather. No clouds this Friday morning, not even a trace of DC's frequent haze. It looked to be another agreeable late spring day in what the more prideful of Washingtonians believed was the Capital of capitals.

He didn't know why he turned to look at the refrigerator at that moment, nor why a souvenir magnet shaped like the Statue of Liberty drew his attention. A dozen other magnets dotted the appliance, four of them cornering a photo of him at age 15, a lanky teen punk garbed head to toe in black. He'd been going through his Goth phase. But the statue magnet was a loner, off in the corner, supporting no photos, notes or other refrigerator riffraff.

The next thing he knew, the vision was upon him.

It was nighttime. He was walking down the middle of a foggy street in the Tribeca neighborhood of Lower Manhattan. In the real world, he'd lived here with his brother Jeremy and an elderly cousin after the death of their parents when he was 12, back before his brother had shipped out to the Middle East with an Army special forces unit.

Although he recognized the area, the geography was screwy. From this vantage point, he shouldn't have been able to see the Statue of Liberty in New York Harbor, miles south of the neighborhood.

But there it was, rising majestically from behind a warehouse converted into loft apartments, looking like it was only blocks away. He couldn't make out its entire structure. The pedestal and foundation were hidden by the building and Miss Liberty's head and raised arm with torch were cloaked in fog.

Usually, his visions corresponded to actual events. Whatever he saw ended up happening within the next 72 hours, although occasionally a vision preceded its real-world counterpart by weeks or months. Most visions involved violence and death. The highway crash was a typical example.

However, this vision was surreal, making it different from the hundreds of other psychic experiences that had pummeled him from age 9 onward. It also lacked a greenish hue, an oddity common to many of his visions, as if he was viewing those typically violent events through green-tinted spectacles.

The Statue of Liberty's presence was weird enough. But it couldn't hold a candle to the feral humans creeping through the fog. Men, women and children, caked in dirt and tattered clothes, scampered along on all fours as if they'd lost the ability to walk upright. None seemed aware of Corbet as he strolled past. It was as if he were invisible.

Buildings, overgrown by predatory foliage, appeared long abandoned. Rusted vehicles caked in grime littered the street, some serving as hovels for the feral people. The stink of rotting garbage and excrement was palpable.

He caught an even worse smell, the putrid odor of dead flesh. Nearby, a decomposing body sprawled across the hood of a Mercedes.

His shoe crunched against something hard. But before he could look down, an intense violet light burned through the fog from above.

The eerie glow came from the Statue of Liberty's torch. It illuminated Miss Liberty's face. But the inviting countenance that had welcomed millions of immigrants was now a hideous creature, an unsettling blend of human and canine features. Its creepy black eyes seemed to stare down at Corbet.

"Dog-face," he whispered, giving the monstrosity the first name that popped into his head.

His utterance terminated the vision. And then he was back in his apartment, staring at that fridge magnet and wondering what it all meant.

4

"DOG-FACE?" TRISH EXCLAIMED, SOUNDING OFFENDED. "Is that what you just called me?"

Corbet whirled, startled by her voice. He didn't know how long he'd been in la-la land. Visions didn't necessarily align with the passage of time in the real world. But considering that Trish stood by the front door, dressed and ready to leave, he'd been gone at least several minutes.

"Sorry," he said. And then he realized the apology implied that he had uttered the name in reference to her. "I wasn't talking about you. I was... lost in thought, dwelling on something else."

"You were like totally zoned out. I thought maybe you were having a seizure or something."

"I'm fine."

"I gotta go. Listen, I had a great time last night. We definitely should do it again. How about dinner at my place, tomorrow night? I bake a mean ravioli."

Corbet didn't try to hide his disappointment. As he'd done numerous times over the years when a sexual partner wanted to build upon a one-nighter, he pitched his voice to project indifference.

"That's probably not such a good idea."

She looked baffled. Then his words and expression hit home. She put up a brave front but it was obvious the rejection stung.

Corbet hated when he had to play the bad guy and ruthlessly cut the cord. But being forthright about dumping them was better than leading them on with vague promises.

She walked out the door without another word. Relief washed over him. She had accepted that they wouldn't be seeing one another again. He'd hurt her feelings but she was a big girl. She'd get over it.

He'd liked Trish. A lot. They'd had a good time after connecting at the nightclub last night, an even better time in bed. But seeing a woman more than once risked the possibility of a relationship.

That was not going to happen.

5

"PRETTY BIZARRE, HUH?" CORBET SAID to Dr. Jarek as he finished describing the vision and his final encounter with Trish.

"Indeed."

The word sounded judgmental, directed more at Corbet's pathological aversion to relationships than at the vision. He was used to being criticized for his one-night-stand lifestyle. And coming from the Doc, a married man for 30-plus years, such a reaction wasn't unexpected.

"But what do you think the vision means?" he prodded.

"Hard to say. Doesn't sound like one of your typical precognitive experiences."

"Yeah, more like a weird dream. Sure hope it was a dream, considering that my visions always come true."

"Dream symbolism can be challenging to decipher. I'm not a Jungian analyst or specialist in that area. I suspect, however, that only you, the dreamer, can unravel the symbols and uncover the hidden meaning."

"I couldn't make sense out of it. Frankly, not sure I'd want to."

Corbet could tell Jarek had little interest in pursuing the matter. The bizarre experience was too much of a departure from Corbet's "normal" visions, the ones adhering to real-world events. Dreams were too vague for Jarek's "just the facts, ma'am" brain.

The Doc wanted the verifiable. He wanted

specifics – the who, what, when, where, and how of a supersensory experience. He believed that many psychics were charlatans who employed their so-called powers in ways that eluded the cold light of scientific measurement. He had no interest in what he called the psychic rabble: spiritualists, crystal gazers, ghost trackers and voyagers to the astral plane.

In all likelihood, Corbet had simply experienced a weird dream. Maybe he'd still been tired from that late-night romp in the sack with Trish. Gazing at that fridge magnet might have plunged his brain into a brief REM cycle, where dreaming took place.

But whatever had happened, it had left an ominous aftertaste. He had the strangest feeling that the world had undergone an axial shift and that his life would never again be the same.

6

THE 43-FOOT-LONG RUSSIAN SERVICE MODULE, Zvezda, was situated at the aft end of the International Space Station. Its foldout kitchen table was being used for a purpose not envisioned by its builders.

The mysterious spacesuit rested on the table. Kayla floated above it, live video from her handheld camera patched through to Destiny Lab and Houston mission control. She was documenting the efforts of Henri and Russian physician Valentin Anikeyev to clear the sandblasted visor by rubbing it with mild acid washes.

NASA, ever cautious, had dictated that Paco and the fifth crew member, Japanese engineer Tanizaki

Kisho, remain in Destiny module. Their crew originally had numbered six, but one astronaut had returned to Earth early on a Russian Soyuz spacecraft because of a death in the family.

"Making progress," Henri announced, dabbing more acid on the scarred faceplate, trying to restore a semblance of transparency. "We should get a look at the occupant very soon."

That the suit indeed held an occupant had become apparent once Kayla and Henri had freed it from the telecom shaft and maneuvered it through the airlock. It possessed bulk, discernible even in microgravity.

Paco came over the intercom. "The Russians believe the suit's from Vostok, from an early test program. In 1960, two Vostok rockets blew up post-launch. At least one of them achieved orbit. The capsules contained test animals, including dogs, probably Siberian huskies or huskie-mixes. They might also have held mannequins in spacesuits."

"Which no doubt is what this suit contains," Valentin said. "Back then, we knew very little about human survival in space. Sending up test dummies to measure radiation and zero-G effects was logical. Not until the following year did Yuri Gagarin make his historic flight."

Kayla kept silent. Valentin, being Russian, perhaps had a personal stake in the veracity of that theory. But she'd heard rumors of a more ominous possibility, that the former U.S.S.R. had secretly put cosmonauts aboard early flights prior to launching Gagarin, the first man in space. Unlike the Americans, the Soviets had divulged their early space efforts to the world only if the missions proved successful. Had a cosmonaut died aboard an early flight, the fact likely would have become a state secret.

Still, glasnost had parted some curtains of the

primordial Soviet space program and no evidence to support such rumors had been unearthed. Most historians dismissed them as urban legends, Cold War remnants of a once superheated space race.

"I'm getting transparency," Henri announced. "The debris scarring has less depth than initially presumed. I can see a mouth..."

He trailed off, astonished.

"My god. What is that?"

Kayla had no idea. It was the creepiest face she'd ever seen, a ghastly blend of human and canine features.

White, pelt-like hair drooped across large jutting ears. Its nose was a black knob with gaping nostrils. The eyes, thankfully shut, were ringed by dark fur. Yet the lips were recognizably human, as was the cracked and shriveled skin.

They all stared at the face, too stunned to comment. Valentin broke the silence.

"Looks like extreme rigor mortis. Almost as if mummified."

"Are there traces found of blood or internal fluids?" Tanizaki asked, his English perfect except for the occasional syntactic burp.

Henri shined a penlight on the face. "Nothing."

Paco, who had been talking to NASA on another line, returned to the intercom.

"Okay, listen up. The Russians believe there may be a serial number, possibly on the back of the helmet."

Henri and Valentin lifted the head and gently twisted the neck, leaned in for a closer view.

"Got something," Henri said. "It's scarred, but definitely a numeric imprint. I read it as three-alpha-five-seven-two—"

Kayla's scream drowned out the rest of his words.

"Its eyes! Look at the eyes!"

The men lowered the head and examined the face. The eyes were closed, everything as it should be. Henri turned to her with a frown.

"It opened its eyes!" she insisted. "Somehow, it must still be..."

She stopped herself from finishing the thought. They were already looking at her like she was crazy.

"My camera! Check the recording!"

"Doing it now," Paco said.

Kayla's apprehension grew. She was sure of what she'd seen. For just an instant, the dog-faced creature had opened its eyes. Strange black orbs, devoid of irises and pupils, had gazed directly up at her.

"Nothing on video," Paco said. "You must have moved the camera at that moment. All we have is a shot of Henri's back."

"I know what I saw. We need to open the suit, check for organic activity."

There was another long pause on the intercom as Paco conferred with ground control.

"Negative on that request," he said finally. "NASA wants us to suspend the examination."

"What? That's crazy! We have to verify what I saw. We have to open the suit."

"What we have to do is slow down, think this through, give Houston time to come up with a game plan."

"A game plan!" Kayla drew a deep breath, forced calm.. A strident voice and fanatic attitude wouldn't help her case.

"I think NASA is right," Henri said. "There could be a contamination threat. We should isolate the suit before we even consider opening it."

Paco agreed. "Let's vacate Zvezda and seal the module. Kayla, rig your camera so we can keep an eye on this... whatever the hell it is."

She had to admit that what they were proposing made sense. And she couldn't blame them for not believing her. If the situation was reversed, she would have been expressing similar doubts.

But she knew what she had seen.

7

DR. JAREK CLAIMED THAT THE extensive interviews with Corbet and other individuals possessing supersensory abilities were part of a classified research initiative underwritten by the federal government. Corbet had been made to sign a nondisclosure document prior to receiving his first paycheck.

But from the beginning he'd had doubts about the purpose of the interviews. He suspected there was a hidden agenda, that these sessions involved more than just collecting information on psychic freaks like himself.

Jarek's phone vibrated on the coffee table. He frowned as he read the message.

"I'm sorry, but something's come up. We'll have to end early today."

He stood, ushered Corbet toward the door. "Why don't we reschedule for tomorrow."

"It's Saturday."

"I can double your fee for coming in over the weekend."

"You're cool, Doc."

He gave Jarek a friendly pat on the back as they proceeded into the hallway and toward the exit that led to the front reception area. Corbet couldn't resist a backward glance to the strange door at the other end of the corridor. Made of steel, it had an inset rectangular screen – definitely some sort of biometric lock. Judging by the house's exterior dimensions, the mystery door accessed a space no larger than four feet by four feet. Jarek said it was a closet for storing classified patient files.

Except it wasn't a closet. The Doc might be whip smart but he didn't have a poker face. Corbet knew he was lying. Something else lay beyond that door.

As they reached the exit, Corbet's thoughts turned to a more pressing matter.

"Speaking of money, I'm a little short this week. I was wondering if you'd be willing to let me have another advance."

"Certainly. See Mildred on your way out. Tell her I okayed it."

Corbet smiled. It was the third advance he'd requested since beginning the sessions, and the third one granted without so much as a question or comment. The Doc not only had secrets, he had money to burn.

As Jarke reached for the exit knob, someone yanked the door open from the other side. Corbet's elation over the advance dissolved into anger as he came face to face with a bull of a man in Army uniform.

Robert Mavenhall had been an Army special forces lieutenant when Corbet first encountered him. Several promotions later, he was a colonel, proving Corbet's contention that in all walks of life, being an asshole was no boundary to advancement.

It had been years since their last confrontation. The colonel's buzz-cut red hair was now edged with gray. His chin had developed early hints of a jowl.

"Hello, Corbet."

The voice was friendly. But the cold eyes suggested that Mavenhall regarded him as little more than a pesky insect.

Corbet confronted Jarek. "What the hell's this asshole doing here?"

"Colonel Mavenhall is involved in my research."

"Better stock up on the body bags. The colonel tends to bring 'em home dead."

Mavenhall ignored the cryptic insult and pushed past Corbet into the hallway.

"Tomorrow then," Jarek said, holding the spring-loaded exit open for Corbet. "Same time?"

"Works for me."

Corbet exited but stuck his fingers in the jamb to prevent the door from closing all the way. He peered through the crack as Jarek and Mavenhall approached the mystery door and placed their hands on the biometric screen. The lock scanned their palms. With a faint hiss of hydraulics, the door slid open. Beyond, a compact staircase spiraled toward the basement.

The men descended as the door closed. Corbet stifled his curiosity and proceeded to the reception area, the domain of Mildred DeTurk.

8

"MILDRED!" HE EXCLAIMED, TURNING ON the charm. "Did I mention when I came in this morning that you're looking exceptionally fine today."

She wore a polka-dot dress and drooping bifocals. Studiously reading an AARP magazine, she reminded

Corbet of an old-fashioned schoolmarm from the pages of some ancient high school yearbook.

She sat in a tiny receptionist's office that overlooked the small waiting room. As usual, no one was there. Since Jarek didn't have a real psychiatric practice, there were never any patients, nor the need for a more discreet entry-exit system to maintain patient confidentiality.

Mildred knew what he wanted and wasn't fooled by the flattery. "We've already given you two advances. Dr. Jarek isn't running an ATM."

"The Doc said to tell you it's okay."

She grimaced as if the cash was coming out of her own pocket.

"Hey, Mildred, come to think of it, how'd you know I want money? You *psychic?*"

She didn't crack a smile. "How much this time?"

"Make it $200. Got a hot date tonight."

Bookmarking her magazine, she withdrew a cashbox from the desk and began counting out 10- and 20-dollar bills.

"Who's the young lady?"

Corbet shrugged. "Haven't met her yet. Catch of the night. What's Colonel Mavenhall doing here?"

"That's classified. You'd better be careful dating all these different women. You could find yourself in a dangerous situation."

"I don't date. I have sex. And don't worry, I've got a strong defensive line. No nine-month blitzes getting through."

"I'm talking about falling in love."

"Ah, romance. The thing is, Mildred, I'm genetically flawed. Something went wrong with my DNA. Got shortchanged on the romantic hormones."

She sneered. Corbet couldn't blame her for not buying his rationale. It was total bullshit and rarely fooled anyone, but he trotted it out anyway whenever somebody challenged his one-night-stand philosophy. Easier than telling the truth, risking a deeper and more painful discussion.

Mildred counted the bills a second time and handed him the money.

"Thanks. Oh, one more thing. That spiral staircase behind the secret door, where does it go?"

"Same place it went yesterday."

"C'mon, tell me what the Doc's really up to. I'll make it worth your while. How's twenty bucks sound?"

Mildred glared. Corbet walked out the front door grinning.

9

"ANY NEWS ABOUT AN ELEVATOR?"

Dr. Jarek posed the question as they stepped off the spiral staircase onto a concrete passageway 80 feet below street level.

"I don't mind going down these steps. But climbing back up... I'm not in the shape I was ten years ago."

Col. Robert Mavenhall doubted that Jarek had ever been in good physical condition. One of the most brilliant minds on the planet yet 50 pounds overweight, he lacked the self-discipline to adhere to a healthy diet and exercise regimen.

"Climbing steps is good for your heart."

Jarek scowled. Mavenhall relented.

"I inserted funds for an elevator in next year's budget. But I wouldn't get my hopes up."

"You can't seriously expect me to believe they can't

find the money?"

Mavenhall spotted a flickering light near a security camera at the far end of the 120-foot passageway. He made a mental note to have one of the Marine guards change it out.

"Not about the money," he continued. "This is a residential neighborhood with more activity than when the agency began back in 1960. Installing an elevator would produce noise and commotion. We've kept this place secret for more than five decades. Not worth the risk of compromising security."

"But we need an elevator."

Three things annoyed Mavenhall the most. Citizens who led the good life in America and still had the audacity to complain was one of them. Sixty years old or not, Jarek needed to suck it up and stop whining.

The other two items on Mavenhall's list were, in no particular order, Americans who lacked national pride and Americans who failed to recognize that taking responsibility for one's actions was the cornerstone of a functioning democracy.

Still, at least Jarek was only an occasional whiner, and only when it came to taking care of his body. Nothing lazy about that genius-level mind. But Corbet Tomms... now there was a walking embodiment of all three sins.

"You should stop wasting time on Corbet. Concentrate on the test subjects we already have."

"He's way above the others," Jarek argued. "Gifted precog, sees things days before they happen. These random visions of his always authenticate."

"Not a team player."

"But he could be the one to make it all the way, qualify for field duty. Let's advance him to the next phase. Bring him down here, see if he can acquire a target."

"I wouldn't trust him to acquire ice cream from a cone."

Jarek gave an acquiescent shrug, unwilling to push the argument.

Mavenhall was Jarek's superior. He could order the scientist to cut Corbet loose. But he loathed using that veto power, particularly in the strange and unsettling arena of psychic research. As Jarek and the other scientists had pointed out, they still knew very little about those rare individuals with verifiable supersensory abilities. Best to keep all options open... even if the option known as Corbet Tomms possessed the maturity level of a self-absorbed child.

They reached the far end of the tunnel. It terminated at another steel door with a biometric lock. Beyond was the headquarters of U-OPS, a tiny agency whose work was as clandestine as the CIA on its blackest night.

10

U-OPS – UNTETHERED OPERATIONS – had been established in late December, 1960, in the waning days of President Eisenhower's administration. Since then, its existence had remained tightly guarded. Even the senators whose black appropriations funded the agency knew little of what went on beneath the unassuming Georgetown house. And only a few officials at the pinnacle of the federal government were privy to the deepest secrets at the heart of U-OPS.

Jarek's psychiatric practice was the agency's latest

front. The cover story, that he treated psychological problems for Homeland Security and Defense Department personnel, provided an explanation for the daily traffic in and out of the building by the researchers and Marine guards.

"Good morning, gentlemen."

Dr. Patrick Appleton, a wisp of a man with blond curls, greeted Mavenhall and Jarek as they entered the circular conference area of the underground facility. They were now standing directly beneath the placid waters of the C&O Canal.

The conference area, ringed by vending machines serviced exclusively by the guards, was nicknamed the Café. Its centerpiece was a large round table bizarrely under the shelter of a yellow beach umbrella. Back in the 1970s, the sprinkler system had malfunctioned, drenching the Café's occupants. Some witty scientist of the era had installed the umbrella.

Surveillance cameras poked down from the ceiling, hardwired to the second-floor security station where the Marine guards were on duty 24/7, ready to respond to trouble. Aside from the sprinkler incident, there'd never been any.

Beyond the Cafe's perimeter, five private laboratory-offices dedicated to various research initiatives could be entered via palm locks.

At first glance, Room Six seemed no different than its neighbors. But looks were deceiving. Room Six was protected by a far more stringent security system, one that employed the latest vascular and facial recognition software, and remote iris-scanning. The biometrics were presently configured to allow access to only three people: Col. Mavenhall, Dr. Jarek and the director of U-OPS, three-star general Juan Carlos Grobbs.

Dr. Appleton was in charge of the psychic initiative, U-OPS's newest program. Using state-of-the-art technology, the program aimed at turning candidates like Corbet into psychic trackers and sending them into the field to locate targets. Like the other researchers, Appleton had no knowledge of U-OPS' deepest secrets, believing that the purpose of the psychic program was to find terrorists and international criminals.

"Abel, I'm glad you're here," Appleton began. "We're doing a target acquisition test. But there seems to be a problem with the new prototype psyts, the 300-series."

Mavenhall checked his watch, nodded to Jarek that they had time. The Room Six telecom computers would still be processing the latest transmission from Preceptor. That transmission was the reason they were down here, the reason Mavenhall had interrupted Jarek's session with Corbet.

Although a message from Preceptor prompted the highest urgency, the computers operated at their own pace. The amount of encoded information in one of Preceptor's transmissions was measured in petabytes – millions of gigabytes – and the custom software needed to process such enormous amounts of data never took less than 30 minutes.

Mavenhall followed Jarek to Room Four, Appleton's compact lab. It was a mess, with papers, books and crushed Pepsi cans strewn across the desk. A workbench bristled with electronic test equipment, circuit boards and computers.

Two wall-mounted Sony monitors displayed live video feeds. The first screen showed a man standing on the path near the old canal, reading an iPad. His name was Higgins. He was Appleton's research assistant and the target for today's psychic test.

The other screen revealed the tracker, a slender ponytailed woman seated alone in a windowless room on the second floor. She wore a pair of thick black goggles with opaque eyepieces the color of sand. In her lap was a large photo of Higgins.

"Subject P-12," Appleton explained, using the woman's code designation. "So far, she's been our best tracker."

"How far apart are target and tracker?" Jarek asked.

"As the crow flies, 278 feet. Just within range for the 300-series."

"So what's the problem?"

"The goggles won't focus. Yet my readouts say they're functioning properly."

Jarek toggled through pages of data on one of the computers. At the fifth screen he experienced a eureka moment.

"It's not the goggles, it's your test subject. Symbiotics aren't aligning. Did you do a drug screening?"

"Not today. She's had addiction issues in the past, but we thought she was over them."

"She's not. I'd guess cocaine, and taken within the last few hours."

Mavenhall wasn't surprised. A high percentage of supersensories suffered from emotional problems, which pushed them toward drugs and alcohol. Substance abuse not only diminished tracking abilities, it rendered them unsuitable for field duty – should any of them even *reach* that stage.

Appleton dialed a number. Onscreen, Higgins pressed a phone to his ear.

"Let's call it a day," Appleton said. "Turns out that Miss P-12 is higher than the Washington Monument."

"Goddamn druggies," Higgins muttered, his voice coming in on speaker.

"Less coddling, more paddling," Mavenhall suggested. The researchers were too lenient with the psychics, allowed them to get away with too much crap. Supersensory test subjects were well paid, even better than individuals like Corbet who'd only reached the candidate stage of the program. Bottom line, they needed better discipline.

Jarek chimed in with an alternate theory. "What we need are drug-free psychics with higher levels of innate talent."

Mavenhall recognized it as another lobbying effort on behalf of Corbet, whose drug screenings had always tested negative. But he saw no upside to reopening that debate.

They left Appleton to deal with the ramifications of the failed test and approached Room Six. Sensors detected their presence. Biometric scanners confirmed their right of entry.

The door slid back and they walked into a vestibule. Mavenhall felt the swirl of overhead fans drawing dust, microbes, and aerosol particles from clothing and exposed skin. Room Six was maintained at low-level cleanroom standards, another signifier of its special nature.

The inner door slid back to reveal a square chamber. This was the heart of U-OPS, the locus of its deepest secrets. Rack-mounted electronics covered the walls, leaving just enough room for two plush chairs fronting a high-definition monitor.

Mavenhall sat and typed in today's security code. The date and time of Preceptor's message appeared onscreen along with the usual precursory data.

Transmission event: #53-11

Transmission configuration: 100 percent video, 0 percent data

Transmission source: unknown

Message processing time: 31.43 minutes

Message ready for access

He realized today's transmission configuration was unusual. Normally, there was a mix of video and data. But this transmission was pure imagery.

The videos were always short, rarely exceeding a minute. U-OPS engineers remained puzzled that it took petabytes of data to display such brief telecasts. The hi-def monitor utilized only a fraction of that data, prompting speculation that the videos were actually intended for some incomprehensible medium far beyond contemporary TV technology.

Mavenhall hit a key. The screen blossomed to life.

The man whose code name was Preceptor was a creature of habit. His videos were recorded in the same elegant study, an anachronism from more than half a century ago. Bookcases of polished mahogany rose behind him. A matching desk bore a manual typewriter and a rotary phone, as well as a brass lamp in the shape of a coiled snake.

As always, Preceptor stood beside the desk with his hands clasped before him. Psychological profilers, permitted to view snippets of the videos, found his pose suggestive of an inner serenity.

Today, he wore a white dress shirt open at the collar, dark slacks and a tweed jacket. Tall and dignified, his wavy brown hair was edged with gray, giving him the look of an elder statesman - perhaps someone who had spent time in the political or diplomatic arenas, or as a tenured professor at some prestigious university. Piercing blue eyes and a healthy tan indicated a man also comfortable with nature, or so the profilers attested.

Of course, there was no way to gauge Preceptor's true age or whether he was an outdoorsman. He looked exactly the same now as he had when he'd first made contact with U.S. authorities back in December 1960. Those allowed to study these telecasts over the past half century had long ago concluded that he was a projected image – in today's jargon, an ultra-realistic digital avatar. They could only speculate about the nature of Preceptor's real identity. Was he human or quasi-human? Some nightmarish alien with six eyes and twelve tentacles? A sophisticated AI, an artificial intelligence?

"Good afternoon," Preceptor began, his voice deep and authoritative. "I wish today's transmission was of a more enlightening nature. But I'm afraid we face a dire situation.

"You are in grave danger. Against all odds, my pilot survived in Earth orbit for 50-plus years, using radar cloaking to hide his presence. Now he's tricked your astronauts into bringing him aboard the International Space Station. He will attempt to reach the surface and carry out the insane plan that was interrupted more than five decades ago by his own arrogance and the incursion of fate."

Preceptor turned to the bookcase, whose selection constituted another mystery. The hi-def pixel density enabled researchers to identify each book by title and author imprinted on the spine.

However, every Preceptor video featured a different selection of volumes. One U-OPS research team did nothing but study Preceptor's metamorphosing library in an attempt to understand whether the mix of books held hidden significance. So far, in terms of drawing any conclusions, the team had struck out.

Not surprising, Mavenhall thought. A recent transmission included titles as disparate as *Dracula, The Elegant Universe, Classic American Railroads Volume III, Paradise Lost, Book of Mormon* and a sadomasochistic how-to manual, *Screw the Roses, Send Me the Thorns.*

Preceptor removed one of the volumes, held it up to the camera so that they could see the title, *The New Dictionary of Thoughts.* He paged through the book until he located a quote.

"There is nothing so minute, or inconsiderable, that I would not rather know it than not.

"The quotation is by Samuel Johnson, esteemed British writer of the 18th century. The philosophy inherent in that quote, the intellectual acquisition of knowledge upon which all advanced civilizations are founded, is anathema to my pilot. He has no love of reason and rationality in the service of cultural exuberance."

Preceptor snapped the book shut. "Your President must undertake a course of action that may well be viewed as political suicide. But the stakes are too high to place personal ambition above the security of seven billion human beings.

"Under no circumstances may the space station crew be allowed to return to Earth. The President must order the launch of an exo-atmospheric kill vehicle to intercept and destroy the International Space Station. Sacrifice of the five astronauts is regrettable. But the action is necessary and time is of the essence. I strongly urge that this action be taken immediately."

The video ended.

"My god," Jarek whispered.

Mavenhall was equally shocked. But he went into action immediately, opening a direct phone line to the Pentagon. A female communications officer answered on the first ring.

"Yes sir?"

"Get me General Grobbs."

"I'm sorry, sir, I believe he's in a meeting with the Joint Chiefs."

"Interrupt them."

11

SOMETHING'S WRONG.

Kayla Ackerman awoke with a start. She crawled out of her sleeping bag, checked her watch. She'd been under for two hours.

NASA had insisted on the unscheduled nap. Neither Houston nor her crew believed that the human-canine creature in Zvezda module, which they'd nicknamed Dog-face, had opened its eyes. The operative assumption, delicately relayed to Kayla by a Houston flight surgeon, was that she'd been tired from a long spacewalk and had suffered a hallucinatory episode.

She didn't believe the prognosis then, didn't believe it now.

Slipping on light blue coveralls, she propelled herself through a series of open portals to Destiny lab.

Henri and Paco were hunched over a console. Tanizaki floated nearby, typing into a tablet.

"What's wrong?" she demanded.

"Do not you feel it?" Tanizaki asked.

"Feel what?"

And then she realized what had awakened her.

"A vibration."

Now that her conscious mind had identified the problem, Kayla could sense it through her skin. Faint and deep, it reminded her of the growl of a subwoofer. Subtle changes in its intensity suggested a repeating pattern.

"A pulse of some sort?" she wondered, peering over Henri and Paco to the waveform monitor they were intent upon. The screen displayed a jagged sine wave, the vibration's electronic signature. Its cycles coincided with the sensations running through her body.

"Started a few minutes ago," Henri said. "Low amplitude, operating down around 8 hertz, below the audible threshold. Apparently the walls themselves are transmitting it through the station."

"Where's it originating?"

"We don't know. Valentin went forward to check the other modules, try to isolate it."

Her heart pounded with fresh worry. "What about Dog-face?"

"Nothing new on the zombie watch," Henri said. "NASA is monitoring Zvezda's video feed. Our spacesuited guest has been behaving like the perfect corpse."

She felt foolish for having broached the matter. Her outburst served only to reveal that even after a nap, she was still obsessing over the incident. She forced her concentration to the problem at hand.

"A motor going bad somewhere?"

The station's walls could amplify and transmit certain mechanical vibrations. On Mir, the former Russian space station, a cosmonaut exercising on the treadmill had been enough to cause the entire station to resonate. But no one was working out at the moment and newer exercise equipment had been engineered to negate such forces.

Tanizaki shook his head. "I do not believe it is a motor. Neither the frequency nor the harmonics align with any of our mechanisms."

Valentin swam through the forward hatch. The Russian held a shotgun mike with a decibel meter for tracking wayward sounds.

"The vibration varies in amplitude from module to module," Valentin said. "But I can't find the source.

Could be originating almost anywhere."

"NASA's stumped," Paco said, removing his headset. "It appears we're in brand-new-glitch territory.

"Oh, and the Russians tracked down the serial number on the back of that helmet. That test suit and two dogs were launched aboard a Vostok spacecraft, Sputnik 6, on December 1, 1960. The capsule achieved orbit and was returning to Earth when it was destroyed, possibly because of a retro-rocket failure or accidental activation of a self-destruct charge."

"Sounds like the Russians need to come up with a new explanation," Kayla said.

An alarm went off – a pulsating tone highlighted by flashing red lights.

"Electrical malfunction in Zvezda," Tanizaki said, jabbing at his keyboard to access more information. "The whole module just lost power, went dark. The cause I cannot ascertain..."

The rest of his words were lost amid a cacophony of screaming sirens.

"Multiple failures, including atmospherics!" Tanizaki hollered, straining to be heard above the racket. "Primary O2 generators and CO2 scrubbing systems are shutting down!"

"Severe electrical fluctuations across the board," Valentin said, scanning another monitor. "We're losing systems in every module. Something's draining our power."

Henri and Paco donned headsets, plastered their hands over the muffs in an attempt to hear the voices of mission control above the sirens. The noise was deafening. Never in the station's history had so many alarms gone off simultaneously.

"Houston, we are declaring an emergency!" Paco yelled into his mike. "Houston, please respond!"

He glanced at Henri, who shook his head. He wasn't

hearing ground control either.

Kayla accessed the alarm system and muted the sirens.

"Com system is down," Tanizaki confirmed. "An interference signal of an unknown type is disabling it."

"Switch to alternates," Paco ordered.

"It is of no use. The interference is affecting the S-band, Ku-band, everything. All ground links are nonoperational."

"That's impossible."

A spark of fear touched Kayla. Impossible or not, it was happening. And losing touch with the ground meant they had to figure it out on their own.

The lighting fluttered, dimming the lab to an eerie yellow glow.

"Backup power has come online," Tanizaki reported. "We are down to 30 percent illumination everywhere except Zvezda. That module remains dark."

"What about life support?" Paco asked. "How long do we have?"

"Twenty minutes," Valentin said. "Twenty-five if we're lucky."

"All right, we evacuate. Let's prep the CRV."

The CRV – Crew Return Vehicle – was a recent addition to the station, a small lifeboat capable of transporting a space station crew back to Earth in an emergency.

"That thing in the spacesuit," Kayla said. "It must have something to do with all this."

Everyone hesitated, wondering if she was right. *Maybe Dog-face did open its eyes*, they would be thinking. *Maybe it is somehow causing these malfunctions*.

Paco shook his head. "Doesn't matter. Under these conditions, procedure says we do a hot evac. Everybody into their ACES."

The Advanced Crew Escape Suit was worn by crews during liftoff and reentry. Lighter and more mobile than the bulky garments employed for spacewalks, the latest generation of ACES could be donned without assistance, although the process took 10 minutes.

Kayla did a quick calculation, arrived at a decision. There should still be enough time to don her suit and strap into the lifeboat.

It wasn't procedure and probably wasn't very smart. But she had to see for herself, had to know. The others were too busy monitoring the malfunctions or activating the CRV to notice her swimming through the aft hatch, heading for Zvezda module. She figured it would take only two or three minutes to check on the status of Dog-face.

12

KAYLA SOARED THROUGH UNITY NODE, a cube-like module with six ports, including the access hatch to the CRV. The power drain had dimmed the lights here as well, but enough illumination remained to guide her.

Heading aft, she reached the next module in line, Zarya. It was the station's first component and had provided power and propulsion during the station's fledgling days.

She swam into Zarya and closed the hatch behind her, per procedure during an emergency. At the far end was the other closed hatch to Zvezda. She slipped a penlight from her pocket, grasped it between her teeth, and swung open Zvezda's hatch.

At that moment, Zarya's lights went out, plunging her into total darkness.

She turned on the penlight and entered Zvezda, shining the beam toward the table. She gasped.

The cosmonaut spacesuit was gone.

Fighting panic, she swung the light to her left. Nothing. She panned right…

And screamed.

Dog-face floated 10 feet away, its helmet off, the black eyes wide open. The spacesuit was peeled down its waist, revealing a torso of withered skin with random patches of white canine fur.

Embedded in the flesh over its stomach was some sort of device. It was shaped like a tuning fork, with the two longer parallel prongs terminating in clusters of tiny shimmering needles. The whole thing glowed with an eerie violet luminescence.

Dog-face lunged. An icy hand grabbed hold of Kayla's neck, squeezed her jugular. She opened her mouth, desperate to suck in precious air. The creature's other hand yanked the tuning fork from its stomach, in the process tearing out bits of its own flesh and spraying them through the module.

For a moment, the creature seemed to study Kayla. Then it shoved the twin ends of the tuning fork deep into her nostrils. A flash of pain was followed by a dry heat that seemed to fill her head, in sharp contrast to the icy hand wrapped around her neck. Barely able to breathe, she could only gaze in terror at the hideous face.

Flashes of light seemed to emanate from the center of her brain. The luminescent bursts pierced flesh and bone throughout her body. She had the eerie sensation that she was being illuminated from the inside out.

Numbness spread outward into her limbs. Fatigue came over her. Consciousness slithered away. She fell into a deep and dark place, far beyond the portals of the world.

13

CORBET HAD ALREADY SPENT A good chunk of Jarek's $200 advance at the trendy new nightclub. First there had been the bribe money to be allowed through the front door. Then an obscene cover charge. Once inside, he'd sprung for rounds of drinks and munchies for the trio he'd hooked up with: an exotic dancer who called herself Tra-Tra and her waitress-cum-actress friends, Helene and Maria.

The four of them sat in a half-moon booth along one of the dance floors, close enough to feel gusts of air swirling from the hyperkinetic dancers cascading past, bodies in sync with hip-hop rhythms blasting from overhead speakers.

The club was P.M. Fugue, one of Washington's newest, located in a former lumber warehouse in a redeveloped section of Southwest DC. It was packed. There'd been a line outside when Corbet arrived and even minor celebs and killer eye candy were being turned away. But the doorman had worked a previous face-control gig at The Icicle and recognized Corbet. For 20 bucks, he'd lowered the proverbial drawbridge.

"Wanna dance?" Helene asked, shouting to be heard above the music.

"Clumsy on my feet," Corbet yelled back, lying his ass off.

Helene was attractive, no doubt about it. And Tra-Tra was killer hot in a girls-gone-wild kind of way. But tonight he was in the mood for a one-on-one, and he'd locked his sights on Maria, the quietest of the trio. Something about the petite redhead suggested she had the right temperament for a complication-free romp.

"Want to get out of here?" he whispered in her ear.

Maria smiled and followed him toward the door.

14

"Is your apartment far?" Maria asked, as they stood outside P.M. Fugue waiting for a taxi.

Corbet shook his head. He'd called for a cab 10 minutes ago and was getting antsy. At least they were going to his place. If it turned out he'd misjudged Maria and she made a fuss when he cut the cord in the morning, he could better distract himself from guilt feelings in the comfort of his own domicile.

"So, what does Corbet Tomms do for a living?" Her tone hinted she was running low on small talk.

"Whatever pays the rent. How about you?"

"I work for this startup, a robotics firm. They're sending me to this big weekend trade show in Manhattan." She glanced at the clock on her phone. "I have to get up pretty early to catch the train."

He craned his neck to gaze up the busy street, trying to will the taxi to appear.

"So, who's paying your rent at the moment?" she asked.

"I work as a paid research subject for this doctor."

"What kind of research?"

"Classified. Can't talk about it. In fact, if I did tell you about it—"

"Oh no, don't say it," she laughed. "If you told me, then you'd have to—"

"That's ra...ra...right," he interrupted, adopting a fake stammer. "I'd have to... kihh... kihh... *kiss you.*"

Her eyes said yes. He gripped her shoulders and moved in for the kill.

Just as their lips were about to touch, a black SUV roared down the street and screeched to a stop at the curb. A tall young woman in a gray business suit hopped out the passenger side, extending her FBI badge like a weapon.

"Corbet Tomms?" she demanded.

"That's right."

He felt Maria pulling away. A sinking feeling warned him the evening was ruined.

"Sir, you're to come with us."

"I don't think so."

"I'll explain once you're ensconced in our vehicle."

"Why don't you go ensconce some bank robbers."

Her lips compressed, not quite a scowl but close. Corbet guessed she was mid-to-late twenties, with a good figure disguised under the bland jacket and pants. Straight blond hair was pulled back into a no-nonsense bun. She had a narrow mouth and piercing blue eyes, sexy eyes. He found himself wondering how she'd look in full-service makeup, and maybe ensconced in a bikini.

"Sir, this isn't a request."

She opened the SUV's rear door, motioned for him to get in.

"Am I being arrested?"

"Not yet." There was no hint of threat in her voice but the meaning was clear. One way or another, he was going for a ride.

Jarek must be behind this, he thought, trying to imagine the reason. Had the Doc and Mavenhall noticed him spying on them as they'd passed through that secure door? Had he violated some arcane national security regulation?

"Is this going to take long?"

"I'm not privy to that information."

He turned to Maria, put on a game face to hide his disappointment.

"Sorry."

"I'll take a rain check."

Corbet hopped in the back seat. The driver, a tall black man with a shaved head, hit the accelerator. The SUV lunged away from the curb.

"Please fasten your seat belt," the woman instructed, strapping herself in up front.

Corbet watched Maria head back toward the club. "Shit! I didn't get her phone number. We have to turn around."

"No time. Dr. Jarek needs to see you immediately. The matter is urgent."

"I was about to get laid. Think that's not urgent?"

15

P.M. Fugue disappeared from view as the driver turned a corner. Corbet ignored the seat-belt request, slithered to the middle of the SUV and hunched forward between the bucket seats. The night was a washout so he might as well have some fun, make the best of a bad situation.

"Do this often?" he asked. "Snatch people off the street before they can have sex?"

"It's an FBI specialty," the woman said, not missing

a beat. "They teach courses on it at Quantico."

Corbet hadn't been expecting a sense of humor. He laid a hand on the back of her shoulder, noted that she wasn't wearing a wedding band.

"You know, I've never been shanghaied by such a beautiful representative of federal law enforcement. I'll bet the two of us could—"

She grabbed the intruding hand, dug a set of sharp fingernails into his flesh. Wincing, he yanked his arm away, massaged the wounded spot. Four red indents on the back of his palm marked her displeasure.

"Feisty. I like that. What's your name?"

"Special Agent Rittenhouse." She nodded toward the driver. "This is Special Agent Reeves."

"Pretend we're at a party and I walk up to you and say, 'Hi, I'm Corbet.' And you say?"

"Agatha."

"Aggie for short, right?"

She didn't answer but he knew he'd guessed right.

"How'd you find me?"

"We have agents checking nightclubs all over town."

Corbet was impressed. They'd gone to a lot of trouble.

Aggie pressed a hand over her earpiece to receive a communication.

"They want you to watch this," she said, turning on a dash-mounted TV.

"They?" Corbet wondered.

A female CNN newscaster appeared onscreen, in the midst of a special report.

"...in what NASA officials characterize as an alarming series of events. If you're just joining us, what we know so far is that the CRV, the emergency lifeboat, undocked from the International Space Station at 7:22 p.m. eastern time, approximately two and a half hours ago. Seventeen minutes prior to that, at 7:05 p.m., an emergency of unknown origin severed all audio, video, and data communications with the ground.

"Since the emergency, efforts to raise the CRV have been unsuccessful. Presumably, the four astronauts and one cosmonaut transferred to the lifeboat, but there is no way to confirm that.

"NASA reports that some telemetry on the space station became functional again moments after the CRV undocked. However, officials stress that many systems remain inoperative.

"The CRV has been orbiting the Earth at an average altitude of 200 miles since undocking. Scientists familiar with the craft believe the loss of ground communications may have caused navigational problems that are affecting the lifeboat's ability to make a safe landing."

The screen split, consigning the newscaster to the left and bringing on a bearded, gray-haired man.

"Joining us from Los Angeles is Dr. Jon Feltenhammer, a spacecraft engineering expert and former MIT professor. Welcome, Dr. Feltenhammer."

"Thank you."

"Doctor, could you give our viewers a brief description of the CRV and how it's supposed to function?"

"The Crew Return Vehicle is about thirty feet in length, with limited capabilities. It's intended to return up to six crew members to Earth during occasions when no other spacecraft are docked at the station. The CRV is a new replacement for the American shuttle vehicles that served that role during the station's earlier years."

A photo of the craft appeared. It looked like a smaller version of the classic space shuttle, but with stubby upswept wings.

"The CRV is designed for unpowered reentry by gliding down through the atmosphere. It utilizes a series of parachutes and a huge steerable parafoil for its final descent. Under ideal conditions, Baja California is its primary emergency landing site.

"The CRV's reentry and landing are intended to be fully automated although it is capable of a manual descent. That the craft remains in orbit may be due to unusual problems switching from automated to manual landing systems."

"Unusual in what way?" the newscaster asked.

"We still don't know what caused the emergency situation aboard the station. However, those problems may have migrated to systems aboard the lifeboat."

"Dr. Feltenhammer, NASA has been reticent about linking the evacuation of the station with the discovery earlier today of a Soviet spacesuit floating in orbit, a spacesuit believed to be at least 50 years old. Reliable sources have confirmed that the crew brought the spacesuit aboard the station, but no videos or photos of it have been released. Is it possible this earlier incident is related to the problems that forced the evacuation?"

"I don't know."

"What about the speculation that the spacesuit was found to contain a corpse?"

"I'd prefer not to contribute to the rumor mill."

It wasn't the kind of juicy answer the newscaster sought. She closed out the interview.

"Thank you, Dr. Jon Feltenhammer. When we return from break, we'll talk with a Ukrainian physicist whose father worked on the original Vostok program—"

Aggie lowered the volume as she received another earpiece message.

"Change of plans," she said, addressing Reeves. "Head for Arlington. We're to rendezvous with a copter that will take us to Dulles."

"The airport?" Corbet protested. "What the hell for?"

"Please fasten your seat belt."

"Or what, you're not going to tell me where we're

going?"

Neither agent responded. Corbet leaned back and reluctantly strapped himself in.

16

CORBET GAZED OUT AT THE Capital in its nighttime glory. In the distance, the Washington Monument rose more than 500 feet above the National Mall.

He'd visited many of the famous sites upon arriving here from Manhattan three years ago, having emigrated from Tribeca. He'd come here with a married couple from his apartment building, a pair of chefs with dreams of a politically-themed upscale restaurant. *A La Politik*, the couple believed, would be a sure hit with the DC crowd. Their contagious excitement had prompted Corbet to become a partner and invest his modest life savings.

A La Politik had flopped after three months, wiping out Corbet's investment. After nasty recriminations as to who was at fault, the husband and wife had stopped talking to Corbet – and each other – and fled Washington.

In retrospect, Corbet should have seen the obvious signs he'd been in over his head, such as zero experience running a business. It hadn't helped that he was a burger-and-fries man and didn't care for most of the exotic dishes on *A La Politik*'s menu.

A Corvette roared past their SUV in the passing lane, doing well over the speed limit. A couple hundred feet ahead, it swerved to avoid a piece of tire tread in the middle of its lane.

The Corvette creased the guard rail in a sizzle of sparks. The driver overcorrected, wrenched the wheel hard right. The car turned sideways and began a wicked series of barrel rolls.

The last roll launched it airborne. The Corvette cleared the guard rail and tumbled into the path of a minivan traveling in the opposite direction. The two vehicles merged in a thunderous explosion of metal and flame.

"Jesus Christ!" Corbet yelled.

Aggie whipped around to face him. "What's wrong?"

As their SUV passed the crash site, Friday night traffic flowed normally in all lanes. There was no evidence an accident had occurred.

Corbet drew a deep breath to calm himself, mentally adjusting to the fact that what he'd witnessed wasn't real, but a psychic vision repeating itself.

"A rerun," he muttered.

"Rerun?" Aggie quizzed.

"They happen sometimes."

"I don't understand."

He fell silent, in no mood to explain.

Reruns were rare. They usually occurred when he found himself in a real-world situation that reminded him of the original psychic event. In this case, the link was obvious. They'd driven past the site of last night's seven-fatality crash, prompting his wired-for-weirdness brain into performing a supersensory encore.

Agent Reeves poked a thumb toward the opposite lanes. "This is where that nasty crash happened."

"Actually, we're already past it," Corbet explained.

Reeves eyed him suspiciously through the rearview mirror.

"Forget it. Ancient history."

17

Henri Renier had absorbed an astonishing array of surprises over the last eight hours. The discovery of the cosmonaut spacesuit, the hideous creature inside it, Kayla's contention that Dog-face had opened its eyes, the bizarre malfunctions forcing them to evacuate the space station. By any standards, it had been an extraordinary day.

But Kayla's odd behavior was taking things to a whole new level.

Like the rest of them, she was in her bright-orange ACES suit, strapped into an acceleration couch in the CRV's tiny cabin. Paco and Valentin sat upfront in commander and pilot's positions. Henri and Tanizaki occupied the middle set of seats, leaving Kayla alone in the rear.

In all the excitement, no one had asked where she'd disappeared to after the onset of the malfunctions. They'd had more important issues, such as making sure the lifeboat could undock from a space station whose power and life support systems were failing at an unprecedented rate.

The undocking had gone off without a hitch, although they still weren't able to communicate with the ground. Complicating matters, the CRV's audio, telemetry and navigational systems had gone haywire the instant Paco and Valentin switched them on.

That meant the lifeboat had to be brought down manually with no navigational assistance from mission control. It was a challenging task, but within their capabilities. All space-station crews prepped for such worst-case scenarios.

But after Paco and Valentin had plotted a course for the primary landing site in Baja California, the manual navigation system refused to accept the coordinates. For reasons that defied logic, the system had locked in a set of new coordinates, a landing site not on their list. The lifeboat had programmed itself to bring them down somewhere within a 7,000-square-mile region of the Appalachian mountains of northcentral Pennsylvania.

Since undocking from the station and assuming a stable orbit, Henri had worked feverishly with Paco, Valentin, and Tanizaki to alter those coordinates. But all attempts to override or reset the system proved futile.

Kayla had not helped with their efforts. In fact, her sole contribution had been to suggest that they accept the validity of the new coordinates and land the CRV in those mountains. She argued that once the lifeboat was closer to the ground, they'd be able to locate an airport or field.

Paco and Valentin disagreed, believing such a scenario too dangerous. But they were running out of time. A decision would have to be made soon. The CRV's life support was short-term, not intended to maintain a crew in orbit for an extended period.

"The Pennsylvania landing site is our best option," Kayla insisted.

Henri craned his head around to face her, curious about the odd lack of emotion in her voice. Everyone was understandably tense. However, since entering the lifeboat, she seemed different somehow.

"Kayla, you sure you're all right?"

"Yes, Henri. There is no cause for concern. Everything is A-OK."

The A-OK remark was unusual. The term had been

popular back in the 1960s with American astronauts in the Mercury program. Contemporary crews rarely used it.

"Is there an issue relevant to my behavior that troubles you?" she asked.

Henri stared at her, at a loss for words. The Kayla Ackerman he knew didn't frame questions in such an odd way.

"Where did you go when you left Destiny Module?" he asked.

"I thought it important to check on the status of the creature in the spacesuit."

It was a reasonable answer. Henri pressed for more information.

"You were gone a long time."

"I had difficulty opening Zvezda's hatch."

"What about our visitor?"

"Status was unchanged."

"It didn't open its eyes again?" he asked, smiling to let her know he was joking.

"I was mistaken in my earlier appraisal," she said, her tone still devoid of any feeling. "It's now clear that I suffered a transient hallucinatory episode from which I have fully recovered."

A chill went up Henri's spine. For the first time, he had the feeling he wasn't talking to Kayla, that the woman seated behind him was a total stranger.

"We can't wait any longer," Paco announced. "We have to go with these landing coordinates, take our chances. Deorbit burn in one minute, 30 seconds."

"Pennsylvania, here we come," Valentin muttered, trying to sound cheery.

Henri took one last look at Kayla, then faced front and tightened his belts.

18

CORBET BOARDED THE PRIVATE JET at Washington Dulles International Airport. He'd never flown in anything smaller than a 747. The cabin, outfitted with four swivel leather seats, felt large and luxurious by comparison. His chair boasted a retrofitted extra, a flatscreen TV with a videoconferencing camera.

Aggie strapped in beside him as the jet took off and climbed into sable skies. Other than pilot and copilot, they were the only ones aboard. Agent Reeves had dropped them at the airport and departed for another assignment.

While waiting at Dulles for the jet to be readied for takeoff, Corbet had eavesdropped on a cell phone call by Aggie. She hadn't realized he'd returned from the men's room and had been standing behind her.

"Yes sir, he won't be any trouble," she was telling someone. "He's pretty much what his file says, always on the make... uh-huh... don't worry, sir, I've handled much worse."

She sensed his presence, ended the call.

"How do you know you've handled worse?" Corbet challenged. "We're barely acquainted."

"First impressions."

"I might surprise you. If I put my mind to it, I could cause lots of trouble."

"It wouldn't be in your best interests to give me a hard time."

"Why not?"

"I'm armed and a crack shot."

"I don't believe you'd shoot me."

"You don't know what I'd do."

His attention returned to the jet as they reached cruising altitude and Aggie took another call.

"Got it," she said, hanging up and leaning across him to turn on his TV. He caught a whiff of her perfume, an unusual scent, reminiscent of tropical fruits. Coconut and lime? Maybe at heart she was an island girl.

"You smell nice. What kind of perfume is that?"

She grimaced and rolled her eyes.

Encountering a sexy woman who regarded him with open animosity was a new experience for Corbet. There was little chance he and Aggie would ever share a bed. Still, her cool demeanor toward him was like a matador waving a red cape, inspiring the bull to charge.

The screen came to life, revealing Dr. Jarek and Col. Mavenhall seated at a round table. The handle of what appeared to be a beach umbrella rose from the center of the table. But the lighting bore a greenish tinge, suggesting overhead fluorescents, not the outdoors.

"Corbet, sorry to spoil your evening," Jarek began.

"What about it, Colonel, you sorry too?"

"Let's try to be professional," Mavenhall urged. "This is too important to allow personal issues to interfere."

Personal issues. Even the phrase left Corbet seething and dwelling on possible retorts. But he kept his mouth shut. Best not to let the prick get under his skin, at least not until he learned what was going on.

"You're probably wondering why you're here," Jarek said.

"Crossed my mind."

"Before we explain, have you experienced any further psychic visions related to the one that occurred this morning in your apartment? The one that felt like a weird dream."

"No."

Jarek opened a folder, withdrew an 8x10 photo, held it up. Corbet couldn't contain his shock.

"That's Dog-face!"

"You're sure? This is the creature from your vision?"

Corbet nodded, unable to tear his gaze away from the hideous countenance. White pelt-like hair, triangular ears sprouting from the back of the head, rings of black fur around the eyes, all in jarring contrast to those all-too-human lips. The clarity of the photo provided more detail than his vision, revealed tiny imperfections in the shriveled skin.

However, there was one critical difference. On the Statue of Liberty, the eyes had been open. Here they were shut. Here, Dog-face looked dead.

"Where did you get this?"

"This photo was digitally enhanced to heighten clarity. Here's the original untouched image, a freeze-frame from a video camera that puts this creature in its proper context."

Jarek held up the second photo, a wider shot showing Dog-face through the grainy visor of a corroded space helmet.

"He was inside that Soviet spacesuit they found in orbit?"

"Correct," Mavenhall said. "I would remind both of you that these images have not been released to the media and that this entire discussion is classified top secret. I trust you will bear that in mind."

"Absolutely, sir," Aggie said.

Corbet gave a halfhearted nod, still trying to get his head around the amazing fact that Dog-face was real.

Jarek continued. "During examination of the spacesuit, astronaut Kayla Ackerman claimed that the creature opened its eyes. The other crew members were unable to confirm her observation.

"A short time ago, ground-based radar and

telescopes tracking the CRV reported it had engaged axial and RCS thrusters, which put the lifeboat on a trajectory for reentry. It then initiated a deorbit burn, the first step in the reentry procedure. The propulsion stage was successfully jettisoned and the craft began a controlled descent.

"NASA's projections indicate it will come down somewhere in northcentral Pennsylvania. The pilot's rationale for selecting such an isolated mountain region remains a matter of conjecture."

"I assume that's where we're going."

Jarek nodded. "We want you there when the lifeboat touches down. NASA is scrambling its people to reach the presumed landing site. But your jet is already in Pennsylvania airspace and should arrive first. We want you to rendezvous with the crew and take part in the initial debriefing, hear firsthand what happened to them up there."

"Uh-huh. And these astronauts, they're just going to hop out of their little spaceship and chat with a complete stranger."

"The crew will be asked to cooperate," Mavenhall said. "You and Agent Rittenhouse will be provided with temporary security clearances. Dr. Jarek and I will pose the specific interview questions. Your job will be to listen."

"Listen for what?"

"We're interested in any psychic impressions you might receive during the debriefing. You obviously have made some kind of supersensory connection with this creature and with these events."

Corbet sensed they weren't telling him everything. The two of them knew more about Dog-face than they were letting on.

Jarek continued. "Be aware, there are potential complications with the landing. The terrain is unsuitable and the weather in that region is less than ideal."

Corbet looked out his window. In the distance, lightning streaks cleaved the darkness.

Less than ideal.

19

HENRI RENIER CLUNG TO THE armrests as the CRV shuddered violently. His sessions in the trainer hadn't prepared him for turbulence of this magnitude. The reentry forces buffeting the lifeboat seemed about to tear it apart. And after months of living in microgravity, the onset of Earth's pull made his bones and muscles ache.

"Twenty-seven thousand feet!" Paco hollered, keeping them abreast of the hazardous descent, allowing Valentin to concentrate on piloting.

There was little to see through the windows. They'd dropped into a dense layer of tropospheric clouds and were now flying solely by radar. Thankfully, that system had not suffered any malfunctions.

A thunderstorm blanketed much of the northeastern U.S. The glider-like CRV was not rated for such extreme conditions. In pre-flight testing, NASA had theorized the crew would always have a choice of landing sites and be able to avoid inclement weather.

"Twenty-one thousand!"

Sheets of rain battered the window. The shaking intensified.

Henri craned his head around to Kayla. The turbulence rocked her back and forth. But her face bore an expression that suggested she was ready to nod off from boredom.

And then he noticed something even odder, an eerie violet glow emanating from the area around her stomach. It was as if some intense light source was inside her spacesuit, powerful enough to ooze through the flexible orange material.

"Kayla, what is that?"

She laid her gloved hands over her stomach, as if trying to hide the glow. But the light seeped through gaps between her fingers.

A gust slammed the lifeboat, almost flipping the craft onto its side. Henri whipped his attention front again, refocused on their dire situation. But he couldn't stop thinking about Kayla and that strange light.

"Twelve thousand!" Ortiz barked.

"We need to slow down," Valentin said. "I'm releasing the drogues."

He flipped a safety switch, punched two illuminated buttons. Henri felt his body press forward against the seat straps as the drogue parachutes ejected out the back and air-braked the lifeboat.

"Seven thousand!"

A series of brutal gusts rocked the craft as they entered the heart of the storm. And suddenly, Henri was weightless again as the lifeboat hit an air pocket, plunging hundreds of feet in a matter of seconds.

"Drogue chutes aren't slowing us," Valentin said. "I'm ejecting the parafoil."

"Not advisable," Paco warned. "Not in this storm, not without a viable landing zone. Otherwise—"

The rest of his words were drowned out by the harsh rumble of disintegrating metal.

20

MAURICE OLAFSON SLOWED HIS PICKUP to a crawl. He could barely see more than a few yards beyond the windshield.

The rain sounded like a thousand marbles as it smacked the roof of his Ford F-150. He could have kicked himself for choosing this route to drive home from his three-to-eleven shift at the bakery. Mercy Hollow Road went over Neckels Mountain in a series of hairpin turns. Still, it was quicker than the road that curled around the base of the mountain.

At least in good weather.

Sheets of rain splattered the windshield with renewed fury. It was no sense driving farther until the worst of the storm subsided. He reached the mountain's apex and pulled onto the shoulder. Up ahead, he could just make out the old stone fire tower, an abandoned monolith rising above the windswept trees.

A distant noise snared his attention, a high-pitched whooshing. It sounded like sheets flapping on the washline in a brisk wind. He knew it wasn't part of the storm.

The sound intensified. He hunched forward, straining to see.

A peculiar aircraft appeared, streaking down from the heavens. It looked like a cross between one of those ultramodern gliders and a stealth bomber with sweptback wings. White on top and dark underneath, it was trailed by plumes of steam from raindrops vaporizing on contact with its hot undercarriage. An immense red and white parafoil unfurled overhead, at least five times the vehicle's length.

Maurice had heard about the troubles at the International Space Station. He knew this had to be the lifeboat they'd been talking about on the radio all evening. But what in god's name was it doing in Pennsylvania, way up here in these mountains? Weren't spaceships supposed to land down at Cape Canaveral or at military bases out west?

The craft sailed past the fire tower. Only then did Maurice realize it wasn't going to land.

It was going to crash.

One of the trailing drogue chutes snared the edge of the tower, ripped free. The craft's undercarriage skimmed a line of evergreens, shredding branches before crossing the road and slamming the crown of a tree on the mountain's downward side.

The last thing Maurice saw before the lifeboat disappeared from view would haunt him forever. The collision ripped a gaping hole in the craft's side. Two astronauts in orange spacesuits, still in conjoined seats, were hurled from the ruptured fuselage. The pair ricocheted violently across the treetops before dropping into the dense canopy.

"Mother of god," Maurice whispered, fumbling on his phone to dial 9-1-1.

21

"The good Lord's taking one hell of a pee tonight, ain't?"

Eighteen-year-old Smitty made the

observation with his face pressed against the Jeep's windshield as he strained to make out macadam through the downpour.

Corbet was in the back seat, Aggie up front with their young driver. The jet had made it in under the weather, landing at a small private airfield near Kelliksville, 10 miles south of the crash site. Smitty, a volunteer with the Kelliksville Regional Fire Police Auxiliary, had picked them up after Aggie had lobbied an overworked 9-1-1 dispatcher for a ride.

"This gotta be the most badass storm we've had in years," Smitty continued, turning to Aggie. "My mom said when it rains like this, it's not just water trapped up there in the clouds like they teach in school. Mom's part Mohawk, plus part hippie on my grandfather's side. He was at Woodstock. Anyways, she says rain like this is really the spirits of the world telling folks they're gettin' too big for their britches, and that a good soaking is letting 'em know who's really in charge."

"Uh-huh," Aggie offered, noncommittal. "Mind keeping your eyes on the road?"

Lightning strobed the heavens, illuminating the forests straddling Mercy Hollow Road, which wound it way ever higher up the side of Neckels Mountain. Smitty had explained that Neckels had been named after a wild, three-legged horse that had lived in these forests during the Civil War.

"Sometimes, people still see the ghost of that horse galloping through the trees," he assured them.

They hit a rut. The Jeep took a wicked bounce, forcing Corbet to grab hold of a roll bar beneath the detachable hardtop. The glove compartment popped open, dropped a road flare into Aggie's lap.

"Wow!" Smitty hissed, pivoting to gaze back at Corbet. "That was wild, ain't?"

"The road," Aggie reminded him.

Smitty swerved onto the narrow shoulder to dodge a fallen branch. Corbet glanced out his side window, into what appeared to be a bottomless pit two feet from the edge of the jeep. Such precipices had been shifting from one side to the other every few hundred yards as Smitty negotiated an endless series of switchbacks. The guard rail was a relic from the early days of paved roads, two rusted cables strung between lopsided white posts. At many spots, the cables sagged to the ground. An out-of-control vehicle could easily plummet over the edge.

Smitty slammed the brakes. Emergency vehicles blocked the road – ambulances, fire trucks, police cars. Four-way flashers, distorted by the heavy rain, appeared as shuddering globules of white, amber and cop red-blue.

They exited the Jeep, hunched forward against the fierce wind. Aggie had procured an extra FBI jacket for Corbet, supposedly waterproof. But the pounding rain took only seconds to seep under his collar, soaking his chest to the skin before they reached the first vehicle, a fire department pumper.

On the hill above, towering pines bent sideways under sustained gusts, looking as if they'd be torn from the earth and swept off to Oz. On the downhill flank, wavering flashlight beams illuminated the crash scene.

They made their way down the embankment. Corbet, lacking a flashlight, stuck close to Aggie. He had to grab onto branches to keep from losing his balance on the slick mud. Even so, he slipped a few times and flopped onto his butt. Aggie suffered a similar fate. Smitty, however, had no difficulty, bounding down the hill with complete disregard for potential mayhem. Maybe emergency workers in hilly communities were required to be part mountain goat.

Dismembered branches littered the ground as they drew closer. Overhead, silhouetted by the lightning, they could make out where the branches had been sheared off by the descending craft. They came upon mangled chunks of debris, including a three-foot section of wing with leaf clusters jammed into its broken edge, giving the weird impression that foliage was growing from the carbon-fiber composite.

They reached the crash site. The main body of the craft was wedged between two trees, a dozen feet off the ground. Frayed parafoil lines draped its flanks like party streamers. Steam wafted from its underbelly. The lifeboat angled defiantly skyward, as if still aspiring to heavenly missions.

The CRV's innards spilled from a gaping hole in the fuselage, making the craft look like a wild animal that had been hung up and gutted. Nestled amid the torn cables and electronics, a dead astronaut hung upside down, still strapped in his seat.

"This is bad," Smitty muttered, raindrops bouncing off his cheeks as he stared up at the body. "*Really* bad."

Two firemen stood below the hole, supporting a ladder propped against the fuselage. An EMS worker stood on the top rung, his flashlight aimed into the craft's shadowy interior. Corbet moved up the slope for a better angle. Inside, amid a twisted tangle of wreckage, he could just make out a pair of rescuers flanking another seat.

"Any survivors?" he hollered.

The EMS worker twisted around. His annoyed expression dissolved at the sight of Corbet's FBI jacket.

"The one in here is still alive. Unconscious, probably internal injuries. We're trying to free him. Trapped under a piece of wreckage."

"Got an ID?"

"Nametag says Renier."

Corbet nodded. That would be Henri Renier, the Belgian.

"Be careful about touching any of that debris," the EMS worker warned, gesturing to chunks of metal at Corbet's feet. "Some of it's still hotter than hell."

A grizzled older cop in a white plastic overcoat stomped toward them.

"Smitty, this ain't no sightseers convention. Hightail your butt back up to the road and grab every roll of crime-scene tape from our vehicles you can find. We need to run a perimeter a couple hundred yards out from the wreckage. I'll see if I can get somebody to give you a hand, but at the moment we're stretched thin. For now, you're it."

"Yes sir," Smitty shouted, dashing back up the hill.

"Pisser of a night," the older cop grumbled, tipping the brim of his cap. A pool of rainwater cascaded out from under his hood.

"I'm Chief Lambert, Kelliksville Regional P.D. So far, we got three fatalities. Paco Ortiz and Valentin Anikeyev were thrown from the craft a couple hundred feet back up the hill. Probably dead before they hit the ground."

He pointed to the body in the dangling seat. "That's the Japanese fellow, Tanizaki Kisho."

"Any place for a medevac to land up here?" Aggie wondered.

"Not in this weather, unless the pilot's got a serious death wish. We have medevacs flying in from Williamsport. They're going to try landing on the old baseball field at the base of the valley, about four miles from here. I've got one of my people standing by to guide 'em in. We'll get the two survivors transferred down there by ambulance."

"Two survivors?" Corbet wondered, looking around

for the fifth astronaut, Kayla Ackerman.

"Yeah, the woman made it. We found her in the woods. Apparently, she was either thrown clear or managed to climb out. Must've been in shock and wandered off. She made it a few hundred feet down the mountain before the first responders caught up to her. Lucky for this rain, cause they might never have tracked her without muddy footprints to follow."

"She's awake?" Corbet asked.

"Was awake. Collapsed when they found her. Medics are trying to get her stabilized before moving her."

Chief Lambert's radio chirped. He reached under his coat, unholstered a mike. "Yeah, go ahead."

A deputy's voice came through. "Chief, it's Gene. I'm down here at the field. A big-assed Army copter just landed with a platoon of soldiers. Their lieutenant says he has instructions to secure the crash site. He's demanding I arrange transportation and haul their asses up there. What do you want me to do?"

"What about the medevacs?" Lambert asked.

"Closest one's still ten minutes out. They're having a hell of a time in this weather. I told this captain I needed to stay put to guide 'em in, but he says his own pilot will do it."

"Find some vehicles and bring the Army on up."

He turned back to Corbet and Aggie. "Storm's not supposed to break for another couple hours, but we'll have media and sightseers up the wazoo before long. This place is gonna turn into circus city."

The EMS workers had freed Henri Renier and strapped him to a stretcher. They strung a rope to a higher branch to belay the stretcher and carefully lowered the unconscious astronaut to the ground.

Lambert shook his head. "Hope that ship wasn't carrying anything radioactive."

"I don't think so," Aggie said.

"I suppose if the wife sees me glowing in my P.J.s tonight, we'll know for sure."

A pair of EMS men emerged from the woods bearing the other survivor. A third paramedic, a heavyset woman with a flashlight duct-taped to her helmet, paced their stretcher with an IV bag.

Like Henri Renier, Kayla Ackerman remained in her spacesuit, a small portion of which had been cut away to feed her an IV line. But in Kayla's case, there was a more obvious reason why the garment hadn't been removed.

A severed branch, 18 inches long and half an inch thick, protruded straight up from her chest. It must have speared through the lifeboat's thin hull, impaling her. Corbet assumed the paramedics didn't want to risk removing it until they reached a trauma unit.

"Miracle she's still breathing," Lambert muttered as the paramedics hustled the unconscious astronaut past them.

Kayla was barefooted. Not only were her boots missing, the legs of her spacesuit had been cut away at the ankles, revealing light blue coveralls underneath. Her feet were caked in mud and covered with deep bloody scratches.

"Why'd you cut off the bottom of her suit?" Corbet asked.

"We didn't," the female paramedic said. "Must have been torn off in the crash somehow."

He peered closer, looking for jagged tear marks. But there were none.

"Hard to imagine she could walk anywhere with such severe injuries," he said.

"Traumatic shock can endow a person with superhuman fortitude," the paramedic offered. "I've seen it before."

As the EMS crew struggled up the muddy hill with

Kayla's stretcher, Aggie made a phone call to Col. Mavenhall.

"No sir, the survivors are in no condition to be debriefed… yes sir, got it."

She hung up, faced Corbet. "We're to stay here, help secure the site."

He nodded absently, unable to shake a growing feeling of unease. Something was terribly wrong, something far more unsettling than the horror of the crash itself.

22

"I'M GOING INSIDE," CORBET ANNOUNCED, heading for the ladder propped against the lifeboat's fuselage.

"Too dangerous," Aggie said.

He ignored her and began climbing. She followed him up.

Corbet eased himself into the battered lifeboat and extended a hand to Aggie. She ignored the offer, swung through the jagged hole on her own.

"What are you looking for?"

"I'm not sure." That feeling of unease was guiding him now.

Debris and tangled wires clogged the floor. A few control panel buttons remained illuminated, probably running off a battery backup system. Corbet headed into the rear of the craft, to the three acceleration seats that had not been torn loose.

Henri Renier had occupied the remaining middle seat. That meant Kayla had sat in one of the rear pair.

Corbet tripped over a cable, banged his shin against a metal brace protruding from the wall. Wincing, he leaned over to massage the sore appendage. The movement directed his gaze toward the floor, where Aggie's flashlight beam illuminated a pair of black boots and the missing leg portions of Kayla's spacesuit.

Corbet frowned. "What's wrong with this picture?"

"She was badly injured," Aggie said, trying to sound convincing. "Probably delusional from shock and pain. Given that scenario, no telling what a person's capable of."

He didn't buy it. Her footwear hadn't been torn away in the crash. The edges of the suit were smooth and faintly blackened, as if they'd been sliced away with a hot knife. That suggested that after the lifeboat had come to rest, Kayla, with a branch protruding from her chest, had removed her boots and trimmed away the bottom of her spacesuit with some unknown device.

Rain drizzled through a gash in the roof, forming a waterfall that ran across the back of Kayla's seat. Corbet found himself transfixed by the flowing liquid.

Consciousness dissolved into that gentle cascade, transporting him to another reality.

23

IT WAS NIGHTTIME. HE WAS standing on that same foggy street in Tribeca. The displaced Statue of Liberty peered over the loft apartments from a few blocks away, the fog again hiding Miss Liberty's face and upraised torch.

As before, the feral humans crept through the mist

on all fours, ignoring his presence. As before, his shoe crunched something hard as that intense violet light burned through the fog from above.

This time, he lowered his gaze to see what he'd stepped on.

A toy ray gun was embedded in the macadam, like some partially unearthed artifact waiting to be excavated. He brushed a layer of dirt from it, revealing a barrel encircled by washer-like rings. It was a Pyrotomic Disintegrator pistol, a relic of his father's 1950s childhood. As a young boy, Corbet had come across the toy in their New Hampshire basement.

He raised his gaze to the Statue of Liberty. The violet torch was identical to his initial experience of the vision. But Miss Liberty's inviting countenance had changed, was no longer a monstrous blend of human and canine features. In place of Dog-face appeared a pleasant African-American woman.

Kayla Ackerman.

The vision ended. And then Corbet was back inside the wrecked lifeboat, staring into that waterfall.

"Corbet, what's wrong?"

"Nothing."

"You seemed to be in a trance."

"I'm okay."

He wasn't. The vision's second manifestation had left in its wake that same ominous aftertaste. Technically, it wasn't a rerun – the statue's face was different and the toy ray gun was a new aspect. Nevertheless, he again had the strange feeling that the world had changed. In some unfathomable way, his life had been switched to a different track.

A shudder went through him. He needed to get out of here. He stumbled toward the exit, ignoring Aggie's pleas to slow down. Not until he reached the bottom of the ladder did his heart stop pounding.

And then he realized there was a new crisis.

"What do you mean you can't find it?" Chief Lambert growled into his radio. "How the hell do you lose a damned ambulance?"

Corbet instinctively knew which ambulance they were talking about.

"Henri Renier's wagon made it to the field," Lambert explained. "They're putting him aboard a medevac. But the ambulance with Kayla Ackerman never showed up."

"Maybe the driver took another route," Aggie suggested.

"There is no other route."

"Does it have GPS?"

"Yeah, but not transmitting. They lost radio contact too. And nobody can reach the EMS crew on their cell phones."

Corbet knew that locating the missing astronaut was profoundly important. He had no idea why.

Aggie read his deep concern, addressed Lambert.

"We'll need a vehicle."

24

THEY HEADED DOWN THE MOUNTAIN in Smitty's Jeep, this time at a slow pace. Their young chauffeur again filled the vehicle with relentless chatter.

"The ambulance driver is Cal Stoltzfus. He's sort of a relative. Cal's married to Gilda Jean, my second cousin. I just saw him at the fire company picnic last month. Our team won the volleyball tournament. I sure hope nothing happened to him. You don't think he got hurt, do you?"

Corbet didn't reply. He kept his attention on the road's downward side while shielding his face from blowback through Aggie's open window up front. She had her flashlight aimed down the embankment to search for signs of the missing ambulance.

It was a daunting task. Her beam didn't penetrate far and the rain had intensified again after a brief lull. If the ambulance had plunged over the sagging guard rail, it could have left no trace. The wreckage might be lying in a ravine hundreds of feet below.

"A couple years ago, this guy in a Mustang went over the edge," Smitty said. "He was trapped for two days before they found him. But he survived so that's a good sign, ain't?"

"Maybe," Corbet offered.

"Ya' think their GPS and radio got busted when they crashed?"

"Maybe."

Corbet was sure the ambulance's disappearance had something to do with the Statue of Liberty's face changing from Dog-face to Kayla Ackerman. But beyond that, the elements of his dream remained a collection of disparate mysteries.

Why did it take place in his old Tribeca neighborhood? Who or what were the feral humans? What was the significance of the toy ray gun? The Statue of Liberty? The violet light?

"You're sure no other roads connect with this one?" Aggie asked.

Smitty shook his head. "Not until you reach the old baseball field down in the valley."

Up ahead, headlights appeared around a bend. A vehicle was approaching in their lane, on the wrong side of the road.

"Maybe it's Cal," Smitty said, sounding hopeful.

It was an ambulance but not Kayla's. An EMS worker was driving. Two soldiers were crammed beside him in the front, no doubt from the Army unit that had landed in the helicopter. Two more soldiers stood on the vehicle's back bumper. They were panning the trees on the downward side with a large portable spotlight, illuminating great swaths of wilderness.

Smitty steered to the opposite shoulder to allow the ambulance with its stronger beam to stay close to the guard rail. The lane change drew Corbet's attention to the road's other flank.

"Hey, hold up!"

Smitty hit the brakes.

"What's that?" Corbet asked, pointing into the trees.

A muddy lane snaked into the woods on the upward side of the mountain. Half overgrown by underbrush, it would have been hard to spot even in good weather.

"That's weird," Smitty said, directing their attention to a pair of weatherbeaten posts flanking the lane. "The chain ain't there. They always keep it locked."

"Who does?"

"The company that put it in the access lane. They got one of them microwave relay and cell towers up on the ridge, about a half mile in. But there's supposed to be a chain strung between the posts to keep out unauthorized vehicles."

Rutted tire tracks were visible in the wet stones. But it was impossible to tell whether they'd been made tonight or weeks ago.

"Was the chain in place earlier?" Aggie wondered.

Smitty shrugged. He steered onto the lane but immediately nailed the brakes.

The chain lay in the underbrush. Judging by the freshly exposed wood on the posts where the eyebolts had been yanked out, a vehicle recently had crashed through the barrier.

Smitty guided the Jeep along the gently ascending lane. Rain blasted the roof, sounding like marbles cast down by some angry god. Lightning irradiated the trees, each flash followed instantly by roaring thunder. Round two of the storm had positioned itself directly overhead.

"This don't make no sense," Smitty mumbled, eyes darting nervously into the surrounding woods. "Cal wouldn't have driven the ambulance up here."

The trees seemed to press in upon them, further constricting the narrow route. Corbet noted another peculiarity. Torn branches littered the edges of the lane, as if the driver was drunk and hadn't been able to keep the vehicle from drifting off the gravel surface.

Smitty also noticed the oddity. "No way is Cal this bad a driver."

Corbet's suspicions crystallized. Cal hadn't been driving. Somehow, the injured astronaut had taken control of the vehicle.

He kept the notion to himself. No sense getting Smitty even more spooked.

Aggie tried her phone. "Something's wrong, I can't get a signal. And this is a secure sat."

"A what?" Smitty asked.

"Satellite phone on a secure military net. I should be able to uplink from practically anywhere, even in bad weather."

Smitty tried to contact Chief Lambert on his dash-mounted unit. But only static issued from the speakers. Corbet and Smitty pulled out their phones.

"Nothing," Corbet said.

"Oh man, this is way too freaky!" Smitty hissed. "We need to go back and get help."

"Keep going," Corbet urged.

Aggie agreed. "Once we reach the tower, there'll be a place to turn around, right?"

Smitty reluctantly drove on.

Corbet wondered if their disabled communications had something to do with what had befallen the space station and the lifeboat, which had suffered similar malfunctions. After all, there was a common denominator.

Kayla Ackerman.

Smitty negotiated a final bend and braked at the edge of a small clearing. Up ahead, a barbed-wire fence ringed a cinderblock shed at the base of the tower. The spiderweb structure soared some two hundred feet into the bleak skies. Aircraft warning beacons shone faintly at its apex.

The ambulance was parked beside the fence. Its engine and lights were off.

"Cal's a standup guy," Smitty said, clenching the steering wheel as if it was a life preserver. "Ain't like him to do something like this."

They exited, leaving the Jeep's headlights trained on the ambulance. Wind and rain whipped their faces as they approached the darkened vehicle. Aggie drew her sidearm, a Glock semiautomatic. Hunching into a two-handed shooter's stance, she approached the cab.

It was empty.

They circled to the back of the vehicle. Aggie motioned to Smitty. The young volunteer's hands shook as he gripped the handles and yanked the door open.

"Sweet Jesus!" he yelled, backing away.

The three EMS workers lay sprawled on the floor. Corbet leaned in and checked the pulse of the nearest one, the female paramedic. He shook his head.

"That there is Cal," Smitty said, his voice quivering as he pointed to one of the men.

Aggie pressed her fingers against Cal's neck, grimaced. "I'm sorry, Smitty."

The second male was dead too. Aggie ran her hand along the victims' torsos and appendages, searching for obvious injuries.

"No broken bones, at least nothing I can detect. No gunshot or stab wounds, either. No traces of blood."

"Look at their faces, above the eyes," Corbet said.

Each victim had a pair of quarter-sized black smudges on the forehead. The circular marks were about an inch apart.

Aggie ran a fingernail across Cal's smudges. "Some sort of burns. I'm guessing that's what killed them."

She reached beneath the gurney and retrieved a tree branch covered in blood. It was the limb that had impaled Kayla Ackerman.

"They must have pulled it out of her."

"Or she pulled it out herself," Corbet said.

He found a flashlight and returned to the cab with Aggie. Their dueling beams froze on the floor beneath the steering well. The remnants of Kayla's spacesuit lie there, sliced to pieces.

"Faster to cut the suit off her body than squirm out of it," Aggie surmised. "I'm guessing whatever device she used to remove the suit was used to kill the paramedics."

"Maybe she also used it to do *that*," Corbet said, pointing to the dashboard radio, which bore another set of those black smudges.

Aggie nodded. "Probably what took out the GPS."

Corbet leaned into the cab. Near the gas and brake pedals were flakes of bloody skin. Most likely, they had come from Kayla's injured feet.

The evidence pointed to a simple yet utterly bizarre explanation. During the drive down the mountain, the astronaut had awakened, killed the ambulance crew, wrecked the vehicle's tracking unit and took over behind the wheel. She'd crashed through the chain, perhaps not realizing the lane terminated at the tower. Or maybe she had known it but wanted to get as far away from the road as possible.

"She didn't want to rendezvous with that medevac," Corbet concluded, gazing into the gloom of the surrounding wilderness. "Whatever agenda she has, it didn't involve being taken to a hospital. And after she escaped, she somehow caused the communications interference to hinder a search."

Aggie nodded. "She needed to get away."

"Whaddya mean she needed to get away?" Smitty muttered, frantically jerking his flashlight around, as if expecting something to leap out at them from the trees. "She's almost dead! How can she be needing to get away?"

Corbet walked to the edge of the clearing to where the gravel ended and the woods began. The rain had morphed the ground into a glimmering sheet of mud. It took him only a few seconds to locate footprints not yet washed away by the storm. They had been made recently by a barefooted person. The tracks led off into the forest.

"These astronauts work out a bunch and stay in real good shape," Smitty said. His hands were shaking, body and mind desperately in need of a rational explanation.

Corbet started to follow the footprints into the trees.

"Don't even think about it," Aggie said, grabbing his arm. "We wait for backup."

"We could lose the trail by then."

"I'm responsible for your safety. I can't allow it."

"I'm not asking your permission." He pulled away from her and continued on.

"Okay, dammit, hold up."

She was right to be so concerned, Corbet admitted. Following these tracks probably wasn't the brightest idea. But he couldn't shake the notion that they had to find Kayla Ackerman before it was too late.

But too late for what?

"Stay here," Aggie instructed Smitty. "Keep trying your radio and phone."

"All by myself? I don't even have a gun."

"You wouldn't want to leave Cal alone out here, would you?" Aggie said, her tone soothing. "He's family, right? So you need to stay here, watch over him. It's the proper thing to do."

"But what if something happens?"

"Holler," Aggie said, jogging to catch up with Corbet.

25

KAYLA ACKERMAN WAS PRETTY SURE she was awake, was pretty sure her eyes were open. But afloat in microgravity and enveloped in utter darkness, she couldn't validate those notions.

However, the darkness rendered her other senses more acute, particularly hearing. Although she couldn't identify the nature of the odd thumps and clangs that seemed to emanate from nearby, they triggered a flood of memories.

The system malfunctions... Paco ordering their evacuation in the CRV... entering Zvezda module to check on Dog-face... encountering the human-canine monstrosity...

The creature attacking... its icy hand grabbing her neck... the twin prongs of the tuning fork device invading her nostrils...

And then nothing, a timeless dark void, not sleep

but something else, a state of consciousness rife with odd stinging sensations, as if a thousand microscopic needles were stabbing into her, penetrating not only flesh but delving deep into organs and bones.

The thumps and clangs grew louder. Someone – or some*thing* – was in the adjacent Zarya module. She suddenly realized that whoever or whatever it was, it was trying to open the hatch between the modules.

Terror overwhelmed her as she imagined Dog-face returning. She flailed her arms and legs, frantic to touch something solid, to ground her fears against a physical object.

Calm down, Kayla! This isn't helping.

She stopped flogging the air, forced slow deep breaths to quell panic. More than likely, her crew mates were coming to rescue her. Soon she'd be safe in the CRV and the five of them would be evacuating the station.

A blinding starburst appeared as the hatch opened with a discordant groan. She squinted at the intense illumination until her pupils adjusted to Zarya's normal lighting.

Two figures in spacesuits floated through the portal. Kayla's fear was replaced by bewilderment. Her crew mates should have been wearing the orange ACES garments. But these were the bulkier EVA suits. Odder still, these suits were white with blue trim, a different color combination than the ones used at the station.

Her confusion intensified until the two male figures drifted closer. They were neither astronauts nor cosmonauts. Asian features, as well as red flag patches with five golden stars, revealed them as taikonauts from the fledgling manned spaceflight program of the People's Republic of China.

Kayla recalled that China recently had launched

one of its Shenzhou spaceships with a three-man crew for an extended orbital mission. Somehow, that craft must have docked with the station.

"What are you doing here?" Her voice sounded weak, as if vocal cords hadn't been used in a long time. "What about the evacuation?"

"You are astronaut Ackerman of the United States?" the first one asked, his English near-perfect.

"Of course! Who do you think I am? And you're Chinese taikonauts. What's going on? How are you here?"

"NASA and its international partners in the space station asked us to enter. Our authority originates from an emergency directive, pursuant to a space treaty signed by the People's Republic of China, Russia, the United States, Japan, the nations of the European Union and—"

"Right, I get it," she said.

"We accessed your station without incident. However, the hatch to this module was damaged from outside. It took us some time to open it."

That explained the thumps and clangs. They must have been using tools to pry open the hatch.

"The mechanism appeared to have been deliberately jammed. We found a pair of dark smudges, as if from the application of some unknown thermal source."

Something bumped against Kayla's elbow. Startled, she whirled around. It was the cosmonaut spacesuit, empty and adrift. The helmet floating nearby. Her mind flashed back to the terrifying events.

"This thing, it's dangerous! Did you see it?"

The taikonauts looked confused.

"Okay, listen, start at the beginning. My crew, where are they?"

They hesitated, as if reluctant to answer.

"Please, I need to know."

A smattering of Chinese passed between the two men. Finally, the English-speaking one explained that an evacuation had occurred hours ago, and that the lifeboat had crashed in the Pennsylvania mountains.

"We are sorry to inform you of these events. According to American news reports, three of your crew mates perished. Henri Renier was the only survivor." The taikonaut hesitated. "However, there is an obvious contradiction in these reports. You also were reported to have been aboard the lifeboat."

Kayla tried to absorb it all, but couldn't get past the knowledge that Paco, Valentin and Tanizaki were dead. She didn't realize she was crying until an expanding cloud of tiny globules drifted away from her eyes.

"Please allow us to help you from this module," he said. "We can administer medical attention to stop the bleeding."

"Bleeding?"

She stifled her sobs, gingerly touched her face. The action dislodged a bevy of red globules clinging to her upper lip. She rubbed a finger across the septum of her nose. More blood drifted from her nostrils.

"I'm sure you will feel better after treatment." The taikonaut hesitated. "And after donning some attire."

Kayla looked down. Only then did she realize she was naked.

26

Corbet and Aggie lost the trail twice amid the dense underbrush and pounding rain. On each occasion, they managed to relocate Kayla's footprints a few yards farther on. The astronaut's general heading remained the same, southwest, according to Aggie's compass.

The farther they got from the tower, the more Aggie tried to convince him to turn back.

"We don't know what we're dealing with here," she argued.

"We have to go on. We can't let it get away."

They'd mutually adopted the *it* moniker without discussion. Whatever they were chasing couldn't possibly be an American astronaut. But not until the footprints began to change did the pronoun seem truly appropriate.

At first, the changes were subtle. Corbet rationalized that the driving rain was responsible. But the deformities eventually became too pronounced to ignore.

Kayla's shoe size was about an eight. The muddy impressions now exceeded that by at least six inches. And the toes had begun to morph together, transforming five human digits into a shapeless blob.

As the tracks progressed, the blob metamorphosed into a new kind of foot, a large triple claw in a wishbone configuration, with two talons projecting forward and the third facing the rear.

Aggie grabbed his arm, brought him to a sudden halt. "All right, that's it. End of chase."

"Its stride is getting longer too."

"Corbet, if I have to handcuff you and drag you out of here, I will."

"You've got a right to be scared. I am too."

"This isn't about being macho, it's about making a sane choice. This is no longer a responsible course of action. We have to turn around. We have to report what's happening out here and get backup."

She was right, of course, her logic indisputable.

This entire night had transcended ordinary weirdness, had become a runaway locomotive steaming into twilight-zone territory. The two of them were out here in the middle of nowhere with no communications, on the hunt for some murderous monstrous thing.

But Corbet couldn't turn back, couldn't risk losing the trail.

"My dream, I had a rerun when we were in the lifeboat. Or, sort of a rerun. There were differences. I was still in Tribeca with the feral humans. But this time I saw the toy ray gun. And the Statue of Liberty was no longer Dog-face, it was Kayla."

Aggie looked at him like he was crazy. He tried to clarify.

"What I'm trying to say is, Dog-face and Kayla are the same person. Only it's not a person, it's not human—"

Sudden movement, off to their left. They spun toward it. But it was just a squirrel, dashing up the trunk of a drooping evergreen.

Corbet went on. "This morning, when I first experienced the image of Dog-face, I thought it was all a weird dream. Then later, when Dr. Jarek showed me the pictures of Dog-face, I thought maybe it was a psychic event mixed into a dream. But now, the more I think about it, the more obvious it becomes that the whole thing really is a vision. But it's a new kind of vision, one that isn't literal, at least not entirely. Instead, it's full of symbols."

Aggie still looked confused. Corbet couldn't blame her, considering he was still trying to piece things together.

"Bottom line – whatever we're chasing, we can't let it get away."

She regarded him for a long moment before finally releasing his arm. They proceeded onward, following the trail.

But it went only a few more paces before disappearing at the trunk of a massive oak. They searched outward from the tree's base in all directions but found no evidence of further tracks. The clawed prints seemed to have vanished in mid stride.

And then, as if on the same wavelength, they raised their flashlights.

Snared on a twig ten feet overhead, flapping in the wind like a miniature flag, was a torn fragment of light blue cloth. The oak's dense canopy prevented their beams from penetrating higher.

"That's a piece of her coveralls," Corbet said.

"Maybe."

"One way to find out."

He grabbed the lowest limb, planted his soles against the tree and walked up the trunk. The bark was slippery and his Converses caked in mud. But the oak was ancient, and studded with enough knots and protrusions to provide decent footholds.

"Corbet, what the hell are you doing!"

He swung his feet over the limb, locked his ankles together and rotated himself up onto the branch.

"Get down from there! This is crazy!"

She was right. It was beyond insane. Yet he felt as if he were walking a tightrope that crossed a chasm of his fears. There was no turning back. To maintain his balance and not fall into those fears, he needed to keep moving forward until he reached the other side.

Aggie backed away from the oak, pancaked her gun and flashlight together. She aimed them into the canopy above him, ready to open fire should the tree contain something besides the remnant of cloth.

Corbet reached a branch that brought him eye level with the fragment. It was definitely a piece of Kayla Ackerman's suit, likely snared by the branch and torn away as she ascended. Gingerly, he extended the flashlight upward, pushed it through a cluster of leaves in an attempt to see higher into the canopy.

A pool of trapped rainwater splashed down onto his face. Startled, he lost his footing. He wrapped his arms around the trunk just in time, preventing what would have been a nasty plunge.

"Goddammit, Corbet, that's enough!"

"My bad."

"Get down from there before you break your neck!"

Her warning tripped an early childhood memory, his mother blasting him with that same reprimand. He'd been perched on a limb, pretending to be high-wire performer in a black walnut tree behind their New Hampshire house as Jeremy cheered him on.

"I'll be all right."

His words sounded hollow. It didn't matter. He had to keep going. Blinking moisture from his eyes, he planted his feet securely on the limb and prepared to climb higher.

A strange animal sound echoed through the forest, loud enough to stand out against the pounding rain. It seemed to be coming from a nearby tree. Corbet froze, his groping palm inches from an overhead branch. The sound approximated a low-pitched gurgling, like someone trying to clear mucus lodged deep in their throat. It rose and fell in cyclical fashion. Loud, faint, then loud again as the cycle repeated.

He wiped the rain from his eyes, trained the flashlight in a wide arc to illuminate the surrounding trees. At first, he detected nothing unusual, just masses of intertwined foliage amid an overall fog of moisture. But as he began to distinguish details among the more distant trees, he spotted something out of place.

The gurgling stopped, as if cut off by a switch.

It was a couple hundred feet away, poised on a

high limb of another soaring oak, slightly above the level of his own perch. He couldn't make it out clearly. Only fragments of its body were visible through the intervening leaves and branches.

Patches of light blue material suggested he was looking at Kayla Ackerman in her coveralls. Yet, what was not hidden by the cloth or the intervening foliage spurned that identification. Those areas were darker and grittier in texture, with little similarity to human flesh.

He pinched the flashlight under his arm to free up a hand and slipped his phone from his jacket. Not surprisingly, the interference hadn't relented – still no signal. But he should be able to snap a photo. He aimed the lens toward the thing, even knowing he wouldn't get much of a shot at this distance and in these weather conditions.

He zoomed in, pressed the shutter. The flash went off. The thing froze, then whirled in his direction. A chill vaulted up Corbet's spine. He had the impression it was looking right at him.

There was a blur of motion. With unnatural speed, the thing rocketed up the trunk and leaped out onto a limb. It made a spectacular 15-foot jump to the branch of a higher and more distant tree.

The sudden movement startled Corbet. His foot slipped off the limb. He released the phone and flashlight, made a frantic grab for an overhead branch.

He missed.

He tumbled out of the tree, slammed butt first into a clump of underbrush.

"Corbet! Are you all right?"

He winced as she helped him up. Nothing felt broken. But he'd definitely earned some bruises.

He picked up his flashlight, whipped it upward. They could hear the thing retreating into the distance, vaulting through the canopy like some jet-powered Tarzan. Its speed rendered pursuit on foot useless.

The sounds of its getaway receded, finally dissolving into a rumble of distant thunderclaps.

"Did you get a look at it?" Aggie asked.

"Not really." His heart was pounding. Probably enough adrenaline coursing through him to power a city. He checked around the base of the tree, located his phone.

The photo he'd snapped showed little more than wet tree branches interspersed with hazy specks of blue cloth. There was nothing to suggest a living creature.

"We have to find it again," he said. "We have to get the whole damn army out here, whatever it takes."

"No argument. But right now we need to go back."

27

Russell Van Zeeland liked the homely nature of this West Wing study adjacent to the Oval Office. Its lack of pretension, a quality he'd valued throughout a four-decade political career, made it perfect for informal meetings. He could sit on the edge of the rough-hewn Teddy Roosevelt desk and close his eyes and briefly imagine he was somewhere other than the White House.

It was important to recall on occasion what life had been like prior to ascending to the surreal office of the Presidency. To have every whim catered to by scores of servants was a far cry from the Missouri farmhouse where he'd spent his formative years. Anything that returned his spirit to those simple roots, even for an illusory moment, helped him to maintain a sane perspective on the world.

And this morning, Van Zeeland sorely needed perspective.

He gazed at the study's sole nod to modernity, a large communications console. The giant flatscreen TV was divided into quadrants that displayed four news channels. Although the audio was muted, the quartet of anchors was fixated on the identical set of interwoven stories. Field reporters near the lifeboat crash site updated the status of survivor Henri Renier, the tragedy involving the ambulance crew and the mystery surrounding Kayla Ackerman. She'd been found alive at the space station, which conflicted with initial reports placing her aboard the doomed lifeboat.

The fantastic nature of the events contained enough morsels for the media to feast on for months. And if the press ever learned that a murderous extraterrestrial was running loose in the mountains of northcentral Pennsylvania...

"Mr. President, we try keeping a lid on this, it'll blow up in our faces," Dan Edelstein said.

"Only if we lack the fortitude to remain strong," General Juan Carlos Grobbs countered.

The two men sharing the study with Van Zeeland occasionally expressed similar opinions. Today was not to be one of those times.

Edelstein, Van Zeeland's closest friend, was national security adviser and White House liaison for issues involving U-OPS. Seated in a Victorian-era chair said to have been used by Abraham Lincoln, he looked like a mild-mannered retired school teacher. But those privy to the inner workings of the White House knew better. Staffers often referred to Van Zeeland and Dan Edelstein as a singular and immensely powerful two-headed entity, nicknamed "The Van-Dan."

The President addressed Grobbs. "Fortitude, General? I think the issues are a bit more complicated than that."

Van Zeeland had inherited the three-star Army officer from the previous administration. He'd often toyed with the notion of appointing a fresh face as director of U-OPS. But Grobbs had Beltway clout, including bipartisan support on Capitol Hill and an impressive list of Pentagon allies. Firing him would have repercussions.

"Preceptor's pilot is running loose in those mountains," Edelstein said. "The first responders at the crash site saw her... or him... or whatever in god's name we're dealing with."

Grobbs airily dismissed the concern. "Local police and emergency personnel are cooperating in the interests of homeland security."

Tall and trim, his buzz-cut hair prematurely white, the general's existence revolved around a near-pathological need for secrecy. It probably would take an act of Congress to learn what he'd eaten for breakfast.

"The locals have been warned about speaking to the press," Grobbs continued. "Kayla Ackerman is cooperating, not that she has much choice. No room for her to be brought back on the Chinese spacecraft, so she's stuck in orbit until the next Soyuz goes up in two weeks. Little danger of her engaging the media. And Beijing has promised not to make any public statements other than bragging about their role in providing assistance."

"Which they'll milk for all it's worth," Edelstein said.

"What about the ambulance crew?" Van Zeeland asked.

"The ambulance was relocated to make it appear the crew died when they plunged down an embankment. That's played well in the press."

"Maybe so, but it won't hold up," Edelstein argued. "We're on shaky ground with this whole misinformation campaign. Someone will get wind of a coverup."

"The steps taken thus far are of an emergency nature, intended only as a short-term solution. Their sole purpose is to buy us time to locate Spartan and deal with the threat he represents."

Spartan. It was the old code name for Preceptor's pilot. Preceptor had informed U-OPS about Spartan five decades ago but had assured them that the pilot of his two-person spaceship had perished in the 1960 incident. Despite the gravity of the situation, Van Zeeland derived an odd satisfaction from realizing that the mighty Preceptor was not infallible.

"What about this young fire-police volunteer?" Edelstein asked. "He saw what really happened to the ambulance crew."

"He remains in protective custody," Grobbs said.

"And what do we do when he's released and decides to go to the press? Or when families of those paramedics start demanding to see the bodies?"

"Modifications are being made to the corpses to disguise the real cause of death and provide evidence they perished in a vehicular accident."

We're mutilating bodies. Van Zeeland grimaced at the idea but couldn't see a way around it. "Do we know what killed them?"

"The weapon that caused the burns remains unknown."

"And what happens when this whole affair does go public?" Edelstein demanded.

"Assuming a successful resolution – Spartan's capture or termination – the White House can invoke national security as a justifiable reason for having misled the American people. That will give us additional time to establish a comprehensive long-term strategy."

"New and improved lies."

"You have a better solution?"

Edelstein hesitated. "At the moment, no."

"Ike should have gone public with the whole damn thing back in 1960," Van Zeeland said. "Would've saved us a huge headache."

"But he didn't, Mr. President. Nor did any of your predecessors."

"I don't need to be reminded of my duties here, General."

Like every Chief Executive since Dwight "Ike" Eisenhower, Van Zeeland had learned of U-OPS, Preceptor, Spartan and the incredible nest of secrets they encompassed on the day he'd assumed the Presidency. U-OPS matters had been kept hidden from the world for more than half a century.

Still, even today Van Zeeland found it hard to accept that the United States had been engaged in clandestine communications for 50-plus years with a crash-landed extraterrestrial – code name Preceptor – and that those communications involved the nation in a profound conspiracy.

Preceptor had made it clear in his earliest videos that should his existence or the reason he'd come to Earth be revealed, his close relationship with the U.S. government could be jeopardized. It was impossible to ignore the not-so-subtle threat. Should the United States make U-OPS matters public, the nation would no longer benefit from the alien's goodwill.

And that goodwill had provided the country with spectacular economic benefits.

Van Zeeland, like his White House predecessors, expended most of his energies on real-world issues. There was always a war, legislation, natural disaster or election campaign to deal with, as well as the 800-pound gorillas: runaway debt, the world's addiction to energy, global warming and terrorism. Addressing those issues was difficult enough. It seemed folly trying to delve into the mind-boggling implications of a visitor from another planet.

Now, however, those implications were unavoidable.

Edelstein received a phone message. He turned to Van Zeeland.

“Henri Renier was just transferred to National Naval Medical Center in Bethesda from that trauma center in Williamsport. He’s been in and out of consciousness but managed to pass along some details.

“That Pennsylvania landing site wasn’t a random choice. A malfunctioning navigation system wouldn’t allow them to come down anywhere else. Somehow, Spartan must have plugged in those coordinates. Either he was unaware – or simply didn’t care – that the lifeboat wasn’t built to withstand such bad weather.”

There was a knock on the door. A female captain entered.

“Excusc me, Mr. President.”

The captain plopped an attache case on a coffee table. “We just received this from U-OPS. Dr. Jarek said it was urgent.”

28

PRECEPTOR TRANSMITTED FROM HIS HIDDEN location at random times, bouncing the signals across global SATCOM via an unknown technology that made it impossible to trace the messages back to their source. Transmissions sometimes occurred monthly and on other occasions, half a dozen times a week, but never more than once in any 16-hour period – a limitation U-OPS investigators believed was due to some technological constraint aboard his damaged vessel. His messages were considered so sensitive that they were rarely sent from Georgetown to the White House via landlines or airwaves, but dispatched by courier.

Today, the captain served that function. She opened the attache case and handed Grobbs a rectangular box twice the size of a cell phone. Grobbs waited until she departed before setting the box on the console and plugging it into a special input.

A virtual keyboard appeared above the box. Grobbs typed in a security code. The news channels vanished from the TV, replaced by today's date and the time Preceptor's message had been received by U-OPS – 45 minutes ago, at 5:50 a.m.

Transmission event: #53-12

Transmission configuration: 99.98 percent video, 0.02 percent data

Transmission source: unknown

Message processing time: 32.58 minutes

Message ready for access

Grobbs hit a key. Preceptor's video began. As always, the alien stood in that elegant 1960s-vintage study. Today he wore a familiar tweed jacket, one of his favorite items of apparel. He appeared more somber than usual.

"My pilot is now among you. Your choice not to destroy the space station and terminate him before he reached the surface has drastically escalated the danger. However, our priority remains the same. He must be stopped from carrying out his insane plan.

"As you now realize, he has potent replication capabilities. He can alter his appearance from his native form to assume various identities, including quasi-human ones. The dog creature was his first replicate, the astronaut his second. A transformation requires physical contact with the lifeform to be imitated.

"Once he abandons a replicate and reconstitutes into his native form, he cannot return to that replicate. Also, each successive replication increases cellular instability, making it more difficult for him to maintain a perfect imitation. This essentially places an upper limit on the number of successful transformations he can achieve.

"The small device he carries is the source of all his technological capabilities. It allowed him to survive in orbit and hide from your tracking systems. It caused the malfunctions that forced the space station crew to evacuate and prevented the crew from utilizing their telecommunications, as well as creating the interference that facilitated his escape. This device also has multiple applications as a potent energy weapon.

"He has incredible powers of resiliency and could withstand intense assault from standard firearms and explosives. I recommend utilizing your latest generation of kinetic radiating weaponry."

Preceptor walked to the edge of his desk, laid a hand on the vintage rotary phone. Researchers later reviewing the transmission would search for hidden symbolism in the action. But Van Zeeland knew it represented nothing more than a savvy politician's way of accentuating the impact of his final words.

"You are confronting a crisis that could determine the fate of your species. Hard decisions may be called for, perhaps great sacrifices. Unfortunately, I cannot offer direct assistance. It is up to you to stop him. I can only urge that you not forget what he is – a merciless enemy unswayed by the tenets of reason. It is unlikely you can take him alive. Do not even try. Termination, not capture, must be your goal.

"Do not underestimate him. He is shrewd, fanatically motivated and extremely lethal. You must destroy him before he locates me and gains a terrible power."

The video portion of the message ended in a scroll of incomprehensible letters and numbers – the data portion of the transmission. Van Zeeland knew from prior messages that U-OPS would need many hours to translate that data into usable information.

"Mr. President," Grobbs began, rising from his chair, "with all due respect, this crisis could have been averted."

"By blowing up the International Space Station? Not on my watch, General."

Edelstein flashed anger at Grobbs. "That decision was made yesterday. It's your role to accept it."

"It's my role to give the President an honest opinion."

Van Zeeland held up his hand, signaling both men to back off. "What's our next step?"

Grobbs handed the President a sheaf of papers from his briefcase. "This is a classified executive order authorizing special mission unit Mantis One to conduct search-and-destroy operations on American soil."

Van Zeeland passed the papers to Edelstein for review. "I presume this is a technicality, considering we already have the military involved in the search."

To explain the presence of soldiers scouring the wilderness, they'd leaked a fake story to the press that the troops were looking for pieces of the lifeboat that had broken off during the descent. The soldiers were unaware they were really searching for a runaway extraterrestrial.

"Mantis One isn't composed of typical soldiers," Grobbs said. "They're the pinnacle of our spec ops forces and have been briefed on the nature of their quarry. They operate out of uniform and have access to Blackjack technologies, including the prototype kinetic radiating weaponry to which Preceptor referred."

Van Zeeland nodded. The top-secret Blackjack Research Complex in Nevada developed advanced combat gear for the Pentagon.

The general continued. "If Henri Renier is right and Spartan deliberately forced the lifeboat to come down in Pennsylvania, Preceptor and his spaceship likely are hidden somewhere in that region. Spartan could lead us to it."

Finding Preceptor and his hidden vessel, and its presumed technological bounty, had been the Holy Grail of the Pentagon since 1960. Until now, no one had even developed a clue to its whereabouts.

Edelstein frowned. "We need to tread delicately here. Preceptor does not want to be found. Not by Spartan and certainly not by us. Finding him could upset a five-decade status quo and produce unpleasant repercussions."

"And so could *not* finding him," Grobbs argued. "We've been through this debate before, Mr. Edelstein. We must continue our efforts to locate Preceptor and his vessel."

"Anything else we need to discuss at the moment?" Van Zeeland asked, ending the exchange before it blossomed into another argument.

Grobbs handed him a file. "Information you requested on the U-OPS operative, Corbet Tomms. He's the first supersensory we've activated for field duty as a tracker. We'll use him as an additional resource to hunt Spartan. Should he locate the target, Mantis One will implement the kill."

Van Zeeland opened the folder, flipped through pages of dense background info and commentary by Dr. Jarek. He froze when he reached the photo documentation.

"Are you sure we want someone like this involved?"

The first photo was a close-up of a good-looking young man with untidy hair and a devil-may-care smile. Many of the others were surveillance images, clearly shot without Corbet Tomms' awareness. Some showed him partying in nightclubs, usually with one or more attractive women.

But the photo that caught Van Zeeland's attention had been snared from an online amateur porn site. It showed Corbet Tomms and two naked beauties in bed. One woman was caressing Corbet's chest while pouring a pitcher of beer into his open mouth. Unable to gulp down the massive infusion of liquid, he was spraying some of the beer into the woman's laughing face. The other woman had her head buried in Corbet's crotch, presumably performing fellatio. The picture was captioned: *Thar she blows*.

Van Zeeland closed the folder. "I'm no prude, but I would question the commitment of someone like this."

"Most of these supersensories are characterized by a high degree of instability and youthful unruliness," Grobbs said. "Unfortunately, it's not a matter of choice on our part. Corbet Tomms experienced visions involving Dog-face and Kayla Ackerman. He's clearly developed some kind of psychic connection involving Spartan."

"Is he manageable?" Edelstein asked.

"Yes. Slacker type, no job to speak of. Like the other psychics, he's been well compensated for the pre-admission interviews he's being doing with Dr. Jarek, to the point where he's believed to be financially dependent on that income. If we offer him enough money, he'll get with the program and keep his mouth shut."

"Be careful what you tell him," Van Zeeland warned.

"He'll be made aware of only the most relevant information."

"And you're sure he knows nothing about Preceptor, the spaceship, the rest of it?"

"He bought the U-OPS cover story, thinks the purpose of the psychic initiative is to develop supersensories for tracking terrorists and criminals. He has no idea what's really going on."

29

MOST OF IT WAS THE same: the foggy Tribeca street, displaced Statue of Liberty, feral humans creeping through the mist on all fours, toy ray gun embedded in macadam, violet light from the statue's torch. However, when he looked upon Miss Liberty, it was neither Dog-face nor Kayla Ackerman.

The face of an unsavory white man now occupied the statue. Snaky tendrils crept up onto the man's cheeks, presumably the ends of a tattoo on his neck or torso.

Movement on the ground caught Corbet's eye. Startled, he tore his gaze away from the statue to confront a little girl standing a few paces away. She was maybe five years old. Long blond hair framed an angelic face. A pale nightgown cloaked her figure.

But she was translucent, as ethereal as the fog. Unlike the ferals, the Ghost Child retained the ability to walk. She strode purposefully toward Corbet.

"We have to go," she said, her voice serene and composed.

"Go where?"

"To the beginning."

She raised her arm, pointed at the distant statue. Her other hand reached toward Corbet. She wanted him to take hold, walk with her.

"I don't understand," he said. "Who are you?"

She didn't answer. Instead, she wagged her tiny fingers, urging him to grip her hand. Corbet backed away. Strolling through this bizarre realm with a pint-sized phantom was not on his bucket list. And there was something inherently unsettling about her, something beyond her spectral appearance. Fear stabbed at his guts.

And then a blast of morning sunlight yanked him back to the real world. He shielded his eyes as the outside door opened, admitting Dr. Jarek and Col. Mavenhall.

Corbet was in a portable trailer. Sparsely furnished, its highlights included a cheap desk with metal legs, plastic chairs and the uncomfortable cot where he'd spent the night. The trailer squatted at the foot of Neckels Mountain, on the baseball field where the army and rescue copters had landed. The field had become an ad hoc operations base for NASA crash investigators and military personnel.

Corbet, Aggie and Smitty had driven here following the close encounter at the tower. He'd been debriefed by Mavenhall, Jarek and other officials until close to 4 a.m. and had collapsed from exhaustion the instant his head touched the pillow.

Jarek shut the door and turned on overhead fluorescents. Corbet slipped from the cot, realized he was naked. Someone had thoughtfully dried and folded his clothes and piled them beside the bed.

He dressed as Jarek opened a small cushioned briefcase. Housed within was a pair of black goggles with opaque, sand-colored eyepieces.

"No thanks," Corbet said. "Never enter virtual

reality before my morning joe."

"Coffee is coming," Jarek said. "And these are not VR. Please try them on."

Corbet sat at the desk and picked up the goggles. They were lighter than they looked.

"We designed them to imitate the stylings of eyewear used for navigating virtual environments," Jarek explained. "This is our newest and most advanced model in what we call the 300-series. It is capable of—"

"Whoa, slow down. First things first. What about that thing on the mountain last night? Did you find it?"

A burly sergeant arrived with the coffee. Corbet took a sip from the styrofoam cup, grimaced. Compared to his usual freshly ground dark roast blend, it was sewage.

Jarek waited for the sergeant to exit before continuing. "There's been no progress in locating the quarry."

"So where did it come from? Why's it here?" He'd asked the same questions during the debriefing, had gotten no answers.

"We know nothing of its origin," Jarek proclaimed.

Corbet knew that part was a lie. Mavenhall, seeming to sense Jarek's inability to present a good poker face, jumped in.

"Code name for the creature is Spartan. Use that nomenclature should you need to refer to it in a public venue. Avoid any mention of an extraterrestrial origin. We need to maintain the highest levels of secrecy."

"Whatever. You couldn't find any trace of it?"

"We lost the trail not far from where you and Agent Rittenhouse experienced the encounter. The remnants of Kayla Ackerman's coveralls and underwear were found half a mile away, most of it up in the canopy. Apparently, the clothes were abandoned once Spartan completed what we believe was a transformation back into his native form."

Corbet nodded. "That gurgling noise, I think it was part of the process of him changing."

"Our conclusion as well. The most likely scenario is that Spartan was rendered briefly unconscious in the crash. Upon awakening, he removed the boots and cut away the foot coverings in order to begin the change."

"Which suggests the process initiates in the lower extremities," Jarek added.

"He's got big-ass feet," Corbet said, remembering those muddy prints. "Probably why he needed to get barefooted."

Mavenhall nodded. "The first responders must have reached the crash site before Spartan could transform, so he fled. When the paramedics caught up to him, he likely feigned unconsciousness and allowed himself to be taken away in the ambulance. When he realized they were going to put him aboard a medevac, he made his getaway.

"Troops are searching the mountains. Unfortunately, it's a daunting task, considering that Spartan's apparent preferred mode of travel is leaping from branch to branch. It rained most of the night, so if he did come down from the canopy, there should be fresh tracks. As yet, we haven't found any. Blood and flaked skin from the ambulance have been forwarded to our labs. We may learn more about his shapeshifting abilities once they're analyzed."

"What about that interference that knocked out our communications?"

"It affected all forms of telecommunication over an area of at least 50 square miles. Presumably, Spartan can activate and deactivate the interference at will."

Corbet nodded. By the time he and Aggie had rejoined Smitty at the abandoned ambulance, their radios and phones had been working again.

"The goggles?" Jarek prodded.

Corbet put them on. He was surprised he could see normally through the opaque lenses. "Like one-way glass."

"A variation of that technology."

Jarek adjusted the temples for a better fit. "They're psychogenic tracking spectacles, psyts for short – spelled p.s.y.t.s. but pronounced 'sights.' They represent the current end product of our supersensory research initiative at U-OPS."

Last night during his debriefing, Mavenhall and the Doc had explained about U-OPS – Untethered Operations – and its focus on psychic research. But reading between the lines, it had become obvious to Corbet that they weren't revealing everything about what went on there.

"All human beings generate what we call symbiotic brain waves," Jarek explained. "These waves, which are invisible to the eye and to most measurement devices, are broadcast into our surroundings. It's as if each of us possesses our own radio transmitter that sends out a unique signal. We now know that symbiotic brain waves form the basis for all types of supersensory perception.

"Precogs like yourself who can glimpse the future, as well as those blessed with a variety of other psychic skills, have an additional capability. Besides generating the waves, they also can receive them."

"Sounds like you've got ESP down to a science."

"Hardly. Many aspects of the phenomena remain mysterious. As a field of scientific research, we're just beginning to scratch the surface. However, we have codified certain features, enough to develop the technology you're now wearing."

"Okay, so I can receive these symbiotic waves. What

next?"

"To activate or deactivate the psyts, blink rapidly three times."

Corbet strobed his eyes. At the third blink, a floating three-dimensional grid appeared in front of his face. It looked similar to one of those targeting systems used by fighter pilots.

The floating grid was spherical and tinted green, but translucent enough to clearly show the trailer beyond. As Corbet panned and tilted his head, the grid remained centered in his field of vision.

Jarek went on. "The technology is difficult to explain in layman's terms. But a good analogy is to think of it as a kind of radar system. Psyts lock onto the source of incoming symbiotic waves from a specific person – the target. Coordinates are displayed on the grid as a pulsating blip. The target's location and distance appear at the bottom of the grid."

"What's the range?"

"That's the limiting factor. They can only lock onto a target within 300 feet. Actually, to be precise, the record measured distance is 301 feet."

Corbet frowned. "So whoever I'm looking for – and presumably, we're talking about Spartan – can't be farther away than the length of a football field?"

"Unfortunately, yes."

"How do I choose him as a target?"

"That part is rather easy. Or, at least it's proven so for other supersensories we've tested. All you need to do is visualize the target's face."

Corbet closed his eyes, formed a mental portrait of Aggie. But when he opened his eyes, the grid remained blank.

"I was looking for Agent Rittenhouse." The last time Corbet had seen her early this morning, she was being led away to a separate debriefing.

"Too far away," Jarek said. "She's on a flight back to Washington. Try visualizing one of us."

He stared straight ahead and planted an image of Mavenhall in his mind. Seconds later, a pulsating red dot appeared on the grid that matched his position relative to the colonel. The linear distance from the target, 9 feet, appeared at the bottom of the grid, along with the colonel's three-dimensional coordinates.

"All right, I'm tracking." He panned his head to gaze directly at Mavenhall. As he did, the blip moved to the center of the grid. "Looks like I've acquired an enemy target."

If Mavenhall was annoyed by the reference, he didn't show it.

"Many psychics find a photo or drawing of the target helpful," Jarek said. "That enables them to better hold a specific image in their minds.

"The goggles are powered by lithium-ion batteries. A plug-in recharger is enclosed in the left temple. The right temple contains an intuitive touchpad control activated by rubbing your finger across it. The touchpad allows you to increase or decrease the size of the sphere, change the grid color to avoid chromatic conflicts with the background, other functions of that sort. There's a tutorial. I'll download it to your phone."

"And be careful with these," Mavenhall warned. "They're a prototype. No spares at the moment."

Corbet blinked again and the grid vanished. He removed the psyts, nestled them back in the briefcase. Then he told Jarek and Mavenhall about the latest vision, his third excursion into that devastated world. He skipped the encounter with the Ghost Child – he wanted more time to process that unsettling exchange before revealing it. He concentrated on the tattooed white man who had appeared on the statue's face.

"I'm pretty sure it means Spartan has transformed

again."

"Can you describe this new countenance?" Jarek asked.

"I think so."

Mavenhall got on the radio, ordered one of his people to find a sketch artist.

"I gotta tell you, your whole plan sounds kind of flaky," Corbet said. "What am I supposed to do, drive around these mountains in the hopes of getting within 300 feet of Spartan?"

"For now, yes," Mavenhall said, finishing his call. "No one must know what you're searching for. We can't risk inciting panic."

That made sense. People would freak if they learned a shapeshifting E.T. was on the loose. There would be a deluge of false leads. Spartan sightings would flow in from all manner of publicity seekers and UFO nuts, not to mention zealous helicopter parents mistaking strangers in the neighborhood for aliens intent on abducting their little Naomi and Sam.

"You'll be given a cover story," Mavenhall said. "You'll travel in the company of one of our agents. Your compensation will be $1,500 per diem."

Corbet acknowledged a spark of pleasure at the prospect of earning that kind of money. Still, he would have done this for free. For reasons that remained elusive to him, he had to find Spartan.

"I want Aggie Rittenhouse as my handler."

"We'd prefer a male agent. Someone you won't try to seduce."

Corbet hid his anger behind a cold smile. "Wouldn't want this mission to fail, would you, Colonel? As I recall, you've been down that road before, made a stupid decision that cost lives. So, don't make another bad call. Get me Aggie."

"You'll do as you're told, preferably without

complaint."

"Like hell. I'm not my brother."

"That's obvious. He understood the importance of duty."

Corbet stood up, got in Mavenhall's face. "You don't have the right to talk about Jeremy. You're not worth the weight of his shit."

The colonel's eyes flashed anger. Corbet prayed he'd throw a punch.

Go ahead, give me an excuse to do what I've wanted to do for years. He'd like nothing better than to start pounding on the asshole.

Jarek saw where things were headed, jumped in as mediator. "Colonel, perhaps a female handler would make for a better cover story. She and Corbet could pretend to be a young couple vacationing in the area."

A knock on the door ended the stalemate. A corporal entered, sprang to attention in front of Mavenhall.

"Sir, the Alpha Command trailer has arrived. General Grobbs is on a secure line. I've been asked to bring you there ASAP."

Mavenhall nodded, barked an order to Jarek as he followed the corporal out the door. "Contact Agent Rittenhouse's plane, have the pilot turn around."

Mavenhall slammed the door shut behind him with such force that the walls rattled.

Corbet had won the battle. But his anger didn't fade.

There was still a score to settle.

30

SHARON THOUGHT SHE'D SEEN IT all during her 35 years of waitressing at Bramble Road Café. But she'd never encountered anyone like the stranger in booth three.

When he'd stepped through the door in jeans and tank top, she figured he was here to fuel up for a Saturday morning shift at the sawmill, the destination of many of her regulars. Yet something about the way he gazed curiously at his surroundings hinted that he wasn't one of the woodcutting grunts.

Tall and lean, he looked to be in his mid-thirties. He also looked like trouble. Tattoos covered most of his exposed flesh, including a leafless tree on his chest and neck, with branches slithering up onto his face. A more violent tat decorated a well-muscled arm, a coiled rattlesnake crushing the life out of a pregnant woman. Sharon took it as one of those vengeance fantasies, the kind deadbeat dads spent their money on instead of sending the cash to the struggling wife and kids.

She'd had some experience with that.

His wavy black hair was trimmed short on the sides and he was overdue for a shave. Mirrored sunglasses completed the image of an antisocial jerk.

She approached his booth. He was staring out the window, his attention riveted to a low-flying helicopter on the far side of the valley.

The air was filled with planes and choppers this morning. Sharon lived 12 miles from Neckels Mountain. On her drive to work, she'd passed oodles of soldiers in trucks and humvees, as well as rubberneckers and media types. The spaceship crash was the biggest disaster to hit the region since Hurricane Agnes had caused massive flooding back in '72.

"Regular okay?" she asked.

The stranger turned from the window and awkwardly removed his sunglasses with two hands, as if unaccustomed to wearing spectacles. He stared at her coffeepot, finally nodded.

She filled his cup. He sniffed at the coffee like it was some hoity-toity wine, then made a *yuck* expression, as if it was the foulest thing in the world. The Bramble served a decent cup of joe, certainly nothing like he was making it out to be. Sharon hoped he wasn't one of those dipshits who got their kicks giving waitresses a hard time.

"Something wrong with it?" she asked, ready to do battle. Since her divorce, she took no crap from dipshits.

"This beverage contains a high concentration of psychoactive molecules."

"Uh-huh." She had no idea what he was talking about. "You want decaf?"

"No." He pushed the cup to the other side of the table, putting it as far away from his nose as possible.

His attention was drawn to the door, to a young couple entering with their arms wrapped around one another. Sharon didn't know their names, only that they were semi-regulars. They were obviously crazy about one another, still in that playful stage of youthful passion that came without heavy baggage.

They sauntered past the booth, giggling about some private joke. The stranger craned his head to follow them, intrigued in a way that Sharon took as unseemly. Weirder still, he arched his head back and inhaled sharply, as if trying to *smell* them. A chill went through Sharon. She had the sense of a predator stalking its prey.

She rapped on the table edge to recapture his attention. "What can I get you?"

He pried his nose away from the couple, gazed blankly at Sharon for a long moment.

"Information," he said finally.

"I meant, what can I get you from the menu?"

"Is purchasing something in addition to the coffee a requirement?"

"If you just want to sit here, that's fine." She wanted him gone but couldn't think of a reasonable way of suggesting it.

"I have no appetite. I took nutriment at an earlier hour."

Was he putting her on with the bozo talk? Yet he seemed so serious. Either way, in the hierarchy of difficult customers, weirdo was better than dipshit. As long as he left that young couple alone.

"I seek historical information pertaining to this region of Pennsylvania."

"What kind of historical information?"

"It is of a personal nature. I would prefer not to divulge details."

"Uh-huh. So, you're looking to do some research."

"Yes. Research."

"Did you try going online?"

"Do you have an Internet-accessible device I might borrow? A smartphone or computer?"

She had a phone in her purse but had no intention of loaning it out, especially not to this character.

"You might want to try a library," she suggested.

"Of course," he uttered, looking like a lightbulb had just gone off in his head. "Libraries of this era not only would reposit analog physical materials in the form of books and magazines, but would incorporate primordial elements of the paradigm transition to digital."

"Uh-huh."

"Where is the nearest library?"

"Calloway." She pointed west. "About 10 miles down the road. The town's main drag is only a couple blocks long so you can't miss it. Look for the strip mall on your left."

He bolted to his feet so fast that she jumped back, startled.

"May I have the check so that I might pay for the coffee and the service?"

Sharp laughter erupted behind them. Two sawmill grunts at the counter had been listening in, could no longer contain their amusement at his oddball talk.

The stranger's cheeks reddened. His eyes flared with rage. But it was the way he bared his teeth like some wild animal that truly frightened Sharon. Her ex used to get a similar scary look when he was drunk or in one of his moods, so pumped up with anger that the slightest provocation would get him slapping or punching.

Worried a fight would break out, Sharon quickly wrote up his check. It came to $1.06 with tax. By the time she handed it to him, his anger was gone, having vanished as quickly as it had appeared.

He rooted in his jeans for a tip, counted out two nickels and a penny.

"Gee. Thanks a lot."

"You are welcome."

He seemed oblivious to her sarcasm. But eleven cents, a measly 10 percent tip? She'd provided all that help and he turned out to be a cheapskate. Besides, 10 percent tips had gone out of style when Sharon was a kid, back in the 1960s.

He strode past the sawmill grunts without a word,

handed $1.06 in change to Dottie at the register. Sharon watched through the window as he strolled across the parking lot. His gait was odd too, kind of stiff, with the knees hardly bending. He looked like someone unaccustomed to walking.

Her final surprise was his ride, a vintage Pontiac Firebird. The kick-ass muscle car was tricked out in two-tone metallic gold paint, a rear spoiler and flame decals.

One of the sawmill grunts joined Sharon at the window. "What planet's he from?"

She shrugged. "Takes all kinds."

The stranger revved the engine, laid rubber as he pulled out. The Firebird's back end skidded wildly as the car accelerated onto Bramble Road, heading in the direction of Calloway.

31

The Bordeaux-red Chevy Trailblazer reeked of comfort. Still, an SUV wouldn't have been Corbet's first choice on a day like this. It would have been more fun cruising around these mountains searching for Spartan in a Mercedes SL convertible, like the one Jeremy had put money down on with his reenlistment bonus. They'd taken it for a test drive but his brother had never been able to complete the purchase. He'd been killed in action five weeks later.

Last night's storm had left an ideal environment for top-down cruising. The skies were purified, the air drained of humidity. Corbet hung an arm out the passenger-side window, felt warm sunlight on his arm.

He inhaled sweet honeysuckle on the breeze.

"Great day," he said to the driver.

Aggie Rittenhouse gave a brisk nod, maintaining the icy composure she'd displayed since they'd set off from the baseball field. Her eyes never wavered from the road, a rambling two-lane course through an endless progression of tree-flecked hills and valleys. They hadn't encountered another car for miles.

"Put the goggles on again," she instructed. "You're missing opportunities for contact."

"Do you have any idea what the odds are of coming within 300 feet of him?"

"Zero if you're not wearing them."

Her suggestion made sense but he was getting tired of her pissy mood.

He'd already donned the psyts half a dozen times, beginning where Spartan's trail had been lost. Although the creature's escape through the canopy had been to the southwest, there was no reason to assume it had continued on that heading. Aggie was following a spiraling route outward from the tower. She'd suggested a low-flying copter to better cover these thousands of square miles of wilderness. Mavenhall promised to arrange it but for now had consigned them to the SUV.

The sketch artist, following Corbet's recollections, had come up with a fair likeness of the tattooed man. Corbet had been using the drawing in conjunction with the psyts to visualize their quarry. But even assuming that whatever face he saw on the Statue of Liberty during his recurring vision correlated with Spartan's current identity, it was always possible the alien had transformed again. If so, attempts to visualize a previous incarnation would be futile. Corbet would need to re-experience the vision and look upon a new face.

And even if he wanted to, bringing on a vision was

not an option. He'd tried that a few times over the years, never with success. His precog experiences remained either random events or adhered to some mystifying schedule beyond his comprehension.

"Are you going to put them on?" Aggie demanded.

"I need a longer break. They hurt my eyes if I wear them too much."

"That's a lame excuse."

It wasn't an excuse. Something about the floating grid caused eyestrain if he kept the psyts on for more than a few minutes at a time. He'd scanned the tutorial Jarek downloaded to his phone, had tried alleviating the problem by adjusting the grid's size, intensity and hue on the touchpad control. Changing the grid lines to a pale shade of blue made for a slight improvement but didn't solve the problem. Unless he took frequent breaks, the eyestrain sprouted into a full-blown headache.

But he wasn't about to argue the issue with Aggie. It would only escalate her foul mood.

He had no idea why she was so angry. She'd barely uttered a civil word since they'd set out. As far as he could tell, he'd done nothing wrong. She'd been this way since returning to the baseball field.

Maybe she needed food? It was close to lunchtime. He was certainly feeling the urge to gut-park a burger and fries.

"Let's stop for something to eat."

"No time."

"Can't expect me to track E.T. on an empty stomach."

She pulled aside her mannish jacket and reached into a fanny pack belted to the front of her baggy trousers. Had she draped her body in a burlap bag, she couldn't have looked less sexy. Perhaps Mavenhall had ordered her to don such attire to discourage any amorous advances from Corbet.

She rummaged in the pack, handed him four broken peanut butter crackers in clear plastic wrap. He popped one in his mouth. It tasted stale.

"Not exactly what I had in mind."

"There's bottled water on the floor in the back seat."

"Gosh, honey, crackers and water. Had no idea we'd be eating five-star."

She scowled. He changed the subject.

"So, what else do you know about Spartan?"

"What do you mean?"

"C'mon, it's obvious I didn't get the whole story. What are they holding back?"

"You'll have to ask Col. Mavenhall."

"He's not into sharing. Who is Spartan? Why's he here?"

"I know what you know. And what makes you think Spartan's actually a he?"

"Just a hunch."

"Violent. Destructive. Sounds like the appropriate sex."

Her tone transcended sarcasm, was tinged with real anger. Her mood was getting under his skin. It was time to have it out with her, push her buttons until she revealed why she was so pissed.

"I guess being forced to be my handler again made you miss out on something, huh? What was it, frat party with the FBI boys down at the Hooverville hotel?"

"You're too clever for me."

"Or maybe something hot lined up with a boyfriend? Or girlfriend? Or other friend of the intimate persuasion?"

"I'm not discussing relationships with someone whose longest one lasted three days."

"Yeah, she was special."

Aggie sneered.

"C'mon, pretend you're one-on-one with Oprah and

it's time to unload. After all the two of us have been through, you owe me some dirt."

"*Owe* you?"

"Yeah. For allowing you to tag along."

Her eyes flashed fire. She was ready for the knockout punch. He released an exaggerated sigh.

"I guess maybe you're just one of those women. You know the type. The ones who get all bent out of shape when a man tries to do them a favor."

"A favor!"

The dam broke. She hit the brakes, rumbled to a stop on the shoulder, spun to face him.

"Listen, Corbet, there's more to this than just you getting your kicks having me reassigned! I took a lot of crap from those debriefers last night for not being able to control you, for allowing you to lead us into a dangerous situation. And they were right. You were my responsibility and I screwed up.

"Female field agents are still a minority in the Bureau, which means we're under more scrutiny. I'm the only woman assigned to U-OPS and I take this job seriously. The FBI is my life. I have career ambitions. And I don't like being manipulated, especially by men who see me for my sex and not for my abilities!"

She stomped the gas pedal. The Trailblazer lunged back onto the road. "I don't even know why I'm telling you any of this. It's pretty clear you're only interested in one thing."

It was his turn to flash indignation. "Meaning the only reason I requested you was that I want to hook up? Look, you're an attractive woman, I can't deny that. But there's more to it. Last night, I felt comfortable being around you. Believe it or not, you even made me feel safe in an odd sort of way."

He hesitated. This was coming out mushier than he'd intended.

"Look, I'm sorry I made things difficult with your bosses. But what happened up there on the mountain, I'd do all of it over again in a heartbeat. And what I said last night, about needing to find this alien freak, that wasn't bullshit."

Her face softened. He pressed on.

"And for the record, that male chauvinism stuff I was just spouting off about, I don't believe a word of it. I was just trying to push your buttons, find out what was pissing you off."

"Good job," she admitted, the anger seeping out. "Pushing buttons. You've got some skills there."

"Thanks. Years of practice."

She looked on the verge of cracking a smile. Corbet took it as an opening, tried to further lighten her mood.

"Don't you just hate these little spats. We really ought to kiss and make up. After all, we've got Naomi and Sam to think about."

"Who?"

"Our two kids. Remember? They're staying at your aunt's for the weekend so mom and dad can go alien hunting."

She didn't laugh. Still, he sensed the emotion was there, just beneath the surface. Before he could coax it out of her, her fanny pack chirped.

It was Mavenhall, calling on her sat phone. She listened for a moment, then motioned Corbet to reach under the dash.

"Yes sir... checking the location right now."

Corbet slid a tablet PC out from beneath the glove compartment. The computer had an advanced GPS navigation system linked to a DoD satellite net. He typed in the directions as Aggie recited them.

"Stay on this route... three-quarters of a mile... second left onto Meckley Lane... eight miles... look for a dirt trail on the right."

The navigator displayed a photo-enhanced map.

"Got it," she said. "Twelve minutes from our present location." She ended the call, hit the accelerator. The SUV screeched around a bend.

"What's going on?" Corbet asked.

"Spartan's been busy," she said. "More killings."

32

THEY REACHED THE DIRT TRAIL in under 10 minutes, drove a mile through dense woods to a hunting cabin overgrown by ivy. Aggie squeezed the Trailblazer between two other SUVs in the small clearing.

A slain deer, barely older than a fawn, was draped over the cabin's porch railing. Dozens of gunshot wounds peppered its flank. Corbet grimaced. It looked like the animal had been used for target practice.

Inside, Rufus Potts was in charge of the FBI investigators. Short and husky, he had the weary and weatherbeaten face of someone who'd seen it all during 25 years with the Bureau. According to Aggie, Potts was one of their top forensics experts. Like the other half-dozen agents in and around the cabin, he was on special assignment to U-OPS under Mavenhall's command.

The gloomy interior was a work in progress. Walls were unfinished sheet rock; bunk beds and a rickety table and chairs were the sole furnishings. There was no electricity. Kerosene lamps hung from the rafters. Two closed doors led to a small bathroom and kitchen.

"Meet Lonnie Roe," Potts said, gesturing to the naked

dead man lying face up at his feet. The victim's neck and powerful biceps were covered in tattoos, including a particularly loathsome one of a coiled rattlesnake crushing a pregnant woman. A high-powered rifle lay by his side.

Aggie turned to Corbet. "It's him, isn't it. From your vision."

He nodded. The sketch was a decent approximation, but didn't do justice to the real thing. The last time he'd seen this man's face clearly, it had been gracing the Statue of Liberty.

A chill went through him as he gazed down at Lonnie Roe. The fear wasn't brought on by the body itself, but by the fact it prompted a sudden recollection of images from the rest of his vision. And as those memories flashed through his mind, front and center stood that creepy little girl, the Ghost Child.

He forced attention back to Potts and the agent's explanation of events.

"Killcd seven or eight hours ago, somewhere between 4 and 5 a.m. Lonnie Roe and his two friends were hunting out of season. Not the brightest bunch. A state game commission officer tracked them here. He found the bodies, called the township police. We intercepted the call, got here first. So far, we've been able to keep things under wraps. My people are scouring the woods, looking for a trail."

"Spartan definitely did this?" Corbet asked.

"Left his signature." Potts pointed to a pair of circular smudges on the side of Lonnie Roe's neck. "Same weapon used on the ambulance crew. High-energy electrical pulse."

"Like a taser?"

"Like the taser from hell. Those burn marks are the contact points. Lonnie Roe's body completed the electrical circuit. Whatever this weapon is, it's got a mean-ass bite. Voltage is likely in the stun-gun range, 50 kilovolts or so. But way higher amperage."

"Those marks look smaller than the ones on the ambulance crew," Aggie said.

"You're right. I don't think these injuries were meant to be fatal, only knock him unconscious. That suggests Spartan can control the weapon's intensity.

"I saw the preliminary autopsy report on the victims at the tower. They suffered internal burns in their frontal cortexes, which were closest to the forehead impact areas. However, the technical cause of death was ventricular fibrillation. The flow of current caused such powerful muscle contractions that their hearts couldn't function. But I've got a hunch we won't find the same degree of thermal damage inside Lonnie Roe."

"Based on the size of his wounds?" Aggie asked.

"Partly. But also based on this."

Potts inserted a gloved finger into Lonnie Roe's nostril. When he withdrew the digit, it dripped with slimy trails of mucus and blood.

"Same thing Kayla Ackerman reported," Aggie said. "Then Lonnie Roe is definitely Spartan's newest imitation."

"Yepper. Why else take his clothes and ID, not to mention his vehicle. Oh, and we may have lucked out there. He's driving a tricked-out muscle car, an '84 Pontiac Firebird with aftermarket paint job and flame decals."

"Not exactly inconspicuous."

"We notified every PD east of Chicago."

"How'd you identify him without I.D.?"

"Lonnie Roe's in the system, got a hit on his prints. Did three years in Graterford for armed robbery."

Corbet spotted a cell phone amid crumpled beer cans on the floor beneath a chair. He knelt for a closer look. It was an older model, practically an antique.

No internet access, just a limited range of basic call features.

"Any idea how Spartan does one of these imitations?" Corbet asked.

"We're talking genetic engineering way beyond human capabilities, so this is 99 percent guesswork. But I think he inserts the prongs of that tuning-fork device up their nostrils to extract a relatively large DNA sample, primarily from mucus but also from the walls of the nasal cavity. He's not gentle about the process, which accounts for the bleeding. Somehow, he uses our human DNA as the basis for transforming himself into a lookalike."

"More to a person than just their genes," Aggie argued.

"Sure, environment plays a big role in our appearances. Kayla Ackerman reported odd flashes of light and the feeling that her body was being illuminated from the inside. So I'm thinking the device also takes some sort of x-ray or electron-beam tomography scan to nail down the externals, characteristics that aren't genetic.

"The scan provides Spartan with a precise, three-dimensional image of the body to be mimicked. In Lonnie Roe's case, things like muscles developed from working out, the tats, an appendectomy scar, other identifiers not determined by heredity. I also think Spartan needs a living victim to do an imitation."

"If that's true, what killed him?" Aggie asked.

"Probably asphyxiated. Landed on his back and choked on his own nasal blood and excess mucus. The astronaut may have avoided that fate because she was in a microgravity environment. Enough blood floated from her nose, didn't clog her airway while she was unconscious."

"Your human DNA theory might explain Kayla

Ackerman and Lonnie Roe," Corbet said. "But what about Dog-face?"

"You familiar with the story about that Sputnik capsule the Soviets lost?"

Corbet nodded. Dr. Jarek had filled them in on the December 1960 incident, the presumed destruction of the capsule because of a retro-rocket failure or accidental activation of a self-destruct charge.

"That capsule contained two dogs," Potts said. "Spartan must have gotten aboard, obtained the canine DNA."

"But Dog-face was partly human," Corbet argued. "Where'd he get the human DNA?"

"Early space programs didn't operate under modern clean-room standards. It's easy to imagine a few human hairs from some Soviet technician being inadvertently left inside the capsule. However, assuming Spartan requires a relatively large DNA sample, those few hairs wouldn't have been enough to perfectly replicate a human."

"He combined the two species," Corbet said, excited to make the connection. "He wanted to look like one of us, but the best he could do was a blend of human and canine."

Potts nodded. "He must have survived in orbit for more than half a century disguised as Dog-face. Some kind of hibernation, maybe. Or else he's got a really long lifespan. Whatever the case, eventually he drifted close enough to the space station to make his move."

Aggie looked skeptical. "Why not just stay in the Sputnik capsule?"

"Maybe it was damaged. Or maybe he figured his best chance of being found was to pass himself off as a dead cosmonaut and hide inside a suit with a sandblasted visor. Count on some curious astronauts to rescue him from the void."

The scenario made sense to Corbet. "Once he's in the space station, he causes the malfunctions that force them to evacuate. But how'd he get up there in the first place? I mean, presumably he's from some distant planet. Where's his own spaceship?"

No one had an answer.

"There's something else you need to know about him," Potts said.

The agent reached into his forensics kit and handed each of them a barf bag. "In case you feel the urge. Don't want you vomiting on the evidence."

Corbet thought he detected perverse amusement on Potts' face as the agent led them toward the kitchen.

33

CORBET HAD A STRONG STOMACH. Still, he was glad they hadn't stopped for lunch. The sight of the carnage was bad enough but it was the stench that got to him. He fought an urge to retch as Potts opened the door.

"Stay on the sheeting," the agent instructed, pointing to plastic pads near the door.

The kitchen was little more than an aisle flanked by sink, cabinets and propane stove. The aisle terminated at an outside entrance. That door hung open, half torn from its hinges. An FBI agent in a hazmat suit knelt on the floor, using a UV gun to scan Lonnie Roe's blood-soaked friends.

What was left of them.

Flies buzzed around the two victims. Their torsos had been excavated from chests to crotches, exposing the spinal columns. Flesh, broken ribs and internal organs were splattered everywhere. Pieces of cracked vertebrae seemed to be all that held together the upper and lower halves of their bodies.

One man's arm had been severed in the attack. It protruded from the sink. A clump of what appeared to be intestines had landed on the propane stove, as if ready for frying.

"He didn't use his weapon in here," Potts said, seemingly oblivious to the odor. "These two were torn apart by hand. Or, more precisely, by claw."

"I've never smelled such bad decomp," Aggie said, covering her nose.

"Way stronger than what you'd normally find in victims dead this short a time. We think the attack introduced alien compounds, caused a chemical reaction that intensified the odor."

"Should we be standing this close without protective gear?"

"We've taken air samples. No aerobic toxins, at least none that are detectable. But if your skin rots or you start growing extra limbs, give me a call."

The agent gestured to the dangling outside door. "That's where Spartan entered. Near as we can figure, the noise awakened these two. They came to investigate and got a nasty surprise. Lonnie Roe must have been the last one to awaken. Either drunk or a heavy sleeper. He had time to grab his rifle, not much else."

Aggie gazed at the floor behind them, which bore no traces of the slaughter. "If he killed the two in here first, shouldn't there be a blood trail leading back to Lonnie Roe's body?"

"Must have cleaned himself up first. I'm guessing he didn't want blood from this pair contaminating the DNA samples he took from Lonnie Roe. A genetic blend might have mixed up the transformation process, similar to what occurred with Dog-face."

"This level of brutality suggests a perpetrator acting from extreme rage."

"My first thought as well. But there's more to this than just a pissed-off alien. I can't be certain until we get the remains into a lab, but each victim appears to be missing about 20 pounds of flesh and internal organs. Best guess is that Spartan's transformations require large amounts of caloric energy."

"Wasn't just rage," Corbet said. "He was hungry."

34

TOWNSHIP PATROLMAN MARCO TABRISI EASED his cruiser through the parking lot of The Shoppes at Calloway, the strip mall where he'd spotted the suspect's vehicle. It fit the description from this morning's FBI bulletin.

The car was parked at the edge of the lot, its trunk facing an embankment. Pennsylvania didn't require front plates so Marco couldn't see the license to confirm. But the car had to belong to Lonnie Roe. How many 1984 gold Pontiac Firebirds with flame decals could there be in this rural county?

Marco wasn't supposed to risk interaction with the suspect, only report the sighting. The bulletin was unusual in that it didn't reveal why Lonnie Roe was wanted, only that he was considered armed and extremely dangerous.

He unhooked the dashboard mike. "This is unit four. I've got a probable ID on that Firebird over at the Shoppes." He explained the issue with the license plate.

"Copy that." The voice belonged to Connie, the department's office clerk and part-time dispatcher. "The BOLO says surveillance only, no approach."

Marco had no intention of violating the feds' 'Be On the Look Out' edict. But he wasn't happy about it. He'd crossed paths with the FBI before and didn't care for the way its agents treated local departments. They were arrogant and too quick to play the jurisdiction card.

He parked the cruiser behind a van at the end of the lot and settled in for the stakeout. The Shoppes at Calloway housed seven storefronts, including a laundromat, sandwich shop, and a hand-me-down outlet run by the United Rescue Missions. Through his own church, Marco volunteered there, helping to spread the love of Jesus Christ to less fortunate souls.

The largest storefront was Calloway Community Library. Marco doubted the suspect was there. Lonnie Roe was an ex-felon with a long record. More the type of man to be found scrawling graffiti in his prison cell than browsing bookshelves.

But just as the thought occurred to Marco, Lonnie Roe emerged from the library. The suspect hopped into the Firebird, ignited the powerful V-8 engine and headed for the exit. Marco pulled out, tailed the car at a discreet distance.

He radioed in. "Suspect's on the move, heading west on Selkirk. I'm following but you'd better get an unmarked car out here. He's liable to get suspicious."

"Copy that. Feds are fifteen minutes away."

The Firebird suddenly tore off down the street at high speed.

"Too late. I think he made me. I'm in pursuit."

Marco hit the accelerator. A hundred yards ahead, the Firebird reached the traffic signal at Waykirk

Avenue. The light was red, a tractor-trailer halfway through the intersection.

Lonnie Roe slammed the brakes, fishtailed, then gunned it through a narrow opening between the back of the trailer and a Ford Escort.

The Escort driver panicked, swerved hard right and plowed into a parked FedEx truck.

Marco eased past the melee, punched it. He no longer gave a hoot about the feds' agenda. This perp was going down.

The Firebird reached the edge of town. Here, Selkirk Road lost its beeline discipline, became wild and curvy. Lonnie Roe reached the first bend, a left-hander into a downhill slope. Locals knew you had to enter the curve slow, decelerating until you were through the apex.

Lonnie Roe plowed into the corner at dangerously high speed. Marco held his breath. The Firebird made it, but skid way over into the opposing lane. Fortunately, no traffic was approaching.

Marco slung his cruiser around the bend and accelerated onto a short straightaway. The Firebird wasn't in the hands of an exceptional driver. All things being equal, it easily should have outrun his Dodge. But he was keeping pace.

A second cruiser joined the pursuit from an intersecting road, cut in between their vehicles. Marco recognized Elgin Taylor behind the wheel. He couldn't ask for a better partner in a high-speed chase. On weekends, Elgin raced a winged sprinter down at Port Royal, the Juniata County oval. Elgin could sling a machine around dirt or asphalt with the best of them.

Elgin closed fast as they approached Selkirk's most dangerous corner, a wicked right-hander flanked by forests. Overhanging branches created a canopy effect, giving the impression of plunging into a green tunnel. Despite warning signs, every few years some kid took the corner too fast and wrapped his car around a tree.

Marco glanced at the speedometer. Close to 90. If the Firebird didn't slow down, no way he'd make it.

Lonnie Roe recognized the danger, started pumping the brakes. Elgin's cruiser closed to within 50 feet.

Way to go, Elgin.

Before the Firebird entered the corner, Lonnie Roe stuck his arm out the window. He had something in his hand, an object that resembled a tuning fork. He aimed it back at Elgin's cruiser.

Quivering shafts of lightning erupted from its prongs, intersected at Elgin's front bumper. Flames erupted from the engine compartment. The cruiser jerked violently off the asphalt. It tumbled through the air in a lazy spiral, snapping overhead branches.

The cruiser landed on the shoulder in an explosion of mud and gravel, barrel-rolling twice before flopping back onto its wheels with a grinding thump.

Marco screeched to a halt. The flames had died away but oil smoke flooded the cruiser's interior.

"I'm okay!" Elgin hollered, kicking open the door, coughing and limping away from the wreckage. "Go get the son of a bitch!"

Marco rammed the gas pedal. Department policy dictated that he call for backup before resuming the pursuit. And common sense should have made him wary of that weird weapon. But he was too angry.

He accelerated through the tricky corner in a controlled four-wheel drift. Just as the rear tires began to lose grip with the asphalt, he eased up on the throttle, then floored it again as he came out of the curve onto the next straightaway.

Immediately, he slammed the brakes. Wheels screeched in protest as his cruiser shuddered to a stop.

The Firebird was upside down 20 yards ahead,

its rear end facing Marco. The engine had shut off, but the front wheels continued spinning, propelled by inertia. Gray smoke plumed from gashes in the exposed undercarriage.

Torn branches littered the macadam. On the outside of the curve, bark peeling from a tree revealed where the Firebird had run off the road. The smashed-in driver's door indicated the point of impact. The Firebird must have slammed the tree with enough force to flip it.

Marco uncradled his rifle, an old Ruger carbine, and got out of the cruiser. Hunkering down behind his open door, he took aim. The Firebird's spoiler had twisted in the crash, impeding his view through the back window of the overturned vehicle. There was no movement, but he wasn't taking any chances, not with a suspect armed with a lightning-bolt gun.

"Lonnie Roe, if you can hear me, throw out your weapon!"

No response. Marco smelled gasoline, realized the Firebird's fuel tank had ruptured. Gas streamed over the rear deck and down across the spoiler. It drizzled to the asphalt, forming tiny pools that merged into a miniature lake.

"You gas tank is leaking," Marco yelled. "Your vehicle could catch fire at any moment. I can't help you unless you throw out your weapon."

Still no answer. The suspect had to be dead or unconscious. No sane person would stay inside a demolished car that was leaking fuel.

Marco was about to approach when a grinding noise captured his attention. The Firebird wiggled on its roof, began rocking from side to side, gently at first, but then at an increasing tempo. Although Marco still couldn't see the interior, he grasped what Lonnie Roe was trying to do. The perp was trying to flip the car back onto its wheels by shaking it from the inside.

That was impossible, of course. Rocking it a bit, okay – he was probably able to accomplish that because most of the Firebird's weight was now overhead, giving him an effective fulcrum. But not even a muscled perp like Lonnie Roe was that powerful.

A loud scraping of metal against asphalt proved Marco wrong. The Firebird tumbled onto its side, then completed the roll and flopped upright with an ugly thud.

God in heaven help us! What kind of man possessed such incredible strength?

The gas ignited. The force of the explosion slammed the cruiser's open door back against Marco, knocking him on his butt. He roared to his feet, backpedaled from the waves of heat cascading off the wreckage.

Something was moving within the fire. Lonnie Roe darted away from the burning Firebird, engulfed in fire and black smoke. Marco watched in stunned amazement as the flaming figure vanished into the woods.

Marco raced after him, caught up as Lonnie Roe burst into a clearing at a deserted farmhouse. It was the old Needham farm, abandoned for decades.

The fire had subsided but had burned away most of Lonnie Roe's clothes and the top layer of skin, leaving him a reddish hulk trailing hot ashes. Marco couldn't fathom how he was still on his feet. The pain alone must have been unbearable.

The suspect battered down the farmhouse door like a runaway train and disappeared inside. Marco followed.

A derelict piano, the only piece of furniture, looked out of place in the debris-covered living room. Lonnie Roe took a flying leap and landed atop it, then whirled toward Marco with his weird weapon.

Marco reacted on instinct, squeezed the trigger. The

semiautomatic Ruger barked six times. At this range, no way he could miss. Six rounds nailed Lonnie Roe in the chest.

The gunfire should have knocked him off the piano, killed him instantly. Instead, Lonnie Roe just stood there, his red face pockmarked with deep burns, eyebrows and scalp hair singed, six bloody holes in his torso. But it was his expression that brought terror to Marco's heart.

A look of raw hatred.

Expelling a cloud of hot smoke from his lungs, Lonnie Roe leaped off the piano and came at Marco like an enraged animal. Marco got off two more shots but the bullets went wide.

Then the rifle was yanked from his hands, hurled across the room. Marco felt himself being lifted over Lonnie Roe's head and carried to the staircase. An instant later he was airborne, being thrown *up* the stairs as if he weighed no more than a rag doll.

A part of Marco's mind seemed divorced from what was happening and marveled at the precision of Lonnie Roe's aim. Marco didn't hit anything. His body stayed centered within the stairwell like a perfectly thrown football.

He sailed past the second floor landing and through the open bathroom door, on an intersecting course with the tiled wall above the tub.

He slammed the wall hard, dislodging tiles and hunks of plaster, then dropped like a rock into the tub. The back of his head cracked against the porcelain. His last thought before consciousness slipped away was that Lonnie Roe wasn't human but a servant of the devil.

Perhaps even Satan himself.

35

CORBET TUNED IN A NEWS channel on the Trailblazer's satellite radio. Not surprisingly, the lifeboat crash and its aftermath remained the top stories.

"President Van Zeeland arrives later this afternoon in this rural Pennsylvania county," the newscaster announced. "The President plans to confer with state and local officials and meet with the EMS crews who initially responded to the crash, as well as with the families of the three paramedics who died tragically when their ambulance plunged over an embankment.

"And in related news, the Associated Press is reporting that a high-speed pursuit less than 20 miles from where the lifeboat came down has ended in a fatal crash. The suspect, who died instantly when his car hit a tree and overturned, is believed to have been wanted for stealing pieces of the lifeboat wreckage. Two police officers were reported injured during the chase."

Corbet lowered the volume. Cover story or not, the Washington bullshit meter was pinging near the top of the scale. "What a load of crap."

"Uh-huh," Aggie said, stopping at a four-way intersection. "Which way?"

"Make a right," he said, checking the GPS map. "The White House needs to make sure everyone's on the same page with their lies. That's the real reason Van Zeeland wants to talk to those first responders. Probably give them a spiel about national security, convince them to keep their mouths shut for the good of the nation."

"What's the alternative? You want the President to start a panic by telling people there's a flesh-eating alien monster on the loose?"

"I'm just sick of all the lies. Remember, it's not just the public being kept in the dark. Mavenhall's holding out on us too." He paused. "Then again, maybe our esteemed colonel is just holding out on me."

"Corbet, I swear, I know what you know."

"So tell me about U-OPS. What else goes on there?"

She told him what little she knew: that she and Potts and a small coterie of FBI agents were on special assignment to the ultra-secret agency, and that it indeed was involved with more than just psychic research.

"I get the impression of deep dark secrets at the center of it all," she added, "things our government is determined to keep from the public at all costs."

"And you have no idea what those secrets are?"

"Not really."

Corbet sensed hesitancy in her words. "But you do know something."

"Just a rumor. Which you didn't hear from me."

"Deal."

"Does the name Preceptor ring any bells?"

He shook his head.

"It's the code designation of a secret source. Supposedly, this source provides our government with highly advanced technology."

"You're talking about alien technology?"

"That's the speculation. Before last night, I would have said it was all just a load of UFO conspiracy crap, like that nonsense about Roswell and Area 51. But now..."

"How'd you hear about Preceptor?"

"Trick or treat."

“Pardon?”

“Bureau nickname for a special kind of undercover op. About six months ago I was assigned a trick or treat, told to get close to this DoD analyst who was suspected of selling classified engineering material to the Taiwanese government.”

“By getting close, you mean seduce.”

She gave a quick nod and continued before he could press for specifics. “When we arrested the perp, I saw some of his materials, including schematics for state-of-the-art electronics, stuff that supposedly was beyond what Earth science was capable of manufacturing. Ancillary documents revealed that the schematics originated from a high-level U-OPS source.”

“Preceptor.”

“Right. But when I mentioned that name to my superiors and they floated it up the chain of command, I started getting memos from people way above my security clearance. I was ordered to forget I’d ever heard of Preceptor. And then, out of the blue, I’m transferred to U-OPS.”

“Sounds like somebody wants to keep an eye on you.”

“That’s my take on it. Since I’d gained access to information I wasn’t supposed to have, moving me closer to the inner circle meant I could be more closely monitored.”

“So, how do we find out more about this Preceptor, about what really goes on at U-OPS?”

“We don’t. In fact, we don’t even try.”

36

Russell Van Zeeland gazed through the bulletproof window of his VH-60N Whitehawk helicopter as it soared above the wild terrain of northcentral Pennsylvania. Looking out over these seemingly endless Appalachian ranges made him even more appreciative of the challenges facing Mantis One and the other assets hunting Spartan.

An aide knocked on the door, peeked into Van Zeeland's private compartment.

"Mr. President, we should be on the ground in 10 minutes."

"Thank you."

The aide departed.

The copter, designated Marine One because of his presence, would be landing at the baseball field co-opted for onsite investigation of the CRV crash by the military and NASA.

Van Zeeland was making the trip without senior staff, not even Dan Edelstein, who was busy coordinating the White House's disinformation campaign and extinguishing media fires. Edelstein also was dealing with senators and congresspeople from both sides of the aisle, many of whom already were accusing the executive branch of hiding pertinent facts.

Too much publicity and too many lies.

Edelstein was probably right. This whole affair was going to blow up in their faces sooner or later. Even if they found Spartan and ended the threat, the firestorm might well take down his administration.

There was another knock. Gen. Grobbs entered.

"An urgent communication," he said, turning on a monitor to reveal the face of Dr. Jarek transmitting from U-OPS.

"Mr. President, we've translated the data portion of Preceptor's morning message. Even considering the source, it's rather unusual, not at all like the advanced technology instructions and schematics he normally sends. Our people are still trying to analyze its finer points. There remains a slight degree of uncertainty over the precise interpretation of some of the minor details—"

"Out with it, Doctor."

"Yes sir. The schematics are assembly instructions for a type of high-explosive incendiary warhead. Preceptor believes that with a crash program, it can be put together within an extremely short time frame – a mere six hours, he estimates. The bomb would be made by combining existing materials from our arsenal."

"A bomb for what purpose?"

"Presumably, Preceptor will update us with that information."

"What's the yield?" Grobbs asked.

"Just one of these warheads could vaporize a couple city blocks. Preceptor wants us to construct at least a dozen. We're to mount them on short-range missiles carried by our most advanced fighter jets."

Van Zeeland faced Grobbs. "Is something like this even doable in such a short amount of time?"

"Preceptor has a good read on our technical capabilities. If he says six hours, I'm inclined to take him at his word."

"Then the question becomes, do we follow his suggestion and assemble these bombs without knowing their intended purpose?"

"Mr. President, if I may," Jarek said. "The 16-hour

technical limitation between Preceptor transmissions suggests that we won't receive the next video or data from him until around 10 o'clock this evening. At that time he may provide clarification, explain the purpose of these weapons. Therefore, I suggest we begin assembly at once. After all, we're under no mandate to use these bombs."

Van Zeeland saw no obvious downside.

"All right, make it happen. Dr. Jarek, keep me informed. Updates every two hours."

"Yes sir."

The screen went blank. Van Zeeland turned to stare out the window. In the distance flew a second Whitehawk, one of the identical decoy helicopters that always accompanied Marine One as a security measure.

"Speculation, General?"

"It would seem probable these bombs are intended for use against Spartan."

"But payloads of this magnitude?"

"We have to assume Preceptor has a plan."

Assembling the bombs would be the easy part, Van Zeeland realized. The greater challenge might come when he had to order them launched at a target.

37

AGGIE SLOWED THE TRAILBLAZER AND steered into the opposite lane to give the young woman a wide berth. She was standing at the edge of the narrow road, withdrawing envelopes from a roadside mailbox. A little girl of about five stood at the woman's side, clutching her hand. Corbet assumed they were mother and daughter.

The little girl was dark complexioned with curly black hair. She bore no resemblance to the Ghost Child. Yet the sight of her swept Corbet's thoughts back to the most recent incarnation of his vision, to that strange encounter.

Who was the Ghost Child? Why did she want Corbet to walk toward the statue with her, *to the beginning*?

Even though the recurring vision was richly symbolic, he couldn't be certain all the symbols related to real-world happenings. Maybe some aspects of the vision were totally random, dream-chunks infused into the overall event. Then again, maybe that notion was wishful thinking, a less upsetting way to think about the vision. It was more soothing to consider it as a series of haphazard events than as a template of the future.

There was another unique quality to the vision: its progressive nature. Each rerun – if that was the right word for them – seemed to plunge him deeper into that feral city, forcing him to experience new aspects of it.

He felt relief when his thoughts were drawn back to the present. The Trailblazer rounded a bend and they arrived at their destination. The road ahead was blocked with wooden barricades guarded by soldiers. Beyond lay the burned-out shell of Lonnie Roe's Firebird. Two agents from Rufus Potts' team were crawling through the Firebird's charred window openings, probably collecting evidence. From a distance, the pair looked like maggots feeding on fresh carrion.

Aggie pulled onto the shoulder, cut the engine. Corbet grabbed the briefcase with the psyts and followed her to the nearest group of soldiers, who motioned them through into the restricted area.

There was a flurry of activity. A black helicopter

swooped in low over the trees and landed on the road beyond the Firebird. Moments later, guards lifted the barricades to allow a Tastykake delivery truck to enter the restricted area.

The sight of the 28-footer reminded Corbet he was still hungry. But the fact the truck had been allowed in suggested the Tastykake logo was fake, and that the vehicle wasn't here to dispense baked goods.

His suspicions were confirmed when the truck stopped and its rear doors sprang open. A ramp dropped down, banged against the asphalt. Eight all-terrain vehicles rumbled down the ramp. They looked like typical four-wheeled ATVs, yet they were unnaturally quiet, probably electric powered.

The lead rider, a blond Adonis with a crescent-shaped scar on his left cheek, raced to the edge of the woods. He brought his ATV to a squealing halt with its front end aimed toward the forest. The other riders followed his lead, forming a neat line with the precision of a drill team.

There were seven men and one woman. All wore casual hiking garb, cargo pants and safari jackets. But they had a badass look about them that reminded Corbet of his brother's Army commando friends.

The rider with the scar raised his arm, pointed toward the forest. The ATVs accelerated into the trees. In a moment they were gone, swallowed by wilderness.

Col. Mavenhall appeared in the door of the copter, waved for Corbet and Aggie to come aboard. They entered the cramped cabin, belted themselves into flip-down metal seats. Mavenhall had changed into outdoorsy civilian clothes but the perfectly creased pants and jacket didn't seem natural on him. He looked like a male fashion model fresh from a Cabela's catalog shoot.

The copter ascended, hovered over a clearing. Corbet

gazed at an abandoned farmhouse below. Several of the ATV riders were circling the house. One of the men was waving a brick-sized implement through the air.

"Who are they?" Corbet wondered.

"Mantis One, special mission unit," Mavenhall said. "Should they locate Spartan, your assistance will no longer be required."

"Thanks, appreciate the pep talk. What's the guy with the thingamajig doing?"

"It's a next generation PID – photoionization detector with exended range. He's attempting to detect gaseous remnants of Lonnie Roe's burned flesh to pick up a trail."

Mavenhall barked orders to the pilot. The copter lunged forward.

"Put on the psyts," the colonel ordered, handing Corbet a mug-shot photo of Lonnie Roe to replace the sketch-artist depiction. "We'll fly within 300 feet of the ground in ever-widening circles to maximize the coverage area."

Corbet donned the goggles, blinked three times. The translucent tracking grid appeared. He studied the photo until he'd locked in Lonnie Roe's face, directed his gaze toward the terrain below.

"Sir, what about the cop who had contact with Spartan?" Aggie asked.

"Should pull through. He and the other injured officer were transferred to Bethesda for security purposes."

"Any evidence of DNA extraction?"

"No indication those prongs were inserted. We're confident a replication didn't occur. And judging by what happened last night with Spartan's Kayla imitation, it seems likely he can't repair a human body if it's badly damaged. He may have been forced to change back into his native alien form."

That made sense to Corbet. And in back country, Spartan could travel faster that way, do his Tarzan act up in the canopy.

"Sir, I have a theory," Aggie said. "Maybe Spartan needs to familiarize himself with our contemporary culture. If he was trapped in orbit all those years, possibly in hibernation, then at least some of his knowledge of our world might be based on what he learned back in 1960."

"We've considered that too," Mavenhall said, opening a laptop and bringing up a paused video.

"One of our scientists with expertise in genetics and embryology has been studying Spartan's replication capabilities. This is a portion of a longer presentation he made a few hours ago. It may help you understand what we're facing."

Corbet gazed at the screen through the psyts' tracking grid. A balding man with thick Civil War sideburns and a rumpled lab coat stood at a lectern, addressing an off-camera audience.

"Skin and blood samples of the fake Kayla Ackerman taken from the lifeboat and the hijacked ambulance reveal traces of alien DNA," the scientist began. "This indicates a replication of astonishing scope, but one that bears a notable similarity to rare chimeric fusions in zygote or blastocyst developmental phases."

Corbet heard muttering from the unseen crowd, followed by an off-camera voice reminding the speaker that his audience was not steeped in embryology.

"Chimera is a zoological term," the scientist clarified. "It identifies an animal possessing two or more genetically unique cell populations – more than one set of chromosomes. It's extremely rare in humans.

"A human chimera might be thought of as fraternal twins occupying the same body. In the very earliest stages of development, two fraternal embryos fuse in the womb. The cells intermingle. Hermaphroditism or other abnormalities can occur if the twins are of opposite sexes, but in same-sex cases, physiological development is often normal. But throughout the chimera's life, it carries two distinct sets of chromosomes. Often, one set is dominant, with the recessive set found only in certain organs.

"A Spartan replicate carries a similar dual set of chromosomes. Blood and mucus extracted from the human to be imitated are commingled with Spartan's own DNA, but in such a way that all surface traits retain the chromosomal identity of the mimicked individual. Spartan's own DNA remains recessive, hidden within the body of the replicate.

"In human chimeras, the dual set of chromosomes provide no special physiological advantages. However, in a Spartan replicate, the alien DNA retains an extraordinary level of control over the replicate's physical and mental functions. How this is accomplished remains beyond the scope of contemporary science, but the evidence would seem to suggest that a replicate is capable of superhuman strength and endurance.

"Several other factors are notable. The elasticity of the chimeric process enables Spartan at any time to return to what presumably is his native alien form. During such a reformation it must be presumed that his own DNA absorbs and eliminates all traces of the replicate DNA. Also, his first imitation, the creature referred to as Dog-face, proves he is not limited to homo sapiens for purposes of replication."

The video ended.

"Any way of identifying a replicate?" Aggie asked the colonel.

"Other than a complex, multi-sample DNA test, no."

"He might have already assumed a new human identity," Corbet said. "If so, Lonnie Roe's photo won't help me find him."

"Possibly," Mavenhall said. "But until we receive evidence of such an occurrence, we stick to the plan and continue the search."

Corbet turned his attention back to the endless square miles of mountain wilderness, wondering who Spartan's next victim would be.

38

O*UTRAGEOUS PRICES FOR TOMATOES*! The thought churned through Edith Ramagano as she turned off Lincoln Road and guided her Volkswagen Beetle along the winding, tree-shaded lane that led home.

String beans and radishes remained bargains, but tomatoes, cabbage and sweet peas seemed more expensive by the week. And blueberries... well, vendors already were predicting escalating prices throughout the season, even for locally grown varieties.

Edith couldn't recall ever seeing such big price jumps. It was highway robbery. Why, soon you'd have to be a millionaire just to afford a Saturday trip to the farmers market!

She reached the end of the lane and eased the Beetle up against the side of the barn. Popping the front cargo hood, she got out of the car gingerly, pausing to massage bare ankles peeking out from beneath the hem of her flowered house dress. These days, old age and arthritic joints made even simple movements a challenge. Still, considering she was 87 years old, there was no cause to complain.

"March strong through the weeks, through the valleys and the peaks," she muttered, reciting one of her late husband's favorite litanies. Herman had a phrase for every occasion. That one he'd repeated a lot, even after the dementia had taken root.

Through most of their 61-year marriage, Herman would utter it in defiance, inspiring the two of them to keep on battling no matter what the odds, to face life's ups and downs with unwavering courage. Of course, near the end, she'd sensed it held no meaning for him and was merely a string of words fused into memory by repetition.

She lifted the grocery bags from the trunk, trying not to dwell further on the cost of produce or on how much she missed Herman. Gripping a bag in each hand, she trudged along the flagstone walkway toward her modest clapboard home.

Halfway there, she spotted the strange mounds.

There were five of them. Spaced about a foot apart, they lay on the gravelly earth in a line that terminated at the barn's closed door. The nearest mound was as big as a cantaloupe, with each successive one smaller. The final mound, closest to the barn, was about the size of an apple.

Curious, she put down her bags and approached. The mounds were even more mystifying at close range. What she'd taken for a uniform gray color was revealed as an odd mixture of hues, including an oily pink and a shade of green as pale as iceberg lettuce.

Edith leaned in for a better look but pulled back abruptly, assailed by a sulfurous odor. The mounds were excrement, the stool of what must be a fairly large animal. It must have been walking while defecating, unburdening itself a turd at a time.

She gazed into the surrounding woods, searching for signs of movement. Decades ago, these family acres had been tilled fields and pastures, part of a working farm that produced corn, barley, pumpkins and cow's milk. But after World War II, her parents had deemed the land too small to remain profitable. Over the intervening decades, nature had reclaimed the fields.

Black bears occasionally roamed the region. Last winter, Edith had spotted one, although it hadn't approached the house. She was always careful to keep her garbage sealed so as not to attract them. Herman had been an avid hunter and Edith had gone out with him a few times. Although she wasn't as skilled at identifying animals by their feces, she was pretty sure these droppings weren't from a bear.

She followed the mounds toward the barn, froze when she saw the door's padlock lying on the ground. It appeared undamaged. Since Edith carried the only key in her purse, someone must have picked the lock.

Fearful, she backed away. But Herman's litany popped into her head and she chided herself. Having lived on this land since childhood, she wasn't about to let herself become a Casper Milquetoast.

She eased closer. Obviously, an animal of the intelligent human variety must have opened the lock. However, that didn't explain the defecation.

Perhaps the mess wasn't real. Maybe whoever had broken into the barn had left it as a sick joke or an attempt to scare her. These days, she no longer pretended to understand young people, who listened to that horrible rap music and enjoyed watching movies about people being tortured.

The barn held only one thing of value, a vintage 1958 Mercury Montclair. The car had been Herman's pride and joy. He'd spent many an evening out here, lovingly restoring it to mint condition. Edith had been told the Mercury would fetch a pretty penny on the classic-car marketplace.

Outrage at the idea it might have been stolen hardened her resolve. She'd once encountered an escapee from the county prison on her property, had sent him hightailing into the woods with stern language and a sturdy hatchet. Of course, that had been years ago, back when she could still chop firewood.

She gripped the door and slid it open. Entering cautiously, she breathed a sigh of relief. The Mercury was still there, squatting in the middle of the earthen floor, boxy and stout in its sheet-metal armor.

Big tail fins and an abundance of chrome dated it to the '50s, Detroit's first golden age of large and ostentatious vehicles. Herman had found it in a junkyard, but his mechanical skills and numerous coats of black paint had restored it to showroom quality. Her grandson came over and drove it around the property every once in a while to keep the gas stirred and the battery charged.

The barn seemed deserted. However, the windows had been boarded up years ago and the minimal light spilling through the door didn't illuminate all the nooks and crannies. Edith wondered if the intruder might be hiding somewhere.

March strong through the weeks, through the valleys and the peaks, she reminded herself. This was looking like a valley, but Herman always said it was those times when you needed to be your bravest.

"You there in the barn!" she hollered. "I've called the police and they're on their way. You'd better scamper out of there pronto!"

Her bluff drew no response. Emboldened, she grabbed a wooden mallet from the pegboard above the workbench. Not that she was going to knock anybody out, but Herman always said that in dangerous circumstances, holding a weapon was better than not holding one. Thieves were cowardly by nature, he claimed, and often could be intimidated.

She glanced at the photo of Herman hanging above the bench. Just seeing his image made her feel braver. He looked so handsome in the picture, dressed in his Sunday best, gazing slyly at the camera from beneath the brim of a felt hat. The photo had been snapped on a vacation they'd taken in Atlantic City, decades before that charming town had disintegrated into a gambling mecca.

Those were good memories. They helped her forget the bad ones, especially that period half a century ago when Herman had fallen under the influence of his Navy buddy, the one with the screw loose in the head. The two of them had adopted Jack Daniels as their mascot, and there'd been drunken nights and sluttish women, as well as that zany business with the UFO. Thankfully, Herman had mended his ways, giving up the bottle and other vices with the help of Alcoholics Anonymous.

Edith raised the mallet and warily circled the car, straining to see into the depths of the barn. One corner was stacked with boxes and a heavy-duty winch for lifting engines. Both made for good hiding places, along with the half loft in the rear that was accessed by a wooden ladder.

The sound of creaking wood broke the silence.

Edith froze. The sound came from inside the barn but she couldn't pinpoint its source. Maybe one of the stray cats that she hung around the property had found its way in here.

"Shoo!" she hollered. "Skedaddle!"

She banged the mallet against a hubcap hanging from one of the barn's supporting posts, creating enough racket to wake the dead and send any sneaky felines scampering. But no strays appeared.

Again, wood creaked. This time, Edith discerned its

point of origin. She leaned her head back and gazed up into the shadowy beams and rafters that crisscrossed overhead.

Her heart skipped a beat. Something massive was perched up there in the darkness.

The thing leaped out of the gloom, gyrating in midair to land on all fours between Edith and the door. It rose to its feet and towered over her, silhouetted against the bright light. She couldn't make out details, but she could see enough to realize it wasn't human.

Seven feet tall. Triangular face. Powerful physique. Nasty triple claws where hands and feet should be.

Terror overwhelmed her. She wanted to scream but no sound emerged. She tried to recite Herman's litany but suddenly couldn't recall the words.

The monster spoke, in a deep voice marred by a background hiss that reminded her of distant waterfalls.

"Dune noth scrim."

She shook her head, not understanding.

"Dune noth scrim, ide juss wonansirs."

Her mind penetrated the distortion, translated:

Do not scream, I just want answers.

"What are you?" she whispered. The fact that it was intelligent and not merely a wild beast made her no less frightened.

"Where is Herman Ramagano?" it demanded.

"My husband? He died two years ago."

Muscles rippled across the creature's thick neck. Clawed hands rubbed against one another, producing a sound like fingernails across a blackboard. Edith sensed that her response had made it angry.

"What did you want with my Herman?" she demanded, her voice quivering with fear.

The monster seemed to calm down. And then it asked about the UFO.

She babbled out everything she could remember. Most of the details she'd only learned after Herman had freed himself from the bottle and the poisonous influence of his Navy buddy. Following a particularly cathartic AA meeting, Herman had divulged the entire saga.

The creature listened intently until she finished. Then it picked up an oily shop rag and took a menacing step toward her.

Edith's mind could take no more. The mallet slipped from her hand, hit the dirt floor with a muffled thud. Her legs buckled and she fell into a merciful faint.

39

CORBET PANNED HIS GAZE ACROSS the endless mountainous wilderness below, trying to will a telltale blip to appear on the tracking grid. But the psyts increasingly felt like a waste of time. Even if Spartan hadn't gone native or found a new victim to replicate, it seemed unlikely they'd pass within 300 feet of him.

He voiced his concerns. Mavenhall was unsympathetic.

Aggie piped in. "Sir, Corbet makes a good point. The speed that Spartan moved through those trees last night, by now he could be 20 miles from the wrecked car in any direction. That's hundreds of square miles of forest to locate a moving target in."

"I trust my instincts," Corbet added. "And they're telling me that Spartan's either in his native form or has transformed into another human. Either way, we'll never find him. And as long as he can endlessly change his identity, he'll always be a step ahead of us."

"There's an upper limit on the number of transformations," Mavenhall said. "Cellular instability increases with each new replicate, making it harder for him to maintain an imitation."

"How do you know that?"

"Analysis of the data."

Corbet knew he was lying. "Holding back information makes it harder for me to do my job."

"We all function within limitations."

"Why don't you cut the bullshit, tell us what's really happening. Who is Spartan? Where'd he come from? Why's he here?" Corbet paused. "And who's Preceptor?"

"Where did you hear that name?"

"I'm psychic, remember?"

Corbet whipped off the goggles. The eyestrain was getting to him again. He needed a break before the inevitable headache came. And Mavenhall's refusal to bring him into the loop was reviving old hurts, reminding him of just how much he hated the inflexible asshole.

The copilot popped his head in from the flight deck.

"Sir, Agent Potts called from the library. They found something."

Mavenhall nodded. "Get us there ASAP."

40

Edith and Herman spun across the crowded dance floor, tripping the light fantastic in the ballroom of Atlantic City's Steel Pier. The big band sounds of Benny Goodman – the maestro and his orchestra live on stage – filled the hall with the rhythms of one of his best, “Stompin’ at the Savoy.” Each time Goodman’s clarinet hit the high notes, Edith felt the notes tickling her flesh, like cooling droplets of summer rain.

She couldn’t recall ever being happier. Herman was a fine dancer, his footwork strong and confident. Edith wanted the song and the night to last forever. But the music stopped abruptly. Herman pulled away, disappeared into the crowd. She spun round and round, looking everywhere for him.

And then she saw him, rushing out the door in the company of his old Navy buddy. The two of them were probably heading for the nearest lowlife bar. Disappointment coursed through her and she felt a profound sense of loss.

As if by magic, the ballroom vanished. Now she stood on the edge of a cliff, looking out over a dark forest. Herman and his buddy stood a few yards away, excitedly gazing at something up in the star-flecked skies. A splotch of golden light descended, growing larger and larger. It seemed to be coming straight toward them.

“It’s our shot at the big time!” Herman’s buddy hollered. “We’re going to be rich!”

Edith wanted to yell back that she and Herman were already rich, that their wealth transcended dollars, that it was encompassed in their love for one another. But she couldn’t get the words out. Something was stuffed in her mouth, preventing her from speaking. She could only watch in growing misery as that seductive fool stoked Herman’s greed and tried to steal him away from her.

The splotch of golden light flew past with a shuddering whoosh, revealing its profile as it descended toward the base of the cliff. It didn't look anything like those UFO drawings that appeared in newspapers and magazines. It wasn't even shaped like a flying saucer.

It looked like a squirming, 60-foot snake.

Yet it was strangely beautiful. The hull sparkled, as if covered in fireflies of every imaginable color. The golden splotch was actually a long vapor trail which, in total defiance of common sense, streamed out the *forward* end of the wiggling snake, ahead of the UFO instead of behind it.

Something soft rubbed her ankle. Startled, she snapped awake from the dream and looked down. One of the area strays, a small cat with gray fur, meowed at her feet.

Chains rattled overhead, spooking the animal. It dashed out the barn door, which had been pulled shut far enough to allow only a sliver of daylight to penetrate. The cat slithered through the opening and was gone.

Edith stood upright, her back pressed against one of the posts. Ropes bound her ankles, chest and arms. The shop rag was stuffed in her mouth as a gag.

The chains rattled again, louder this time. She strained at the ropes but the bindings were too tight. She couldn't break free.

March strong through the weeks, through the valleys and the peaks.

The incantation had a calming effect, enabled her to gain a foothold on her terror.

The monster hung upside down from the rafters, its clawed feet clutching a length of automotive chain looped around a beam. Hanging up there beside it was her Volkswagen Beetle. Like some crazed mechanic, the monster was stripping engine and body parts from the suspended car.

Directly below was the Mercury Montclair. Its

trunk was open. Within the spacious cargo space sat a boxy machine three feet across and two feet high. Judging by the slew of unconnected cables and wires sprouting from the machine, it was being assembled from parts stripped off the Beetle. Even in the gloom, Edith recognized a bent section of VW tailpipe and pieces of the rear suspension.

The monster climbed headfirst down the chain, hovered above the open trunk with a rear fender detached from the Beetle. As Edith watched in fascination, it effortlessly bent the metal fender into a conical shape.

The monster pointed a tuning fork-shaped device at the seam, where the ends of the cone overlapped. An intense light erupted from the two prongs. The way sparks flew from the fender reminded Edith of welding. The monster inserted the cone into an opening in the machine so that its wider end protruded from the Mercury's trunk.

Edith grasped the machine's function. The cone was a thruster nozzle. For reasons that defied comprehension, the monster was building some kind of jet engine in the trunk of Herman's vintage car.

She prayed that once that task was finished, it would take flight in her Mercury and soar far away.

41

THE HELICOPTER TOUCHED DOWN IN the strip mall's parking lot. Corbet and Aggie followed Mavenhall past a gaggle of curious onlookers gathered at the entrance of Calloway Community

Library. A heavyset woman with big hair and a crucifix around her neck argued with a state trooper guarding the door.

"I'm the librarian," the woman insisted. "I simply *must* get in there."

"Sorry, ma'am. The facility will reopen as soon as possible."

The trooper ushered Corbet and company inside. The library was ridiculously compact in comparison to the expansive libraries Corbet was used to in New York and Washington. The motley collection of wooden shelves and revolving paperback displays couldn't have held more than a few thousand books, videos and CDs. Its annual budget probably wouldn't cover a Senator's lunch tab.

Two agents wandered through the stacks, either searching for evidence or taking advantage of some free reading time. Agent Potts stood behind the checkout counter, engaged in a heated phone conversation. Corbet overheard enough to realize Potts was frustrated that the cops couldn't locate a Mrs. Koppenhaver, the librarian.

He caught the agent's attention, gestured outside. "She's waiting to get in."

Potts cupped the phone. "No, that's the afternoon librarian. Mrs. Koppenhaver volunteers in the mornings. She was here when Spartan arrived. We're trying to track her down."

Corbet and Aggie followed Mavenhall to a frumpy beanpole of a woman in a wheelchair. She sat before one of the computers used by patrons. One hand blazed away at the keyboard while the other violently whipsawed the mouse.

"What have you got, Ferris?" Mavenhall asked.

"And a good afternoon to you too, Colonel. What we got is one uber aficionado of flying saucers. Spartan googled the bejesus out of UFOs. Clever son of a bitch. Tried to cover his tracks, hide what he was searching for." She threw them a crooked smile. "But not clever enough."

According to Mavenhall, Decca Ferris was on loan to U-OPS from Primo Americanus, a stealth group of quasi-governmental hackers who freelanced for the NSA and other shadowy agencies.

Ferris clicked the first URL from a scrolling list of websites, bringing up a gaudy screen crammed with movie images of alien vessels. Corbet recognized stills from several flicks: *Independence Day, Forbidden Planet* and *The Day the Earth Stood Still* – the original version.

"These are the sort of websites and blogs he visited."

"Why not use his tuning fork device to get online?" Corbet wondered. "He can do just about everything else with the damn thing."

"It must have limitations," Ferris said. "He obviously can interfere with fixed and mobile transmission frequencies across wide portions of the RF spectrum – cell phones, Internet, microwave, who knows what else. It's also possible he can tap into some of those frequencies, potentially eavesdrop on telecommunications within a limited area. But I suspect that in most instances, he needs our technology to interpret the data. For example, the modern world is saturated with television broadcast signals, but you can't see them without the appropriate translation device. You need a computer, TV, smartphone, whatever."

Corbet recalled that the phone found in Lonnie Roe's hunting cabin was an early model, lacking even a basic video screen. That could explain why Spartan had come to the library to get online access.

Ferris toggled through the websites and blogs. The pages were united only by their dedication to all things alien. Many looked like the work of cranks, including a husband-and-wife blogger complaining of how hard life was on Earth since they'd emigrated from the planet Cawala Seven, as well as an adversarial effort by an Arizona-based association dedicated to halting the secret immigration of space people.

Weirdest of all was a rant entitled "Worried in Oklahoma," by someone calling himself *OkieJoeyUFOey*. The writer believed that whenever he urinated, microscopic starships were ejected from his penis. Although he was careful always to immediately flush the alien vessels down the toilet, he worried that they could be congregating into a powerful armada at a Tulsa wastewater treatment plant near his home.

"How many more of these?" Mavenhall demanded.

"Hundreds. Spartan went through them much faster."

"Let's do the same, cut to the chase."

Ferris jumped to a website dedicated to Project Blue Book.

"Here's the first site where he spent quality time."

"What's Project Blue Book?" Corbet asked.

"Old Air Force investigation," Mavenhall said. "Blue Book and its predecessors analyzed UFO sightings from 1947 until the project was discontinued in 1969. Most were explained away as airplanes, meteors, freakish atmospheric conditions or unreliable narrators."

Ferris nodded. "However, according to this site, about 700 of the 12,000 documented sightings remained in the category of the unidentified. Anyway, Spartan searched for sightings that occurred in this part of the country back in 1960. He didn't get any hits so he went googling again. And that's when he stumbled on this."

She brought up the site of a Pennsylvania historian who had scanned copies of a small-town newspaper,

The Purple Mountains Majesty Gazette.

"Defunct since the mid sixties," Ferris said. "Published weekly by a local farmer moonlighting as a journalist. Lots of patriotic rants about evil Commie pinkos mixed in with harvest reports and farming advice.

"Spartan examined the issues from late 1960. The final one he accessed was from the third week of December. It's the only edition that had a UFO-related item."

The 12-page tabloid was down-home. Two stories shared the front page, one on Soviet infiltration of American industry and other on Mabel Thompson's prize-winning, 555-pound sow. Ferris clicked on the icon for the tabloid's back page, a mix of fillers and local business ads. Most of the fillers displayed tongue-in-cheek humor, including the one she highlighted.

Holy Flying Saucers!

Herman Ramagano of Lincoln Road is said to have recently spotted a mysterious object falling from the nighttime skies.

We think Herman's one lucky son of a gun! **The only saucers most of us see at 3 a.m. on a Sunday morning are the ones we're dreaming about**. **You know, the ones beneath our morning cups of freshly perked pre-church coffee**!

"After this, Spartan lost interest in UFOs," Ferris said.

He found what he was looking for, Corbet concluded.

Herman Ramagano had witnessed the alien's spaceship landing in these mountains. Spartan, somehow separated from his vessel and stranded in orbit, must have known the general region where his vessel came down but not an exact location. That explained why he'd put the lifeboat on a course for this part of Pennsylvania.

Yet finding the missing spaceship must represent only part of Spartan's plan. Was he also searching for Preceptor? Was Preceptor, perhaps blessed with an equally long lifespan or the ability to hibernate, still aboard the hidden ship?

And why had the two aliens come to Earth in the first place?

The more they learned, the more questions Corbet had.

Ferris accessed an online phone directory. "The next thing Spartan did was look up Herman Ramagano's address."

Mavenhall got on the radio with someone, read from the screen. "We have a high-probability target. Herman Ramagano. Seven-six-eight-eight Lincoln Road. Take no action, surveillance only. Report when you're in position."

"Excuse me?"

The female voice came from behind them. A primly dressed white-haired woman stood with Potts, balancing herself on a cane.

"This is Mrs. Koppenhaver," Potts explained. "She was volunteering at the library this morning when our suspect arrived."

"He was very polite," Mrs. Koppenhaver said. "Very formal. He asked to use the computer and then left."

"Yes, thank you," Mavenhall said. "The agents will take your statement."

"I couldn't help overhearing you mention Herman Ramagano. I'm afraid you won't find him at that address. He's up in Hilldale Cemetery. Passed on a few years ago. His wife Edith never bothered changing the listing. She lives by her lonesome out at that old farmhouse."

Mrs. Koppenhaver hesitated, as if reticent about further disclosures.

"What is it?" Corbet urged.

"I don't like to speak out of school. But Herman's gone so I suppose it can't hurt. You see, back then he was the biggest drunk in the county. Everybody knew it. So when that business with the flying saucer happened, nobody gave it much credence."

"Where did he claim to see this UFO?" Corbet asked.

"He never said. He bragged about it, but refused to reveal the location. He apparently had some big plans. I remember him telling my grandfather that soon the whole world would know about his UFO. But nothing ever came of it."

"Did Herman Ramagano have any close friends?" Aggie asked. "Someone other than his wife he might have confided in?"

"Yes, his old Navy buddy. But he's not a very nice man." The librarian's face soured. "Edgar Brown is a sick pervert, still skirt-chasing at his age. It's disgusting. Several of the young girls who clerk at Bosley's Supermarket say he makes suggestive remarks and touches them in inappropriate ways. He should be arrested for sexual harassment."

"Do you know where Mr. Brown lives?"

She scrawled the address, handed the note to Aggie.

"I doubt he'll talk to you. He hates authority figures. Last year he attacked a zoning officer who came to his door. He doesn't trust the government."

"Can't imagine why," Corbet offered, drawing a dark look from Mavenhall.

Potts ushered the librarian away. Mavenhall turned to Aggie.

"Edgar Brown sounds right up your alley. You and Corbet will pay him a visit."

"We need to go to that farmhouse," Corbet argued.

"Not your mission."

Decca Ferris interrupted before Corbet could

protest further.

"Colonel, one more thing. After Spartan looked up that address, he did a final search. Found his way to these pages."

She brought up a series of sites listing the populations of large metropolitan areas throughout the world. Depending on what parameters were used to define boundaries, the data varied. But in general, Tokyo, Seoul and Mexico City ranked near the top, with New York and Los Angeles the most densely populated in the U.S.

"What was he looking for?" Aggie wondered.

Ferris shrugged.

Corbet tried to fit this latest piece of the puzzle into an expanding jumble of disparate facts. But it only left him more confused than ever.

42

THE MONSTER HAD FINISHED CONSTRUCTING the jet-engine contraption in the Mercury's trunk. It now stood in front of Edith, regarding her with an indecipherable look. Although the barn remained shrouded in gloom, she finally got a clear look at it.

The skin was dark and grittier than human flesh, more like course sandpaper. Upper arms and thighs were exceptionally well-muscled. A flap of skin descended from its midsection to cover the groin, hiding any sex organs. But some sixth sense cued her that the monster was male.

Its chiseled face boasted a familiar arrangement of sensory organs, but with differences. Its nose resembled a beak, but one that split into three nostrils instead of two. It had no hair, only slabs of loose skin covering the scalp and drooping down to cloak boxy ears. The mouth was little more than a horizontal slash above a jaw that came almost to a point, giving the face a distinctly triangular look.

The monster parted its lips, revealing a gaping mouth filled with a double set of teeth. The front set resembled fangs, reminding Edith of that old Dracula movie with Bela Lugosi.

Initially, the eyes were black and totally alien, possessing no irises or pupils. But then the monster blinked and the eyes suddenly changed, as if some inner eyelid had opened. White corneas appeared, with irises as green as summer grass. Edith sensed cold intelligence behind those orbs. Yet there was something else, something that hinted of a deep and smoldering anger.

A clawed hand removed her gag. The monster raised the tuning fork to her face.

"Please don't," she whimpered.

She cried out in pain as it shoved the twin ends of the tuning fork up her nose. Strange flashes of light filled her head. But the light didn't emanate from outside her body, wasn't perceived through her eyes. It seemed to come from deep within.

She slumped forward. Looking down, she realized her torso and limbs were being made transparent with each flash of light. She could see her own bones and muscles, organs and tendons. It was as if she was being photographed from the inside out.

Just before she slipped away into a netherworld devoid of dreams, she heard a gurgling sound.

43

CORBET STOOD UNDER THE FUELING canopy of a convenience store, impatiently waiting for Aggie's return. She'd gone into the lavatory with an overnight bag. He'd already filled the Trailblazer's tank, could have pumped five more vehicles in the time it was taking her. They were only minutes from Edgar Brown's trailer park and he wanted to get the interview with the old pervert out of the way. It felt like a waste of time.

An agent had retrieved Aggie's SUV from the Firebird crash site and driven it to the library. Mavenhall had taken off in the copter to oversee the Mantis One commandos, who were on their way to the Ramagano farmhouse. At last report, a recon satellite passing over the property had detected no visible activity. Edith Ramagano's VW Beetle was not in sight. According to a neighbor, that was not unusual – she often ran errands on Saturdays. Global Hawk UAVs were being tasked for flyovers and soon should provide more detailed imaging.

Corbet's attention was drawn to a woman emerging from the ladies' room. For a moment, he didn't recognize her.

Aggie had transformed. Hips swayed provocatively in a tight black miniskirt, her pleasing wiggle accentuated by stiletto pumps. A turquoise blouse with plunging neckline highlighted cleavage. A heart-shaped purse completed the exotic ensemble.

She'd let her hair down. Blonde tresses fell across

her shoulders. Mascara and shadow rendered those piercing blue eyes larger than life, like the dreamy orbs of some Japanese manga princess.

Corbet wasn't the only one ogling her. Two teen boys radar-tracked her until she reached the Trailblazer and got behind the wheel.

"Are you coming?" she asked.

He stopped staring at her long enough to hop into the passenger seat.

"Think Naomi and Sam would approve?" she asked.

"What?" He hardly heard the question, was still entranced by her metamorphosis.

"Our two kids. Remember? They're staying at my aunt's for the weekend so we can go alien hunting?"

She kept a straight face as she threw the travel bag in the back seat and accelerated out of the lot.

44

ELISABETH "LIS" ROCHELLE ENJOYED HER profession. She had ascended to its heights by approaching tasks the same way she approached her hobby of chess. Study the board and the opponent, and relentlessly attack until the enemy king was checkmated.

Of course, there were profound differences between chess and her day job. As a rule, losing table matches didn't result in fatalities. Still, those strategies had served her well during a nine-year military career. Mastery of chess had given her the gumption to overcome the extra hurdles facing a woman in the testosterone-charged world of special operations, where big dicks ruled the board.

Mounted on her high-tech steed – a specially modified all-terrain vehicle – Lis waited in the woods with the seven male riders of Mantis One's "A" squad. Tucked under a sugar maple, she could just make out the target buildings a few hundred feet away.

She checked her watch. 13:40. Shouldn't be much longer. She hated inactivity. But waiting was part of the game and she'd grown accustomed to it. Spec ops assignments often consisted of hours or even days of boredom interrupted by explosions of violence.

Waiting was annoying because it permitted her mind to wander. Right now she found herself dwelling on the fact that the shapeshifting Spartan was an enemy unlike any the team had ever faced. She wished the unit's other two squads were operational, which would triple the unit's force pervasion. But "B" and "C" squads were still undergoing special weapons training at Blackjack and wouldn't land in Pennsylvania until this evening.

"Lis, what's happening?"

The lazy drawl of the unit's commander, Captain Doughy, sounded in her earpiece. Doughy had founded Mantis One, was the only leader the elite search and destroy unit had ever known.

His voice instantly refocused Lis on the mission. By rote, all fear, doubt and other emotions that could endanger an op were suppressed.

"Nothing yet," she replied, checking the small screen under her handlebars that displayed real-time tactical data from a Global Hawk UAV. The unmanned aerial vehicle would soon be in position over Edith Ramagano's house and barn at 60,000 feet. The Global Hawk had see-through capabilities via synthetic aperture radar and the latest package of electro-optical and infrared imaging sensors. That combination could penetrate buildings, should reveal any surprises that might be waiting for them inside.

Doughy, perched sidesaddle on his ATV a few yards away, leaned back against a tree. He looked totally relaxed, almost ready to drift off. His appearance of serenity, even in combat, was a trait Lis and the other team members could never quite seem to emulate.

People outside the realm of special operations assumed the crescent-shaped scar on his cheek was a war wound. But Lis knew the truth, that it had occurred in the checkout aisle of a supermarket in his West Virginia hometown.

On leave, Doughy had been shopping for his pregnant wife when a former Marine high on crystal meth had gone crazy. Wielding a 7-inch Ontario combat knife, the man had stabbed a clerk and two customers. Doughy heard the commotion and intervened. Taking the blade in his cheek to save a seven-year-old child from harm, Doughy had proceeded to disable the maniac by fracturing both his wrists and pulverizing a kneecap. The apocryphal part of the story, told in awed tones to Mantis One initiates, was that following the attack, Doughy had declined medical treatment and calmly finished his grocery shopping.

Lis' screen flickered. The Global Hawk had reached its position. An overhead view of the Ramagano property appeared. She studied the color-enhanced image, automatically ignoring the reddish-gold heat signatures of the squad and their ATVs, as well as what she guessed was a nearby family of slumbering cats.

"Imaging online," she said. "House looks empty. Could be someone in the cellar, though. Sensors can only read accurately down as far as the first floor. Two heat signatures in the barn. One definitely organic. Might be Granny."

The second hot spot in the barn was too big for a person. But she didn't think it was Spartan in his native alien form either. She adjusted the image, applied some resolution-enhancing tricks gleaned from her early days as a missions analyst at Fort Bragg.

"Second signature is mech. Probably a stationary vehicle with the engine running."

"Driver?" Doughy asked.

"Can't tell."

"All right, we go in ten, on my signal. Pedro, Icks – you've got the barn door. Plug weapons *now*."

Lis opened a hidden compartment in front of the seat and whipped out a compact white gun made from carbon-fiber composites. The barrel was capped with a translucent marble, had no opening for a bullet to pass through. She snapped in the boxy charger, heard the telltale hiss as it mated to the spot where a magazine would be inserted in a normal automatic weapon.

The Go-9 kinetic radiating gun was anything but normal. So far wielded only by Mantis One, the short-range Go-9 was a prototype energy weapon, courtesy of the mad scientists and engineers at super-secret Blackjack Research Complex.

She snapped the gun onto the swivel handlebar mount and looked toward Doughy for the signal.

He raised his hand, waved them forward.

The ATVs charged from the woods into the small clearing. Six of them stayed in motion, circling the barn. Pedro and Icks roared to a stop, leaped from their steeds and rushed the door to yank it open.

On her screen, the mech signature in the barn accelerated forward.

"Coming at you!" she hollered.

Her warning and lightning reflexes saved the lives of the two commandos. Pedro and Icks leaped to opposite sides as a vintage black Mercury smashed through the door in an explosion of splintering pinewood.

Lis glimpsed the driver as the Mercury roared past, heading for the winding egress lane that led out to Lincoln Road. It was an elderly woman. She matched the description of Edith Ramagano.

Kelly was the closest rider to the escaping car. He swiveled the Go-9 on its mount, took aim at the driver.

Edith Ramagano swerved violently into Kelly's ATV. The grinding hit twisted the steed sideways. The ATV caught a rut, tumbled end over end, landing the commando in a nest of brambles at the edge of the woods.

The Merc reached the lane. The five remaining mounted commandos pursued. Lis noted that the car's trunk lid was open. A plastic tarp covered an object protruding from the cargo space.

The two lead riders, Brick and Tomas, opened fire. Their Go-9's shrieked like dental drills. Jagged bursts of white light streamed down the barrels.

But the lane had too many curves and potholes, and the Go-9 had a bizarre recoil. The gun didn't kick back, it kicked sideways. The geek designers at Blackjack couldn't even predict which way the barrel would swing following a discharge. "Quantum forces in flux," was how an instructor had explained it to Lis.

Brick and Tomas missed the Merc by two yards. A clump of bushes and a wilted evergreen took their errant hits. The foliage burst into ruby-red flames.

Brick and Tomas allowed the weapons their violent swivels then yanked them back into firing positions. But the Go-9 had another shortcoming – it took nearly three seconds to recharge between shots.

Edith extended the tuning fork weapon out the Merc's window. Shafts of lightning erupted from the prongs, intersected in the woods up ahead. The energy beam sliced through the base of a towering black walnut like a giant scythe. The tree fell, missing the back of the Merc by less than a yard.

Brick and Tomas braked frantically but it was too late. Their ATVs smashed into the fallen tree, catapulting them over the handlebars. They crash-landed on gravel at the side of the lane.

Doughy, Lis and the last commando, Ruck, were the only ones still mounted. They managed to stop in time. Lis realized Doughy was barking orders into his headset, but she and Ruck weren't hearing him. That probably meant com interference. They'd been warned Spartan had the capability of creating an interference perimeter of at least 50 square miles.

Doughy ripped off his headset, shouted, "Lis, you're with me. Ruck, check casualties."

Lis followed Doughy's ATV around the fallen tree and back onto the lane. But the Merc had vanished from sight.

45

EDGAR BROWN'S TRAILER WAS STREAKED in grime, years overdue for a wash. The yard resembled a junk pile: rusted stove, smashed doghouse, imploded television. A pickup truck occupied the driveway, its metallic blue paint withered to the color of dead sky.

The trailer squatted at the end of a street, separated from the park's other mobile homes by an empty lot. Judging by the neat appearance of those properties, neighbors probably appreciated the buffer. Near the door, a crude lawn sign featured a drawing of an upraised middle finger and the words *Zone This*!

Corbet and Aggie ascended the stoop. Venetian blinds cloaked the windows. There was no bell. Aggie knocked hard.

The door opened, revealing a tall gangly figure in bibbed overalls. A TV in the background bellowed the sounds of a baseball game.

"What the hell do you want?" the figure growled.

Despite his tone, Edgar Brown didn't fit the sex-fiend image described by Mrs. Koppenhaver. Strands of white hair peeked out from beneath the brim of a Pittsburgh Pirates cap. He could have stepped from the canvas of a Norman Rockwell painting.

His eyes wandered up and down Aggie's body, finally settled on regions north of her neck. The sight of a drop-dead sexy woman on his stoop inspired a reassessment of his gruff manners. When he spoke again, the surliness was blunted.

"What can I do you for?"

"Edgar Brown?"

"Yeah. I win something? You here to give me my reward?"

"Oh, no sir, nothing like that." Aggie adopted an apologetic tone. "First, please forgive the outfit. I was just on a rather unusual undercover operation and my boss didn't even give me a chance to change into regular clothes." She sighed. "I'm been running around like a crazy person all day."

Edgar Brown's face darkened. "Undercover? You some kind of cop?"

"FBI," Aggie said, playing the role of ditzy female to the hilt by pretending to fumble in her purse. "Oh god, where is it? I hope I didn't leave it in my regular clothing. Oh no, here it is."

She pulled out her badge, allowed the old man to study the photo ID while introducing Corbet as her assistant.

"We're here about an old friend of yours, Herman Ramagano."

"Hermie's dead."

"Yes, we're aware of that. Back in 1960, Mr. Ramagano witnessed a UFO sighting. We have some questions about the incident."

Edgar Brown scowled.

"I know this sounds a bit unusual," Aggie continued. "But we're being asked to check out all sorts of oddball things."

"This got something to do with that lifeboat crash?"

"Rather silly, I know." She faked a weary tone. "But my bosses need to cross their T's and dot their I's. That means even investigating a flying saucer report from way back when."

"Sound like a bunch of government asswipes."

"On their good days. Listen, I promise we won't take up much of your time."

Corbet thought the old man was going to slam the door in their faces. But he'd underestimated Aggie's trick-or-treat skills. Some combination of sexy outfit and eager-to-please smile proved irresistible to the old lech.

Edgar Brown flicked on a ceiling light and ushered them inside.

46

LIS AND DOUGHY ROARED OUT of the woods and onto Lincoln Road. The Merc had about a quarter mile lead on them.

Communications were still down; they couldn't call in backup or air support. Lis could only hope that the Global Hawk was tracking the action from high overhead, and that Alpha Command was arranging for the road ahead to be blocked. Or, better yet, for the Merc to be blasted into junk by a scrambled fighter jet.

If not, it was up to the two of them to catch the target and take care of business.

Lis nailed the accelerator to keep up with Doughy. Her speedometer climbed to 80. The ATVs were probably as fast as the Merc, but at these speeds, none too stable. Her frame rumbled. Handlebars shook. She held on tight, pushed it to 85.

They rounded a bend onto a long and relatively straight section of road. Lis caught movement in her rearview mirror. Far behind them, two more ATVs had joined the chase. Probably Pedro and Icks, restored to their steeds after diving from the path of the escaping Merc.

Up ahead, their quarry braked hard. Protesting tires squealed, emitting bluish smoke as the Merc came to almost a complete stop.

The ATVs closed fast. Lis swiveled her Go-9, was just about to depress the trigger when the Merc made a 90-degree turn onto an intersecting road.

She and Doughy slowed but still took the corner at a good clip, fast enough for their ATVs to bicycle. Lis leaned hard in the opposite direction until four wheels again connected with asphalt, then punched it.

Up ahead, the Merc roared into a covered bridge crossing a narrow river. Once again, she and Doughy lined up their guns.

Spartan/Edith reached the middle of the bridge. Then she smashed her hand with the tuning fork straight up through the Merc's roof, shattering the metal. The device, balanced on a single prong in her open palm, began to pirouette like some super-fast child's top.

A screeching noise filled the air. A wave of pulsating energy expanded outward from Edith's hand, slammed the bridge decking behind the car. Massive slabs of timber and a thousand splinters exploded into the air.

Lis couldn't stop in time, realized too late that the entire midsection of the bridge had been blown away. She and Doughy dropped out the bottom, tumbled downward amid a cascade of rubble toward the rain-swollen river, 40 feet below.

Lis leaped from her steed, twisting her body to hit the muddy water feet first. She slammed the surface hard, went under. Fortunately, the river was deep enough and she didn't impact the bottom.

She popped her head out of the water. Doughy surfaced nearby, signaled he was okay. The priority now was retrieving their weapons. To prevent the top-secret Go-9s from falling into enemy hands, they were equipped with self-destruct modules. If she and Doughy couldn't recover the guns, they were ordered to destroy them.

Fortunately, the ATVs retained enough buoyancy to stay briefly afloat. She and Doughy were able to unlatch the weapons from the handlebar mounts before the two vehicles sank beneath the waters.

Weapons in hand, they swam back to shore. Pedro and Icks had arrived, helped pull them out of the drink.

"Status of com links?" Doughy asked, calmly running a hand through his blond mane to squeeze out the river water.

Icks shook his head. "Still can't reach Alpha Command."

"Back to the barn. Regroup."

Doughy hitched a ride with Icks, Lis with Pedro. She took a last look beyond the disintegrated bridge to the far side of the river. The Merc was gone, on a road that appeared to wind its way deep into the mountains.

47

"LET ME TELL YOU, OUR boss can be a pain," Aggie said. "He really keeps us hopping."

She sat on the edge of an ugly yellow recliner in Edgar Brown's trailer. Faking a wince, she lifted her left foot over her right knee and massaged the ankle. Edgar, on the sofa opposite her, leaned forward to take advantage of the view.

"It's just one assignment after another," Aggie whined, demurely crossing her legs an instant before the old man could gain an upskirt peek. "Some days I never even have a chance to catch my breath."

"What sort of assignments?"

"Sorry, that's classified." She unleashed a girlish giggle. "If I even talked about it, I'd get an official spanking."

Edgar's face lit up.

While Aggie kept the old man intrigued with her vamp act, Corbet wandered through the trailer. Most of the furnishings were flea-market specials. Still, the place was reasonably tidy compared to the exterior.

An open curtain at the back revealed a made bed. A rectangular bulge delineated the bathroom, with one wall serving as divider for the modest kitchenette. A holstered revolver hung with the pots and pans above the sink.

"Don't know if I can help, but glad to try," Edgar Brown offered, enraptured by Aggie's charms. "Can I you offer you a drink? A beer?"

"Oh, no thanks, Mr. Brown. We're not allowed while on duty."

"Mr. Brown was my old man. You can call me Edgar."

"Thanks, Edgar, I appreciate that. I always like to keep these interviews friendly and informal. First off, you didn't have any other recent visitors, did you? I wish I could say the FBI was perfect, but sometimes we screw up the paperwork and double-team the same interview."

"Ain't nobody else been here for days."

Which would include Spartan in a new human disguise, Corbet thought. Although it seemed a long shot that Spartan would have learned about Edgar, he was impressed at how Aggie had elicited the information.

"You knew Herman Ramagano a long time?" she asked.

"Since we were kids. Fought in the Korean War together."

"I saw your service record. A silver star. You must be very proud."

"I was a frogman with the UDTs. Hermie too. We went in ahead of the amphibious landing at Inchon, scouted the mud flats and cleared mines."

"Underwater demolition teams?" Aggie looked impressed. "Weren't they the forerunners of the Navy SEALS?"

"Damn straight."

Corbet continued checking out the trailer. Edgar scowled in his direction a few times, unhappy about the blatant snooping. But each time, Aggie recaptured his attention with an exaggerated compliment or by leaning forward in a way that accentuated her cleavage. She had the trick-or-treat act down to a science.

"So what can you tell us about the UFO your friend witnessed?" Aggie asked.

"Hermie might have mentioned it. Don't remember much else."

"Did he tell you where the sighting occurred?"

Edgar shook his head.

Corbet gazed at three 8x10 picture frames. One held Edgar's silver star, the others vintage black-and-white photos. The first picture showed two young men in crisp white Navy uniforms flanking an attractive Korean woman. Scrawled across the bottom was a caption.

Hermie and Edgar with a hot patootie. Seoul, 1952.

The second picture seemed equally innocuous, a wide shot of a somewhat older Herman Ramagano in a woodsy setting, posing beside a Ford station wagon with a fishing rod and a snared trout. Branches were devoid of leaves, suggesting late fall or early winter. Just visible past the trees was an expanse of water.

The caption read:

Hermie at Bellhopper's Lake, Pearl Harbor Day, 1960.

And below, in smaller lettering:

Didn't catch the big one, had to settle for a trout.

Corbet stared at the photo, intrigued by the date. Pearl Harbor was December 7th, which meant the picture was taken shortly after the Sputnik 6 capsule had been lost in orbit and around the time of Herman Ramagano's UFO sighting.

Yet there was something else about the image, something Corbet couldn't put his finger on. He studied it closer, extracting details: empty beer bottles scattered in the dirt, a cooler atop the station wagon, a black crow on a distant branch.

And then he saw what his subconscious mind had picked up on. Partially visible in the back of the station wagon were two silver cylindrical objects.

Scuba tanks.

He reread the caption, connected the dots. The "big one" had nothing to do with angling for fish. It was a cryptic reference to the UFO, which Herman Ramagano must have witnessed only days earlier. Edgar, who would have taken the picture, hadn't come to Bellhopper's Lake with his old Navy buddy to go fishing. That was a cover story for their real intent.

The two seasoned divers had come to search for the UFO.

Herman Ramagano had bragged about the sighting but had been shrewd enough not to reveal the location. Realizing he was the sole witness, Herman must have confided only in Edgar. They'd dreamed up a plan.

The flying saucer craze had been in full bloom during that Cold War era. Major magazines such as *Life* and *National Geographic*, as well as newspapers and the three TV networks of the time, would have paid handsomely for articles and photos relating to the existence of UFOs. Edgar had brought along the camera to document their efforts, which they'd hoped would culminate in finding an alien spacecraft beneath the waters of Bellhopper's Lake.

But their plan had fizzled. For whatever reason, they'd never located Spartan and Preceptor's ship.

Corbet tried to contain his excitement. "Nice photo of you and Hermie at the lake. Must have been a pretty mild December day for the two of you to go diving, huh?"

The look of suspicion on Edgar's face clinched it. Corbet needed no further proof that his suppositions were on the money.

"Guess if you and Hermie had caught the big one, you'd have been sitting on easy street. That didn't happen, obviously. But I am curious about a few things. Did you outfit the camera for underwater use? Were you planning to do interviews about your big discovery, or hire someone to write the article for you? Maybe that guy from *The Purple Mountains Majesty Gazette*?"

"I don't know what you're talking about."

"Sure you do. Hey, after all these years, why not come clean?"

"You calling me a liar?"

"If the shoe fits."

Edgar rose angrily from the sofa. "Get the hell out of my house. Now!"

Corbet signaled Aggie with a nod that it was okay. They had what they needed. Edgar followed them to the door, eyes glued to Aggie's butt. Pissed off or not, his libido was still in hot mode.

"No need for you to go," he offered her, trying to sound magnanimous but not quite pulling it off. "Lot more I can tell you about Hermie."

"Thanks anyway. I think we have what we needed."

But Edgar refused to give up the chase. Smiling lewdly, he laid a hand on the back of Aggie's shoulder. She grabbed hold of the intruding palm and dug her fingernails into the withered skin. The old hound let out a snarl but quickly released.

"Should have warned you about those nails," Corbet said.

Edgar, nursing a sore hand, slammed the door shut behind them. In the yard, Aggie whirled to Corbet. "You think the ship is under that lake?"

"I'm positive it is."

She retrieved the sat phone from her purse to call it in. A frown came over her.

"No signal."

Corbet checked his phone. It was dead too. The interference had returned. He didn't know what that meant, knew only that they had vital intel that needed to be passed along.

Information was a two-way street. As they raced for the Trailblazer, he considered ways in which he might use what he'd learned as leverage to break through Mavenhall's veil of secrecy.

48

Alex Wong couldn't believe his good fortune. After two weeks of dating, he still got a rush of good feelings simply by being in Mandy Herrera's presence. Even texting her made his heart happy.

They'd known each other since ninth grade but had only hooked up this junior year at Kelliksville High. She was vibrant and smart, and although his tradition-minded parents hadn't met her yet, he felt certain they'd approve. Of course, they wouldn't be told that he and Mandy intended to go all the way, that they intended to lose their virginities well before the sanctity of marriage. *Possibly even tonight*, Alex thought, provided he could get through her final layer of apprehensions.

They sat on a pair of ancient swings at Drayer's Playground, holding hands, staring out over the empty basketball court. The playground was nearly deserted, unusual for a Saturday afternoon until Alex remembered there was a big soccer game over at the high school stadium. Only a bunch of little kids scampering in the tot lot on the far side of the court marred the silence.

But even on a good day, Drayer's was rarely full. It was an old playground, the last remnant of an elementary school that had been torn down years ago and whose stone foundations could still be seen in the distance. Because the playground was on the edge of town and surrounded by forests, it was often an after-dark hangout for the local druggies.

"Want to know what I'm thinking?" Mandy asked, her brown eyes smiling, making his heart race.

"Absolutely positively."

She leaned over, pressed her lips against his. They kissed long and hard. Alex felt familiar stirrings. God, how he wanted her!

Bushes rustled behind them. They broke apart as an elderly woman in a flowered house dress burst from the narrow strip of woods that separated the playground from Miner's Road. Her dress was spotted with dirt and what appeared to be dried blood. She kept her right arm hidden behind her back.

She took a step toward them, raised her head and *sniffed.* Alex got the weird impression of a predator checking out a potential meal.

He hopped off the swing. She came closer and revealed the hidden arm. It was covered in a blood-soaked towel from hand to elbow. Weird bumps and protrusions had swollen it to nearly twice a normal circumference.

The old lady compressed her legs. She looked like an athlete preparing to make a standing long jump, to spring at them. Alex instinctively stepped in front of Mandy to shield her.

At that moment, seven male runners emerged onto the playground from one of the trails that snaked through the surrounding woods.

"Breather," shouted the lead runner.

The old lady froze at the sight of the intrusion.

Whipping the misshapen arm behind her, she ducked back into the woods.

The runners halted in front of Alex, leaned over to catch their breaths or swig water from aluminum bottles. Alex recognized them from school. All were on the track team, heavy-duty jocks. He knew they considered him a nerd. He hoped they felt the same way about Mandy.

He whirled back toward the strip of woods but the old lady was gone. An engine fired up. Through the trees, he glimpsed a vintage black car with tail fins roaring off down Miner's Road. A tarp covered a bulky object protruding from its open trunk.

"Let's go home," Mandy said, fear tinging her words.

She'd been spooked by the strange appearance of the old lady. Alex felt the same way but wasn't about to admit it, not in front of the macho runners.

He knew the old lady had been about to attack them, that the arrival of the runners had saved them from some unknown fate. He wondered if he should tell someone about the incident, maybe report it to the police. But what exactly would he say?

Excuse me, officer, but an elderly woman with a mutant arm tried to jump us while we were necking.

Best to forget the whole thing, not make trouble.

The runners took off, sprinted out across the basketball court. Alex turned to Mandy, hoping her mood wasn't spoiled for this evening.

"Pick you up tonight?"

"Absolutely positively," she said, managing to smile again.

49

Aggie got the Trailblazer up to 70 on a few stretches of back road that shouldn't have been driven at half that speed. But they reached the baseball field at the foot of Neckels Mountain in under 20 minutes.

The field had undergone a stark transformation from when Corbet had seen it this morning. Dried out from the storm except for a few puddles, it had morphed into a ragtag miniature town. More than two dozen portable trailers, either unmarked or with NASA emblems, stretched from home plate to the outfield. Sealed vestibules connected many of the trailers, linking them in scrabble-board formations. Telecom arrays sprouted from their rooftops.

Chainlink fencing topped with coiled barbed wire enclosed the field. Soldiers guarded the gated entrance. Camera crews and reporters from around the world filled the parking lot areas, jostling with one another and with hundreds of spectators for better viewing angles.

Aggie threaded the Trailblazer past the media circus. A guard slid open the gate, directed her to park near a herd of Humvees. They were met there by Major Bander, a liaison to Col. Mavenhall.

"We need to see the colonel immediately," Aggie said. "We have vital information related to Spartan."

Bander, a black man with a preternaturally youthful face, ushered them across the field while providing a rundown of the failed assault and Spartan's escape in the vintage Mercury.

"Fortunately, no serious injuries to our commandos. Edith Ramagano was found unconscious in the barn. She's been taken to a local hospital. Someone was sent with her for debriefing. *If* she wakes up."

"When did communications come back?" Corbet asked.

"Just a couple minutes ago," Bander said, angling toward a trailer labeled *Alpha Command* that was parked along the second base line. A non-uniformed security detail stood outside, three imposing Men-in-Black types wearing dark suits and Raybans. The MiBs came alert at the sight of Corbet and Aggie.

"We need to see him right away," Bander said.

The MiBs relaxed. One of them got on the phone while another held open the door.

Aggie hesitated. "I should change first."

"No time," Bander said, urging them into the trailer.

Alpha Command was jammed with telecom gear and manned by soldiers at consoles. All were young males. Heads swiveled in unison to gawk at Aggie and her outfit.

"Stay focused, people," their captain growled, appearing from behind a partition. The captain was older and the only female. She shot Aggie a disapproving glare before whirling to one of her men.

"Kapelski, any sign of that Merc?"

"No, ma'am. And most assets are back online."

"UAV imaging?"

"Functional. Two Global Hawks in coverage, two more being tasked. But that old car has disappeared."

"Old cars don't disappear, Kapelski, they don't even fade away. Find it!"

"Yes ma'am."

Bander motioned Corbet and Aggie to a door at the far end guarded by another MiB, who scanned them with a mag wand.

"I'll need your gun," he said to Aggie.

"Colonel Mavenhall knows I'm authorized to carry—"

"Your gun," he repeated, his tone sharper.

Aggie surrendered her Glock. The MiB opened the door and they entered a closet-sized space, a vestibule connecting Alpha Command with another trailer. Bander accessed a control panel on the second door and punched in a code.

The door snapped open, revealing a well-appointed conference room with sound-deadening drapes. Two men occupied the narrow table. Neither of them was Mavenhall.

Corbet didn't know the first man. He was in uniform, a three-star Army general with buzz-cut white hair. The second man, in suit and tie, Corbet recognized. He sat at the head of the table. He seemed older than his numerous media appearances suggested.

His presence explained the MiBs. They were Secret Service agents, here to perform their sworn duty of safeguarding Russell Van Zeeland, President of the United States.

50

AGGIE WAS EVEN MORE SURPRISED than Corbet at the sight of the President. She tugged at the hem of her miniskirt, as if trying to make it longer. She looked like a schoolgirl caught by the principal for inappropriate attire.

Van Zeeland frowned. "FBI relax its dress code, Agent Rittenhouse?"

"Yes sir," she said, folding arms across her chest in an attempt to hide cleavage. "I mean, no sir they haven't." Her cheeks reddened. "I'm really sorry, sir. The getup was for an undercover operation that we—"

"Relax," Van Zeeland said, motioning them to sit and introducing General Grobbs. "Your immediate superior, Colonel Mavenhall, is coordinating search efforts."

Corbet took the chair closest to the President, resisted an urge to correct the man for referring to Mavenhall as his *superior.* Aggie slipped in beside him.

Van Zeeland cut to the chase. "I'm told you have vital information about Spartan."

"We believe we have a lead on the location of the UFO he's searching for," Aggie said.

"More than just a lead," Corbet said, not intimidated sitting three feet from the President. Instead, he felt lucky to have an opportunity to bargain for more information.

"We *know* the location," he continued. "But first I need to know what you know about Spartan and Preceptor, why they're here, what they want."

Van Zeeland darkened. "This isn't a trading post, young man."

"And this isn't just about finding that ship."

Aggie, appalled that Corbet was giving the leader of the free world a hard time, kicked him under the table. Corbet winced and rubbed the sore ankle with his other foot, but pressed on.

"These aliens have something to do with a vision I've been having, a vision of an apocalypse. You need to tell me—"

"No, you need to tell us!" Van Zeeland snapped.

Corbet realized his tactic wasn't working, that the President had no intention of playing this game. Four faces glowered at him. Aggie, Major Bander and

Van Zeeland seemed merely pissed. But Gen. Grobbs looked ready to propose waterboarding.

Corbet had no choice. If he didn't come clean, Aggie no doubt would reveal all.

"The spaceship is hidden underwater at Bellhopper's Lake." He told them the whole story, about Herman Ramagano having seen it splash down one night, about Hermie and Edgar's secret plan to dive for it on Pearl Harbor day, 1960.

When Corbet finished, Grobbs snatched up a phone and recapped the tale to someone on the other end of the line.

"Full surveillance, clear out any friendlies," the general ordered. "SEAL teams prepped and ready to dive in one hour."

Aggie interrupted. "Sir, a heads up. If Spartan can tap into telecommunications within a limited area, it's possible he can penetrate and eavesdrop on our secure nets."

Grobbs incorporated her warning into his instructions. "Limit com chatter to a bare minimum. Multi-code transmissions only. Also, have this Edgar Brown brought in for further questioning." He glared suspiciously at Corbet. "We need confirmation."

Grobbs ended the call, motioned Aggie toward the exit. "The two of you have done a fine job. Remain at the field for reassignment."

Corbet stayed in his seat. They weren't going to dismiss him before he'd had his say.

"Mr. President, this isn't just a matter of finding Spartan. There's more to it than that. If we're to have any chance of preventing what I've seen in my vision, you need to tell me what's really going on."

Van Zeeland hesitated. Corbet forged on.

"Preceptor's still aboard that ship, isn't he? He's hidden under that lake, secretly providing our government with advanced alien technology. And Spartan wants something from Preceptor or from that ship, something he's going to use against us."

"These matters are not your concern," Grobbs said.

"Like hell they're not! I'm sure you have good reasons for keeping us out of the loop. But you need to understand something about my visions. They always come true. Now granted, this vision is different, less literal, full of symbols. So maybe it won't come to pass. But if it does, then some really bad shit is heading our way.

"I need to understand these symbols, decipher their meaning. I need to know about the feral people and the toy ray gun and the other stuff, what it represents." He didn't mention the Ghost Child and the disturbing emotions she engendered. "I need to know why Spartan's face keeps appearing on the Statue of Liberty. And to do those things, I need you to tell me everything."

Van Zeeland pushed back at his chair and stood up. He seemed to want to start pacing.

Grobbs scowled. "Sir, you can't be considering this."

"What if he's right?"

"They don't have security clearance."

"They do now. I just gave it to them."

"With all due respect, Mr. President, you're making a critical error."

"If so, it won't be my first. Tell them."

51

GROBBS WASN'T A HAPPY CAMPER. But given the President's dictate, he had little choice.

"What I'm going to reveal is based on information supplied by Preceptor. Consequently, much of it is unverifiable. However, in the five-plus decades since Preceptor initially made contact with us, we have no evidence he's ever lied.

"Preceptor and Spartan come from a multi-planet interstellar civilization they call the Consortium. The two of them were sent here on a mission to improve our science and engineering capabilities by supplying aspects of their advanced technology to Earth's most stable and democratized nations. Their overall purpose is to elevate our technological prowess so that someday, in the distant future, Earth will have progressed enough to be offered membership in the Consortium."

"The very distant future," the President added. "Preceptor has indicated that it will take centuries of technological development before we're considered sufficiently advanced to join them."

Grobbs continued. "The United States is one of the main beneficiaries of Preceptor's largess. However, we know that a number of other nations have also received his technological gifts. The Consortium carries out these missions via small spaceships with two-person crews. In our case, Spartan was the pilot and Preceptor the mission specialist, responsible for transmitting the technological data to us."

"Mainly in the form of blueprints and schematics," the President said. "The Consortium has a policy of not overloading a civilization with too much new technology in too short a time, which they believe creates social unrest. They parcel out these techno-gifts slowly, give us time absorb the advances."

Grobbs continued. "Because of the great distances involved, the crews are often out of touch with their home bases for centuries. Extended lifespans and hibernation techniques apparently make such undertakings possible. However, it's also been speculated that Preceptor is an artificial intelligence and essentially immune to the aging process."

"If he's an AI," Corbet wondered, "why would he need a pilot?"

"Our researchers have asked that very question. A computerized entity capable of such sophisticated communications would certainly seem able to navigate and control a spaceship. The bottom line: we simply don't know.

"At any rate, these two-person crews operate under strict prohibitions and can neither land nor have physical contact with a species they're assisting. They're required to remain hidden in orbit and limit contact to one-way transmissions."

"Preceptor talks, you listen," Corbet said, fascinated by the revelations. "So what went wrong?"

"Spartan had a different agenda. Despite being so technologically advanced, Preceptor admits that the Consortium is not perfect. It suffers from many of the same types of turmoils and conflicts that beset our world. Chief among its enemies are militants opposed to the very idea of the Consortium. These militants want to restore an earlier era when planets were isolated from one another, and when many of them were lorded over by ruthless dictatorships.

“Spartan is one of the most dangerous of these militants. He infiltrated the Consortium as a mole in order to create disruption and havoc from within.

“Their ship arrived in Earth orbit in 1960. For a short time, they monitored our TV and radio broadcasts, learned our languages and customs. Then Spartan revealed his true colors. He imprisoned Preceptor and attempted to land the ship to carry out his plan. But unknown to Spartan, their ship boasted a security feature, a fail-safe mechanism designed for just such a contingency. This fail-safe mechanism made it impossible for the vessel to land on Earth.”

Corbet nodded excitedly. “Spartan needed another way to reach the surface! That’s why he rendezvoused with Sputnik 6. That capsule was his ride down!”

“Correct. He boarded the Soviet capsule shortly before Sputnik was to begin its descent. Preceptor believes he originally planned to replicate one of the dogs, eject the original into space and land in the Soviet capsule. But after he found human hairs inside the capsule – human DNA – he altered his plan.”

“Dog-face,” Aggie said.

“Yes. A better choice for a replicate. For Spartan’s purposes, human hands with fingers were more useful than paws.”

“If he had landed in that Sputnik,” Corbet surmised, “Soviet recovery crews would have been in for a hell of a shock.”

Grobbs nodded. “It’s likely he would have killed the recovery team to facilitate his escape. Later, once his mission here was completed, he probably would have returned to his own ship by sneaking aboard another Soviet or American rocket launch, perhaps disguised as an astronaut or cosmonaut.

“However, his plan never reached that juncture. Something went wrong with Sputnik 6. It suffered a mishap, probably a retro-rocket misfire or detonation of its self-destruct charge. Whatever the cause, it blew up while the two spacecraft were still docked.

"When it happened, Spartan had already transformed into Dog-face and donned the test-dummy spacesuit. Preceptor believes he had a few seconds advance warning before the explosion and was able to exit the capsule. But he didn't make it back to his own ship in time. The blast burned the outside of his suit and hurled him into an erratic orbit.

"The explosion destroyed the capsule and critically damaged his own vessel, which plunged out of control toward Earth. Rather fortuitously, however, the blast disabled the fail-safe system and freed Preceptor, who managed to regain control at the last minute and bring the crippled ship down in one piece."

"Which brings us to Herman Ramagano," Corbet said. "He's riding around late one night, probably drunk. He sees a UFO splash down in Bellhopper's Lake."

Grobbs nodded. "Preceptor says his ship was too badly damaged to ever again achieve orbit. Trapped here on Earth, the only thing he could do was carry out the original mission. For fifty-plus years he's done just that, secretly transmitting data and video to us from his hidden ship."

"Exactly what sort of advanced technologies are we talking about?" Corbet asked.

"A bit of everything," Van Zeeland said. "But mainly advances in fields we were already working on. Lasers, computer chips, medical devices. Methods for increasing electrical power generation and agricultural yield. Satellite rocketry, telecommunications, automotive design, high-rise construction... the list goes on. It's safe to say that much of the spectacular evolution of technology over the past half century can be traced to Preceptor."

"And you've kept this all secret," Aggie said, stunned by the implications.

Grobbs shrugged. "Preceptor wanted it that way. There was an implied threat that should we reveal his existence, we would no longer receive these gifts. He believes our society as a whole is not yet ready for total revelation."

"But doesn't anyone ever get suspicious about where this data is coming from?"

Van Zeeland explained. "Our government – and the other nations that receive Preceptor's gifts – serve as clearinghouses. For the most part, we don't develop these technologies ourselves. Instead, we break apart the data and anonymously leak small portions of it to university or corporate researchers working in that particular field. In most cases, the researchers eventually develop the technology on their own.

"The process of leaking this information works surprisingly well, even better since the advent of the Internet. By spreading the data around, we also maintain a competitive research environment that benefits everyone."

"That's why you created U-OPS," Corbet said.

"The agency oversees Preceptor's transmissions and helps coordinate the dissemination of these technologies."

"But U-OPS has another agenda, doesn't it?"

Grobbs jumped in. "Preceptor continues to deny us the Consortium's greatest achievements. Interstellar spaceflight, advanced genetic engineering – those and numerous other technologies remain off limits to us. The United States should not be held at the whim of an alien civilization."

Grobbs and Van Zeeland exchanged sharp looks. Corbet had the impression the two men weren't on the same page.

"Should another nation locate Preceptor's ship," Grobbs continued, "they could capture its technological bounty. If that happened, American global competitiveness could be severely impacted. Overnight, the United States could find itself reduced to Third World status."

Another piece of the puzzle became clear to Corbet. "The U-OPS psychic program, recruiting and training supersensories. Its real agenda is to train psychic trackers to locate that ship. Get *all* of Preceptor's technology."

Grobbs didn't answer. But Corbet knew he was on the money.

He glanced at Aggie. She looked dazed, as overwhelmed as he was by these incredible revelations. Yet Van Zeeland and Grobbs hadn't answered the most fundamental questions, the ones that might help Corbet make sense of his vision.

"But why is Spartan here?" he asked. "What's his plan for us?"

"Spartan's goal," the President said, "is to carry out an attack against our entire species, to bring down all of human civilization."

"My god," Aggie whispered. "Why?"

"That we don't know," Van Zeeland admitted. "Even Preceptor has been unable to explain Spartan's rationale. Spartan obviously has traits in common with earthborn terrorists. Like all such fanatics, his actions don't necessarily succumb to rational explanation. He's driven by his emotions, by a deep hatred and anger toward the Consortium."

Corbet suspected there was more to it than that. If Spartan's beef was with the Consortium, there had to be a reason why he'd go to all this effort to plan an attack on humanity.

"Do we know any specifics about the nature of this attack?" Aggie asked.

"Only that it will involve a WMD," Grobbs said.

"Weapon of mass destruction," Aggie whispered.

"Yes, and one capable of having global impact. Although Preceptor long ago assured us his ship contained no such WMDs, he admits to possessing the raw materials for constructing such weapons in numerous forms – chemical, radiological, biological, nuclear. However, as an additional security feature, the ship carried no devices that could be used to set off any of these weapons."

"Spartan needs a trigger," Corbet said. "And he has to acquire that trigger here on Earth. That's why he needed to reach the surface in the first place."

"Preceptor refers to the trigger as a catalyst. Once Spartan gets hold of this catalyst and returns to his ship, he'll have all the ingredients for creating a weapon of terrible power."

"His target must be a city or cities," Aggie said. "At the library, he researched the world's largest metropolitan areas."

He's here to cause the apocalypse, Corbet realized with a chill. The chaos in Manhattan from his vision was itself a symbol. It represented a level of devastation that would impact the entire world.

And if Spartan locates that catalyst, finds Preceptor and the ship...

We're running out of time.

52

HILDA BAUSHER RARELY HUNG LAUNDRY on Saturdays. But she needed to prepare for the Battle of the Bulge.

Mondays were the traditional washday, had been for four generations of Bausher women who'd lived in this modest row home along Honeysuckle Road in Appleton, Pennsylvania. But every rule had an exception. This Monday, she and Hank would be driving to North Carolina for the infamous World War II German offensive.

Hilda withdrew the final item from the washbasket – a pair of Hank's size 46 Jockeys – and pinned them to the backyard line. This wouldn't be the last of her quartermaster duties. She still had to iron her husband's authentic vintage uniforms. Historical reenactment festivals involved lots of prep work.

A girlish giggle came from nearby. She glanced into Betsy Fackler's yard, two houses away. Behind the shed near the back fence, hidden from any prying eyes at the kitchen window, was Betsy's 16-year-old son, Timothy. He was playfully tickling his girlfriend, Trixie, also a tenth grader at Eastfield High.

Hilda smiled as the teens started necking. By coincidence, Buddy Holly's "It's So Easy" shuffled onto her iPod. Hilda recalled dancing to the song when she was their age.

It's so easy to fall in love, she hummed along. *It's so easy to...*

She trailed off, curious about the black car creeping

down the rear alley. A vintage Mercury, a late 1950s model. Buddy Holly might have driven one just like it.

Lots of folks hereabouts owned classic vehicles. But this one wouldn't win any cruise night awards. There was a jagged hole in the roof above the driver, and the car was as dusty as a reenactor's uniform after a day of mock fighting. A lumpy object covered by a tarp protruded from the open trunk.

The Merc eased to a stop. The driver, a little old lady in a soiled dress spotted with dried blood, hopped out. Ignoring Hilda, she walked toward the picket fence behind Betsy Fackler's yard. She kept her right arm out of sight behind her back.

Hilda took off the headphones, riveted by the strange sight. Timothy and Trixie, feverishly sucking face, didn't notice her approach.

"You two!" the old lady called out. "Come over here."

The teens bolted apart, probably thinking they'd been discovered by some disapproving scold. But they relaxed when they laid eyes on the interloper.

"I wish to speak with you."

The teens obliged, strolled to the fence. Keeping her right arm hidden, the old lady halted on the other side of the barrier. Abruptly, she arched her head forward. And then she did something really odd. She *sniffed* at the young lovers. Hilda wondered if she suffered from some form of dementia.

A smirk appeared on the wrinkled face as she revealed the hidden arm. Even though it was covered from hand to elbow in a blood-soaked towel, the arm looked badly swollen. Either that or it was horribly deformed.

"Jesus, lady," Timothy said, his voice full of genuine concern. "Are you all right?"

"A-OK," the old lady replied.

At that moment, Hilda knew that something was

dangerously wrong, even though she couldn't put her finger on the nature of the threat. She turned back to the house to call for Hank. But then she remembered he'd gone to the Home Depot in Kelliksville to pick up supplies for their trip.

The old lady let the bloody towel fall to the ground.

Trixie shrieked.

The hand was half human, half something else, something monstrous. A spiked claw six inches long protruded from the flesh between the thumb and forefinger. The knuckles oozed blood. The skin was rubbed raw, as if she'd punched that fist through a wall.

The old lady lunged at the fence, wrapped the claw around Timothy's neck. Her other hand – the still-human one – snagged Trixie's throat.

Hilda screamed as the old lady, with impossible strength, lifted the two teens high in the air and yanked them over the fence. They struggled to break the choking grips by kicking and punching at their assailant. But their efforts proved futile.

The old lady dragged the teens over to the Merc and bashed their heads against the side of the car until they were unconscious. She whipped open the Merc's back door and shoved the two limp bodies into the back seat.

"Stop!" Hilda yelled, finally recovering her wits.

The old lady got behind the wheel and started the engine. Hilda ran toward the alley, waving her arms helplessly as the Merc accelerated away. It screeched around the corner at high speed.

Neighbors rushed out their back doors. By the time Hilda calmed down enough to explain what had happened, the old lady and her victims were gone.

53

TABBY PULLED THE TENNIS BALL from a clump of wet sand and hollered to Otis.

"Here boy! Go get it!"

She threw the ball as far as she could down Bellhopper's modest beach. The golden retriever bounded after it with his usual frantic excitement, kicking up wads of sand as he followed the ball's arc.

It wasn't much of a beach, not like down at Wildwood and Ocean City where Tabby's parents took her every summer. The lake was linear-shaped and extended around a bend to the dam breast, where it was deepest. Daddy said Bellhopper's wasn't a natural lake. It had been made by engineers who'd dammed a confluence of small streams a hundred years ago to control flooding. The beach was manufactured too, with sand trucked in so the lake could be used for recreation.

Tabby waved to Mommy and Daddy in their sailboat drifting a couple hundred feet offshore. Sailing was boring and she'd been happy to stay on the beach and play with Otis. Besides, there wasn't much of a wind today so instead of sailing and swinging the jib back and forth, her parents just floated along. Mommy would be keeping an eye on her, she knew. But Tabby was 8 years old and could take care of herself.

Bellhopper's was almost deserted, kind of surprising on such a nice spring afternoon. Mommy and Daddy were the only ones on the water. Two men were fishing on the opposite shore, and she could hear the drones of dirt bikers on a nearby trail, but that was it. When the school year ended and the county stationed its summer lifeguard, the beach would be packed with bathers and the water crammed with small boats.

Otis dashed back to her with the tennis ball clamped in his jaws. He nuzzled her ankle, annoyed her attention was elsewhere and not dedicated 100 percent to *the game*, which she was to keep playing until *he* decided it was time for a break.

She hurled the ball again, realized at the moment of release that she'd thrown it too hard. Otis skidded to a halt when the ball disappeared into the far trees.

"Go get it!" Otis was funny sometimes and needed to be reminded he had a powerful nose.

The retriever hesitated. He began to growl.

"What's the matter, boy?"

The growl turned into incessant barking. Maybe the dirt bikers, or an animal, had spooked him. Tabby ran down the beach, worried he might sprint into the woods in pursuit of whatever had him riled. She wasn't afraid for his safety. Otis could handle pretty much any critter found in these parts. But last summer at Bellhopper's, Louise Trotter's dog had encountered a skunk. What a stinky time that had been.

She reached Otis and grabbed his collar. Then she heard it – a mechanical noise that filled the air, growing ever louder.

A big military helicopter in camouflage paint roared out from beyond the woods. The copter was flying so low its landing skids almost touched the treetops. Otis reared up and barked furiously. Tabby struggled to maintain a grip on him.

The copter flew out over the water, heading straight for the sailboat. Mommy and Daddy stood up in surprise as the craft hovered above them. A giant net dropped from its belly, completely enshrouding her parents.

Ropes trailing up to the copter's open door pulled taut, tightening the net. The copter rose straight into the air, lifting Mommy, Daddy and the sailboat right out of the water.

Tabby screamed and let go of Otis. The retriever bounded to the edge of the water, his shrill barks protesting the abduction of two-thirds of his family. The copter and its dangling captives flew past the fisherman on the far side of the lake and disappeared beyond the distant trees.

A pair of strong hands grabbed Tabby from behind. Shc screamed again as the big soldier hoisted her into the air, threw her over his shoulder, and carried her toward the woods. Otis snarled and leaped to her defense. But another soldier appeared and shot a silent gun at the retriever, hitting his flank with a dart. Otis whimpered as his feet went out from under him and he collapsed onto the sand. Tabby burst into tears.

"Shh!" the soldier hissed. "Just a tranquilizer. Your dog will be okay."

Tabby wanted to believe him, wanted to ask why all this was happening. But she couldn't stop crying long enough to get the words out.

54

CORBET SAT IN THE CABIN of Mavenhall's copter as it ascended from the baseball field. The craft banked into a long sweeping turn. He gripped the tray on his lap to prevent spilling his dinner remnants.

He'd realized how hungry he was prior to takeoff.

The copilot had scrounged up an MRE – Meals Ready-to-Eat in military parlance. Jeremy, having grown cynical of such army food, used to say the acronym stood for Meals Rejected-by-the-Enemy.

Although it was late in the day and the MRE was a breakfast version, Corbet had been too famished to be fussy. The cheese omelet, hash browns and bacon were decent enough. The instant coffee left much to be desired.

Mavenhall had retreated to the flight deck to confer with the crew, leaving Corbet alone back here with Aggie. She stood in the rear of the cabin, gripping a safety rail to maintain her balance as she changed into less exotic attire. He tried to do the gentlemanly thing, look away as she stripped to panties and bra. But he couldn't resist a peek.

She caught him looking. Their eyes met, held one another for a long moment.

Corbet was surprised by the intimacy inherent in that brief contact. It transcended sexual desire, went beyond emotional borders he'd spent years fortifying, made him realize he wanted something more from Aggie. The feeling left him confused and unsettled.

Aggie also seemed disconcerted. Before she broke eye contact and turned away, he glimpsed puzzlement on her face.

The copter emerged from its sweeping turn and leveled off.

"I think the President was secretly impressed by that outfit," Corbet said, grateful to return to solid footing.

"Fat chance. I meet the leader of the free world dressed like a hooker. He's always going to have that image of me in his head."

"Trust me, next time he's alone with the first lady, he'll beg her to play trick or treat."

She grinned as she finished donning jeans, an all-weather jacket and her Glock. But Corbet couldn't shake off what had just happened between them.

He had a pretty good notion of *why* it had happened. Spartan could well be on the verge of causing an earth-shattering apocalypse. Confronted with the possible end of the world, it wasn't surprising that a mind could do strange things, awaken restricted emotions. For Corbet, a secured border had been breached. His one-night-stand philosophy had taken a hit. Aggie, in her own unique way, must have experienced something similar.

Mavenhall entered from the flight deck.

"Bellhopper's Lake is secured. ETA, seven minutes. The lake has been cleared of civilians and a two mile perimeter established. Spartan will not reach it by vehicle or on foot without being spotted. Even if he changes back into his native form and travels through the canopy, we'll see him if he gets close. The entire region is now under a full complement of imaging assets. SEAL teams with portable submersibles will arrive shortly to enter the water.

"Edgar Brown was brought in for questioning, but he's being obstinate. Refuses to talk until he's consulted with his lawyer."

"You don't need that old lech to confirm," Corbet said. "Trust me, the ship's under that lake."

"Hidden in less than 45 feet of water?"

Mavenhall had reason to be skeptical, Corbet admitted. UAVs had scanned Bellhopper's but found no trace of a submerged spacecraft. The ship must be concealed in a way that confounded the world's most advanced spy assets.

Mavenhall gestured to the unopened psyts briefcase.

"Can't do much with them at the moment," Corbet said, instantly on the defensive. "In case you didn't notice, we're already flying way above 300 feet."

"Put them on anyway. Best to be prepared for all contingencies."

"Odd advice coming from you, *Lieutenant*," he said, deliberately reverting to Mavenhall's rank at the time of Jeremy's death.

Aggie changed the subject before Mavenhall could react to the taunt. "Sir, what if Spartan activates that interference again?"

"Let him. The interference will confirm he's in the area, possibly enable us to pinpoint his location at the center of the interference zone. And should telecommunications go down again, our forces have been instructed to converge on Bellhopper's and initiate a prescribed sequence of independent operations. This time we're ready for whatever Spartan throws at us."

Corbet had his doubts. Spartan was shrewd. He might figure a way to elude them. There was also the unsettling possibility that he'd already reached the lake and boarded the hidden vessel.

The copilot popped his head into the cabin. "Sir, Alpha Command intercepted an emergency call to the state police about a weird kidnapping. Two sixteen-year-old kids were snatched by an old lady. Descriptions are dead on. It's Edith Ramagano, driving that Merc."

Mavenhall returned to the flight deck with the copilot. Corbet and Aggie squeezed into the door frame behind them. The copilot, monitoring radio traffic through his headset, recited the highlights.

"Kidnap victims are a Timothy Fackler and his girlfriend, Trixie Beloti. Happened about fifteen miles south of our position. Alpha Command is trying to get the staties and local cops in neighboring jurisdictions to put up roadblocks."

The copilot hesitated, receiving more information.

"Sir, they say we're the closest airborne unit. They want us to go off-mission, divert to the kidnapping site."

Mavenhall nodded. "Do it."

"Hang on," the pilot said, banking the craft sharply.

"What's he want with a couple of kids?" Aggie wondered.

Corbet grimaced. "Let's hope it's not dinnertime."

55

VAN ZEELAND REMAINED ALONE IN the trailer. He'd asked not to be disturbed unless there was urgent news. He needed some quiet time, a chance to mull over the events of the day, perhaps arrive at options not yet considered. But as he paced back and forth within the narrow enclosure, he couldn't get his mind off the terrifying reality that Spartan was close to achieving his goal, and that Van Zeeland's own inaction might have been a contributing factor.

The President must order the launch of an exo-atmospheric kill vehicle to intercept and destroy the International Space Station.

In hindsight, he wished he could rewind the clock 24 hours and revisit his decision. Yet even now, he couldn't be sure he was capable of giving an order that would have reduced the space station and its crew to vapor.

Gen. Grobbs perceived him as a weakling, as a man unable to make the harsh life-and-death decisions required of a President. Other critics gave credence to an even more insulting claim, that he put his career ahead of national security.

Wiping out the space station likely would have ended his political life and driven him from office. No way would he have been able to rationalize killing those astronauts to the American people, even if he told the truth and revealed all he knew about Spartan and Preceptor. Resignation – or impeachment – would have been the inevitable result.

Nevertheless, that wasn't the reason he'd refused to carry out Preceptor's drastic solution.

Corbet Tomms had expressed reservations about his vision, whether it indeed was a literal interpretation of an apocalyptic future. The young psychic had good reason to doubt the validity of his prescience.

Humanity's future was *not* preordained. There was always the possibility of fresh discovery, of unexpected information arriving to reveal new possibilities, new decision trees. *Nothing is settled until the dust clears*, a political mentor back in Missouri had once told him.

It was a belief worth clinging to.

56

AGGIE SPOTTED EDITH RAMAGANO'S MERCURY. She let out a holler from the flight deck doorway, directing the others' attention to a tiny black rectangle on a winding road far below. The Merc was identifiable from this height by the discolored spot on its roof. It was where Spartan had punched a hole to wield his energy weapon against Mantis One.

"Get us higher," Mavenhall ordered. "We don't want to risk being seen."

The copter leaped upward like an elevator on steroids. Corbet gripped the flight deck's handrails and hung on. The pilot banked the craft to stay on the Merc's tail as the road curved around the base of a steep hill.

The copilot got on the radio. "Whiptail Zebra to Alpha Command—"

Mavenhall depressed the transmit button, cutting him off. "Let's assume worst case scenario, that he's broken our security codes and is monitoring radio traffic in the area. We don't want him to know he's been spotted. Let's just see where he's going."

The copilot gestured to a moving blip on one of his tracking systems. "Doesn't appear to be heading for Bellhopper's. This road is strictly backwoods, goes nowhere near the lake."

The blip froze. Below, the Merc pulled onto the shoulder at a T-junction. The intersecting road was blocked off by a wooden barricade. Judging by the cracked, weed-infested macadam, it was long abandoned. The road curved out of sight, winding its way into a small valley.

The copilot activated thermal scanning. "Vehicle has three occupants. Driver plus two in the back seat."

"It must be those kids," Aggie said. "They have heat signatures. They're still alive."

"Not necessarily," Mavenhall said. "A corpse will retain body heat for a short time."

The car door opened. The driver got out. The copilot switched his screen to telescopic imagery. The figure far below was definitely Spartan in his Edith Ramagano guise.

The old lady effortlessly yanked the barricade from the ground and moved it aside. She returned to the Merc but hesitated at the open door. Corbet couldn't be sure, but he got the impression she'd glanced upward in their direction.

"I think we've been made," he warned.

"She can't see or hear us," the pilot assured them. "We're flying with the sun at our backs and whisper-mode is engaged."

As if bearing out his appraisal, Edith got back behind the wheel and drove onto the abandoned road. But immediately, the car stopped. She got out again and replaced the barricade.

"Doesn't want to be followed," Aggie concluded. "But where she's going?"

"It'll be dark in an hour or so," Mavenhall said. "She could be looking for a place to hide out until then. Better chance of reaching the lake under cover of night."

Corbet was starting to get a sense of Spartan's thought processes. And he knew the colonel's conclusion was wrong.

Spartan doesn't need to hide. He's not afraid of us.

The alien's sole concern was completing his mission. Sure, he'd run away from them last night at the tower. And today he'd escaped from that cop and from the Mantis One commandos. But he wasn't avoiding confrontations out of fear, but because they brought him no closer to his goal of finding the missing spaceship.

Corbet got a feeling that something was terribly amiss. *What's he doing so far from the lake*? It made no sense.

Mavenhall requested a map of the area that might reveal a destination. But before the copilot could comply, Edith whipped her gaze skyward and pointed an object up at them. Corbet instinctively knew it was the tuning-fork device.

"Get us out of here!" he hollered.

The pilot couldn't react in time. Twin streaks of

lightning leaped from the prongs of Spartan's device. A blinding flash filled the cockpit, followed by violent shudders that almost knocked Corbet off his feet. And thenthe controls were blinking and sirens were wailing and the copter was accelerating forward at an awkward angle.

"Can't hold her," the pilot said, his voice surprisingly calm.

The copilot radioed Alpha Command. "Whiptail Zebra has been hit by hostile fire. Position is grid reference..."

He trailed off, shook his head. "We're not getting through. Interference is back. All com channels are—"

The copter bucked. The flight deck shuddered. Corbet grabbed an overhead handrail to steady himself. They were still moving forward at high speed but losing altitude. The forest canopy drew perilously close.

"Hang on," the pilot said. "We're going down."

Just as he got the words out, the craft flipped onto its vertical axis, aiming itself skyward. Corbet lost his grip, tumbled out of the flight deck into the main cabin along with Aggie and Mavenhall. The three of them slammed against the rear bulkhead. Aggie bounced off Corbet's chest, knocking the wind out of him.

He glimpsed treetops through a window. An awful grinding noise filled the cabin as the tail rotor chewed branches.

The copter hit the ground with a bone-jarring crack and flipped forward, end over end. The back of Corbet's head banged into something hard and metallic. Vivid sparks filled his vision as awareness dissolved.

57

SpecFour Myron Jones still had trouble believing the entire com system could be knocked out with a single punch. But there was no arguing the fact that their nets had been laid low for the second time today by the mysterious interference. Whoever this Spartan was, he had some kick-ass electronic warfare toys.

"Dammit, people, give me something!" the captain snarled. "There's got to be a way to cut through this interference!"

The Cap tended to holler a lot but she was okay in Jones' book. Better than those officers who never said a word then wrote you up for some bullshit violation.

"Get creative, people! Solve the problem!"

Jones would have loved to oblige. But the interference was mystifying. Only one of his consoles, a phased array radar system, remained functional and continued to track targets. But all voice and data transmissions were being blocked.

A screen flashed a warning. A copter in his airspace had vanished.

"Cap, we just lost Whiptail Zebra. Dropped off radar in the mountains about thirty miles west of here."

"That's Col. Mavenhall's bird. Alert search-and-rescue."

"But ma'am, how? Everything's down. I can't even make a call—"

"Pretend it's 1812 and nobody's heard of radios!"

Jones needed no further prompting. He dashed out

the door and sprinted across the baseball diamond, weaving through the maze of trailers. All around him, he sensed soldiers and NASA types frustrated by nonfunctional telecom.

He reached the helicopter pad. But the two Sikorsky birds outfitted for search and rescue were gone. In their place was a trio of imposing Whitehawks: Marine One and its two decoys.

He ran toward the nearest Whitehawk, abruptly realized that wasn't the smartest move. Marine guards and Secret Service agents drew weapons, screamed at him not to come closer.

Jones froze and raised his hands, praying he wouldn't get shot. It would be a bitch getting taken down by friendly fire.

The Marines surrounded him. The agents hung back, but kept their MAC-10 submachine pistols at the ready. A sergeant demanded to know what kind of stupid-ass shit Jones was pulling by making a banzai charge at the President's fleet. He explained about needing one of the Sikorskys to reach a downed bird.

"They moved them to another field," the sergeant said, pointing toward the baseball diamond's home plate.

"How far from here?"

"Seven or eight miles."

"Great," Jones muttered, sprinting back in the direction he'd come. First, he'd have to find a Humvee to drive him to the alternate field. Then he'd have to convince a crew to get their bird in the air, which they might be reluctant to do without official orders from Alpha Command.

One thing for sure, it wasn't going to be a quick search and rescue.

58

CORBET AWAKENED, LYING ON HIS back. He had a headache and a few bruises. But as far as he could tell, no bones were fractured.

Their helicopter, what was left of it, had landed upright. A tree limb had speared through a porthole window, spreading leaf clusters into the wreckage. Foliage blocked views through the other windows and interior lights had failed. In the near darkness, he could see little more than the outlines of objects.

He spotted Aggie, crumpled atop an extra flight suit dislodged from an overhead compartment. She wasn't moving. He crawled over to her, heart pounding with worry.

"Aggie! Are you okay?"

Her eyes popped open. She focused on his face, a good sign.

"Can you move? Anything broken?"

She squirmed upright, shook her head. "I think I'm all right."

Relief coursed through him. Before he could dwell on the fact he'd been more concerned about her safety than his own, the copilot limped in from the flight deck. The man winced in agony and clutched his right leg. The limb was twisted at an odd angle, suggesting a nasty shinbone fracture.

"We need to get out of here," he hissed. "Fuel leak."

Corbet sniffed. The rich odor of kerosene filled the cabin.

The copilot yanked on the door handle. It wouldn't

budge. Corbet and Aggie rushed to help. The three of them leaned their weight against the door and pushed. It burst open, flooding the cabin with fading daylight.

The exertion almost overwhelmed the copilot. He grabbed Aggie's arm for support. "I need your help. My pilot..."

She followed him to the flight deck. Corbet spotted Mavenhall lying motionless in the back of the cabin. For an instant, he entertained a dark fantasy that his long-time nemesis was dead.

Nobler instincts took hold. He rushed to Mavenhall's aid.

No way could he carry the colonel, who outweighed Corbet by a good 50 pounds. He took hold of Mavenhall's wrists and dragged him toward the door.

Aggie and the copilot got there first, struggling to support the barely conscious pilot. An ugly sliver of bone protruded from the pilot's right elbow and his torso was covered in blood.

A severed electrical cable fell from the ceiling, its exposed end still live. Sparks flashed as it danced across the metal flooring.

"Hurry!" the copilot urged.

They squeezed through the door. Corbet caught a glimpse of the flight deck as he pulled Mavenhall away from the craft. An uprooted tree had smashed through the windshield, demolishing the cockpit. It was a miracle the crewmen had survived.

They battled dense wilderness to get away from the wreckage. The tangled undergrowth was bad enough, but the laws of friction gave Corbet extra trouble. Mavenhall kept getting snagged on upthrust roots and slithering vines as Corbet dragged him. Finally, they reached safety behind a limestone outcropping.

"I forgot something!"

Ignoring Aggie's protests, he dashed back to the

copter and scrambled through the hatch. He quickly located the briefcase with the psyts. But as he was about to exit, he heard ominous crackling noises. Tiny sprouts of flame waltzed across the flight deck. It wouldn't take much for one of them to ignite that leaking fuel.

He leaped through the hatch with the briefcase, sprinted for the outcropping. He almost made it.

The blast stung his eardrums and shoved him violently forward. He half-dove, half-tumbled behind the outcropping. Exploding debris whizzed past overhead.

He peeked out from behind the rocks. The copter had morphed into a golden fireball. The flames spewed a wiry cloud of black smoke upward into the canopy. He turned away from the carnage, gazed down at the unconscious Mavenhall.

"You owe me, you son of a bitch."

To Corbet's surprise, Mavenhall opened his eyes. The colonel seemed to want to say something. But he couldn't manage it. A cheek muscle twitched and then his eyelids closed again. Corbet couldn't tell if his own words had registered.

The pilot was also out cold. Aggie drew a pocketknife from the copilot's first aid kit, sliced open the pilot's shirt to expose the badly fractured arm. She wrapped a tourniquet above the protruding bone and smacked an emergency trauma bandage over the wound.

She turned to help the copilot. He pushed her away, gestured toward Mavenhall.

"Take care of the colonel. I'll handle tourniquet pressure."

Aggie ran her hands over Mavenhall's head, chest and appendages, checking for obvious injuries.

"Took a blow to the back of the scalp. Could be a concussion."

"Someone will see the flames," Corbet said. "They'll find us quick."

The copilot crushed that hope. "Not likely. This whole area is even more isolated than where the lifeboat came down. With that interference knocking out com nets, could be awhile before a rescue party gets here. The fire will burn out quickly and it'll be dark soon."

Aggie nodded. "I'll go for help."

"Head due west. You should intersect that road. We traveled a good linear distance from where Spartan nailed us. Might have to hike two or three klicks."

She turned to Corbet. "You stay here and—"

"He goes with you," the copilot insisted. "No lone wolves. We stay in groups whenever possible."

Aggie cast a skeptical eye toward the copilot's injured leg.

"Don't worry about me, I can handle things." He patted his sidearm and drew a flashlight from a thigh pocket. "We'll be fine."

Aggie took a compass bearing. Corbet grabbed the psyts from the briefcase and followed her into the trees.

59

LIS WAS MAD ENOUGH TO shoot somebody.

Before joining Mantis One, she'd spent three years with Special Operations Command out of Fort Bragg. Under the aegis of SOCOM, she'd done SEAL training and counterinsurgency ops in the Gulf, had guest lectured at a "Women in Combat" seminar for the CIA's Special Activities Division and had testified before secret Congressional committees.

And now she'd been reduced to babysitting.

Lis knew the order had come from Mavenhall. She also knew that Capt. Doughy had objected. That didn't make her feel any better. The colonel's decision was sexist, pure and simple. Since Edith Ramagano was a woman, Mavenhall's reasoning went, a female babysitter was needed.

And so Lis sat in the private room at Mercy Memorial Hospital in Kelliksville with the unconscious 87-year-old, idly paging through a *Good Housekeeping* magazine. She kept telling herself the assignment was important. Granny could have vital information about Spartan. Someone with the security clearance to discuss U-OPS-related issues needed to be here if she woke up.

But that didn't lessen Lis' frustration, not one goddamn bit. She should be at Bellhopper's Lake with Mantis One and three platoons of Army Rangers, all awaiting the arrival of SEAL teams with special submersible vehicles. Instead...

A nurse entered the room to change Edith's IV drip.

"Any word on that copter?" Lis asked. One had been tasked to fly Granny to Bethesda. It should have arrived half an hour ago.

The nurse shook her head. "Some kind of communications mixup, I hear."

Until Edith was transferred to the naval medical center, a local doctor was in charge of her case. He was a young hotshot, openly resentful of the presence of a nonuniformed female soldier.

Lis had gleaned little from the doctor, who seemed mystified that Edith remained unconscious. In response to Lis' questions, he'd spouted medical mumbo-jumbo, something about "unusual activation of inhibitory neurotransmitters resulting in deep sedation."

The nurse departed. Lis returned her gaze to the

magazine.

"Where am I?" Edith Ramagano asked.

Lis bolted from her chair, leaned over the bed as the old lady's eyes fluttered open.

"You're in Mercy Memorial. Do you remember what happened to you?"

Fear touched Edith's face. She grabbed Lis by the wrist, held on tight.

"That thing... that monster... I thought I was going to die!"

Lis patted her hand. "You're safe now. You're going to be all right. But you need to tell me about this monster. Did it speak to you, ask you anything?"

"It wanted to know all about the UFO, the one my husband saw."

The nurse and the hotshot doctor rushed into the room, summoned by a beeping monitor above the bed. Lis stood by impatiently as the doctor shined a penlight in Edith's pupils and stethoscoped her chest.

"I'm going to ask you some questions," he announced, speaking loudly as if addressing a deaf person. "Can you tell me your name?"

"Edith Ramagano."

"Do you know where you are?"

"Mercy Memorial."

"Can you tell me where you live?"

That was enough for Lis. Her debriefing carried a higher priority. Edith was awake and talking – that was all that was important.

"Both of you out of here," Lis ordered. "Right now."

The nurse scowled. The hotshot ignored her. Lis was in no mood for pleasantries. She grabbed the doctor's arm, wrenched it behind his back and frog-marched him out the door amid his stunned protests. The nurse followed quickly, wide-eyed.

"Call security!" the hotshot sputtered.

"You don't want to do that," Lis warned, sweeping back her windbreaker to reveal her sidearm. "Until I say otherwise, this patient is under federal protection, off limits to hospital personnel."

She slammed the door in their startled faces, drew the shades and turned back to Edith. "Sorry about that, Mrs. Ramagano."

To her surprise, the old lady gave a vigorous nod. "Ask your questions, young lady."

The fear departed Edith's face, replaced by grim determination. She might be elderly but she was no wimp. Lis took her for part of a dying breed: old-fashioned country folk, tough and self-reliant.

"This monster, what exactly did it want to know about the UFO?"

"Where it came down, where my Hermie saw it hit the water. You see, my husband had been out late that night. Drinking." She scowled with the memory. "He'd pulled over to the side of the road to relieve himself when he heard this whooshing sound. He looked up and there it was. He said it resembled a squirming snake."

"A snake?"

"That's what he said. A snake with sparkling skin, as if covered in fireflies of every imaginable color. And it had a golden vapor trail that streamed out the front end, not the back end like a normal jet."

The description of Spartan's vessel sounded too bizarre to accept at face value. After all, Edith's husband had been drinking. Then again, they were dealing with unknown alien technologies. Anything was possible.

"Hermie didn't actually see the splashdown. He said it dropped into the forest about a mile away. But he was certain it hit water. It caused a massive waterspout, high enough to be viewed above the tree line."

She ran her tongue around the inside of her lips. "My mouth feels funny. Why did it stick those prongs up my nose?"

"First, tell me about what happened after the UFO came down. Your husband and his friend went diving for it?"

Edith grimaced. "I wouldn't call Edgar Brown a friend."

"But the two of them went to Bellhopper's a few days after the splashdown, right?"

A faint smile touched Edith. The question apparently had tripped pleasant recollections.

"Bellhopper's. I used to go swimming there when I was a young girl. After I got married, Hermie would take me fishing at that lake. We used to catch the biggest trout you can imagine. I'd make my own special seasoned batter and we'd pan fry them until they were lightly browned. It was the most scrumptious fish you can imagine."

Lis was about to jump in and terminate the nostalgia tour when Edith adopted a puzzled look.

"But Bellhopper's isn't where the UFO came down."

60

Daylight was almost gone. The sun had fallen behind the treetops, infusing the wilderness with a soft amber glow. Soon they'd need Aggie's flashlight to navigate.

Corbet had no idea how far they'd come. The trek was sluggish. The forest seemed morbidly dense, a sibling to one of those equatorial jungles that swallowed all who dared enter. Knotted clumps of undergrowth and ground-hugging vines snared their ankles. An endless succession of hills left Corbet panting. Aggie, in better physical condition, reduced her spirited pace several times to allow him to catch up.

They reached the apex of another incline. But instead of a respite, a level jaunt where he might catch his breath, the terrain beyond rose at an even steeper angle.

"Hey Supergirl, I need a break." He kept his voice low in case Spartan was close.

"We should keep moving," Aggie said.

"Two minutes."

She relented. Corbet sat on a fallen log encrusted with moss, hung the psyts on a knotted branch. He'd activated the goggles several times since setting out from the copter wreckage, using a photo of Edith Ramagano in an attempt to target Spartan. He'd gotten no hits, only fresh bouts of eyestrain and the inevitable headaches that followed.

Aggie plopped down beside him, offered a water bottle. "Must have been hard back there with the colonel."

"Hard?"

"Saving his life."

Corbet took the bottle, drew a long swig instead of answering.

"So what's the story with you two?"

He handed the bottle back, changed the subject. "That femme fatale act of yours. Boyfriends ever get jealous?"

"If you're trying to ask whether a trick or treat entails sleeping with a target, the answer is... none of your business. And you're one to be talking about relationships. Not exactly an area of expertise."

"Guilty as charged. I'm genetically flawed, got shortchanged on the romantic hormones."

Yet even as he trotted out the familiar rationale, it felt more hollow than usual, a ridiculous lie. He turned away, stared into the trees, aware of a strange new feeling. As painful as the idea was, he found himself wanting to tell Aggie the truth.

She seemed to sense he was on the verge of disclosure. Her voice softened.

"Why do you hate the colonel so much? I know it has something to do with your brother."

"You've read my file."

"Jeremy Tomms, Army special forces. Killed in Afghanistan. But the rest of that report's been redacted."

Corbet made a final attempt to steel himself against revelation. He failed. The story flowed out of him.

"I was totally messed up as a kid. This psychic stuff, these visions... it was pretty rough trying to get a handle on being a precog, seeing things that hadn't happened yet. After our parents died in that crash when I was twelve, things got even worse. For a while I thought I'd go crazy, end up spending the rest of my life in some mental institution.

"But I had Jeremy. Ten years older and the goddamn rock of Gibraltar. He was always more like a dad to me than a big brother. He got me through the bad times, probably kept me from losing my mind."

As Corbet spoke, old hurts drifted to the surface. But there was no turning back.

"Wasn't just that Jeremy died. It's that I saw him die. I was fourteen when I had a vision of his squad being ambushed in an Afghan village, two days before it happened. I was so scared."

He remembered the terrible fear, how he'd hidden in his room for hours, so overwhelmed he couldn't even think of what to do.

"We'd been living in Manhattan with our cousin, who was supposedly my legal guardian when Jeremy was away. But our cousin was old and had his own issues. Early-stage dementia, I found out later. Anyway, I finally got my shit together enough to realize it was up to me to act.

"I called Jeremy's unit but I couldn't reach him. They told me he was on an op, that it could be a week or more before he could take a personal call from home. I bitched and whined, told them how important it was that I got through. Of course, I didn't say why, at least not then. Didn't want them thinking I was a whack job.

"They finally connected me to Jeremy's commanding officer. I begged him to cancel the op, bring the squad back before it was too late. He demanded to know why.

"So I told him about the visions, that I'd seen Jeremy's squad getting ambushed, seen my brother die. I described the village where the attack was to occur, and I guess he was familiar with it. He demanded to know how I'd gained access to 'classified material.' He warned that if Jeremy had told me, we'd both be in a lot of trouble."

Corbet stopped. His guts ached. The pain was as awful as it had been on that terrible day.

"I couldn't convince this officer I was on the level. The asshole finally came to the conclusion that it was some perverse teenage joke. He chewed me out for bothering him then hung up. I tried to get through again but he wouldn't take my calls.

"Two days later, Jeremy's squad walked into the ambush. He took a bullet in the head, died instantly."

"The officer was Colonel Mavenhall?"

"He was only a lieutenant back then."

"That's why you avoid relationships, don't let

anyone get close. You're afraid you might see their future, see something bad happen to them."

He nodded.

"But isn't that true for all of us?" Aggie argued. "Everybody dies. One way or another, everybody risks the pain of losing someone they care about."

"It's not the same. Most people don't see it happen ahead of time. The experience is different. I can't explain it any better than that. But seeing an event from the future, seeing it precisely, knowing it's going to happen..."

He shook his head. "People like Dr. Jarek, they think my ability to experience these visions is a gift. But it's not."

"Did you ever manage to change something you've seen, make the future different from the way you'd perceived it?"

"No. Never."

"Then even if you'd warned your brother, you couldn't have saved him."

"I've thought about that. A lot. The thing is, maybe there are exceptions. Maybe there is a way to change the future." He unleashed a bitter laugh. "Considering current events, we'd better hope so.

"But with Jeremy I never got the chance to find out. Mavenhall made sure of that. Years later, I tracked the son of a bitch down, confronted him outside a restaurant. I don't know what I was expecting. Maybe an apology. Or maybe I just wanted him to stand there so I could scream at him for killing my brother.

"I got no satisfaction, of course. He told me to get a life and walked away." Corbet paused. "The last thing I said to him was that someday, somewhere, I was going to watch him die."

Aggie rose from the log. "We should get moving."

Corbet stood up. His hands were sweaty and he

felt lightheaded. Reactions, no doubt, to having unburdened himself after all these years of hiding behind mental ramparts, of keeping those painful truths sequestered. Yet he also felt a sense of relief that he'd come clean to Aggie.

He realized he hadn't told her everything. He still hadn't revealed to anyone the most disquieting part of his vision, his encounter with the Ghost Child.

Aggie headed uphill. He followed, donning the psyts and blinking to activate the tracking grid.

The moment he visualized Edith Ramagano's face, a pulsing red dot appeared on the grid's outer perimeter. Corresponding data printed out across the bottom, the target's three dimensional coordinates and linear distance.

"I got him! Just within range. 290 feet."

Corbet pivoted until the blip moved to the center of the grid, pointed in the direction he was facing. Aggie checked the compass.

"South-southeast. Way off our heading."

"Doesn't matter. We need to go after him."

"I have a pistol, you're unarmed. Bad odds."

"We have to try. Who knows how long it'll take to get help out here. And he has those kids. We could be their only chance."

"We don't even know if they're still alive. Our priority is reporting Spartan's position and contacting search and rescue."

"I don't think Spartan's trying to reach Bellhopper's."

"What are you talking about?"

Corbet revealed what had been troubling him since they'd spotted the Merc heading onto that abandoned road. It made no sense that Spartan was way out here, far away from the lake. Unless...

"I may have been mistaken about where the spaceship came down. If so, it's up to us to stop him."

Aggie hesitated. She would be thinking back to the grief she'd taken from the debriefers last night for allowing Corbet to lead them into a dangerous situation at the tower.

"Do we really have a choice?" he prodded.

Her resolve hardened. She unholstered the Glock, double-checked the magazine.

Corbet knew that the two of them going after Spartan on their own was crazy. Yet he couldn't help himself. The same compulsion that had forced him to track Spartan last night on the mountain was again driving him.

They turned onto the new heading, south-southeast.

61

LIS RACED HER HUMVEE FROM the parking garage beneath Mercy Memorial Hospital, whipped the wheel hard left onto Kelliksville's main drag. The back end slid out, almost hit a parked Toyota.

She gunned the accelerator. The Humvee bit macadam, accelerated to 60 in a 30 mph zone. She didn't care. She wasn't stopping, not for local cops, not for anyone. She needed to reach the field and update them on Edith Ramagano's startling revelation.

We have the wrong goddamn target.

Lis tried her radio again. Nothing. Although Kelliksville was outside this latest interference zone, Alpha Command wasn't. She couldn't get through. The closest unit she'd reached was a National Guard platoon 17 miles south of town. But the unit had lost touch with its commanding officer, and the young NCO in charge couldn't locate a copter to ferry Lis from the hospital.

She skidded the Humvee around another corner, tried to calculate how it would take to reach the field and get Alpha Command to redeploy to the correct target.

Too long.

62

CORBET AND AGGIE PEERED AT the vintage Merc from behind a tangle of huckleberry bushes. The car was parked 30 feet away, in the middle of the abandoned road. The mysterious object protruding from the trunk remained covered by a tarp.

Detritus littered the area: beer and soda cans, fast-food packaging, a pair of underpants tacked to a tree. The place must be party central for local kids.

There was no sign of Edith/Spartan. The two kidnapped teens were alive in the back seat. Cloth gags covered their mouths. They appeared to be bound, judging by their frantic twisting and turning. But they couldn't break free.

Corbet donned the psyts again, reconfirmed Spartan's position. The Edith replicate was about 175 feet ahead, past where the road made a gentle curve and vanished beyond a cluster of evergreens. But the tracking grid indicated something odd.

Edith was in motion, moving perpendicular to their position. She'd walk about 30 feet in one direction then double back, an endlessly repeating pattern. At the completion of each back-and-forth cycle, two muffled cracks could be heard.

"What's she doing?" Aggie whispered.

Corbet had no idea. Even with Edith out of sight, he feared she was too close for them to attempt to open the Merc's back door and rescue the teens. Yet they couldn't just keep hiding here in the bushes. The sun had set; red and gold bands on the horizon already were morphing into purplish streaks. They had to do something before darkness fell.

Corbet removed the psyts, signaled Aggie to stay put. She shook her head but he ignored her objections. He crept toward Spartan's position, keeping low to the ground within the cover of the woods. Much of the shaded earth remained damp from last night's storms, helping to camouflage his footsteps. Even so, he trod lightly to avoid stepping on any twigs.

A man-made object appeared in the midst of the dense forest: the rusting hulk of an ancient steam shovel. At one time, the entire area must have been a clearing. The extent of the surrounding growth suggested the shovel had been here for decades. A tree grew straight up through its cab, the trunk angling through a windshield devoid of glass.

Just past the shovel, the road ended at a ragged, two-foot-high stone wall. In front of the wall, the macadam revealed where a less formidable wooden barricade had been ripped out.

Corbet inched closer. A pile of rocks came into view, remnants from some sort of mining operation. Limestone, he guessed.

Edith stood at the rock pile. The replicate's right hand was bloodstained and crudely deformed, with a dark spiked claw between the thumb and forefinger.

He recalled Mavenhall saying that Spartan was limited in the number of transformations he could undergo, and that cellular instability made it harder for him to maintain a replicate. Maybe when he'd punched a hole in the Merc's roof to attack the commandos, the injury had caused some freakish crossover between the two chromosomal sets.

Edith picked up two rocks from the pile, each about the size of a basketball. Balancing one in each palm as if they weighed next to nothing, she walked 30 feet to the stone wall and plopped the rocks on top, one at a time. That explained the two muffled cracks, one right after the other. But he couldn't fathom Spartan's intentions, why he apparently was replacing the wooden barricade with one made of stone.

What was he, some deranged safety advocate? Was he worried a car might crash through the flimsier wall?

Corbet crept closer, slithered behind a tree. He finally could make out the far side of the wall, realized why a barrier was needed. There was no more road, just a 50-foot drop to the surface of a dark body of water.

Comprehension came in a flash. The limestone rocks, the road ending at a cliff, the primordial steam shovel...

It was a submerged quarry.

Long ago, workers must have delved too deep to extract the limestone and broken through into an underground stream. Whether the water had seeped in over time or came gushing through in a torrent, the outcome had been the same. The quarry had flooded.

He gazed out over the still waters. The failing light gave the surface an inky blue tinge. The quarry was roughly kidney-shaped, maybe 250 feet end to end. It was enveloped by wilderness except for the abandoned road, which was the only spot where a vehicle could get close.

This is where Herman Ramagano saw the UFO splash down. Preceptor and his spaceship are hidden under these waters.

Corbet realized in a sickening instant the nature of his screwup. He'd misinterpreted the photo caption in Edgar Brown's trailer, jumped to the wrong conclusion.

The caption had read: *Hermie at Bellhopper's Lake, Pearl Harbor Day, 1960. Didn't catch the big one, had to settle for a trout.*

Corbet assumed Edgar and Herman had searched for the UFO at Bellhopper's. But now he realized nothing in the caption proved the lake was where they'd employed the scuba gear. The more likely chain of events that day: they'd climbed down into the quarry, donned the gear and spent the better part of that December 7th searching beneath these waters. Only after failing to find Preceptor's ship had they driven to Bellhopper's to soothe their disappointment with fishing and beer.

He retraced his steps back to Aggie, an idea forming about how to rescue the teens. He tried conveying it to her with hand signals but she didn't understand. She finally whipped out her phone, gesturing to Corbet to explain his idea in text.

She read the screen, nodded in agreement. They crept toward the car, approaching from the rear. Corbet was tempted to remove the tarp, see what was hidden in the trunk. He wondered if it might be the catalyst for Spartan's WMD.

But first priority was freeing the teens. Fortunately, the Merc's doors were unlocked. He thought of getting behind the wheel and driving the four of them out of here, decided the idea was too risky. There wasn't enough space to turn the vehicle. He'd have to steer in reverse along the decrepit road. And Spartan certainly would hear them the moment he started the car.

It was a moot point. The ignition keys were missing.

The girl, Trixie, spotted them first. Eyes damp from

crying widened with fresh terror. If she hadn't been gagged, she would have screamed.

Corbet made the shush sign to the teens as he gripped the door handle. He waited for the noise of Spartan adding two more rocks to the wall.

Crack.

Judging the timing of the second crack, he whipped open the door at that precise instant. He held his breath and gazed toward the bend in the road, poised to run if Edith appeared. But the ploy seemed to have worked. The sound of the second rock plopping onto the wall had camouflaged the opening of the door.

The teens' wrists were knotted with rope. They were belted into the seat with leather strips, the kind used to power equipment in old-style machine shops. Edith must have procured the bindings from the Ramagano barn. The '58 Merc predated seat belts so the replicate had punched holes in the cushions to pass the leather strips through, probably attaching their ends to the vehicle's frame.

Aggie sliced through the bindings with her pocketknife. The leather was tough, the task slow. Corbet didn't have a knife so he kept an eye on the road, knowing they were running out of time. At some point, Spartan would finish building the wall and return.

They freed Trixie first. Corbet helped her from the car while Aggie leaned in to cut Timothy's bindings. The girl was wobbly: her legs had fallen asleep. Corbet helped her stagger to the edge of the woods, made another shush sign as he removed her gag.

Aggie liberated Timothy and gave him her compass. She motioned the teens to stay off the road and hike due west, and to not stop until they reached civilization. She scrawled an Alpha Command phone number on a slip of paper, signaled the teens to call the number as soon as they were able.

Trixie and Timothy hustled off into the woods. Watching them go, Corbet fought an instinct to follow, to get the hell away from here. But as potent as that instinct was, he knew that he couldn't run away. Spartan was close to his goal. If he reached that ship, it could be all over. Somehow, they had to stop him.

Corbet returned to the car and gingerly eased the tarp to the ground, exposing the strange contraption in the trunk. The boxy machine was bolted to the floor and looked to have been assembled from automotive, plumbing and electrical parts. Its surface was crisscrossed with wires and rubber tubing. Bent segments of vehicular tailpipe had been welded together and attached to the end cone.

The cone certainly appeared to be a thruster nozzle, suggesting the contraption was some sort of jet engine. Yet the vintage Merc, even with its sleek tailfins, didn't look capable of achieving flight. Corbet remained mystified as to the contraption's purpose.

He looked at Aggie, knew she was thinking the same thing. This machine could be Spartan's WMD catalyst. Sabotaging it could mess up his plans or at least slow him down. He doubted they could destroy it, but maybe they could damage it enough to force Spartan to make lengthy repairs. That could buy precious time, give military forces a chance to get here.

Aggie leaned into the trunk, started slicing wires with her knife. Corbet turned his efforts to the rubber hoses. The first one came loose from its gasket with only a mild tug, but its companion proved stubborn. He grasped it with both hands and twisted hard.

The instant it popped loose, he realized he'd made a terrible mistake. The tube was pressurized, ejected a blast of hot air. Startled, he jerked away. His elbow cracked against the raised trunk lid with a loud bang.

He uttered a silent curse, whipped his head toward the road. There was no sign Spartan had overheard the noise. And then his peripheral vision caught movement in the trees on their flank.

The Edith replicate charged out of the forest at them, galloping on all fours. Corbet froze for an instant at the sight of an elderly woman in a house dress bounding toward them like a mad dog.

Aggie whipped out her Glock, knelt low in a two-handed shooter stance and fired. Edith ignored the slugs tearing into her. Leaping atop the Merc, she used the roof as a springboard to lunge down on them with the force of a blitzing linebacker.

She slammed into Corbet's chest. He went over backwards, felt pebbles of loose macadam chewing into his scalp as it cracked against the road. He glimpsed Aggie falling beside him, the gun flying from her hands as she landed hard.

He tried to sit up but collapsed in a spume of dizziness. The last thing he saw before consciousness slipped away was Edith leaning over them, sniffing at their bodies like some hungry animal.

63

CORBET AWAKENED IN THE MERC'S back seat, unable to move. A length of rope bound his wrists. Strips of leather encircled ankles, waist and chest, pinning him tightly to the cushions. Beside him, Aggie was immobilized the same way.

She craned her head toward him. "You okay?"

He nodded, trying to fight off the stampede of grisly

fates trampling through his mind. Leading the pack was the unholy notion of being eaten alive.

The vestiges of sunset had disappeared. A tapestry of stars peppered the heavens. A flimsy crescent moon hovered above treetops on the far side of the submerged quarry.

Had the teens made it back to civilization? If so, Mantis One and the other military units could be on their way here. Rescue might be only minutes away.

Or hours.

Or not at all.

A shudder went through him. In his visions over the years, he'd seen many people die. Most had perished in bursts of violence, like Jeremy. Corbet had borne psychic witness to shootings, stabbings, fires and car crashes, even a Cessna plowing into an icy mountain. He'd seen death by poison, smoke inhalation and explosions. But for the first time, it felt as if the grim reaper was on his own doorstep.

He shook his head, refusing to succumb to such bleak thoughts. There had to be a way out of this.

Movement beyond the windshield caught his attention. A dark silhouette appeared on the road up ahead. Only when it strode to within a few yards did he recognize it as the replicate.

Edith slipped into the Merc's driver's seat, started the engine.

"What do you want with us?" Corbet demanded, knowing such bluster wouldn't save them. But defiance was pretty much the only weapon he had left.

Edith turned on the headlights and swiveled to face them. Her wrinkled face projected calm. Corbet had to remind himself that he sat only feet away from a murderous alien creature.

"It is best that you try to achieve a state of physical relaxation," Edith said, her voice as serene as a Zen master. "The force of impact will be better absorbed with musculature in repose."

Corbet didn't have time to decipher her meaning. She shifted into first gear, released the clutch. A rooster tail of dirt flew out from under the rear wheels. For an instant, the Merc stood still, its tires spinning madly.

Treads bit into the ancient macadam. The car jerked forward. Edith shifted up through the gears as they skidded around the bend, accelerating toward the wall at the edge of the cliff.

Corbet experienced one of those gestalt moments, a number of disparate elements fusing into a singularity of terrifying comprehension.

The wall drawing closer, the 50-foot drop into the quarry waters visible beyond it...

Those long boards from the original wooden barricade now propped on the wall to form an ascending ramp...

A childhood memory of an auto thrill show, the daredevil drivers launching their cars through the air...

"Oh shit."

It was the only response he could think to utter against the absurdity of what was about to happen. Aggie hollered something equally inane as the Merc's front tires clapped against the boards.

The car rocketed up the ramp, got airborne, sailed out over the submerged quarry. Gravity took swift command. The front end arced downward. Corbet felt a weightless sensation in his guts, like the start of a high-speed elevator descent. But unlike that experience, here there would be no cushioned landing.

As the nose dropped, headlight beams illuminated the dark waters below. He grasped the meaning of the replicate's final words.

The force of impact will be better absorbed with

musculature in repose.

Even if he could have relaxed in such insane circumstances, there wasn't time. The car slammed into the water with a thunderous splash. Sharp pain tore through Corbet's midsection as he was thrown violently forward against the makeshift seat restraints.

A tremendous waterspout roared up past the windows. The car teetered on its front end for a moment, threatening to flip backward onto its roof. But either luck was with them or Spartan understood the physics governing vehicular cliff diving. The Merc released a low groan, fell right side up. The undercarriage pancaked the surface and the car bobbed gently in the agitated waters.

Corbet swiveled his head, glanced behind them. The top of the cliff they'd launched from was etched against the dark skies. From this perspective, it was obvious why the ramp had been necessary, why Spartan couldn't have just driven off the edge. Halfway down the cliff, a limestone shelf protruded out over the waters. Without the ramp, they wouldn't have gained enough distance to clear the shelf and would have landed on rock.

Liquid gurgled in from below. Cold water swirled across their feet, creating fresh panic.

We're not going to drown. Spartan wouldn't have gone to the trouble to strap us in if he intended to kill us like this.

However rational that notion, it seemed at odds with the reality of the situation. The water rose quickly, its coldness prickling the flesh of his ankles, then his knees. It slithered over the seat, submerging his crotch.

He glanced at Aggie, saw fear on her face that matched his own. The water climbed relentlessly, reached their stomachs, enveloped their chests.

Spartan raised his device, held it aloft above the dashboard. A weird light oozed from the two prongs. Like some fantastical form of a luminescent gas, the light spread out to fill the dwindling space between the rising water and the Merc's roof.

The flood ended with their heads just above the water line. Spartan kept the device extended, and the way he leaned forward with it brought to mind some ancient mariner on the bow of his ship, holding a lantern to penetrate dense fog. But the device wasn't only for illumination. Somehow, it was creating an air pocket, a breathable shelf that extended from just below their necks to the car's roof.

The air pocket held its shape as the Merc slipped beneath the surface. Spartan had survived in orbit for decades in that Soviet spacesuit, probably by employing similar technology. The strange light even sealed the jagged hole in the roof where Edith had punched her fist through. Not a drop of water penetrated that opening.

The car's battery shorted out. Headlights flickered and died. Corbet caught a final glimpse of the crescent moon above the trees. And then there was only that ghostly radiance, illuminating their slow descent into the depths.

64

"How deep are we going?" Corbet asked.

The question felt ridiculous even as he uttered it. But he needed to say something, if for no other reason than to maintain sanity in an insane situation.

The light provided enough illumination to see beyond the Merc's windows, revealing air bubbles leaking from undercarriage crevices. Only a gentle rocking motion gave evidence they were still descending.

Fresh anxiety surfaced. The vein of trapped air seemed to be growing stale. He and Aggie were breathing hard, sucking more oxygen with each gasp. Their rapid exhalations would soon fill the air pocket with carbon dioxide, creating a cycle of decreasing o2 and increasing Co2 ending in suffocation.

Then again, maybe the air was fine. Maybe they were simply on the cusp of well-deserved panic attacks.

"How deep?" he demanded.

Spartan surprised him by answering. The Edith-voice had the composure of a tour guide.

"Maximum depth will be 117 feet."

Corbet lacked precise knowledge of the effects of depth and pressure on thin-walled objects, such as submarines and old cars. But he'd seen enough underwater action movies to know that bad things happened when you went too deep. The enemy sub usually imploded, crushed like a paper cup.

A shudder rose up his legs, transmitted through the soles of his submerged feet. The Merc released a mournful groan as it settled onto the quarry floor, presumably 117 feet below the surface.

Spartan continued to hold up the device. As Corbet looked closer, he realized the replicate wasn't merely gripping it in a static embrace. Fingertips drummed the handle with dizzying speed, as if typing rapid-fire commands into an invisible keyboard.

The Merc rose off the bottom and jerked forward, pressing Corbet and Aggie into their seat backs. The acceleration relented as the car reached cruising speed. It swam gracefully through the water, a yard above the rock-strewn quarry floor.

A pulsating hum and loud whooshing reverberated through the interior. Corbet craned his neck around to the trunk, the source of the sounds. A stream of pressurized liquid was being ejected through the conical nozzle.

The contraption wasn't a jet engine for aerial flight. It was a hydrojet, a propulsion system for underwater travel.

Somehow, it was being controlled by Spartan's device. The Merc's tail fins probably afforded the car stability for gliding through the depths, which could explain why Spartan had elected to convert this streamlined vehicle rather than Edith Ramagano's clunky VW Beetle. It also seemed likely that the hydrojet, obviously repaired after Corbet and Aggie's sabotage attempt, had nothing to do with a catalyst for the WMD.

The illumination from Spartan's device served as an underwater spotlight, probing the dark waters ahead. Edith banked the Merc to avoid the skeletal remains of a construction shack, a leftover from the quarry's operating days. Most of the timbers had been eaten away, but the brick foundation remained intact. Parked nearby was an ancient flatbed truck that looked to date from the 1940s, the era when the quarry must have flooded. It was rusted through at spots and layered in grime, but a faded logo remained readable on its door.

Ray Gunn Excavating Co.

In less perilous circumstances, the irony of the name might have elicited a chuckle. Corbet realized he'd just solved part of the mystery of his vision. The Pyrotomic Disintegrator pistol he'd found embedded in Tribeca macadam – waiting to be *excavated* – was a symbol for Ray Gunn Excavating, a company likely out of business for decades. Perhaps the toy ray gun also served as a psychic representation for Spartan's weapon or for the energy guns Mavenhall said the Mantis One commandos employed.

A symbol with multiple meanings.

He wondered if such plurality applied to other elements of his vision. Did the feral people, Statue of Liberty with its violet light and the Ghost Child also have multiple meanings?

Answers would have to wait. The Merc glided past the truck, heading straight for a massive boulder rising from the floor. Spartan banked again, this time a harder turn that shifted the air shelf inside the Merc, lowering it on Corbet's side and elevating it on Aggie's. In an instant, Aggie was completely submerged.

The car straightened. The air shelf leveled out. Aggie popped from the water sputtering.

In front of them, a towering wall appeared – the far side of the quarry. Studded with rocks and pockmarked with fissures, it rose through the aquatic gloom like the rampart of some long-lost castle. Spartan slowed the hydrojet and aimed the car at a horizontal fissure.

He guided the car into the black cavity. Metal creaked against stone as the Merc tunneled through the tight opening. The rock tore apart the jagged metal sticking up from the damaged roof, creating an even larger hole. Corbet steeled himself for a high-pressure flood through what was now a two-foot gash mere inches above them. But the invisible barrier from the device's light held steady and there were no leaks.

The fissure widened. Suddenly, they were free of obstructions. The Merc ascended, spinning gently as it rose, revealing that they were in a circular shaft about 40 feet across. The smoothness of the walls suggested nature's handiwork. Prior to the quarry's flooding, the limestone workers must have breached this hidden cavern.

Corbet suspected that Herman Ramagano and Edgar Brown, despite their underwater skills, would not have entered the fissure. Cave diving was an extreme sport. And back in 1960, with more primitive equipment, even someone of Edgar's grit would have been wary of exploring a submerged cave a hundred feet down in a flooded quarry. Besides the obvious dangers, how could the two men possibly have imagined that Preceptor's spaceship was in here? Although the ship's presence somewhere ahead of them now seemed obvious, Corbet still had difficulty understanding how a vessel constructed for travel in outer space had been able to make its way through the narrow crevice.

His thoughts returned to the present. Above them, the water appeared to end at a perfectly flat horizontal barrier. Corbet instinctively braced for a collision only to realize at the last instant he'd been fooled by an optical illusion.

The car passed through the barrier. It wasn't an obstruction.

It was the surface.

65

The Merc erupted in a shroud of liquid. Moaning and spluttering, as if indignant at being deprived of its watery environment, the car skimmed across the surface of the underground lake. The hydrojet nozzle, now above the water line, howled as it continued to spit pressurized air. The car shot across the lake and up onto a beach of smooth rock.

Spartan killed the engine. The water drained fast, exiting by the same pathways it had entered. The replicate waited until the level had receded to their ankles before flinging open its door and stepping out into the cool musty air of the cavern. Edith's soaked dress clung to her figure, making her look even older, and impossibly frail.

Spartan opened the back door. Aggie flinched as the replicate pointed the device at her. A toothpick of white light lanced from one of the prongs. Spartan controlled the beam with surgical precision, using its laser-like energy to cut through her bindings.

In a few seconds, the two of them were free. Edith stepped away from the car, gestured for them to exit.

Their legs were a bit shaky, stiff from the ordeal. Corbet gripped the roof for support, shivered from a combination of drenched clothes and damp air. Spartan's light illuminated the dry portion of the cavern receding into the distance.

The cave was maybe 15 feet wide and at least that high. Chunky stalagmites rose from its uneven floor, suggestive of human statues whose features had been wiped away by a millennium of erosion. Stalactites in hues of rose and amber descended from the ceiling, slimmer and more colorful than their floor-dwelling sisters.

Spartan weaved through the forest of formations but hesitated when he realized Corbet and Aggie weren't following.

"You must come this way," Edith instructed.

Corbet's leg strength returned. He took a few steps toward the replicate, then stopped and gazed back at the lake, tempted by the possibility of escape. But without scuba gear, diving to the bottom of this sump and then making their way back up to the surface of the flooded quarry was suicidal.

Still, Spartan could be leading them to a far grislier fate.

Aggie stood fast and voiced their concerns. "We saw what you did to those hunters at the cabin. Maybe we'd rather drown than submit to cannibalism."

"It was not a cannibalistic act," Edith replied. "We are not of the same species."

"So that's how you rationalize it," Corbet said.

The replicate regarded them in silence for a moment, as if realizing its response had escalated their alarm.

"I require no additional nourishment. You were not brought here for that purpose."

"Why are we here?" Corbet demanded.

Spartan didn't reply. Instead, the replicate pivoted and headed deeper into the cave. Corbet and Aggie traded looks, realized they had no choice but to follow. The device's light was already fading, casting deep shadows across the Merc and the stone beach. In short order, their world would turn pitch black.

"Anything in your pockets?" he whispered.

Aggie shook her head. "He took my gun, phone, flashlight. Everything but this."

She pulled up a wet sleeve to reveal an analog wristwatch. Still working, it boasted an illuminated dial – woefully inadequate for underground navigation. Corbet's phone and wallet were gone, as well as the psyts. Not that there was any use for the goggles at the moment.

They scurried to catch up with Spartan. As they closed to within a few feet, Corbet resisted an urge to grab a loose rock and smash the back of Edith's skull. But other than releasing his pent-up anger and frustration, he sensed no good would come of such an action.

The cavern floor rose steadily. At some places, the ascent forced them to climb over small ledges.

Grabbing hold of stalactites to maintain their balance, they managed to keep pace with Edith, who negotiated the challenging terrain with the skill of a mountaineer.

Corbet spotted green-skinned salamanders dashing about. He doubted the tiny amphibians had entered through the deep-water route. Their presence suggested that the trek was bringing the three of them closer to the forest floor. Small crevices probably explained how the salamanders had found their way down here.

The mineral formations began to peter out as they rounded a bend. Up ahead, the cavern terminated in a spacious chamber with a smooth domed ceiling. Squatting in the center of the chamber was a bizarre object.

Preceptor's ship.

To suggest that the vessel defied pop imagery of what alien spacecraft were supposed to look like would have been extraordinary understatement. Corbet guessed it was 60 feet long, end to end. However, considering it was coiled up on the floor of the chamber like a sleeping serpent, his estimate was only ballpark.

The snake-ship was about eight feet in diameter. The outer end of the coil – presumably its "head" – tapered to a rounded point. The hull sparkled, alive in a rainbow of colors that seemed to constantly change into new and startling hues. Corbet had the impression the vessel had been grown, not manufactured.

Spartan aimed the device at it. A high-pitched whine filled the chamber, piercing enough to make Corbet and Aggie cover their ears. The sound and the discomfort faded as the snake-ship's head end seemed to liquefy. The dissolution spread, creating an aperture the size of a large manhole cover. Spartan nudged them toward the shadowy opening.

Corbet went first, scared yet fascinated. A part of him realized he might well be the first human in history to enter an alien spaceship. But as Aggie and Spartan followed him inside and the liquefied portal melted back into place, another part of him realized they were trapped.

66

THE REPLICATE EXTINGUISHED THE DEVICE'S light. The snake-ship's interior lit up, yet in a manner that made it impossible to determine the source of the illumination. There were no obvious lamps or wall panels. The air itself seemed incandescent.

Stranger still, as Corbet panned his head, the light became brighter in whatever direction he faced and darker toward the edges of his peripheral vision. The phrase "intelligent radiance" popped into his head – light that only appeared when and where required.

He expected to see control panels or acceleration couches or at least some familiar trappings of space travel. But the circular interior was empty, nothing more than a constantly curving tunnel just high enough to walk upright in. The tunnel spiraled ever inward toward the coiled center.

The interior was drier and warmer than the cavern. Odors seemed unnaturally amplified. Corbet could detect Aggie's tropical perfume as well as a spice-laden potpourri dominated by something reminiscent of oregano.

The concave floor was another oddity. It looked solid yet their feet sank in as they walked. He had the impression of treading on a thick mattress. He gingerly touched the walls and ceiling. They possessed the same mushy quality.

Spartan urged them forward. They traversed the entire 60 feet and arrived at the "tail" of the coil, which also tapered to a rounded point.

"No Preceptor," Aggie whispered in his ear.

Corbet nodded. Maybe Preceptor was hiding in the cavern. Even more tantalizing, maybe he was hatching a plan to overcome Spartan and perform a daring rescue.

Desperate fantasies. A more likely scenario was that Preceptor had hightailed it far away from the cave the moment he realized Spartan was on his way here.

The thought touched off an intriguing notion. What if Preceptor also had the ability to disguise himself as a replicate? Perhaps he'd abandoned the snake-ship years ago. Maybe he'd been operating it by remote control while concealed in human form out there in the real world.

But something told Corbet the idea was unlikely. Preceptor would stay close to his vessel.

"So where is he?" Corbet challenged. "Where's your shipmate?"

"That is of no consequence."

Corbet was surprised to hear annoyance in that controlled voice, the first time a recognizable emotion had seeped through the replicate's cool exterior. He decided to press the issue, maybe prod Spartan into revealing something about his plans.

"I suppose Preceptor was upset when he learned you were a mole. If the Consortium is anything like Earth, traitors are considered a pretty low form of life."

Edith's face crinkled with anger. Aggie tugged Corbet's arm, silently urging him not to provoke the alien. But Corbet figured they had nothing to lose.

"Of course, I'm sure you have your reasons for committing treason. Most traitors come up with some pathetic rationalization."

Spartan's rage bubbled over. "The one you call my shipmate is the traitor! He is the instrument of a vile interstellar hegemony that plunders all that it touches. Your civilization must be destroyed. A blow for freedom must be struck!"

There was no disguising the hatred in those words, the zealotry. The President could be right. Spartan's actions might be incomprehensible from a rational basis. He was driven by his emotions, by hostility and rage.

"But how does attacking us help?" Aggie asked, keeping her tone level and soothing, playing good cop to Corbet's bad one. "We've done nothing to hurt you. Please, we want to understand. Maybe there's an alternative."

The replicate tired of their attempts to draw him out. Fingertips again danced across the device.

A translucent barrier formed, a smoky window-wall that trapped Corbet and Aggie in a compartment about eight feet long. The replicate remained on the other side, gazing dispassionately at them, like an experimenter with new lab rats.

Edith inserted her deformed hand into the mushy ceiling and closed her eyes. She stood silent for a time, one hand plugged into the ceiling, the other jabbing at the device, inputting information or commands.

"At least I pissed him off," Corbet said. "That iceman act was getting tiring."

"You've got a gift."

"A gift?"

"For pushing people's buttons, getting them mad at you."

"It's a disease. I'm taking antibiotics for it."

"Better up your dosage."

They both knew the humor was a release, a way to

deal with their bleak predicament.

Edith opened her eyes, withdrew the buried hand. Clutched in her fingers was a transparent, hourglass-shaped vial. About four inches long, it resembled an old-fashioned egg timer. But instead of sand, the vial contained a glowing white vapor. Corbet had a hunch that the vessel itself had created the vial, engineering it to whatever specifications Spartan had typed into his device.

Whether or not that assumption was correct, the snake-ship represented a level of scientific knowhow far beyond Earth science. As impressive as Preceptor's technological gifts might be, they likely paled in comparison to the Consortium's true capabilities.

Preceptor and Spartan's mission to their planet was equivalent to the United States aiding some Third World country by providing indoor plumbing. While it represented a technological advancement, the grantee nation had a long way to go before splitting atoms or launching satellites.

The idea sparked a vague echo of a thought, something to do with Spartan's reason for going to all this trouble to attack the human race when his real enemy was the Consortium. But before the thought could coalesce, Spartan pressed one end of the vial against the window-wall that separated them.

The glowing white vapor was sucked from the hourglass and propelled through the barrier. The osmosis transformed the gas, which emerged on their side as an expanding stream of tiny effervescent particles. It spread quickly through their compartment.

"Hold your breath," Aggie urged, backing away from it.

"Uh-huh. Then what?"

She had no time to respond. The particulated vapor was already swarming over them. They sucked down great gobs of air, covered their mouths and pinched their noses.

The particles adhered to their skin and wet clothing. Corbet felt it creep across his hands and face like microscopic insects. He tried batting them away but the effort was futile. They clung like leeches.

He couldn't hold his breath any longer. The air exploded out of him. He heard Aggie release a moment later. And then the particles were flowing into his mouth and nose.

Paranoia ran rampant. He imagined dreadful poisons and flesh-eating microbes consuming internal organs.

Not in his wildest imagination could he have predicted what actually happened.

67

AN ONSLAUGHT OF SEXUAL HUNGER.

He'd never felt such instantaneous arousal, not at this intensity. He looked at Aggie and *wanted* her, wanted to make love to her right here, right now.

Her face revealed she was under a similar spell. Licking her lips, breathing hard, face raw with desire – she wanted him. Yet through his own fading rationality, he perceived she was fighting her urges, refusing to surrender mental acuity.

"Must be... some kind of... aphrodisiac," she whispered, struggling to get the words out.

"Must be," he said, seeing her as the most beautiful and desirable creature in the universe.

"Spartan wants this." Her breath came in jagged gulps. "He... wants... us... to..."

"Yeah."

"We have to... fight it."

"Yeah. Have to."

Mutual resistance dissolved. Their bodies crashed together, flesh meeting flesh with unbridled fury. He groped at her wet jacket and blouse, wrenched them down across her shoulders. She undid his pants and shorts, yanked them to his knees. He mashed at her breasts, brutally caressing. She grabbed his butt, fingers clawing.

Lips opened. Tongues devoured. She pushed against him. He tripped over his fallen pants and fell backward onto the marshmallow softness of the floor. She landed atop him, the two of them in the throes of animal lust. Final barriers of fabric were torn asunder and then he was inside her, pure power sex, bodies pounding like jackhammers.

He sensed colors, a spectral array tickling his skin, an impossible sensory jumble amid the coitus, hues from every shade of the rainbow and beyond, tangerine ochers and liquid rubies, toxic greens and ice-charmed blues, colors so unimaginably strange that proper nomenclature would never suit.

They achieved orgasm at the same instant, bodies screaming with belligerent satisfaction. And then it was over as quickly as it had begun, and they were pulling away from one another, relieved to be free of a monumental force over which they'd had no control.

He rolled onto his back, saw and felt the mist of tiny particles retreating from his mouth, clothing and flesh. The particles seemed different somehow, darker, heavier, inexplicably transformed.

He looked up, realized Spartan was calmly watching them from the other side of the window-wall.

The replicate again pressed the hourglass vial to the transparent barrier. The particles swarmed toward that spot, compressing into a gaseous jet stream that took on a familiar hue, a shade of violet identical to the light emanating from the Statue of Liberty's torch in Corbet's vision. Before Corbet could consider what that meant, the vapor lanced through the glass and was recaptured within the vial.

Spartan tucked the vial in a pocket of Edith's house dress and withdrew his device from another pocket. He touched the two prongs to the window-wall. The barrier lost its translucency, morphed into a white partition identical to the rest of the compartment in which they were trapped.

As the glow of their lovemaking faded, a bleak thought hit Corbet.

We're of no further use to him.

68

THE VAN-DAN – PRESIDENT VAN Zeeland and national security adviser Dan Edelstein – strode briskly through a hallway in the West Wing basement. *It* was headed for the Situation Room, where U.S. presidents going back to Kennedy monitored crises. The Sit Room was *the* intelligence management center, a place enabling command and control of U.S. forces anywhere in the world.

Van Zeeland, having returned to the White House on Marine One only minutes ago, realized the world was now in crisis mode.

"Press is in an uproar," Edelstein said. "Without

hard news, speculation's been running rampant about what our military is really doing in those mountains. CNN is reporting that special forces are involved. Everyone wants to know why we staked out that lake."

Van Zeeland knew the media would have to be given some kind of story, and soon. But at the moment, there were more critical issues.

A soldier swept open the door and they entered the Sit Room. A large mahogany table dominated the ample space. Gen. Grobbs, who'd flown back to Washington earlier, occupied a seat at the far end, flanked by a dozen senior officials from the military and intelligence communities. The perimeter housed flat-panel TVs for videoconferencing and tiers of communications consoles manned by junior officers.

Van Zeeland took his place at the head of the table, addressed Grobbs. "Give it to me."

"Mr. President, the interference disappeared a few minutes ago. Telecom has been restored to all field units. Our forces are being redeployed from Bellhopper's Lake to the flooded quarry and should be in position as we speak. SEAL teams will be entering the water shortly.

"Search and rescue located the downed chopper a few miles from the quarry. Colonel Mavenhall and the two crewmen have been found. None of their injuries are life-threatening. The kidnapped teenagers were also rescued and are being debriefed."

"Corbet Tomms and Agent Rittenhouse?" Van Zeeland asked.

"No sign of them. Edith Ramagano's account of what Spartan constructed in the trunk of the car, as well as evidence gathered at the scene, suggests the vehicle was modified for underwater travel."

"Spartan took them into the quarry?"

"That's the most likely scenario."

"Options for a rescue?"

Grobbs' face hardened. "Even if they're still alive, they can't be allowed to jeopardize the mission. Spartan's termination trumps all priorities."

"You're saying we don't even attempt a rescue."

"I'm saying they're casualties of war."

69

AGGIE AVOIDED CORBET'S GAZE AS they dressed, reluctant to make eye contact. He sensed she was embarrassed by what had occurred, not the act itself but the utter loss of control, the surrender to a passion so overwhelming that it deserved its own category on the spectrum of human sexual excitement.

"Any ideas?" he asked, zipping up his pants. "About how we might get out of here?"

"No. But something tells me Spartan got what he wanted. Somehow, our lovemaking was related to the catalyst he needed."

"Guess he'll let us go now."

She ignored the quip, combed fingers through her hair to restore damp tendrils to a semblance of discipline. "I'm thinking the catalyst must be organic in nature, which suggests he's constructing a biological WMD. That vapor could have been transformed by our passion. Maybe something in our DNA along with the very act of our having sex chemically altered its makeup."

"I guess that makes sense."

"We should have fought harder, tried not to... let it happen." She trailed off, sounding wistful.

"I couldn't have fought it. Could you?"

"Probably not."

"And catalyst or no catalyst, it wasn't an entirely bad experience."

He'd intended it as a compliment, but her eyes widened with surprise. Then he realized she was staring at something behind him.

He whirled. Standing three feet away was a tall dignified man in a tweed jacket, hands clasped serenely before him.

"Preceptor," Corbet whispered, knowing there was no other possibility. "How did you get in here?"

"He's not real," Aggie warned. "He appeared from thin air."

Corbet reached out, touched the tweed jacket. His fingers tingled as his hand passed through the material and into Preceptor's chest. The 3-D apparition boasted astonishing depth and clarity.

Preceptor's voice was deep, magisterial. "I don't have much time. My pilot has cut off my external communications but is momentarily distracted. You must listen carefully.

"He has created a terrible weapon, a biological plague from a class of genetic mutaters we call neuropoxies. It is an aerobic contagion in the form of that violet-colored gas, crafted to act solely against species with high-level cognitive functions. He will use it to alter the human genome and exterminate human intelligence.

"Within days of infection by this neuropox, a human will begin to lose the ability to think, to reason, to use tools, to perform a thousand other functions of a mentally evolved species. Any form of procreation will transmit the contamination to future generations. The progeny of an infected parent, even a baby from an uncontaminated human egg fertilized in vitro, will be affected once it reaches the fetal stage. The infant will be born with the same crippling defect, physically normal but unable to develop beyond the intellectual level of a wild dog, incapable of rising above animal instincts and simple emotions."

The feral people. Corbet's vision had provided a glimpse of just such a future.

"Your science is not advanced enough to negate such a destructive alteration of the genome. No matter what steps are taken, an infected child or adult will suffer devolution into a pre-cognitive state of existence. No matter where the neuropox is released, it will spread like wildfire, multiplying itself by chemically attaching to oxygen molecules. In a matter of weeks, your entire atmosphere will be contaminated. Within months, nearly every human on the planet will be infected.

"There is no cure, no immunization. The neuropox ultimately will penetrate most sealed environments. Nothing short of containment facilities for biohazards would ensure against contamination. But the neuropox has an atmospheric half-life measured in centuries, so even the tiny fraction of your populace quarantined within such sites eventually would succumb once their air ran out and they were forced to emerge. Long before that day arrives, your global civilization will have collapsed. For all intents and purposes, Homo sapiens will vanish from the Earth."

"My god," Aggie whispered.

"If the neuropox is released, all hope is lost. As soon as it disperses into the atmosphere it will be unstoppable."

"The catalyst Spartan needed to complete this neuropox," Corbet began, "he got it from us, didn't he?"

"The raw materials he procured here, but they had to be tailored to act upon the human genome. The aphrodisiac caused a specific blend of chemical pheromones to be secreted during your lovemaking. Those pheromones provided the catalyst that made the neuropox effective against your species."

Preceptor regarded them with sympathy, as if aware they might be feeling a burden of guilt. "You had zero control over the passion he induced you to feel. Even if you had known its purpose, that it was the final ingredient of a plague meant to destroy humanity, you would not have been able to resist."

"That's why he kidnapped the teens," Aggie said. "It was supposed to be them having sex. We were replacements."

"Where are you?" Corbet asked. "Hiding in the cave?"

"I am here."

"Here where?"

"All around you. You are inside me."

"You're the spaceship?"

"I am what you would call an AI, an artificial intelligence. What you refer to as the spaceship is actually my corporeal form."

Corbet took the revelation in stride. Nothing could surprise him anymore.

"If you're the ship, why do you need a pilot?" Aggie asked.

"I don't. But the Consortium believes harmony is achieved when natural and processed lifeforms operate in tandem. In our culture, they work side by side, each with specific responsibilities for enhancing the greater good. But my pilot betrayed that trust."

"Is there anything we can do to stop him?"

"There is still time, still a chance for your species. The neuropox must go through a short gestation period to reach toxicity before it can be released."

"How short?"

"Fourteen hours. At this very moment, he is utilizing

my external communications systems to access your Internet. He is finalizing a search for large events and gatherings in major cities throughout the world. He seeks the perfect location for releasing the neuropox once gestation occurs."

Fourteen hours. And then my vision becomes inevitable.

Preceptor continued. "I was badly damaged many years ago in the explosion of the Sputnik spacecraft. I can no longer achieve orbit. However, I do retain a degree of mobility. My weakened state provides your military forces a tactical advantage that may enable them to—"

The apparition vanished in mid-sentence.

"Preceptor?" Corbet called out. "Preceptor, can you hear us?"

No reply.

"Spartan must have forced him to end the transmission," Aggie said.

Corbet suspected she was right. That suspicion escalated when the compartment began rocking back and forth.

"We're moving," he hissed.

A small section of outer wall morphed into a window in the shape of a lopsided diamond. Through it they watched in fascination as the snake-ship uncoiled and began squirming across the cave floor. The rocking movement became more pronounced, making it impossible for Corbet and Aggie to remain standing. They lay down on the cushioned floor, extended arms and legs like outriggers to maintain balance as the crawling vessel picked up speed.

Moments later, it curled around the beached Merc and slithered into the water.

70

THE SIT ROOM POWWOW CONTINUED as the men and women at the table debated options. Van Zeeland's thoughts kept drifting toward what was at stake.

Spartan likely has reached the hidden spaceship, presumably has the WMD and its catalyst. Our species could be on the brink of extermination.

Grobbs nodded to Air Force General Helio Rosario, a compact man with a shock of white hair. Rosario was Chairman of the Joint Chiefs of Staff.

"Mr. President, we've agreed on a tactical response," Rosario said. "We have F-35 fighters flying sorties over the region. They've been outfitted with short-range missiles employing those high-explosive incendiary warheads proposed by Preceptor, which we managed to assemble a short time ago. We need your authorization to launch."

"Into the quarry?"

"Yes sir, if our ground forces fail to neutralize Spartan."

"What kind of civilian casualties and damage are we looking at?" Van Zeeland asked.

"The region is sparsely populated and we're in the process of clearing out all friendlies within a five-mile radius. Provided we can evac our ground forces in time, a best-case scenario would be zero deaths and minimal injuries and property damage.

"The formula Preceptor provided for the incendiaries is an unusual mix of thermobarics and FAEs – fuel-air explosives. Both munitions operate on similar principles. Their chief characteristics are tremendous blast overpressure and high-temperature fireballs. Presumably, Preceptor believes this combination will be effective against..."

Rosario trailed off as Dr. Jarek appeared on a monitor, his voice urgent.

"Mr. President, our computers finished processing the latest transmission from Preceptor, which was received about 35 minutes ago. It contains a short video and a massive amount of data, a far higher percentage than he's ever sent us in a single transmission. Translating this much data into usable information will take weeks. I'm dispatching the video portion to you by secure courier—"

"No time," Edelstein said. "Put it onscreen."

"Yes sir." Jarek fiddled with some off-camera controls. His own face vanished, replaced by Preceptor standing in that familiar retro study. For the first time in Van Zeeland's experience of viewing these videos, Preceptor looked worried.

"My pilot has located me. He likely will have boarded by the time you view this message. Because this will be my last transmission, I've included a wealth of technological advancements, data that under normal circumstances would have been sent to you over the next few years. But our crisis calls for an accelerated process.

"I believe my pilot will soon procure the raw materials and catalyst to create the WMD. He will immobilize me and attempt to launch the ship, escaping to whatever target he ultimately selects. Many of my systems remain damaged and inoperable. I am capable only of suborbital flight at limited speeds.

"These constraints provide your military forces a tactical advantage, a chance to defeat him. A coordinated, midair attack by your fighter jets using the warheads assembled per my earlier instructions may succeed. Your missiles not only will destroy my ship and its occupants, but vaporize whatever WMD my pilot has crafted.

"The plan has challenges. Some of my cloaking systems remain operational and my pilot will make use of them. Your tracking devices will not easily locate their target, except by the initial disturbance caused by the ship's emergence from the quarry. For your attack to succeed, you must wait and watch for my signal. It will come in the form of pulses discernible across the visual frequencies of the electromagnetic spectrum."

Preceptor walked to the bookshelf behind him and withdrew a volume. Van Zeeland couldn't make out the title. But when Preceptor spoke again, it was with an air of resignation.

"My cessation likely will impact the Consortium's ultimate agenda for your world. But I say with all sincerity that providing these advancements to your civilization over the past half century has been a rewarding experience. I wish your species only the best. May you continue progressing toward a notable future."

The transmission ended. The room erupted into activity. Grobbs and Rosario opened phone lines to convey Preceptor's instructions down the chain of command.

Van Zeeland and Edelstein traded stunned looks. Preceptor was sacrificing his life to end the threat to humanity.

71

CORBET STARED OUT INTO THE watery darkness. The snake-ship had entered the underground lake at a sharp angle but quickly leveled out as it dropped through the sump. When they reached the crevice that connected to the flooded quarry, the vessel seemed to alter its configuration, becoming slightly thinner in order to squeeze through the narrow opening. In the compartment where he and Aggie were trapped, the ceiling came closer to their faces.

And then they were through the crevice.The compartment morphed back to its default shape. The snake-ship picked up speed as it angled straight upward, knifing through the dark waters to reach the surface.

Clumps of the floor rose up around Corbet and Aggie, enveloping their supine bodies in cocoon-like shells that left heads and arms free. He sensed the enclosures were Preceptor's version of acceleration couches, custom-molded to human physiques.

The snake-ship broke the surface. Through the diamond-shaped window, Corbet glimpsed a raft overturned by their explosive emergence. Three SEAL divers tumbled through the air, crashed hard into the dark waters.

Acceleration increased. The vessel seemed to squirm its way up into the clear sable skies like a flying serpent.

72

All eyes in the Sit Room locked onto a young captain, the chief communications officer. He sat before a bank of computer screens providing play-by-play descriptions as the chase unfolded.

"Target bearing east northeast...

"Altitude, 4,400 feet and climbing...

"Air speed increasing... approaching 2-8-0 miles per hour..."

He fell silent. When he spoke again, confusion marred his words.

"We're receiving conflicting flight data from other resources. Drone Three has the target heading north at an altitude at 3,100... Air speed 1-6-5... But AWAC Delta reports that it's flying south at 9,350 feet, air speed 6-1-0."

"It's using electronic countermeasures," Grobbs concluded.

"Yes sir, that's AWAC's analysis. Target seems to be broadcasting an unknown type of HIRF."

Van Zeeland nodded. Their own forces used high intensity radiated fields to confound enemy radar and tracking systems. Preceptor had warned of such a thing.

"Any sign of that signal yet?" Grobbs asked.

"No sir. But if he transmits those pulses – paints himself as a target – we'll take him down."

The young captain sounded too confident. Any number of things could go wrong, Van Zeeland realized. And even if Preceptor succeeded in revealing his true coordinates, their fighter jets could be forced to launch those incendiary missiles over a more populated region than the quarry. Humanity's survival could come at a hellish cost.

Edelstein broached the concern. "Do we have updated info on potential collateral damage?"

"Impossible to determine," Gen. Rosario said. "Not until we get incontrovertible data on position, altitude, speed and bearing."

"Once Preceptor transmits the pulses, we won't have much time," Grobbs warned. "We dare not hesitate, Mr. President."

"Got him!" the captain yelled. "Target has painted itself. Speed and position confirmed by all resources."

"How soon till the F-35s' missiles can intercept?" Grobbs asked.

"Less than two minutes."

"Put the commander on speaker."

The voice of the F-35 pilot, leader of his four-craft squadron, boomed across the Sit Room. "White-delta-four, we have visuals transmitted from AWAC Delta. Target is roughly cylindrical, sixty feet long. Lit up like a Christmas tree, every color of the rainbow."

The commander paused. "Approaching missile lock. Request authorization to engage and fire."

All heads turned to Van Zeeland. He wondered if the words he was about to utter would someday go down in history as a pivotal moment: the day the human race saved itself from oblivion.

But even as the thought touched him, he felt a tinge of shame that he could even consider his own place in posterity. Not only was Preceptor sacrificing himself to destroy a traitorous shipmate, the missile attack likely would result in at least two other casualties: Corbet Tomms and Agent Rittenhouse.

"Do it," he ordered.

73

THE SNAKE-SHIP LEVELED OUT AT a steady altitude. Corbet and Aggie now hung face-down from the ceiling in body-hugging acceleration shells. Preceptor was flying upside down, at least relative to their position.

The diamondesque window that had been located to one side of their compartment magically shifted its position, sliding downward to what was now the floor, providing Corbet and Aggie with a birds-eye view of the mountainous terrain. They glimpsed occasional splotches of light below, probably isolated homes and farmhouses. Corbet guessed they were flying about a mile up.

He angled his head toward Aggie, forced a grin.

"Hanging in there?"

"Uh-huh. You?"

"Dealing."

Preceptor's 3-D projection returned as abruptly as it had disappeared. Now the AI stood atop the window, craning his neck to gaze up at them, his face a mere foot from Corbet's. The close perspective revealed minute imperfections: age lines, an errant eyelash, a tiny mole on his left earlobe. The level of detail made it hard for Corbet to accept he was looking at a holographic illusion.

Preceptor continued where he'd left off. "As I was explaining before the transmission was interrupted, my weakened state provides your military forces a tactical advantage. Many of my sensors are blind and I cannot outrun your fighter jets. I have neutralized any attempt by my pilot to initiate evasive tactics—"

"Whoa, hold on!" Corbet said. "What's that about fighter jets?"

"A squadron is closing fast. They've launched an attack."

"How long do we have?" Aggie asked.

"Fifty-eight seconds. Termination is now assured. My pilot cannot prevent the inevitable."

Corbet drew a sharp breath, struggling to accept the reality of his own death in less than a minute. "You commit suicide, take Spartan with you. Seven billion people get to keep their intelligence."

"Pretty good trade," Aggie whispered.

Preceptor looked sad. "I am sorry it must be this way."

"Yeah," Corbet muttered. "Us too."

Aggie stiffened her resolve. "Why does your pilot hate the Consortium so much he would destroy the human race?"

"I know only fragments of his true background, what he deigned to reveal. Great personal tragedy reduced him to bitterness and rage. On his home world, a terrible war among his own people decimated the planet. He lost his entire family and many friends. He blames the Consortium for supplying the technological advancements that made that war so destructive."

Corbet realized Preceptor hadn't entirely answered Aggie's question, hadn't addressed Spartan's reason for attacking Earth. Why destroy humanity when his feud was with the Consortium?

"I'd like to be standing up," Aggie said. "When it happens. Can you free us from these harnesses?"

Preceptor took a step backward. The lower portion of the shells fell away first, allowing their legs to dangle. When the upper halves released, they dropped feet-first onto the window, bouncing lightly. The glass – or whatever the substance was – had the same cushiony quality as the walls.

Corbet met Aggie's gaze. Without a word, they wrapped their arms around one another, held on tight. Corbet wanted to say something to her in those final moments, something profound, something more real than anything he'd ever said to a woman.

I'm in love with you.

But he couldn't get the words past his tongue. Even now, a lifetime of avoidance prevented such candor. The best he could manage was...

"Hell of a way to go out."

A second window appeared, this one in the tail of the snake-ship. Corbet saw four bright dots with fiery tales flying in symmetrical formation. The quartet of missiles was closing fast.

A shuddering roar filled the compartment as the missiles approached. Aggie gripped him tighter, buried her head against his shoulder. Above the noise, he thought he heard her whisper something. It sounded like "I love you" but he couldn't be sure.

Say it, he told himself. *Say it while you still can.*

"I love—"

That was as far as he got. The window beneath them dissolved. A blast of cool night air whistled through the compartment. And then they were dropping out the bottom of the ship.

Amid the shock of freefall, Corbet registered a host of impressions.

Aggie still in his embrace, the two of them plunging as one through the cool night air...

The snake-ship rocketing straight up into the heavens, its sleek body pulsating with a thousand unearthly hues...

The four missiles changing trajectory from horizontal

to vertical, relentlessly pursuing.

His back slammed into cold liquid. Needles of pain rippled across his spine. Aggie landed atop him, driving him under, enveloping him in a smothering aquatic membrane.

The shock of impact wrenched her away from him and ripped the air from his lungs. When he inhaled, there was only water.

Can't breathe! *Going to die*!

Before panic could take him, powerful arms gripped his shoulders. He was yanked out of the water and thrown into a rubber raft. Choking and coughing, he expelled water from his mouth and nose and sucked down precious air. He sensed Aggie there beside him, breathing hard.

The two men in the raft were soldiers. They looked up. Corbet followed their gazes.

High above, the fiery trails of the four missile trails intersected. For a timeless moment, they seemed to disappear, as if absorbed by some invisible object.

Then the sky exploded.

A thermal cauldron as bright as the sun obliterated darkness. It was so intense they had to shield their eyes. The surrounding wilderness came alive in daylight greens and browns. The waters beneath the raft turned vivid chartreuse, reflecting the luminance of that unnatural sun.

The brilliance relented, faded into a bubbling cloud of orange-gold flame. The shock wave hit an instant later. But it was mild, little more than a blustery wind that created ripples on the water's surface. And then the spectacle was over and the heavens decayed back into natural darkness.

Corbet grabbed Aggie's hand. They looked at one another, started laughing, a giddy release of tension that transformed into tears of joy.

The two soldiers wrapped Corbet and Aggie in their jackets, paddled the raft to shore. The soldiers didn't speak, just let Corbet and Aggie keep laughing and crying, recognizing that they were undergoing a post-traumatic reaction.

Their emotional release was over by the time they reached the shoreline, a sandy beach occupied by half a dozen more soldiers and two Humvees draped in camo netting. Corbet and Aggie uttered profuse thanks. The soldiers smiled.

"Where are we?" Aggie asked one of them.

"Bellhopper's Lake."

74

THE SIT ROOM SPEAKERS EMITTED garbled static, an unhealthy sound that reminded Van Zeeland of a sickly child struggling to breathe. The voice of the F-35 command pilot abruptly cut through the noise.

"All sensors negative," the F-35 squad commander announced. "AWAC Delta confirms zero trace of biological or radiological residue. Target is vapor."

Gen. Rosario turned to Van Zeeland with a triumphant grin. "Mr. President, the threat is neutralized."

Cheers broke out across the Sit Room. Civilian and military, men and women, all spouted congratulations and gave one another high fives. Van Zeeland felt remote from it all as did Edelstein. Grobbs also declined to participate in the celebration.

The three of them were thinking ahead, to what the

loss of Preceptor represented. The United States, and probably other nations who'd been sent Preceptor's final data transmission, would enjoy a bonanza of technological advancements for at least a few more years. But the five-decade stream of alien gifts had come to an end.

Van Zeeland also found himself dwelling on damage control, on how they might corral the media and keep U-OPS and its mission confined to the shadows. But he held no illusions. Total secrecy of the type they'd enjoyed before the crisis would no longer be possible. There'd been too many points of exposure. The press had a plethora of leads. Reporters, in their zeal to assemble the entire story, would come at the government with guns blazing. His administration would take hits, possibly a fatal one.

Edelstein read his thoughts. "Hell of a mess to sweep up."

"We don't have a broom that big."

"On the bright side, at the end of the day we're still here."

Van Zeeland managed his first smile in what seemed like ages. No matter what the future had in store, tonight humanity had survived its greatest peril.

75

CORBET AND AGGIE SAT ON the shore huddled in blankets, sipping hot chocolate and shivering to stay warm. The man in command of the soldiers, an amiable staff sergeant with the star name of Kerry Grant, squatted beside them and outlined the night's events.

Sgt. Grant's squad of Army Rangers had been left at Bellhopper's Lake to pack up equipment and sweep the area clean of military flotsam after the rest of his company had redeployed to the quarry.

"The two of you were lucky you landed right next to our raft," Grant said. "Otherwise, we probably wouldn't be having this conversation."

Corbet knew luck had nothing to do with it. Preceptor had targeted their drop to give them the best chance of being rescued.

"What were your men doing out on the water?" Aggie asked.

"Fishing. Some locals we cleared out earlier said the state keeps Bellhopper's well-stocked. I dispatched two of my men in the raft to confirm that intel." Grant adopted a sly grin. "Fresh trout for dinner would have been a bonus.

"The next thing we know, that thing is swooping in 60 feet above the water and the two of you are dropping out the bottom of it. Want to tell me what the hell you were doing inside it?"

"Sorry," Aggie said. "Classified."

A corporal approached, handed Corbet and Aggie khaki uniforms.

"Better get out of those wet clothes," Grant said, departing with the corporal to give them privacy.

It was the first time Corbet and Aggie had been alone since their rescue. They changed beside one of the Humvees.

"Preceptor went out of his way to save us," Aggie said. "He must have taken control of the ship from Spartan in those final moments."

"Taken control of himself, you mean."

"It's hard to get a handle on thinking of him like that. An intelligent spaceship." She slipped on the khaki pants, gazed out over the still waters. "Do you think he felt anything?"

"What do you mean?"

"I guess I'd like to believe he sacrificed himself to save us, save humanity. But maybe he was just a fancy machine. Maybe it was simply following its programming, carrying out a series of logical actions."

Corbet shrugged. The question might never be answered.

They finished changing. Grant ended a radio call, addressed his squad.

"All right, listen up. Orders from Alpha Command. They're sending a copter to pick up our two dropouts. As for that flying snake-thing, the missiles, the explosion - none of it happened. Ditto for our two guests. They were never here. We all spent a quiet night by a peaceful lake and saw nothing unusual."

Grumbling broke out among the soldiers.

"Why ain't I surprised," one private muttered. "By tomorrow they'll be telling us we weren't even in Pennsylvania."

"Way it's got to be, guys."

The cover-up continues, Corbet thought, sitting on a rock at the water's edge.

U-OPS and its myriad of secrets should be revealed. The human race had a right to know how close it had come to being wiped out. Still, that decision wasn't his. Last night on the jet, he and Aggie had been prompted to sign security clearances for all U-OPS-related matters.

Corbet could always leak the story. Yet he knew he wouldn't do that, and not because he feared dire consequences for violating national security. Mavenhall was right about one thing. His brother had understood the importance of duty. Jeremy would never have betrayed an oath, signed or otherwise, and wouldn't have respected anyone who did.

Aggie sat beside him. “Penny for your thoughts?”

The phrase jarred Corbet from his reverie. He smiled as an old memory surfaced.

“Haven’t heard that expression since I was a kid. My mom used to say it, usually when I was being moody. Usually after I had a vision. That was before she realized my visions came true, when she thought they were just daydreams. A little later, when she realized I had the ability…” He trailed off, shook his head. “Eventually, she and Dad didn’t want to know about what I was seeing, told me to keep it to myself.”

“Your visions scared them.”

“Scared us all.”

“Even Jeremy?”

“Maybe a bit. I don’t know. But he was always the brave one, always strong. Always willing to listen to his frightened little brother.”

Aggie leaned over, kissed him on the cheek. “I think Jeremy would have been proud of you.”

“Yeah. I hope so.”

Memories of Jeremy prompted a new insight. “My vision didn’t come true. The future was different. That must mean it wasn’t a real vision after all. Or maybe it was a cross between a real vision and a spooky dream.”

He stood and gazed into the star-flecked heavens. Despite his words, he harbored doubts.

76

Charlie Kleinfelter rarely picked up hitchhikers. Too many damn druggies out on the road these days. But he'd been trying to get home since mid-afternoon and now it was almost 4:30 a.m. and he was dog-tired and having trouble keeping his eyes open. The radio wasn't helping. And he'd already downed four cups of coffee, which was a couple more than the doctors recommended.

Coronary problems had forced him to go cold turkey on cigars and donuts. But he needed caffeine. The docs just didn't understand the challenges of a 63-year-old whose business took him all over northern Pennsylvania and New York's southern tier, selling and servicing dairy refrigeration equipment.

This week had been especially rough. He should have been back home in Bloomsburg by midday. But his final route client, Zelner Farms, had insisted he stay for their anniversary shindig. Zelner was one of his biggest customers. He could hardly refuse.

The hitchhiker stood with thumb extended on the dark road up ahead, caught in the headlight beams of the panel truck. Charlie figured a good dose of conversation was the perfect way to keep alert during these final hours on the road.

He pulled over. The hitchhiker hopped into the cab, nodded thanks. He looked barely out of high school. Charlie wondered if he was a runaway.

The kid's attire was decent, at least compared to many of his contemporaries. The denim jacket looked new and the blue jeans weren't hip-hoppin' halfway down his butt cheeks. Rail thin and short, he had thinning blond hair and soft delicate features. Charlie took him for one of those homebound sorts whose idea of the great outdoors was watching The Travel Channel.

"Thank you," the kid offered. "The ride is appreciated."

"I'm Charlie."

"Lucas Tyrell."

"Where you headed, Lucas?"

"East."

Charlie pulled back out onto the road, a lonely two-laner.

"We're going south at the moment, but we'll be picking up I-80 East soon."

"That would be fine."

He was certainly polite enough. Charlie doubted he was a runaway.

"Got folks back east?"

"No. Just visiting a friend."

"I can take you as far as Bloomsburg. That work for you?"

"Yes."

"You hear anything about that big explosion up north?"

"No."

"They said on the radio an Air Force fighter jet on maneuvers blew up. I saw the flash and heard the boom. Supposedly lit up the whole damn sky for miles."

"It must have been quite spectacular."

The kid was less talkative than his sister's old Chatty Cathy doll, which uttered simple phrases when you pulled its string. For the next 10 miles, Charlie kept trying to jump-start a real conversation. But the kid refused to bite, courteously responding to every question or remark but then clamming up. Charlie finally gave up the effort and they drove in silence.

The kid came alert as they rounded a bend. "There's a rest area up ahead. Could you pull over? I must relieve myself."

Charlie wasn't in the mood for another delay, even a short piss break. But he couldn't exactly refuse. He pulled onto the shoulder of the deserted rest area. It was little more than a small clearing with a pair of lopsided picnic tables.

"Make it quick, huh."

"Of course. Do you have a flashlight?"

Charlie motioned to the glove compartment. The kid retrieved the flashlight and hopped from the cab. Charlie turned on the radio, hoping to get another update on the explosion. But he didn't have satellite service and the few stations he could tune in were playing wall-to-wall music.

"Hey mister, come here!"

The kid's urgent whisper carried across the clearing. Charlie squinted into the darkness, spotted him at the edge of the forest waving the flashlight.

"Hurry! You've got to see this!"

Charlie's hackles went up. Maybe the kid wasn't so nice and polite after all. Maybe he was trying to sucker Charlie into the woods for god only knew what purpose.

He shut off the engine and pocketed the ignition key. Before stepping from the cab, he reached under the seat for the 18-inch length of rebar he kept for self-defense. He'd never had to use the makeshift club, but he felt safer knowing it was handy.

"Hurry, mister!"

Slipping the rebar down the back of his pants, Charlie followed the bobbing flashlight beam into the woods. The kid halted a couple yards in, shined the beam at the base of a maple tree.

Keeping his guard up, Charlie leaned in closer. A line of five grayish mounds dotted the earth. The gray color wasn't uniform but was streaked with odd colors, shiny pinks and greens that seemed to sparkle under the light.

He jerked back as he caught a sulfurous odor. The mounds were some kind of crap.

"Kid, what the hell have you been eating?"

"No, it's not mine. I was taking a leak when I saw the glow."

"Glow?"

He turned off the flashlight, throwing them into total darkness. Sure enough, the mounds generated their own light, a ghostly sheen that reminded Charlie of luminescent paint. He wondered if they'd come from that Air Force jet? Some kind of weird debris thrown miles from the explosion. If so, the stuff could be radioactive.

"Kid, let's get outta here."

A rustling noise. From overhead. Lucas turned on the flashlight, whipped it up the maple's trunk. The foliage was too thick to make out anything beyond the lowest rung of branches.

But something was up there, something big. Leaves and twigs rained down on them. Whatever it was, it was coming toward them fast.

Charlie sprinted for the clearing, sensed the kid right on his heels. He couldn't recall the last time his legs had propelled him so fast. For the first time in years, he ran with no thought as to how his bad heart might be handling the strain.

He heard a loud thump, knew the thing had reached the ground. He sensed it was right behind them, closing fast.

He made it to the clearing but tripped and fell to his

knees. His cell phone popped out of his jacket pocket, slid across the gravel. Before he could even think of retrieving it, a shriek pierced the night air.

Charlie whirled. Something nightmarish had caught the kid from behind, knocked him face down at the edge of the woods. Man-sized, its body resembled a giant salamander. But atop its head was a pair of tentacles that ended in triple claws.

The monstrosity grabbed the back of the kid's neck with one of the claws and mashed his face into the ground. Charlie forgot all about the phone. He dashed the last few feet to the truck, fumbled in panic for the ignition key.

And then a second monster revealed itself. This one, however, was entirely inside Charlie, gripping his chest like a steel clamp. He was having another heart attack.

The last thing he saw was a patch of gravel rushing toward his face.

77

CORBET AWAKENED ON A COT in another trailer at the baseball field, groggy from a second night of insufficient slumber. Sunlight pouring through the windows revealed the trailer was empty. A contingent of NASA engineers investigating the crash had been bunking here when Corbet had staggered through the door in the wee hours of the morning.

Corbet and Aggie had spent most of the night in separate debriefings. He'd been quizzed about every aspect of their ordeal, had been asked to repeat his story for multiple interrogation teams. He'd divulged everything, even the intimate details following the inhalation of Spartan's super-aphrodisiac. No sense trying to hide the fact he'd engaged in hot sex with an FBI agent in the bowels of an intelligent snake that was really an alien spaceship.

He squirmed off the cot and got dressed. He was about to head outside in search of coffee when he spotted an object suspended in midair at the far end of the trailer.

It was a scale model of the International Space Station, hanging from wires. Probably a keepsake of one of the NASA gang. Corbet had seen numerous images of the station. But this three-dimensional version, a mix of modules, heat deflectors and solar panels, struck him as primitive and clunky. The snake-ship – Preceptor – had forever altered his conception of what constituted advanced technology.

We're not even close to being their equals. He fingered one of the model's solar panels, sent the station into a gentle spin. No matter how many high-tech gifts the world had received from Preceptor, planet Earth would remain a pale shadow measured against the Consortium's stunning achievements.

The notion again triggered a vague idea, something to do with the reason Spartan had directed his fury at the human race. But before he could ensnare the thought, the model and the trailer lost focus and disappeared into a fog.

Once again he was striding down that dark Tribeca street. As in previous incarnations, he saw the feral humans scampering about and the ray gun embedded in asphalt. The violet light from the Statue of Liberty's torch pierced the fog. But before he could look up to see if the statue bore a new face, peripheral vision spotted the Ghost Child.

She approached as before, her angelic appearance in stark contrast to the fear she seemed to project.

"We have to go," she said.

"Go where?"

"To the beginning."

The other elements of the vision repeated. She pointed at the displaced statue. Her other hand reached toward him.

"I don't understand," he said. "Who are you?"

Again, she extended her hand, urging him to accompany her. This time, he held his ground. Still, he couldn't bring himself to take hold of those tiny fingers.

She regarded him silently for a moment. Her stare was unnerving.

"Fall for the future," she instructed.

The words chilled him. He wanted to turn and run but fought the urge. No matter how frightening, he had to see this through. He had to allow the vision to progress to its next phase.

He reached toward her. But just as their hands were about to touch, some invisible object smacked the side of his face.

"Snap out of it, man!"

Yanked from the vision, Corbet found himself back in the trailer, confronting a beefy sergeant whose crinkled eyes betrayed annoyance. Corbet grabbed the man's raised arm before it could administer a second slap.

"Corbet Tomms?" the sergeant demanded.

"Yeah, goddammit!"

"You're wanted. Let's go."

The sergeant ignored Corbet's questions about what was happening and led him outside. They jogged across the field to a big Pave Low helicopter.

Aggie stood at the cabin door, motioning him to

hustle. He sprinted the final few yards and hopped aboard. Jeremy had gone into combat in Pave Lows, which could transport three dozen troops. But the back of the cabin revealed that this copter had a different function.

Two technicians in civilian garb, a male and female, manned consoles of mystifying equipment. The pair were under the command of an Army captain named Wilkins, whose shaved head and steely eyes reminded Corbet of Marlon Brando's character from *Apocalypse Now*.

Corbet squeezed into a seat up front between Aggie and Agent Potts. The whining turboshaft engines lifted the copter aloft.

"Bioterrorism command post," Potts said, nodding in the direction of Corbet's curious gaze.

"What the hell's happening?" he demanded. "Where are we going?"

"No flight plan yet," Aggie said. "They just want us in the air."

Potts opened his laptop. A grisly image filled the screen.

Two naked men lie on the ground, face up. The first one had smooth, youthful skin. The second man was older and bore a long surgical scar down his chest. Both men's faces had been obliterated, eyes, noses, mouths and ears dissolved into hideous brown puddles of seared flesh.

"The disfigurements were done with the tuning fork device," Potts said. "Faces were burned off to prevent identification. Same with fingerprints. Estimated time of deaths, between 4:30 and 5:30 this morning."

"Spartan's alive," Corbet whispered. The recurrence of his vision had suggested things were amiss. But it was still a shock.

"A tractor-trailer driver found the victims at a rest

stop 20 miles south of the quarry. They were hidden under a pile of brush at the edge of the clearing. Pure dumb luck they were discovered. Spartan must not have realized the older victim lost his phone during the attack. When the rig driver stopped to take a leak, he heard it ringing and answered. Turned out it was the wife of the older man, calling to check on why hubby was running late. The rig driver, bless his suspicious soul, searched around and came across the bodies.

"Hubby is Charles Kleinfelter. Sells dairy equipment. We believe Spartan hijacked his panel truck and continued driving south toward Interstate 80. We've got the license and vehicle description out to all PDs within a thousand miles."

"Spartan's changed into another replicate," Corbet concluded.

"The younger victim. Even with that melted face there's evidence Spartan inserted the device. Unfortunately, clothes and ID were taken from both bodies, everything but that phone. The wife says Kleinfelter was traveling solo, which means the unknown male was probably a hitchhiker. We've sent DNA to medical, institutional, and governmental resources. If we're lucky, he's in the system."

"Spartan has a good head start," Aggie said. "I-80 is an east-west route, but we have no idea which direction he's traveling."

"East," Corbet said. "New York City, where my vision takes place."

"Maybe," Potts said. "But for all we know, he's on his way to Pittsburgh or Chicago. Or he could have turned south, headed toward Philadelphia or Washington. Or even boarded an international flight to a larger city."

Corbet realized they were right. At best, New York as the target was based on circumstantial evidence. Spartan could just as well be getting on a plane for

Tokyo, Seoul, Mexico City or one of dozens of other heavily populated metropolitan areas. And even if they pinned down his destination and uncovered his newest identity, they'd still have to locate him within a large urban population.

Col. Mavenhall sauntered in from the flight deck, a large bandage on the back of his neck the only evidence of his injuries. Corbet felt the familiar spark of animosity at the sight of him.

Mavenhall displayed a series of photos on a tablet computer. The images were tinged green – night-vision photography – and appeared to have been taken from high above the quarry.

"A drone snapped these a few hours after Preceptor's ship launched," the colonel said. "Unfortunately, what they reveal was only made discernible a short time ago following imagery enhancement."

The photos showed a blurred creature resembling a salamander. In sequence, they revealed it emerging from under the water, crawling over loose rocks at the shoreline and climbing straight up the cliff wall. Presumably, the creature had scurried into the forest without being seen by the troops remaining at the quarry.

"Length is estimated at six feet. Asian giant salamanders can reach that size, but obviously wouldn't be found in Pennsylvania waters. Clearly, this is Spartan. He must have transformed aboard the spacecraft and made his escape prior to liftoff. He hid underwater until most of our soldiers left the area."

"There were salamanders in the cavern," Corbet said. "He could have caught one, combined its DNA with his own for the transformation."

Aggie nodded. "Preceptor said many of his sensors were blind. That would explain how Spartan got off the ship undetected."

"Edith Ramagano was Spartan's fourth transformation," Corbet mused, "which means the salamander was his fifth replicate. If he's moved on to number six, that cellular instability has probably worsened. He had trouble keeping the Edith imitation looking entirely human. He may not be able to transform again."

"We need to ID that younger victim."

Corbet silently cursed himself. In his latest vision, he'd been so intrigued by the Ghost Child that he hadn't looked up at the Statue of Liberty's face. He didn't have the heart to tell Aggie and Potts that he'd probably squandered an opportunity to uncover Spartan's newest identity.

"The neuropox takes fourteen hours to gestate into its toxic form," Aggie said. "He can't release it until then."

Corbet nodded. "And when you and I were trapped on the ship last night, I'd guess the time was about—"

"Ten o'clock exactly."

"How can you be so sure?"

"I checked my watch."

"You checked your watch?"

"Afterwards."

"We have until noon to stop him," Mavenhall said.

Corbet glanced at the time. 9:29 a.m. *Two and a half hours.*

78

VAN ZEELAND HAD GONE TO bed secure in the knowledge that the world had been saved. This morning upon awakening, he'd been told it had not.

The Sit Room was filled with the same faces as last night, including Dr. Jarek via teleconference. Gen. Grobbs was leading the discussion, scrawling red lines with a laser pen across a computerized global map. The lines connected the rest stop where Spartan's latest victims had been found to dozens of major cities.

"Best case scenario, we identify him aboard a transoceanic flight," Grobbs said. "We shoot the jet down over the ocean."

Van Zeeland grimaced, not looking forward to making that decision. Of course, at this juncture, there were no good scenarios.

"What's the CDC's take?" he asked.

A tech officer hit a button and the normally serene face of Inez Hernandez appeared onscreen. But today, the Centers for Disease Control director looked frazzled.

"Mr. President, our people have been reviewing the data," she began. "Unfortunately, it's not much to go on."

"Just give us what you have."

"Yes sir. An airborne plague of the type described released into a large crowd in a big city would be unstoppable. We've run pandemic simulations using every available tracking model and they produce roughly the same outcome. If this neuropox is as contagious as speculated and can bond with oxygen molecules, it would spread fast.

"Upon release, 98 percent of humans throughout the world would be contaminated within three weeks, the majority of the rest of them within three months. Assuming that only sealed environments of the highest standard, such as Level 4 biosafety facilities for containing infectious agents like Ebola virus and the other hemorrhagic fevers, would ensure against transmission, a few thousand people worldwide might be protected for a considerable period. But they'd have to emerge from these facilities sooner or later. And when they did..."

She trailed off. There was no need to state the obvious: the fundamental extinction of human intelligence.

"Recommendations?" Edelstein asked.

"I'm sorry to say we have none, other than making sure this neuropox never sees the light of day."

"Thank you, Doctor," Van Zeeland said. "Please stay available."

The TV went blank. Hernandez wasn't cleared for U-OPS-level discussions. Of course, in short order such distinctions could become meaningless.

79

THE PAVE LOW SLICED ACROSS a series of undulating mountain ranges. Corbet gazed out the window, trying to see things from Spartan's perspective.

Where are you going? What's your target? Why do you want to destroy us?

The last question remained the most puzzling. It was also, at the moment, the least important. Right now, *where* trumped *why*.

Corbet believed New York remained Spartan's most likely destination. It was the closest megalopolis and fundamental to his vision. And a U.S. target made sense, considering the unlikelihood that the hitchhiker carried a passport. But to convince the others – and himself – that Spartan intended to release the neuropox in the Big Apple, he needed evidence, or at least a more persuasive thread of reasoning.

Aggie and Potts stood in the rear of the copter with Mavenhall and Wilkins. All were intent on a large screen showing dozens of metropolitan areas on a global map. Corbet glanced at the clock. A little over two hours remained until the neuropox gestated.

The notion of time returned his thoughts to something that had been bothering him since the encounter with Preceptor. The AI had said the neuropox would spread like wildfire wherever it was released and that once airborne, the plague would be unstoppable. Yet Preceptor also said that Spartan had searched for the perfect location: a large event or gathering in a major city.

Those two remarks contained an inherent contradiction. If it didn't matter where the deadly vial was uncorked, why wouldn't Spartan simply hide out in the mountains until the 14 hours were up and then release it? Why take the added risk of killing those two men at the rest stop and traveling to a potentially distant target?

Corbet had assumed the contradiction had a simple explanation, that the reason Spartan sought a large crowd in a major city was to maximize the number of people initially exposed. Although the end result would be the same, the spread of the contagion would be accelerated, fast-tracking humanity's demise.

But what if that has nothing to do with Spartan's reasoning? What if he has another purpose in selecting a particular city and event?

The alien was driven by anger and hatred. He walked a razor-thin line between diabolical reasoning and barely controlled rage. Losing family and friends in a terrible war on his home planet had caused such a distressful state. Spartan blamed the Consortium for supplying the technological advancements used to wage that war.

The answer came to Corbet in a flash. *His choice of locations has nothing to do with the spread of the neuropox. It's all about achieving an emotional release.*

"Technology!" he shouted, rising to his feet. "That's the key to where he's going!"

Aggie, Mavenhall and the others turned to him with puzzled looks.

"I need to see a list of every major event in every city," Corbet demanded. "But start with New York. That's still his most likely target."

Mavenhall nodded to Wilkins, who accessed a digital map of the metropolis. The captain laser-penned the first of several starred locations.

"Airports. JFK is the busiest international gateway in the U.S. Average daily passenger count in excess of 100,000, as well as tens of thousands of employees. An airport also would hasten the global spread of the neuropox—"

Corbet waved his hand, rejecting the possibility. "What else?"

Wilkins spotlighted a location in the Bronx. "Yankee Stadium, seating for 50,000. Red Sox are in town for this afternoon's game—"

"Next," Corbet snapped, not knowing the precise reason he was dismissing these likelihoods. But he trusted his instincts, trusted that he was somehow keyed into Spartan's thought processes.

Wilkins shifted the beam southward to Manhattan. "Two strong likelihoods here. Central Park. Free retro rock concert. NYPD reports there are already some 20,000 people gathered. Opening group takes the stage at one. Estimates run as high as 100,000-plus by midafternoon when the major acts are scheduled.

"And, Jacob Javits Convention Center. Final day of a new international trade show for consumer electronics. The next wave of what's coming for the home, that sort of thing.

"We also have a number of smaller venues. A circus at Madison Square Garden that might draw 15,000. An ethnic street fair in Queens..."

Corbet barely heard the rest of Wilkins' list. In one gestalt burst of comprehension, he knew Spartan's target.

"The consumer electronics trade show at the Javits! That's where he'll release the neuropox."

Skeptical faces met his pronouncement.

"And you know this how?" Mavenhall demanded.

"Instinct. You've got to trust me."

"Like we trusted you on Bellhopper's Lake?"

"I screwed up on that one," Corbet admitted. "I had just enough information to jump to the wrong conclusion. But that was before I got a sense of who Spartan is, how he thinks, what motivates him.

"Preceptor never said as much, but I don't think Spartan ever had any intention of returning to the Consortium. He plans to die here. Earth was always a one-way ticket for him. He's a crazed fanatic, driven by emotions, by his rage. From the beginning, this was a suicide mission."

"How does that relate to the Javits?" Potts wondered.

"Think about it. He infiltrates the Consortium as a

mole and journeys lightyears across the galaxy. And then he gets stuck in orbit for half a century. Imagine all that time, all those years of nursing his hatred yet never straying from his ultimate goal.

"But now he's reached the end of the road. It's his moment of triumph, the very pinnacle of his twisted life. Combine that notion with what he wants to do to the human race. He seeks to destroy our ability to think, to reason, *to use technology*. The Consortium wants just the opposite for us, to increase our technological proficiency.

"What better place for Spartan to wreck the Consortium's plans than at a technology trade show, a place where the future is on display? What better place for the fulfillment of his vengeance?"

"That sounds flimsy," Wilkins said.

"It is, considered from a strictly logical perspective. But Spartan's not acting on logic here, he's guided by his emotions. He'll *enjoy* unleashing the neuropox amid all that cutting-edge technology, knowing that much of it will never come to pass, knowing we'll be reduced to wild animals incapable of using any technology. He'll take *pleasure* ensuring that what happened on his own planet – a war caused by an influx of Consortium technology – doesn't happen on Earth."

Aggie, Potts and Wilkins seemed to be buying it. But Mavenhall remained skeptical. Corbet approached the colonel until they were face to face.

"This time, you need to accept that no matter how outlandish my idea might sound, I know what I'm talking about."

For a long moment, Mavenhall regarded him with a steely gaze. Finally, the colonel turned to Wilkins.

"Set a course for New York. Maximum speed. Inform all units the Javits is our primary target."

80

THE PAVE LOW WHIZZED PAST a spindly trestle that extended more than two miles out into Sandy Hook Bay in northern New Jersey. The trestle, with railroad tracks and a road, forked into a trio of smaller piers where three combat support ships were docked.

"Earle Naval Weapons Station," Mavenhall said, pointing to the onshore portion of the facility toward which they were heading. "We're about seven miles southeast of Staten Island."

This was as close as they would get to New York in a military craft. From here, it would be civilian markings only to avoid alerting Spartan, who may already have reached the city.

If I'm right, Corbet thought, acknowledging a flicker of doubt. The entire search effort now hinged upon his prediction. If he'd guessed wrong, they likely wouldn't get another shot at stopping Spartan in time.

The Pave Low touched down on a grassy field amid a cluster of buildings. Corbet and Aggie followed Mavenhall toward a small civilian helicopter that would make the final hop into Manhattan. Potts and the agents spread out to board a fleet of other waiting copters.

Corbet noticed soldiers unloading heavy containers from another Pave Low and wrestling them into the back of an unmarked panel truck. Each container was the color of burnished aluminum and the size of a commercial refrigerator, and had a glass porthole above the door latch.

"BCUs," Mavenhall explained. "Bio-containment units. We'll use them to secure Spartan and the neuropox."

Corbet scowled. "And he's just going to jump into one of those things?"

"We'll use persuasion."

Two dozen commandos jogged toward Mavenhall in two-by-two formation. They wore civilian attire and carried their compact white ray guns, which had barrels ending in translucent marbles. Several of the commandos were bandaged.

Corbet recognized their leader, the man with the crescent scar on his cheek. He approached Mavenhall, gave a casual salute. The rest of his Mantis One team halted behind him at a respectful distance.

"Sir, we're at full strength. All three squads now Go-9 proficient, ready to engage."

"You've been briefed on mission parameters, Captain Doughy?"

"Yes sir. What about the target's potential ability to eavesdrop on us?"

"Cyber Command is generating new encryption logarithms that hopefully will secure our com system. All assets will switch over to a new net shortly. Beyond that, not much we can do."

Doughy motioned toward the lone female commando. "Lis?"

She dashed over to Corbet, handed him a small duffel bag. Inside was the pair of psyts he'd lost at the quarry. They were dirty and scarred. He wondered if they still worked.

"I'm told these are important," Lis said.

"Can't play Grand Theft Auto without 'em."

"Kick some ass," she said, throwing him a cold smile before hustling back to her place with the men.

"The very survival of the human race is at stake,"

Mavenhall instructed the commandos. "Upon target acquisition, you are to disregard any and all directives for operating in a civilian-rich fire zone. Clear?"

"Yes sir," Doughy said. "Friendlies expendable."

The captain rejoined his commandos. They jogged away, leaving Corbet with the feeling that humanity's prospects were bleak.

81

LONNIE WAS EXCITED EVEN THOUGH he'd ridden on the Staten Island Ferry bunches of times. But whenever Mommy was going to Manhattan he pleaded with her to take the big orange boat instead of driving into the city. Today, they sat on the port side passenger deck. They were out in the open air which Lonnie liked. He could look over the railing and see the big skyscrapers getting closer.

It was extra windy this morning. Mommy zipped his jacket all the way up to his neck. Her hand brushed his chest, tickling him, making him giggle.

"Mommy, give Lonnie hugs!"

Her face swelled into a sunshine smile. Lonnie fell into her arms, making sure not to squeeze her too hard on account of he was so much bigger and stronger. The last time Mommy had measured his height against the ruler inside his bedroom door he was six feet, two and one-half inches tall. And Mommy always said that even though he was almost 18, he was still a growing boy and could get even taller.

"Okay, enough huggies" she said, releasing him. "Now, I'm going inside for a few minutes, but I'll be right back. I want you to stay right here. Promise?"

Lonnie wagged his head. He watched her walk down the passageway until she disappeared through a door, then returned his gaze to Upper New York Bay. In the distance he could see one of his favorite things, the Statue of Liberty. He had a book at home about the statue. Although he couldn't understand a lot of the big words, Mommy had read the book to him bunches of times. He knew all about the statue, how the French had given it to the people of America as a gift, how it had been delivered by frigate in 1885.

It measured 305 feet, six inches from the base of its pedestal to the tip of its torch. It had seven rays on the crown on Miss Liberty's head, one for each of the continents. He knew lots of other stuff about the statue too, which he liked to tell people about. They'd often break out into sunshine smiles and tell Lonnie what a smart boy he was. That always made him feel good.

Lonnie knew deep down he wasn't as smart as other people his age. But most of the time he didn't care, cause Mommy said he was a special boy. Sometimes mean kids called him dumb, and that hurt his feelings, but he got over it quick when Mommy gave him hugs. Still, sometimes he wished he could be the smartest person in the whole world on account of he couldn't always understand grownup talk.

The ferry was approaching Liberty Island and would pass within a mile of it. Lonnie glanced around him to see if there might be anyone interested in learning all the neat stuff he knew about the statue. But hardly anybody was outside today on account of it was so windy. A young couple stood near the bow, but they were pretty far away.

The only other person around was a young man in a dusty denim jacket two seats away, staring out over the water. He looked to be about Lonnie's age, although not nearly so big.

"Excuse me, Mister."

The young man turned to him slowly. "Yes?"

"Mommy and I are going to the circus today at Madison Square Garden. Is that where you're going?"

"Perhaps."

Lonnie thought *perhaps* was a funny answer. Maybe the man was lost and didn't know exactly where he was going.

"The Statue of Liberty weighs 225 tons," Lonnie informed him.

A woman's faint voice sounded from underneath the man's jacket. She was saying odd stuff that Lonnie couldn't understand.

Q-T-4 Quantico. Priority Zeta. We have fingerprint confirmation on suspect. Tyrell, Lucas O. Age 22. Photo ID to follow.

The words made the man angry. His fingers tightened into fists. His face turned red.

Lonnie got scared. He didn't like it when people got angry. And the two of them were alone out here on the deck. The young couple near the bow had disappeared. He wished Mommy would hurry back.

The man reached into his jacket and pulled out a cell phone and a device resembling a tuning fork. A second voice, this one male, emerged from the phone's tinny speaker.

Alpha Command to Quantico, we are switching to alternate encrypted net. Suggest further information on suspect be withheld until after changeover.

Q-T-4 Quantico, the woman replied. *Understood. Over and out.*

The man pointed the prongs of the tuning fork at the phone and started tapping his fingers on the handle. He looked like he was typing but doing it so fast his fingers were almost a blur. Lonnie was so curious he forgot all about being scared.

"What are you doing?"

The man didn't answer. Odd sounds were now coming from the phone, a bunch of squeaks, hisses and beeps. The man kept typing but only the funny sounds came, no voices. That seemed to make the man even angrier. Finally, he got so mad he threw the phone over the railing into the ocean and shoved the device back under his jacket.

And then something really strange happened. The man's legs started quivering, like he was real nervous and couldn't keep still. Odd little bulges appeared on his neck and arms. It seemed like something inside him was trying to push its way out from beneath the skin.

The man gritted his teeth and clenched the bottom of his seat, as if trying to control himself. The quivering stopped. The bulges shrank until his flesh looked normal again.

Lonnie wasn't scared anymore. He was more worried about the man, who maybe had some kind of medical condition. Maybe he had epilepsy like Lonnie's cousin Joanne.

"Mister, are you okay?"

The man turned, stared blankly at him.

"Yes," he said finally. "A-OK."

The man got up and walked to the railing. Lonnie suddenly realized the two of them had something in common.

We're both special.

As the ferry drew closer to Liberty Island, the man smiled. Yet it wasn't a sunshine smile, all bright and cheery. Lonnie figured the man felt bad about his condition and was putting on a pretend smile to cover up that he was hurting inside.

"Soon you will be free," the man whispered.

At first, Lonnie thought the words were directed at him. But then he realized the man was speaking to the Statue of Liberty.

82

THE COPTER LANDED IN MANHATTAN at West 30th Street on the Hudson River, a heliport that hosted sightseeing flights. Corbet, Aggie and Mavenhall entered a waiting van lettered for a furniture delivery company. Innocuous on the outside, the interior was outfitted as another bioterrorism command post, a civilian version run by the CDC's Epidemiological Intelligence Service.

Mavenhall took a call from Gen. Grobbs at the White House. "Yes sir... photos have been distributed to all search units. Yes sir, knowing what he looks like gives us the advantage."

Corbet studied the license photo of Lucas Tyrell on his phone, tried committing it to memory. The ID had been made through a DNA match from a Buffalo school district where Tyrell had worked briefly as a teaching assistant.

The young man's delicate features made him look younger than his 22 years. The soft chin, fine blond hair and uncertain expression gave the impression of shyness, of someone not comfortable in his own skin.

Corbet glanced at the time. 10:55.

Mavenhall ended the call and turned to them. "Drones and satellites have been tasked to cover the length of Manhattan."

"Not likely they'll spot him from overhead," Aggie said.

"A long shot," Mavenhall admitted. "But we have street-level surveillance too. And we're tied into all major governmental and corporate CCTV systems."

The van arrived at the Jacob Javits Convention Center. The complex, squatting on the edge of the Hudson River, resembled a stack of glass cubes with the corners sliced off. Designed by the architectural firm of Pei Cobb Freed & Partners and opened in 1986, it occupied six city blocks from 34th to 40th streets. It was an imposing public space, longer than the Empire State Building was tall, and with more than a million square feet of exhibition and meeting space on four levels.

The van deposited Corbet, Aggie and Mavenhall at a rear loading dock. They were met inside by Potts. Another agent fitted Corbet and Aggie with flesh-colored earpieces and hidden mikes while Potts updated them on the search.

"We found Charles Kleinfelter's truck on Staten Island, two blocks from the ferry terminal."

"He took the ferry into Manhattan," Corbet concluded, relieved to have solid evidence that New York was indeed the target.

"We've got people at both terminals. Last arriving ferry docked a short time ago. Emptied before we could search it."

"Why not just drive all the way into the city?" Aggie wondered. "Take one of the tunnels."

"Since 9/11, the tunnels are protected by highly sophisticated surveillance tools," Mavenhall said. "He could know that."

"Maybe," Corbet said. "But that's not why he took the ferry. He wanted to cruise past Liberty Island, see the statue firsthand."

"Why?"

"It goes back to his reason for targeting the Javits, about this being his moment of triumph. In some twisted way, the statue symbolizes freedom to him."

Mavenhall frowned. "You're making a lot of assumptions."

Corbet knew it sounded that way. Yet he felt increasingly attuned to Spartan's thought processes.

Another insight came to him. The reason his vision took place in Manhattan wasn't just because Spartan had chosen it as a target.

It's the last place I lived where I felt like I had a family.

A wave of sorrow washed over him. Until this moment, he hadn't realized how losing Jeremy only two years after his parents' deaths had robbed him of an elemental structure, a sense of belonging. He'd retreated from the pain of those losses by avoiding close relationships, anything that reminded him of family. That and his fear of experiencing another vision where he lost someone close had driven him to embrace solitude.

He looked over at Aggie and the sorrow vanished. In some fundamental way, she'd changed him, restored a part of his lost humanity.

And now it might be too late.

83

TRUDI FARR GLANCED UP FROM painting her nails at the young man entering the store. Her first customer of the day was attractive – in a gentle sort of way – but monumentally style-challenged. His blue denim jacket and jeans bore a dusty sheen as if he'd been wrestling in the dirt.

Trudi normally didn't open See-Farr Antiques & Collectibles on Sunday mornings. But she figured on doing biz today because of the retro rock gala, even though Central Park was a good five miles from her Tribeca store. She had friends distributing fliers at the concert. She hoped to draw some customers after it ended.

She finished doing her nails in a blend of Purple Viceroy and Lilac Lust while keeping a wary eye on the young man. Most of the store's offerings were too big to steal, but she'd been ripped off enough to realize thieves could be brazen. She'd once caught an old man trying to slip out with a vintage Sunbeam toaster under his trench coat.

The young man wandered along the narrow aisles until his attention was drawn to a vintage Philco TV. Trudi had been in the biz long enough to peg him for a browser not a buyer. Most serious retro collectors were boomers and didn't dress like slobs. Still, the way he was looking at the console suggested genuine interest.

"It's an early color set," she said. "1960 model. But if you're a black-and-white aficionado, I've got a '57 Dumont in near-mint condition."

"No, thank you. I was merely struck by the styling. It's indicative of an era I once studied."

"Made some cool stuff back then, huh?"

"Yes. Cool stuff."

Trudi considered herself a good judge of people. But there was something off about this young man, something that didn't click.

"Looking for anything in particular?" she asked.

"I'm told that in addition to selling antiques and collectibles, you offer a service."

Trudi smiled. She should have grasped the truth the moment he walked through the door. His lame clothing and awkward demeanor were a giveaway.

He was probably right off a Port Authority bus from some priggy little town. Maybe he'd had a strict upbringing like Trudi's, where sexual thoughts were considered impure. He'd probably been saving up for his first trip to the Big Apple, his first chance to cut loose from parental control and fulfill his most wicked desires.

"Well now," she said, capping the polish and blowing on her nails. "Who exactly has been doing all this telling?"

"Pardon?"

"Who told you I sell something besides antiques and collectibles?"

"A young lady I encountered. She called herself Misty Matrix. In the course of our conversation, I gathered the name was fictitious."

"Really?" Trudi rarely encountered a newbie this naïve. "Where'd you see Misty?"

"On a corner near a McDonald's restaurant three-and-one-half blocks south of here."

"Sure it wasn't four blocks?"

He just stared, oblivious to her humor.

"Listen, hon, I know what you're hot for, okay? The thing is, I'm the only one watching the store today. Now if you want to set up a session tomorrow—"

"It must be now." He dug into a pants pocket, handed her a crumpled wad of cash.

Trudi counted the bills. $400. Way above what she usually charged. Certainly enough to close the store for a while.

She locked the front door, set the window dial to read Back at Noon and threw her arm around his shoulder. He flinched.

"Hon, you need to chill. Get any more uptight and the mortician's going to mistake you for worm meat and start embalming."

She guided him toward the door at the back of the showroom. "Anything in particular you have in mind? A special fantasy you've been dying to explore?"

"I want it to feel... comfortable."

"Comfortable it is," Trudi said, smiling as she urged him down the hallway toward her bedroom.

"This is my first visit to New York."

"Never would have guessed," she said, putting on her most effervescent smile. "Now, you just relax. Trudi's going to make you feel like a million bucks."

84

Corbet and Aggie jostled past waves of humanity streaming along the Level Two concourse. Banners hanging from the Javits' tubular-frame walls touted OmegaExpo – the trade show's name – as one of the biggest gatherings for the consumer electronics industry.

It was 11:14. In about 45 minutes, Spartan's neuropox would be ready to unleash.

They took an escalator down to the first exhibition hall. Booths featured all the big names in hardware and software – Sony and Microsoft, GE and Apple, Google and IBM – as well as countless smaller companies looking to brand the future while creating lucrative stock options. An incredible potpourri of gizmos and gadgets were on display, all the latest advancements for the state-of-the-art householder.

The Javits was in the midst of an expansion and renovation. A few areas were roped off and stacked with construction supplies. But that hadn't impacted attendance.

An ocean of faces filled the vast space. The air quivered with overlapping conversations. The throngs mirrored New York's melting-pot diversity. Male and female, young and old, their attire ran the gamut: tailored suits, chinos and sandals, shorts and blouses, turbans and robes.

Technology on parade included screen-less 3-D televisions, home automation systems and mobile robotic servants. An up-and-coming fabber company – a firm specializing in personal-fabrication technologies – showcased sets of electronic building blocks that could be quickly assembled into items as varied as two-way radios, handheld copiers and portable microwaves. An appliance manufacturer offered virtual reality tours inside its $14,000 refrigerator, enabling visitors to become mini-avatars that explored its coolest feature, a 64-flavor automatic ice cream maker.

Corbet donned the psyts. Fortunately, they wouldn't attract undue attention in this crowd. OmegaExpo attracted a hefty geek contingent. Participants wandered through the halls wearing VR goggles and other high-tech headgear.

The plan called for Corbet and Aggie to proceed through the facility one hall at a time, shadowed by undercover Mantis One commandos and agents. If Corbet got a hit with the psyts, he would report the location and back off, allowing the armed contingent to move in for the kill. The rest of the Mantis One commandos and agents were spread throughout the complex. Mavenhall and Potts were coordinating the hunt, monitoring surveillance cameras from the security command center.

Although Spartan knew Corbet and Aggie's faces, the psyts' 300-foot range should enable him to locate the alien before it spotted them – provided that Spartan hadn't transformed again. But in light of that increasing cellular instability, the consensus was that he wouldn't risk another genetic makeover that could leave him with physical deformities like those that had plagued the Edith Ramagano replicate.

Local authorities, including uniformed Javits Security and NYPD officers, had been kept out of the loop. Spartan could become suspicious if he sensed a uniformed officer eyeballing him. It was felt that their best chance was to take him by surprise.

If Lucas Tyrell was spotted outside the Javits, he wouldn't be impeded from entering. Special forces platoons were hidden in nearby trucks and vans. Once Spartan was confirmed to be onsite, the soldiers would secure the exits, trapping him inside.

In theory, it was a good plan. Still, there were weaknesses. Mavenhall worried that Spartan could stay away from the Javits until after the neuropox gestated. Under that scenario, the replicate might enter the complex and release the plague before anyone could stop him.

Yet Corbet didn't believe it would go down that way. Spartan would want to be here in advance of gestation. He'd want to savor his vengeance within this high-tech wonderland, knowing he was about to strike a blow against the Consortium by destroying the future on display within these halls. Once the plague was dispatched into the atmosphere, the alien would have little interest in watching humans' evolutionary descent. His demented pleasure would be achieved prior to release.

A more formidable challenge was the Javits' size, complexity and mobile crowds. There were so many places to search besides the exhibition halls: scores of meeting rooms, the main concourse, marshaling areas, food courts, retail spaces, rest rooms and ballrooms. It was feasible that two people in constant motion would never pass within 300 feet of one another in the time allotted.

"Young male, nine o'clock," Aggie whispered. "Yellow shirt, glasses. He's fixated on you. Turn and make eye contact."

Corbet swiveled his head, spotted the man immediately.

"No, it's OK. I don't know his name, but we've run into each other at clubs in DC. He designs video games."

The man smiled and waved. Corbet acknowledged the greeting and quickly moved on, intent on avoiding conversations that could mow down precious minutes.

85

"Mr. President," Gen. Grobbs began. "There is a scenario that, however extreme, we must consider."

Van Zeeland hung up the phone. He'd just finished a conference call to European Union, Japanese, Canadian and Brazilian leaders. It hadn't gone well.

The leaders were skeptical of the cover story about an Air Force jet blowing up over Pennsylvania. Van Zeeland hated lying to important allies, particularly when most of them were believed to be beneficiaries of Preceptor's technological gifts over the decades and knew the truth about last night's incident.

They probably had received customized versions of Preceptor's final message to the world, although none would admit it. As in the U.S., everything relating to Preceptor was a state secret, jealously guarded.

"What scenario, General?"

Grobbs stood up and leaned over the Sit Room table, eyes fixed on Van Zeeland. "Now that we possess strong circumstantial evidence that Spartan's target is the convention center, a contingency plan for containing biological WMDs needs to be given operational weight."

"Spit it out."

"The same mix of thermobarics and FAEs used to vaporize Preceptor's vessel can be used against ground targets. If we confirm Spartan's location at the Javits but our forces can't neutralize him before the neuropox gestates, we need the option of a B-2 strike with a specially-equipped missile."

Van Zeeland wasn't surprised the military had come up with such a plan. "What kind of collateral damage would we be looking at?"

"Considerable," Grobbs admitted. "The missile would be outfitted with multiple warheads to ensure coverage. The Javits and portions of the surrounding neighborhood would be vaporized. Death toll could reach 100,000. Concussive effects would produce a large number of injuries well beyond the blast radius. We don't have time to work up accurate numbers on property damage but it's safe to assume losses in the tens of billions, perhaps higher."

Edelstein looked appalled. "Unacceptable, General. The United States will not launch such an attack against its own citizenry."

"I believe it's the President's decision, Mr. Edelstein, not yours."

Van Zeeland scanned the room, searching for other opinions. Several of the men and women had family in

New York and even clandestine evacuation warnings might come too late to save those relatives. Yet no one spoke except Edelstein, a lone voice of dissent.

"There must be another way," the other half of the Van-Dan pleaded.

Van Zeeland wished there was. Should the world be saved from the neuropox by less extreme means, his administration just might survive the revelation of U-OPS secrets and the ensuing political firestorm. But if triumph came at the cost of bombing Manhattan, his presidency would go under the guillotine. Congress would probably begin impeachment proceedings before he could even tender his resignation.

Guilt stabbed at him for viewing the crisis through such a selfish lens. But having spent most of his working life in elected office, he knew he could never truly separate altruistic concerns from personal ambitions. The best an honest politician could hope for was to acknowledge his or her own ego and strive to keep it tamed.

"Get the B-2 in the air," he instructed. "Make sure the crew knows what's at stake, that they may be asked to massacre tens of thousands of American citizens. I don't want anyone growing a conscience at the last minute and refusing to carry out a Presidential order."

86

"SOMETHING'S WRONG," CORBET WHISPERED INTO his mike. "This is taking too long."

It was 11:38, twenty-two minutes to zero hour. He and Aggie had been trekking through the Javits for what seemed an eternity. Moving swiftly, they'd covered the main exhibition halls on Levels 1 and 3, the North annex, the food courts, and a score of meeting rooms, as well as the Level 4 galleria and adjacent river pavilion overlooking the Hudson. They'd just returned to Level 2 for another trek along the 1,000-foot concourse fronting the Eleventh Avenue entrances.

He'd gotten no hits from the psyts. Search teams and surveillance cameras had identified several young men with a resemblance to Lucas Tyrell and agents had quietly pulled them aside for interrogation. But none turned out to be their quarry.

"Maybe he hacked into our new encrypted net," Aggie suggested. "Maybe he knows we're here and decided it's not worth the risk, and selected a backup target."

Corbet shook his head. "Even if he knows we're here, he won't run, not this time. He's outsmarted us from the beginning. It's made him overconfident. He won't be scared off."

"Presuming the Javits is indeed his target," Mavenhall interjected.

Corbet didn't respond. Further arguing was a waste of time. Spartan was here. He was sure of it. Yet as the relentless minutes ticked down, doubt gnawed at him.

We should have found him by now.

Amid those doubts, a deeper concern grew. It was a worry that been brewing since this morning, since they'd learned Spartan had survived.

"Proceed back upstairs to Hall 3-B," Mavenhall ordered. "That will put you closer to the center of the complex, maximize your tracking radius in all directions."

Corbet followed Aggie onto the escalator, trying to ignore the beginnings of another headache. He'd been pushing the envelope, willing himself to battle through the eyestrain and keep the goggles on for longer periods. But as they headed up to Level 3, the pounding in his temples grew unbearable.

He whipped off the psyts. Mavenhall immediately protested. Corbet snapped at him.

"I need a break so back the hell off!"

Aggie tried to tamp down his frustration. "We'll get through this. We'll find him. We still have twenty minutes."

"Do we?" Corbet revealed his deeper concern. "What if all this is hopeless? What if we're not going to find him and you were right all along?"

"Right about what?"

"You said yesterday that even if I'd been able to warn my brother, I couldn't have saved him. All these years I've been telling myself that Jeremy died because I couldn't get through to him in time. But maybe that had nothing to do with it. Maybe the fact Mavenhall wouldn't pass along my warning, maybe all of that was preordained."

His mike was live. The colonel was listening. Corbet didn't care.

"If my visions always come true, if the future's inevitable, then it doesn't matter what we do here today. Spartan's already won."

"It's not hopeless," Aggie said. "You said yourself this vision is different from the others, full of symbols. It doesn't lock us into a specific destiny."

"Wishful thinking."

"I won't believe the world's coming to an end."

"You're missing my point. It doesn't matter what you believe. Having faith in a better tomorrow isn't enough."

"Maybe not," she said, grabbing his hand and gazing into his eyes. "But dammit, Corbet, I have faith in you."

The words pierced the heart of his despair. He realized again just how deeply in love he was with this woman who'd come into his life less than two days ago.

"Over your little tantrum now?" she asked.

"Yeah." He managed a smile as they stepped off the escalator. "Let's find the son of a bitch and wreck his day."

They entered the first aisle of Hall 3-B. It was the largest of the exhibition areas, capable of holding more than 5,000. Like the rest of the Javits, it was jam-packed with humanity.

His headache relented. But as he was about to don the psyts, a pint-sized wheeled robot darted from a booth and stopped in front of him. Looking like a distant cousin to R2D2 of *Star Wars*, the robot extended a tray of hors d'oeuvres in a silver-plated hand.

"Sir, excuse me," the robot announced, its voice mimicking the formal mannerisms of a British butler. "Would you care for an appetizer, courtesy of I-Robbie Robotics?"

Corbet shook his head and moved to one side to step around the machine. Servos whining, the robot wheeled sideways to block him.

"Sir, I do apologize, but even if you do not desire a delicacy, would you be so kind as to complete a brief survey? You're guaranteed to win a prize, possibly an all-expense-paid trip to Disney World."

"Sorry, I'm in a hurry." He felt silly making small-talk with something controlled by microprocessors.

"Please, Corbet," the robot begged, its voice switching to a baritone that sounded like Charlton Heston from *Ben-Hur*. "If I don't drum up more business, they'll replace me with a human."

He frowned. "How do you know my name?"

"Come over here and find out," the voice taunted,

this time slipping into the sexy purr of a Southern belle.

Laughter erupted from the I-Robbie Robotics booth. The multi-voiced robot had a camera in its domed head, which was displaying Corbet's suspicious face on a giant screen. A crowd was enjoying the show.

"I wouldn't want to be disappointed again," the Southern belle added.

More laughter erupted as Corbet glanced toward Aggie for direction. Before either of them could act, two agents who'd been shadowing them sprinted into the booth and whipped aside a curtain at the rear.

The hidden wizard was revealed. The robot's controller was an attractive young woman. Startled by the intrusion, she let go of her computer joystick, freezing the robot.

"It's okay!" Corbet yelled. "I know her."

"Stand down!" Aggie barked.

It was Maria, the petite redhead he'd met Friday night at P.M. Fugue. He recalled her saying she worked for a startup robotics firm and would be doing a weekend gig for them in Manhattan.

The agents backed off. The booth manager, a spin-doctoring pro, hopped onto a chair and raised his voice to announcer level.

"It's okay, folks, just a little excitement to keep things lively! Remember, I-Robbie Robotics is your source for tireless domestic help. Our Sugarhunk line of service butlers features programmable voices, and are operable by remote control or in auto mode. We guarantee they'll never ask for a raise!"

Corbet double-timed it away from the booth to avoid further entanglements with Maria.

"Seventeen minutes," Aggie said, checking her watch. "Hope we don't run into any more of your acquaintances."

"Bad luck." Yet he wondered if the encounter with Maria symbolized the closure of some psychic circle, a linking together of disparate elements.

Up ahead, the aisle was blocked by hundreds of onlookers. All were intent on a small stage where a bikini-clad blond danced to the rhythms of a hip-hop song.

The blond was ringed by a 3-D camera setup that was creating a life-sized image of her, a holographic twin performing the identical dance by her side. Blurred edges distinguished the doppelganger from its flesh-and-blood counterpart. The 3-D technology wasn't bad. But Corbet had seen better.

They reached the edge of the crowd. He reformed an image of Lucas Tyrell in his mind's eye and donned the psyts. But his attention was captured by two young men visible in the distance through the translucent grid. Corbet raised the goggles, stood on tiptoes to get a better look at the pair.

Both men resembled their target. The nearest one wore Raybans and a New York Giants cap with the brim pulled low, as if trying to hide his features. Corbet eased through the crowd to get a better angle.

His improved position brought the young man's companion into view, a slip of a girl in jeans and a halter-top. The way she held his arm and used his shoulder as a pillow suggested young love in full bloom. No way they'd just met.

The second possibility stood farther away, behind the pair. Corbet could only make out a partial profile of his face, but something about it reminded him of Lucas Tyrell.

The crowd shifted, giving Corbet a better view. Had the situation not been so dire, he might have laughed at his error. What he'd taken for a potential suspect wore a peasant blouse and ruffled skirt. Casually sexy, with flowing brown hair, she was the type of woman who might have caught his eye during a night of clubbing.

"This crowd's too thick," Aggie said. "Let's backtrack, try the next aisle."

Corbet nodded. But as he turned around, he bumped into a very pregnant brunette loaded down with bags of show handouts.

"Sorry," he offered.

"No harm done," the woman said, patting her huge belly and breaking into one of those beatific smiles that only expectant mothers seemed capable of producing.

Corbet was suddenly hit by the reality of the neuropox's effect on future generations. Babies born to infected parents would bear the crippling genetic defect, inhibiting their mental growth and preventing them from rising above animal instincts and simple emotions.

This woman could give birth to a child incapable of achieving the normal plateaus of human development. Doomed to live by instincts alone, it would never acquire a basic education, never learn to read and write, never appreciate music or aspire to the nobler ideas that defined Homo sapiens at its best.

Sadness touched him as he slipped past the pregnant woman. Thoughts returned to the Ghost Child from his vision. He now understood at least one aspect of what the little girl represented.

She was a symbol for the fate of the entire human race. Her spectral form alluded to the fact she no longer occupied the present. Robbed of temporal substance, she existed only in the past and in the future, as an icon of what humankind had lost and a precursor of what it was to become.

87

"Approaching 15 minutes to zero hour," Gen. Rosario announced to the Sit Room. "The B-2 is within range, Mr. President. The crew will implement upon your order."

Van Zeeland turned to Grobbs. The general wore a headset, was in direct contact with Col. Mavenhall at the Javits. "Anything?"

Grobbs shook his head.

"Our psychic may have been wrong," Edelstein said. "Spartan may have picked another target."

Van Zeeland reluctantly agreed. They should have found the alien by now.

Gen. Rosario continued. "Sir, if we can't confirm Spartan's location by 11:52 at the latest, you'll need to give the order. The B-2 will be launching from a good distance in case Spartan reactivates the interference. The missile flies at subsonic speed. It will require nearly three minutes just to reach the target."

"That still gives us some extra time."

"The noon deadline must be considered an estimate. We need to incorporate at least a small margin of error."

"This is crazy," Edelstein protested. "You want to bomb the Javits even though we can't confirm Spartan's inside?"

"We have to take our best shot," Grobbs said. "Considering we're facing the termination of our species, is there really a choice?"

Edelstein looked distraught, unable to come up with an alternative. The clock hit 11:45.

"Mr. President, we have hundreds of our people at ground zero," Rosario said. "If we want to enable them to get clear in time, the evacuation order must be given now."

"They should be able to continue searching for at least a few more minutes," Van Zeeland said.

"Yes sir, technically that's true. However, a last-minute warning would be problematic. If Spartan senses a sudden rush toward the exits, he might get suspicious and also retreat from the target area. We can't risk that. Any evacuation must appear casual, unhurried."

"Our people are aware of the air strike?"

"Only Colonel Mavenhall," Grobbs said. "But if it's your decision to continue the search, he'll remain at his post until the end."

88

CORBET AND AGGIE BACKTRACKED FROM the crowd at the holographic stage show, keeping as far as possible from the I-Robbie Robotics booth to avoid another time-sucking encounter with Maria. Not that it likely mattered at this point. Aggie's words of support had provided a brief respite. But a sense of hopelessness was again settling in.

We're not going to find him.

His thoughts flashed back to Preceptor's grim prognosis.

Within days of infection by this neuropox, a human will lose the ability to think, to reason, to use tools, to perform a thousand other functions of a mentally evolved species.

Corbet supposed that even the feral people would continue to seek out mates, and that the debilitated new version of Homo sapiens would keep procreating. Maybe he and Aggie had established a bond strong enough to draw them together in the aftermath. Provided, of course, they survived the worldwide collapse of the social order.

Then again, losing his intelligence might revert Corbet to a lifestyle similar to what had defined him up until this point: casual sex with an endless succession of partners, no emotional entanglements.

He didn't want that, not anymore. He gazed at Aggie's profile, tried to memorize every detail of her face to create an emotional resonance that would outlast the disintegration of his intellect in a post-apocalyptic world.

He came to a sudden halt. An idea trickled into his awareness, straining to achieve form.

Aggie's profile...

The details of her face...

The idea that she might look different to him...

The idea exploded into consciousness. He raced back toward the crowd enjoying the 3-D dance.

"Where are you going?" Aggie demanded.

Ignoring her, he panned across the gathering, searching desperately for the face he'd seen minutes ago, the face he'd initially glimpsed only in profile.

The face that looked like a female version of Lucas Tyrell.

It can't be, a voice in his head warned. *It can't be that simple.*

But maybe it was. Maybe Spartan had learned his Lucas Tyrell replicate was compromised. Maybe the cellular instability made another transformation too risky. Maybe the alien had done the next best thing, had taken advantage of Lucas Tyrell's small size and delicate features to change his outward appearance into a passable version of a woman.

Corbet pushed through the crowd's outer boundary. But there was no sign of the sexy young woman with the peasant blouse and ruffled skirt.

She had to be close. He donned the psyts, reactivated the tracking grid and closed his eyes. Forming a mind's eye image of Lucas Tyrell's face, he mentally reconstructed it with feminine features.

He opened his eyes. A blip appeared on the grid.

"I got him!" He pointed to the far side of the crowd, recited the data readout. "Linear distance 95 feet!"

Aggie and Mavenhall barked in his earpiece, demanding to know more.

"Lucas Tyrell's in drag!" he hissed, describing the transvestite's attire. In the background, he could hear Mavenhall spouting orders to other search teams.

Corbet spotted their quarry. She was up ahead, standing at the far perimeter of the crowd. Her back was to them.

A middle-aged couple stepped in front of Corbet, blocking his view. He squeezed between them to keep her in sight.

The man took offense. "Hey, watch where you're going!"

Lucas Tyrell overheard the disturbance, started to turn.

Corbet ducked to avoid being spotted. But a pair of agents on his right flank were steamrolling through the crowd, creating a ruckus. The girl who wasn't a girl spun toward them.

The cat-and-mouse game was over. There was no longer a reason to hide. Corbet stood up and took off the psyts.

For a moment, there was no reaction on Lucas

Tyrell's feminized face, no sense of recognition. But then came the faintest of nods, as if Spartan was acknowledging that for the third time in as many days, their paths had crossed.

The replicate opened her purse, whipped out the device, aimed it at the stage. Twin arcs of lightning erupted from the prongs. The air tingled with static electricity.

The arcs intersected in front of the dancer and her holographic twin. A shuddering *boom* rocked the hall. The 3-D doppelganger disintegrated in a cauldron of bubbling color.

The concussion lifted the flesh-and-blood dancer off her feet, sent her cartwheeling into the crowd like a human propeller. She careened through two rows of spectators, mowing them down.

Screams erupted. The crowd became a squirming mass of bodies running away from the stage. Corbet lost sight of Spartan, realized the alien had created pandemonium to engineer an escape.

The man who'd hollered at Corbet got tangled in somebody's feet, fell on his face. His female companion was slammed from behind and landed atop him.

Lis and two other commandos appeared with their strange weapons, yelling at the crowd to clear a path.

More people tripped and fell, were run over by the stampede. Corbet leaped atop a two-deep pile of human beings, hating to increase their suffering but needing an elevated perch to see over the crowd.

He spotted the replicate. Spartan had broken free of the melee, was racing down the aisle. Lis and the commandos were 50 feet behind, struggling to push through hundreds of panicked individuals.

Four agents appeared on the far side of Lucas Tyrell, approaching from the other end of the aisle.

"The girl!" Corbet shouted, pointing out the target.

"Shoot her!"

The agents drew handguns. Spartan was faster. The replicate raised an arm over her head and pirouetted the device on her palm.

Hideous screeching filled the air. A wave of pulsating energy erupted, cascaded into the agents. The section of floor beneath them exploded. The quartet tumbled through the air in a storm of blood and debris.

Lis and the commandos broke free of the crowd. Spartan whirled, fired the twin streams of lightning at them.

Two commandos went down. Puffs of black smoke wafted from their chests as the beams lanced through them, intersecting behind their backs to complete the deadly circuit.

Only Lis was left alive. She dropped to her knees, assumed an odd shooting stance. Leaning forward with the gun butt pressed to her shoulder, she gripped the front of the barrel and curled her other hand around the trigger.

Before she could shoot, a frightened teenage girl cradling a baby entered her line of fire.

"Out of the way!" Lis shouted.

Spartan didn't hesitate. The twin shafts of energy curved around the girl, missing the baby's head by inches.

Lis leaped to the side. The move saved her life. The beams intersected, but on her right thigh instead of her chest.

Her leg spasmed. She fell, screaming.

But somehow she got off a shot. From her weapon, a piercing whine and a burst of white light filled the hall. She missed Spartan, but the blast ripped apart a chunk of flooring, spraying the replicate with fragments of tile. One piece went deep into Spartan's shoulder. Blood sprayed from the wound. The replicate let out an unearthly screech, more anger than pain.

That cellular instability seemed to run amok. Spartan's right leg and left arm shook violently. A compact appendage sprouted from the side of the replicate's neck. It terminated in a misshapen human hand, seven long fingers with no thumbs.

Spartan whirled toward Corbet. He dove to the floor as the lightning erupted again. As he hit the deck, the psyts flew from his hand and were crushed by the stampeding crowd.

The alien turned and ran. Corbet stood up, shaken but unhurt, relieved by his good fortune. Then he realized he hadn't been the target.

Aggie had been standing behind him. She was sprawled on her back, unmoving. The right side of her jacket beneath the shoulder revealed a pair of black smudges. Nearby lay her Glock, the top of its barrel smoldering, as if it had caught one of the electrocuting beams.

"Aggie!"

He rushed to her side, shook her motionless body. Some mad, grief-stricken part of him willed her to open her eyes, willed her to return to him.

"Aggie! No... No!"

His grief morphed into despair...

And despair into murderous rage.

He whirled toward the retreating figure. Spartan was heading for a closed maintenance door at the far end of the aisle. Corbet ran to the fallen Lis.

The commando's face was wracked by pain. Still clutching her energy weapon, she tried to stand. She collapsed as she put weight on her injured leg.

"Give it to me!" Corbet yelled, pointing at her gun.

Lis hesitated.

"Gimme the goddamn thing!"

She smacked the weapon into his palms.

"Kinetic radiating weapon, takes three seconds to recharge between shots. Make sure you brace yourself. It's got an offset recoil unlike anything you've ever..."

But Corbet was already running after Spartan. The commando's final words were lost in a miasma of vengeful fury.

89

THE SIT ROOM HAD SUCCUMBED to a nervous hysteria. Agitated whispers flickered through the air. Everyone was glued to overlapping bursts of radio chatter from the Javits. Only Grobbs seemed immune, shrouded in monk-like calm.

"Where the hell did she go?" a radio voice wondered.

"Multiple casualties!" someone else hollered. "We need medics!"

"Last confirmed location is—"

"You're breaking up, Tomas! Say again!"

"Repeat, last confirmed location, Level 3—"

"Goddammit, he's not up here!"

The frequency-hopping telecom traffic ended abruptly, enveloping them in silence.

"What's happening?" Van Zeeland demanded.

All eyes locked onto the young captain monitoring the nets. "Sir, I don't know. We lost all communications from our units in midtown Manhattan. I'm running diagnostics to determine a cause—"

"Don't bother," Grobbs said. "He must have activated the interference again. We won't be able to restore communications in time. We need to order the B-2 to launch its missile."

Van Zeeland glanced at the clock. 11:50.

"We can wait another few—"

"No sir, he could be trying to exit the building as we speak. We can't risk him escaping."

Grobbs picked up the phone, a direct line to the bomber crew. "Give the order, Mr. President. Now."

Every face in the room turned to Van Zeeland. He shook his head and prayed he wasn't making the worst decision of his life.

"No. We wait."

90

CORBET GRIPPED THE ENERGY WEAPON with both hands and lunged through the open maintenance door. Spartan had shot off the lock and disappeared inside.

It was a small janitor's closet with no other exits. That hadn't stopped the alien from blasting a hole through the back wall and escaping into a dark shaft.

The good news was that Spartan was running away. The neuropox must still be gestating. Had the plague been ready for dispersal, he would have had no reason to retreat.

Corbet entered the shaft, aware he was on his own. His radio had stopped functioning. Spartan was hitting them with the interference again, which meant there was no way of informing the other teams of his whereabouts. He didn't care. No one could help him now anyway.

He tried to control his rage, not dwell on Aggie's fate. He needed to think rationally, figure out what

Spartan would do.

Knowing that his identity was compromised, the alien would have to assume the Javits was surrounded. Troops would be lying in wait at every exit. Even with his device and superior strength, he'd be hard-pressed to withstand a large contingent of soldiers.

He won't try to get out of the building.

Avoiding further confrontation until the neuropox gestated made sense. His priority would be safeguarding that vial.

He'll find a place to hide.

The pandemonium in Hall 3-B should have alerted the crowds to exit the facility. But Corbet had heard no alarms going off, no announcements urging evacuation. The interference must be knocking out those systems as well. In all likelihood, thousands of people would still be inside when Spartan unleashed the plague.

Not that it ultimately mattered. In fact, nothing mattered anymore.

Except killing the bastard.

Corbet made his way along the narrow passage. It was just high enough to stand upright. An overhead river of suspended pipes, cable conduits and sealed vent shafts dangled inches from his head. The passage was dimly lit. Low-wattage bulbs spaced every 30 feet provided just enough light to navigate.

A series of wet spots dotted the floor. The glow from one of the bulbs revealed the spots bore a reddish tinge. It was Spartan's blood. Lis had done some damage.

Corbet moved forward at a quick pace. There didn't seem to be any obvious hiding places. Spartan couldn't come leaping out at him. Still, he kept the gun raised, ready for surprises.

He reached a fork where a side tunnel intersected. Seeing no more signs of blood along either shaft, he hesitated, uncertain which way to go. He took a guess, chose the diverging route.

This tunnel was even narrower, barely wide enough for a broad-shouldered man. Overhead, a parallel set of electrical conduits gave the impression of an upside-down railroad track.

Fifty feet along, the tunnel terminated at a wall. The conduits made a 90 degree downward turn, plunged into a vertical shaft. A steel-runged ladder was bolted to the side.

He leaned over the edge. The shaft was unlit. He could see maybe 10 feet. Beyond that was a well of darkness.

Spartan's a climber. This would appeal to him.

It was as good a guess as any. He tucked the gun under his arm, swung hands and feet onto the rungs and began the descent.

A dozen feet down, the shaft intersected another horizontal passage. Corbet paused on the ladder, squinted into the dark tunnel. He could just make out a pale glow in the distance, maybe a hundred feet away.

He strained to pierce the gloom, looking for signs that Spartan had come this way. He swiped his finger across a nearby wet spot, held the finger up to his face. But the lighting was too dim to ascertain if it was blood.

He licked the finger. Immediately, he spat, wiping a sleeve across his tongue to get rid of the aftertaste. Not blood, something vile and metallic. Oil or grease.

He faced another decision: continue descending or take this diverging route. Before he could choose, a faint sound filtered through the horizontal passage. He leaned into the tunnel, straining to hear.

A chill went through him. He'd encountered the sound once before, on Friday night up on the mountain. It was the same gurgling noise Spartan had made up in the tree when changing back into his native form.

He eased off the ladder, tiptoed down the passage. The distant light emanated from a low-wattage work lamp strung up beside a closed door. The gurgling intensified as he approached.

Blackened metal on the door's lock indicated the mechanism had been burned through. Corbet gripped the knob, yanked back the door and lunged inside.

It was a lavatory, unfinished. He'd accessed it through some kind of service portal. He was in a part of the convention center that was undergoing expansion and renovation.

A line of stalls were in place but sinks and toilets remained stacked against a wall, awaiting installation. Some of the floor was finished with tiles. But in other sections even the subfloor was missing, exposing electrical conduits and plumbing.

The room had no other egress. A carpenter's outline on plasterboard marked the site of a future door, the lavatory's connection to the outside world.

The gurgling emanated from the farthest stall. The door was closed. The replicate's attire lay on the floor outside. Along with the ruffled skirt, peasant blouse and shoes, there was a wig, padded bra and special panties with a gaff for hiding the male bulge.

Spartan had put great effort into his transvestite costume. But no further disguises were needed. The alien would make his last stand uncloaked, his true identity revealed for all to see. Once the neuropox was released and humanity's demise assured, perhaps he'd leave the world in a suicidal blaze of glory. Or perhaps he'd fight to the death, gaining perverse pleasure in his final moments, knowing his destroyers were equally doomed.

Corbet raised the gun. Adrenaline pumping, he tiptoed across the floor, inching closer to the stall. He hoped the gurgling noise would keep Spartan from hearing his approach. His best chance to take Spartan was during a metamorphosis.

He reached the stall, being careful not to get so close that his feet could be glimpsed through the door's open bottom. The gurgling continued unabated. His arrival had gone unnoticed.

More luck was with him. Spartan must have figured he'd eluded any pursuers. He hadn't bothered latching the door. It was slightly ajar.

Corbet lifted his right foot, kicked with all his might.

The door slammed inward. Spartan was hunched down at the back wall, nestled against the waste pipe and cold-water line for the uninstalled toilet. Corbet froze, momentarily too stunned to pull the trigger.

The nightmarish image imprinted on his brain in one gestalt instant. Bulging muscles. Sandpaper skin. Gaping mouth with a double set of teeth, the front ones straight from vampire land. Black eyes without irises or pupils.

But it was the triangular face that was truly monstrous. Still being genetically sculpted from human to alien form, it was a clump of open sores, each leaking rivulets of inky fluid. Worse, the eyes, nose, and mouth of Lucas Tyrell remained discernible, flowing like mercury across the mutating visage.

Below the neck, the transformation appeared complete. One clawed hand gripped the device. The other held the neuropox vial. The vapor within glowed violet.

The gurgling stopped. The vampire mouth opened wide, emitted an snarl of animal rage. Spartan whipped up the device, pointed the prongs at him.

Corbet squeezed the trigger.

A burst of white light. A shrieking whine that made his teeth hurt.

The energy blast caught Spartan on the right side of his lower torso. The monstrosity fired an instant later.

A static charge filled the air, made Corbet's hair stand on end. His gun's offset recoil saved his life, throwing him sideways instead of backward. The device's twin arcs missed his head by inches, intersected on the wall behind him.

The blast wave hurled Corbet out into the middle of the lavatory. He crash-landed on an unfinished section of floor, cried out in pain as his shin cracked against a water pipe.

Spartan limped from the stall, a seven-foot tower of rage. Dark fluid oozed from the torso wound. Human and alien features continued their struggle for dominance on that horror show of a face.

Corbet twisted around, squeezed the trigger. Nothing happened. Then he remembered Lis saying something about a three-second recharge.

Spartan whipped up his device. On Corbet's weapon, an LED flashed green.

They fired at the same instant.

91

GROBBS LOST HIS ICY COOL, glared at Van Zeeland from the far end of the table.

"Mr. President, do the right thing. Give the order now."

It was 11:54. Van Zeeland still hesitated. For all they knew, Spartan had been taken down, the threat eliminated.

"We're still in contact with the B-2?" he asked.

"Yes sir," Gen. Rosario said. "They're well beyond the blackout perimeter."

"Mr. President, it's time," Grobbs said, his tone rising in frustration. "Give the goddamn order!"

Van Zeeland stood. The few officials still in their seats rose with him. Every face in the room seemed caught between anticipation and dread.

"Launch," the President ordered.

Grobbs snatched up a phone. "Able Victor One, you are go for Operation Deliverance."

The general paused, waiting for confirmation. Then...

"Missile away. Three minutes, seven seconds to impact."

"God help us all," Edelstein whispered.

92

CORBET'S AIM WAS DEAD-ON. SO was Spartan's. From this distance, neither of them could miss. They didn't. But neither shot reached its target.

The electrical arcs from Spartan's device and the blast from Corbet's gun somehow neutralized one another. But their energies didn't dissipate. Instead, they melded together into a violet-tinged light that leapfrogged across the lavatory's unfinished floor. The light touched Corbet's bare hands and face, stinging his flesh like angry hornets.

The floor lost its solidity, became an undulating wave. Tiles splintered. Jagged shards sailed through the air. Pipes split open, blasted pressurized streams of hot and cold water across the walls and ceiling.

The floor turned as brittle as sheet glass, gave way with a thunderous crack. Corbet, Spartan, and the entire lavatory spilled into an abyss.

Corbet nestled his head in his arms, shielding himself from the cocoon of debris tumbling with him. The coalescing energies had destroyed more than just the floor. Supporting beams must have been weakened too, collapsing under the lavatory's weight.

The mass picked up speed. Corbet braced himself for the inevitable landing. Pain whipped his thoughts back to the real world as he hit bottom in a din of cracking porcelain and groaning steel. He ricocheted off a dislodged sink, tumbled head over heels to land hard against a carton of supplies.

He staggered to his feet. A wave of dizziness threatened to bowl him over. He grabbed hold of a rebar protruding from a chunk of fractured concrete, hung on until the vertigo passed.

They'd landed in a basement. Like the lavatory, it was unfinished. Conduits, pipes and vent shafts awaited final connection. A dimly lit utility corridor led off into the distance.

The broken pipes created a series of waterfalls cascading down from the remnants of the lavatory. Corbet was already soaked. The deluge smothered the debris cloud, drowning the dust and forming a shallow stream. The water flowed out into the corridor, lured by a bubbling drain.

Much of the rubble had landed in a twisted heap in the center of the floor. Spartan was nowhere to be seen – he must be buried under the pile. Corbet's last-second bounce had saved him from a similar fate.

Wincing, he took a step toward the corridor. Although no bones seemed broken, he was bruised and throbbing, a walking cyst of pain.

Behind him, the gurgling noise restarted.

Corbet searched frantically for the gun. It had slipped from his fingers during the fall. He couldn't find it.

He spotted something else, a small object submerged in three inches of water, aglow with violet light. The neuropox vial was caught in the current, picking up speed as it flowed toward the drain.

As Corbet watched in horror, a loosened chunk of concrete dropped from above. It fell into the fast-moving stream, landing right on top of the vial.

Fearing the worst, he dropped to his knees and lifted the heavy chunk out of the water. Miraculously, the vial was intact. The substance that enclosed the neuropox was significantly tougher than normal glass.

He snatched the vial from the stream. It was surprisingly heavy and ice cold. But the vapor remained sealed inside. He hoped that meant the neuropox was still gestating.

Behind him, the gurgling stopped. The debris pile groaned and twisted. Clawed hands ripped their way free.

Spartan rose from the rubble, a terrifying phoenix. The transformation was complete, the last remnants of Lucas Tyrell eradicated. Black eyes, cold and featureless, locked onto the vial in Corbet's hand.

Spartan blinked. The eyes changed, became something akin to human. White corneas blossomed and within them, vivid green irises. There was no disguising the anger and hate in those glimmering orbs.

The alien had lost his device. One clawed hand gripped the side of his torso where Corbet's energy beam had scored a hit. Yet even with Spartan weaponless and injured, Corbet knew he was outmatched.

Gripping the vial, he turned and slogged through the corridor. Loud splashing came from behind him. He glanced around. Spartan was on all fours, bounding toward him, sending up plumes like a jet ski.

The alien was closing fast. In seconds it would be over.

Up ahead was a narrow ascending staircase. But he'd never reach it in time.

He arrived at the drain. Water spiraled into the round opening. The drain was covered by a metal grille but the gods of reconstruction were smiling on him. The grille was new, wasn't screwed down yet.

He wrenched it out to expose the submerged drainpipe, plunged the hand with the vial deep into its turbulence.

"Stay back!" he warned. "Stay back or I drop it!"

Spartan halted three paces away, rose to his full height. Smoldering green eyes focused on Corbet's face, then on the drain. The alien was calculating his chances, weighing the odds of pouncing and snatching the vial before Corbet could release it into the sewer system.

"Dune noth befoolsh en yuwall liv."

It took Corbet a moment to comprehend the odd speech with its background of hissing waterfalls.

Do not be foolish and you will live.

"Not foolish," he warned, pointing his other hand at the submerged vial. "Come any closer and I let it go. Understand?"

Spartan got the message. He backed away, squatted in the stream.

The alien spoke again. "Give me the vial and you are free to go."

Even if Spartan kept that promise, Corbet wasn't about to hand it over. He should simply open his fist and release the damn thing. With any luck, the vial was small enough to get sucked past a drainage trap or other obstructions. It could end up in the depths of the storm sewer system, maybe ultimately at the bottom of the Hudson.

Letting go of the vial had one big drawback, however. Corbet would relish his heroic action for about five seconds, which was about how long he figured it would take Spartan to tear him limb from limb. Committing suicide wasn't an attractive option. There had to be another way, some means of breaking the stalemate while still keeping the neuropox out of Spartan's grasp.

But if there was a viable Plan B, it wasn't coming to him at the moment. Stalling was the only option that came to mind. Sooner or later, help would find its way down here. He needed to keep the alien engaged, keep him talking.

"How do I know you'll let me go if I hand it over?"

"Last night I let you to live."

"Only because it served your purposes, so don't insult my intelligence. And by the way, what have you got against intelligence? You're a smart son of a bitch. Why rob the human race of it?"

The triangular face contorted into what Corbet took for a brooding expression. "Your species perceives intelligence as a gift, but it is a curse. That vial offers your salvation."

"Salvation?"

"From the Consortium. Centuries from now, when your world becomes technologically advanced enough to be offered membership, they will make open contact. But their motivations are not noble. The Consortium will exploit your intelligence, trap your species in perpetual bondage."

"They're going to enslave us?"

"A more sophisticated form of servitude. The Consortium conquers not by force, but by the cunning methodology of the plutocrat. The advancements you're being given are intended to increase your productivity and set the stage for economic subjugation.

"Your species, your entire planet, will be turned into a manufacturing hub whose primary purpose is supplying products and services to the Consortium's ruling classes. It is similar to how your own richer and more advanced countries use and abuse Third World nations."

Corbet felt something hard and metallic rub his submerged wrist. He glanced into the drain. A four-inch piece of broken pipe had lodged against his arm.

Shouts echoed from somewhere behind and above them. Commandos or agents must have found their way into the remnants of the lavatory.

Keep him occupied, Corbet thought. *Keep him talking.*

"I still don't get it. Why destroy our brainpower?"

"Intelligent species become addicted to technology. This concentrates wealth in the hands of the few and renders the majority economic pawns. Such societies ultimately degenerate into ever more violent wars."

Like the way it happened on your planet.

"The loss of your intelligence will ensure your liberty. Once your species is freed from self-awareness and allowed to return to its wild nature, the Consortium will abandon its plans for Earth. Future investment in your planet will be deemed unprofitable."

Corbet finally saw through to the heart of Spartan's rage. The alien hadn't been able to save his own species from the Consortium. In his twisted mind, the human race was a surrogate for that salvation.

Never mind that billions of us will die in the collapse of civilization.

Spartan was insane. His plan was the offspring of deep personal suffering and a festering hatred that had anesthetized empathy. Even so, his craziness bore a kernel of rationality. If Earth was truly fated to be turned into some Third World factory for an alien civilization, his solution made sense from a certain demented perspective.

More shouts came from above, closer this time. But in Corbet's submerged hand, the vial suddenly lost its coldness, grew warm to the touch. Instinctively, he knew what the temperature change signified.

Gestation was complete.

Spartan seemed to sense it as well. The alien compressed his powerful arms and legs against the floor, preparing to attack.

The piece of broken pipe remained lodged against Corbet's arm. He wiggled his hand, manipulated the pipe past the vial until it was pinched between his thumb and index finger.

"I understand now," he said, slowly pulling his arm out of the drain. "Intelligence is a burden and you're just trying to help. So...

"It's all yours!"

Corbet whipped up his hand, threw the pipe behind Spartan while palming the vial. The alien made a grab for what he thought was the neuropox. He missed. The pipe splashed into the water behind him.

The ploy gave Corbet precious seconds. He dashed into the staircase, bounded up the steps two at a time. His pain-wracked body protested the exertion, wanting him to stop.

I stop I die.

He made it halfway to the closed door at the top of the stairs when a shriek of alien wrath filled the air. His deception had been exposed.

Seven steps to go.

Behind him, violent splashing. Spartan was in pursuit.

Five steps...

Three...

He grabbed the knob. Luck was with him. It wasn't locked. He whipped open the door, lunged out into a brightly lit corridor. Dozens of OmegaExpo patrons were milling about, puzzled by their nonfunctional phones but otherwise oblivious to the recent turmoil.

Spartan caught Corbet from behind. A claw raked his upper back. The pain was excruciating, worse than anything he'd ever experienced.

He jerked forward, heard a mournful tearing sound – his own flesh being flayed from his back. His cry of agony was drowned out by crowd screams as they saw what pursued him.

93

SHOTS RANG OUT AS THREE agents punched through the wall of fleeing civilians and opened fire with pistols. Corbet staggered forward with the vial, trying to get out of their line of fire.

The projectile gunfire didn't bring Spartan down. Alien legs tensed like coiled springs. Spartan pushed off the floor, catapulted 15 feet through the air, landed amid the agents in a tornado of slashing claws. In seconds, they were on the floor, wounded or dead.

Corbet hobbled after the retreating crowd. His back pulsated, the pain nearly unbearable. Tears filled his eyes, almost blinding him.

He reached an ascending escalator, lunged onto the moving stairs. He glanced back. Spartan had reached the foot of the escalator. The alien body compressed again, preparing to leap.

Corbet raced up the final few steps, stumbled out onto a deserted mezzanine. The low ceiling ended a few yards ahead as the mezzanine opened into a spacious concourse ringed by overhead balconies.

Instinct warned him to turn. Spartan was airborne, coming at him. Corbet twisted sideways, managed to evade a slashing claw. But one of those powerful legs caught him in the chest, sent him hurtling out onto the concourse. He landed on his back, igniting fresh waves of torment.

He struggled to stand but made it only to his knees. His brutalized body had reached its limit.

And then he lifted his gaze to the overhanging balcony and saw something that gave him hope. Spartan was still a few feet under the balcony. Corbet, with all his remaining strength, raised the neuropox vial over his head like a beacon.

“C’mon, you psycho freak! Come and get it!”

Spartan lunged at him, a blur of rage. The moment the alien emerged into the open, the two dozen commandos and agents perched on the balcony opened fire.

“Trick or treat, asshole,” Corbet hissed, diving to the floor.

Thunder echoed through the concourse. Spartan writhed beneath a hailstorm from kinetic radiating guns, assault rifles and machine pistols. Corbet shielded the vial against his chest. He tucked into a fetal position, making himself as small a target as possible.

Energy blasts and bullets tore through alien flesh. It seemed like every square inch of Spartan was being simultaneously pulverized. Blood geysered from a hundred wounds. The commandos’ weapons did the most damage, blasting away chunks of flesh, exposing sinew and bone.

Spartan staggered back under the balcony to escape the fusillade. But Capt. Doughy and four more Mantis One commandos lunged off the escalator, blocking his escape. Their weapons screamed. The blasts forced Spartan back into the open concourse and into the withering overhead barrage.

It was too much for even the alien's powerful body to absorb. Corbet caught a final glimpse of those furious green eyes before they slithered shut and Spartan collapsed to the floor.

Doughy's shouts rose above the din, ordering them to cease fire. A blessed silence filled the concourse.

Spartan's body metamorphosed, but in a manner unlike his previous replications. It was as if some ultimate cellular instability had been triggered, driving his DNA into wild transmutation. Within seconds, head, torso and appendages compacted into a dense blob of protoplasm the size of a medicine ball.

Corbet uncurled from his fetal pose, surprised he hadn't been hit by any ricocheting bullets. And then he realized he'd congratulated himself too soon. Bloody holes in the front and back of his right shoulder revealed a shot had gone clean through.

He opened his fist with the neuropox vial. It was still warm to the touch. But the violet gas remained safely contained.

The human race had been spared.

94

COMMUNICATIONS HAD BEEN REESTABLISHED WITH the Javits. But everyone in the Sit Room still struggled to make sense of the muddled reports cascading from the speakers.

Gen. Grobbs cupped the mouthpiece of his phone. His booming voice pierced the info-fog.

"They got him! They got Spartan! The neuropox is safe!"

Van Zeeland glanced at the missile countdown display. Twelve seconds to impact.

He bolted the length of the table, snatched the phone from Grobbs' hand.

"Able Victor One, this is the President! Abort! Abort!"

95

MAJOR BANDER STOOD IN THE middle of barricaded Eleventh Avenue with two companies of Army Rangers, watching hundreds of civilians pour from the exits. Emergency systems in the Javits had come back online following the termination of the interference. Sirens nearly drowned out the cacophony of evacuation.

And then he heard a more ominous sound, the whine of an approaching subsonic missile. He looked up, saw the telltale streak over the western skies beyond the Hudson. Impact would occur in a matter of seconds.

There was no sense running. Escape wasn't possible.

The missile suddenly went into a precipitous dive, as if its guidance system had received a last-moment course correction. Instead of slamming into the convention center, it hit the river behind the complex with a thunderous clap.

The impact created a waterspout that rose above the building's highest point, its 15-story-tall lobby. Bander remained still, ready to accept the inevitable followup detonation that presumably would wipe out multiple city blocks. He'd suspected the generals would employ such a tactic. It's what he would have done.

But no explosion came. The missile's controller not only had altered the missile's course in those final seconds, he'd disarmed the warhead as well. The only aftereffect was cool moisture from the diffusing waterspout, falling upon Bander's face like the gentlest of rains.

96

CORBET'S ADRENALIZED BODY QUARANTINED THE worst of the pain, enabling him to sit up. Commandos and agents crowded around him. Others kept their weapons trained on the bloody sphere into which Spartan had reverted, alert for signs of movement.

A familiar face bullied its way through the group.

"The vial," Mavenhall demanded.

Corbet extended his hand. Mavenhall signaled to someone behind them. A bearded man in a hazmat suit approached Corbet. Six similarly dressed specialists followed, three to a group. Each team manhandled a fridge-sized bio-containment unit mounted on a dolly.

The first team parked its BCU at Spartan's body. The other team nestled its unit next to Corbet.

"Remain perfectly still," the bearded man ordered, his voice muffled behind the hood. "I'm going to remove the vial from your hand."

Corbet wagged his head. Even that slight movement triggered a tsunami of agonies, including a new pain on his left thigh. He looked down, saw a blood-soaked rip across his pants where he'd been grazed by a ricocheting bullet.

The bearded man extended a tool resembling a nutcracker toward Corbet's palm. He clamped its padded jaws around the tiny hourglass, moved the vial away from Corbet's fingers with the caution of someone handling nitroglycerin. One of the hazmat men unlatched the BCU. There was a loud hiss as the door with the porthole whisked open.

At that moment, Spartan came alive.

A writhing tentacle shot out of the spherical blob, so fast that none of the commandos or agents had time to react. The tip of the tentacle sprouted a triple-clawed hand that snatched the vial from the startled hazmat chief.

A claw lanced downward with the force of a nail gun, puncturing the top of the vial. Corbet watched in dread as a trickle of violet gas oozed from the tiny hole.

Doughy and the commandos opened fire. Their energy weapons severed the tentacle. The vial fell from the clawed hand.

Mavenhall snatched the vial before it touched the floor. Clutching it to his chest, he lunged toward the

BCU. But his action had come too late. The vapor wormed out from between his fingers, began to envelop his palm.

Knowing he was contaminated, Mavenhall didn't hesitate. He threw himself into the BCU and yanked the door shut.

Pneumatics squealed, sealing the door. Exterior LEDs turned green, indicating the BCU's atmosphere was contained. As far as Corbet could tell, none of the gas had escaped into the outside air.

He made eye contact with Mavenhall through the porthole. They stared at one another from opposite sides of the glass, both aware they now occupied separate realities across a chasm that could never be breached. For the first time in Corbet's life, he perceived Mavenhall without anger and hatred.

He gave a nod, acknowledging the colonel's selfless act. And then the multiplying neuropox filled the BCU's interior, shrouding Mavenhall in a cloud of violet.

Corbet heard someone talking, realized an Army medic was leaning over him. But the man's speech was garbled, the words incomprehensible

Sounds faded. Vision blurred. A dense fog enveloped him.

He felt Aggie's touch. They were together again, cradling one another within some wondrous realm beyond life and death. And then even those feelings dissolved, leaving him with a sensation of falling into an unknown future.

97

NIGHTTIME. THE FAMILIAR STREET IN Tribeca. Just ahead, towering over that converted warehouse, the Statue of Liberty rose majestically, its head and torch arm cloaked in fog.

The feral humans crept through the mists on all fours, oblivious to his presence. The overgrown buildings and rusted vehicles; the stink of garbage and decaying flesh; the toy ray gun embedded in macadam – it was all the same, icons of this strange realm that melded elements of the past and future into a skewed reflection of the real world.

The violet light blazed from the statue's torch, burning away the fog to reveal Spartan in his native alien form. Glaring down at Corbet, the countenance seemed malignantly alive, as potent as ever.

The Ghost Child appeared on cue, translucent and unearthly, long blond hair framing her angelic face, nightgown cloaking her figure.

"We have to go."

"Go where?"

"To the beginning."

She pointed at the statue, reached her hand toward his.

"I don't understand," he said, determined not to retreat even though the fear was as strong as ever. "Who are you?"

"Fall for the future."

He met her gaze, realized for the first time that she was more than just a stand-in for humanity's fate, more than just a symbol of a lost past and a debased future.

He pushed through his fear, reached out and took hold of her tiny hand. Her fingers, initially cool to the touch, rapidly warmed, as if his body heat was flowing into her. She began to lose her translucent quality, slowly solidified into a normal little girl. Strangest of all, she looked vaguely familiar.

"Who are you?" he asked again.

Her answer was to turn and walk toward the Statue, leading Corbet toward the distant colossus. Spartan's face seemed to grow angrier as they approached. The light from the torch became more intense, narrowing into a beam that spotlighted the two of them. Corbet had to squint to see where he was walking.

Yet somehow, together, Corbet and the little girl began to absorb that light. The torch's energy dissipated. Its power faded. Corbet thought he heard a distant shriek of alien rage.

Spartan's face disintegrated, crumbling into a rain of dust and dirt. In its place, the real Miss Liberty emerged. Her torch took on a golden hue, obliterating the last traces of violet and melting away the remaining fog. That new light spread through the city like a healing sunrise. Signs of apocalyptic death and decay vanished. Feral humans rose triumphantly to their feet.

A new day came upon the world.

98

MORE THAN TWO WEEKS HAD gone by since the events of that fateful weekend. Since he'd lost Aggie.

Corbet drove north on Interstate 95 in the rented car, heading for the familiar destination on the outskirts of Baltimore. He'd made this trek daily since his release six days ago from Bethesda.

The day was beautiful, crisp and clear, the temperature hovering in the low 70s. He hung his arm out the window, inhaled sweet honeysuckle. The scent reminded him of traveling with Aggie in the Trailblazer.

Sadness touched him as he thought of her. He averted further emotional distress by returning his mind to yesterday's meeting with Dr. Jarek. Their talk had answered some lingering questions and filled in missing pieces of the far-ranging puzzle the media had dubbed the Spartan Affair.

President Van Zeeland had divulged most of the story involving Preceptor and Spartan to the world a few days after the events at the Javits. His revelatory prime-time speech had inspired some in the press to call him the first Presidential whistleblower in history. Some commentators and bloggers praised his courage for exposing secrets dating back to the Eisenhower administration.

Others, however, suspected his decision was a shrewd political calculation. The American public tended to forgive individuals who admitted guilt and took full responsibility for their mistakes or failures.

And naturally, the political contingent on the other side of the Congressional aisle demanded Van Zeeland's resignation for helping to sustain a massive, five-decade deception.

But the President's travails paled in comparison to the promise of the eventual coming of the Consortium. The media was awash in stories about what would happen to humanity, how the world would be impacted, who would benefit and who would lose out.

Still, Corbet sensed the uproar over future alien visitors would die down relatively fast. An event not slated to occur for hundreds of years would fade from the public consciousness in the wake of the latest tales of catastrophe, criminality and celebrity misdeeds. Humans just weren't wired to be concerned about events so far beyond their own lifetimes. Already, much of the social discussion had shifted to various individuals involved in the Spartan Affair, relegating big-picture issues to the background.

Those individuals included astronauts Kayla Ackerman, who'd returned safely to Earth aboard a Russian Soyuz spacecraft, and Henri Renier, who was expected to make a full recovery from injuries suffered in the lifeboat crash.

The media had also tracked down and interviewed Trudi Farr, owner of See-Farr Antiques & Collectibles in Tribeca. Ms. Farr, a male-to-female transvestite, had enabled Spartan's final metamorphosis, the one not involving genetic mutation. Her newfound fame had led her to a stint as a contestant on an upcoming reality show.

Even Smitty, the loquacious fire-police volunteer, had gained a measure of notoriety via appearances on a late-night talk program. Supposedly, he had a publishing deal in the works for a book based on his experiences, *The Night I Tracked a Monster.*

Jarek had agreed with Corbet's appraisal of the Consortium's far-future encounter with the human race: the event would shrink from the public eye. However, the Doc believed it would achieve escalating importance within niches of the scientific community.

"And there are other important aspects to consider," Jarek said. "From the Consortium's point of view, their plans for us might not happen as forecast.

"First of all, Spartan's idea that our entire planet will become some sort of Third World manufacturer serving their ruling classes represents an extreme viewpoint. Preceptor always promoted a more benign view. It was his belief that when the era of full contact finally arrives, Earth would enter into an equitable and mutually profitable partnership with the Consortium."

"But Preceptor was an AI, a machine programmed by them," Corbet argued.

"Yes. But what I'm getting to is that the truth is rarely discovered at the extremes, out where the zealots live, out where Spartan made his home. The search for truth requires skepticism, a willingness to challenge our most cherished belief systems.

"Consequently, we also must consider that Preceptor may have represented a philosophical extreme. U-OPS always took his upbeat portrayal of the Consortium with a grain of salt. We realized that the arrival of an interstellar civilization harbored unknown dangers for our way of life. Historically, at least here on Earth, cultural collisions have tended to favor the civilization possessing the higher level of technology."

"So we could suffer the fate Spartan warned us about," Corbet said. "Economic subjugation."

"Not necessarily. What I'm saying is that the truth probably lies somewhere between the visions outlined by Spartan and Preceptor. Neither as awful as Spartan's nor as wondrous as Preceptor's.

"And there's another factor. The cessation of Preceptor's technological gifts to use may force an alteration of the Consortium's entire timetable. Even though Preceptor's last transmission provided an enormous amount of data – years worth of advancements – it falls far short of the totality of technology they'd presumably planned to give us over the next few centuries.

"Will they send another vessel to continue our technological evolution? Perhaps. But the very fact that Spartan interacted with our culture and warned us of such a worst-case scenario will make our descendents more suspicious of the Consortium, more wary of all future interactions.

"Put another way, the entire Spartan Affair may have introduced an unknown X factor into the Consortium's equations for our future. Maybe this X factor will prompt them to postpone or even abandon their plans for us. Our world may have lost its luster to them. To paraphrase Spartan, future investment in our planet might be deemed unprofitable."

Corbet returned his attention to the highway as he neared the exit. Jarek's ideas and the media uproar were fascinating to speculate about. But at the end of the day, Corbet wasn't going to lose sleep over it.

That particular problem – his insomnia – had other root causes. Flashes of intense pain from his clawed back often caused him to bolt awake in the middle of the night. Prescription painkillers would subdue his physical agony. But then he'd lie awake in bed, thinking of Aggie.

He exited I-95, found his way to the Kensington-Slade Acute Care Home. Manicured lawns and flowerbeds surrounded the modern two-story building. He parked near the main entrance and retrieved a bouquet from the back seat.

The receptionist at the front desk recognized Corbet from previous visits and didn't bother having him sign in. He headed down the hall to 17-A.

"Hey girl," he said, smiling as he entered Aggie's private room. "Brought you some fresh flowers."

He laid the bouquet on her windowsill amid other arrangements and get-well cards. Many were from her fellow FBI agents.

He approached the bed. Although it hurt him to see her like this, he made an effort to stay upbeat.

"Yellow roses and orange tulips," he said, gesturing to the bouquet. "Your dad said when you were little, you really liked that color combination."

Corbet had met Aggie's parents on previous visits. But today, the two of them had the room to themselves. She looked as beautiful as ever, lying there with her eyes closed, a model of serenity. Only the rack of monitors beside the bed and the IV tubes and wires attached to her flesh revealed that she wasn't merely asleep.

He pulled up a chair, sat beside her.

"My back is feeling pretty good today," he began. "Remember yesterday, when I told you it was hurting like hell? Well, I checked with one of the docs and he thinks changes in humidity might account for why it bothers the hell out of me one day and not the next. Today is dry and yesterday was rainy, so that could explain it.

"All in all, though, I can't complain. The physical therapist gave me some exercises to do to accelerate the healing. I'm going to work at those until I'm back to one hundred percent. Well, maybe not a hundred percent, but as close to perfection as I can get. I'll have a scar the rest of my life."

He paused, wiped a bit of spittle from the edge of her mouth with a tissue. Crime scene investigators had concluded that one of the beams from Spartan's weapon had hit Aggie's Glock before completing its circuit and lancing into the flesh below her shoulder. That electrical ricochet had spared her life.

The first day he'd come here, it had felt odd talking to a woman in a coma. But since then, the one-way conversations had come to seem perfectly normal. And just because the docs said Aggie couldn't hear him didn't make it so. Maybe some of his words were getting through, reaching into her slumbering consciousness, connecting on some primal level.

As he had during previous visits, he spoke to her about many things, some serious, some not.

He talked about his last vision, where the Ghost Child seemed to become fully human, and how the two of them had witnessed Spartan's demise. He admitted that puzzling questions remained about his final excursion through that altered reality. In particular, he still wasn't sure what the little girl meant by those phrases, *to the beginning* and *fall for the future.*

He moved on to less serious topics, chuckling as he related how Smitty was enjoying a brush with fame. He expressed gratitude to the press gods for his own continuing anonymity. So far, Smitty and others he'd encountered over that fateful weekend had been persuaded not to disclose Corbet and Aggie's involvement.

President Van Zeeland's public confession also had held back certain information, including the clandestine training of psychic trackers through U-OPS. That initiative would remain in the black ops fold. Jarek and his researchers hoped the supersensory program could be redirected toward tracking enemies of the human variety.

"And speaking of anonymity, Aggie, I caught one of the news channels last night. They were saying that the soldiers and agents at the Javits who took down Spartan were helped by an unknown man, a civilian. However, no witnesses have as yet been able to identify this mysterious individual."

Corbet chuckled. "Lucky me, huh? Just because the President went into tell-all mode doesn't mean I'm ready to follow his lead. Honestly, fame, fortune and the media spotlight aren't things I'd much care for. Well, okay, that's not entirely true. The money part would be pretty cool. But it wouldn't be worth all the crap I'd have to put up with.

"But hey, girl, I'm monopolizing the conversation. Didn't come here today just to talk about Corbet Tomms. How are you doing? Nurses treating you okay? You'll tell me if you have any problems, right?"

Behind him, someone cleared their throat. Corbet stood up to face Ella DeCarlo, the staff doctor in charge of Aggie's case. A middle-aged woman with ash-gray hair and pince-nez glasses, she'd struck Corbet as ultra-competent. Googling her had confirmed his initial impression. She was a renowned expert on treating comatose patients.

"Hey, Doc. How goes it? I think our girl's looking better today. I'm seeing some color in her cheeks."

Dr. DeCarlo forced a smile, as if not wanting to dash his hopes. "How about you, Corbet? How are you feeling?"

"Recovering nicely from the crash," he said, sticking to the government's cover story, that he'd been involved in a car accident.

The Pentagon had invented a different tale of woe for Aggie: accidental electrocution while on a classified assignment. Corbet had the feeling Dr. DeCarlo didn't buy into either of the lies. But considering that the Kensington-Slade Acute Care Home had major contracts with the feds for treating injured soldiers and agents, she was savvy enough not to rock the boat.

"I have some news," Dr. DeCarlo said. "It's not good, I'm afraid. Frankly, I'm unsure whether you should be the first one I notify. But I'm going to take a chance and bend the rules. Something tells me you're the appropriate person.

"We've been doing routine blood tests on Aggie. This morning we found something unexpected. She's pregnant."

It was the last thing in the world Corbet expected to hear.

"How long?" he whispered.

"Best estimate, a little over two weeks. Still in the embryonic stage."

"Two weeks? That's when Aggie and I... when we were..."

He trailed off, knowing he was the father, knowing that the child had been conceived during that mad, aphrodisiac-fueled sex within the spaceship, within Preceptor.

"I'm afraid the prognosis for the embryo is poor. As I explained the other day, the nature of Agent Rittenhouse's injuries, that electrical shock, caused unusual complications. She was lucky even to have survived such a jolt. And in her condition, transferring the embryo to a surrogate mother isn't a recommended option."

Corbet felt lightheaded. He sat back down. "There's nothing you can do?"

"I'm afraid not."

"But what if Aggie comes out of the coma?"

"Certainly in that case the embryo would have a good chance to reach fetal stage and beyond. But please don't get your hopes up. As I explained earlier—"

"Yeah," he said, cutting her off. He didn't need a rehash of the diagnosis, of the thousand-to-one odds against Aggie ever waking up, odds that grew slimmer with each passing day.

"Would you mind leaving us alone?" he asked.

"Certainly. I'll be around if you want to talk."

"Thanks."

Dr. DeCarlo shut the door on the way out, giving them privacy.

Corbet leaned over the bed, kissed Aggie on the cheek. He wanted to tell her that it would have been a beautiful baby and that she would have made a great mother. But he choked on the words and closed his eyes, and settled for silence.

And in that silence, a vision came upon him, a vision unique in that it represented a symbolic journey, a passage of years rather than a singular period. The vision revealed snippets of his life in an ever-changing array. It was like some incredible version of time-lapse photography.

He saw himself making love to Aggie inside the spaceship, inside that white womb that was Preceptor.

The scene changed. He saw Aggie awake and very pregnant.

The images came faster, Aggie's belly expanding until she lay in a maternity ward, giving birth. The focus shifted at that point to their newborn, a daughter. Corbet watched in fascination as she grew from helpless infant to crawling baby to curious toddler taking her first precarious steps. The changes continued until their daughter blossomed into a little girl. She had long blond hair and an angelic face.

"The Ghost Child," he heard himself whisper.

The vision ended. Corbet opened his eyes. Excitement coursed through him. At last, he understood.

He took hold of Aggie's hand, explained it to her.

"The little girl, the Ghost Child, she's more than just a symbol. She's flesh and blood. She's ours, Aggie.

She's our child!"

It was all so clear now. He was surprised he hadn't put it together sooner.

"The Ghost Child, she showed me the way. She took me back to her own conception, *to the beginning*. But it was really you, Aggie, who made it all possible. Not just because you got pregnant. But because you were the one who made me believe in what was to come. You made me *fall for the future*.

"My visions, they always come true. I know that now. The future that I see can't be changed. It's preordained. But I never saw this future through to its end, not until this very moment.

"Do you understand, Aggie? Do you know what this means? Only one thing can happen now, one possible outcome. You're going to wake up. You're going to come out of this coma. You have to because that's the only way our little girl gets born! That's the only way my vision comes true!"

A medical device over the bed started to beep. Multicolored waveforms pulsated with renewed vigor.

Aggie's eyes flickered, cracked open. Her lips crinkled into a faint smile as she saw his face.

Dr. DeCarlo and a nurse rushed into the room and checked the monitors. They turned to Corbet with astonished looks, as if witnessing a medical miracle.

Corbet preferred to think of it as destiny.

But whatever had happened, he felt enough confidence in its power to begin thinking ahead to the day when Aggie was fully recovered, the day they could begin building a life together.

Of course, before that occurred, there would be numerous issues to resolve. For starters, they'd have to agree on a name for their little girl.

He thought Naomi sounded like a good prospect.

99

SENATOR AUDACIA BEAUMONT, CHAIRPERSON OF the new top-secret oversight committee for all Spartan-related matters, peered out the window as her helicopter circled in for a landing. The valley below, pinched between a pair of craggy mountain ranges, looked even more inhospitable than the rest of this Great Basin region of northern Nevada. At their elevation – above 5,000 feet – hardly any trees grew, just clumps of Prickly Pear cactus and loose sagebrush on parched earth.

"Leave it to the Pentagon to find a hellhole like this," she said to Conchita Perez, chief counsel for the committee and the only aide with the security clearance to accompany Audacia on this fact-finding mission.

"Yes ma'am," Conchita replied, eyes glued to her laptop.

The copter swooped below the peaks of the flanking mountains and banked gently to trace the valley's natural curvature. Audacia spotted a pair of coyotes perched on a ledge, as still as statues. The animals seemed to be staring at the isolated ranch the copter was approaching.

Blackjack Research Complex didn't look like much from the air. Besides the main house, there was a barn with a dilapidated roof, two small outbuildings and a corral penning half a dozen saddle horses. A gravel lot behind the house provided parking for about two dozen vehicles, most of them pickup trucks or SUVs.

The copter spiraled in for a landing. Audacia and Conchita disembarked before the rotors stopped turning, shielding their eyes from the dust storm created by the blades. They scurried toward the house and onto the screened front porch where Gen. Grobbs and his newly promoted aide, Col. Bander, stood waiting.

Grobbs stepped forward to shake her hand. “Senator Beaumont, welcome to Blackjack. I hope your flight wasn’t too boring.”

“Not at all. Beautiful country. Don’t think I’d want to live out here, though. It’s so incredibly isolated.”

“Just the way we like it. Would you care for refreshments?”

“We’re fine.”

“Then let’s get started.”

Grobbs led them into the house, which was divided into a series of offices and labs that performed research on high-desert flora and fauna. It was all part of the Pentagon’s cover story for Blackjack, whose real work went on far below.

The four of them proceeded to the back of the house and into a nondescript elevator. When the door closed, Col. Bander inserted a key into the control panel and typed a security code.

The elevator dropped fast. Audacia experienced a brief moment of near weightlessness.

“How far down?” she asked.

“Two hundred and ten feet to the primary lab,” Bander said. “The rest of Blackjack’s research occurs on the intermediate floors.”

“And the main lab area is effectively secured against any kind of surface penetration?”

“Yes ma’am. Protected 24/7 by hidden security assets, impervious to any imaginable disaster. It could even withstand a direct hit by a high-yield thermonuclear bomb.”

The elevator decelerated to a smooth stop and the

door whisked open. Grobbs led them down a short corridor to a steel door with biometric locks. This time, the general had the entry key, which he used in conjunction with a vascular/facial recognition scanner to gain access.

The door opened into another corridor. They passed a series of locked offices and entered the primary lab. It was a spacious half-moon-shaped chamber manned by half a dozen researchers, each one in a partitioned space full of exotic control panels with joystick controls.

The circular portion of the perimeter featured three blue-tinted window panes. All were too cloudy to see through. Audacia recognized the technology: the latest version of electrochromic glass, capable of going from opaque to transparent with a controlled burst of electricity.

"Each researcher has a specific area of expertise," Bander explained. "The joysticks enable remote handling of the hazardous materials through manipulator arms in the various containment areas. The telemanipulators also can control dozens of interchangeable robotic systems."

Audacia approached the first opaque window. "Is this where you keep it?"

"Yes, ma'am," Bander said. He accessed a control panel beneath the window and punched in a three-digit code. The smart glass surrendered its cloudiness, became fully transparent.

The chamber held Spartan's remains. The protoplasmic blob and the severed tentacle claw rested atop latticed pedestals. One of the researchers was working a manipulator arm whose jointed mechanical fingers gripped what appeared to be a pair of 10-inch metal chopsticks. As Audacia watched in fascination, the researcher plunged the two needles into the blob.

"A stimulation test," Bander explained. "We

periodically apply electrified needles in an attempt to induce a reaction."

"You mean it's still alive?"

"Yes, ma'am. Both the blob and the severed arm exhibit faint signs of activity at the cellular level."

"If we can unlock its secrets," Grobbs added, "we may open up a whole new era in the field of genetic engineering."

Audacia watched another researcher with a second set of remote arms draw syrupy fluid from the tentacle with a syringe. The syringe was placed on a conveyor belt, which carried it from the chamber through a sphincter-like opening.

"The contents of the syringe will be analyzed elsewhere," Bander said. "I don't know the purpose of this particular experiment. If you're interested, I can find out."

"No need." Audacia said. "What about safety protocols? Any chance of the organism breaching the containment area?"

"Zero possibility," Bander said.

His tone suggested the matter wasn't even worthy of debate. Audacia countered with a wry smile.

"You're claiming absolute certainty, Colonel? In my experience, there is no such thing."

"Of course. But I believe we come as close as humanly possible. All aspects of Blackjack that deal with hazardous materials are, at minimum, biosafety Level 4. The glass is multi-layered, impervious to penetration by anything less than concentrated high-velocity weapons fire. And we don't allow guns down here."

"Specimens are examined in separate sealed chambers," Grobbs added. "All testing is done remotely, including the introduction of live animals."

Conchita frowned. Audacia recalled that she was a

longtime PETA member.

"What animals?" Audacia asked.

"Mostly mice at this early stage," Bander said. "Experiments to gauge whether extraterrestrial organisms can have any effect on the earth-grown variety. So far, the most interesting development involves a family of mice who've inexplicably acquired a taste for Spartan's feces, samples of which were discovered at the Ramagano farmstead and at that rest stop where those killings took place." The colonel paused for effect. "The mice seem to prefer Spartan droppings to cheese scraps."

Conchita grimaced. Audacia allowed herself a faint smile at the idea of crap-loving rodents and moved to the next window. Bander rendered it transparent.

The second chamber contained Spartan's tuning-fork-shaped device. It floated in the air, suspended between a pair of circular plates that Audacia assumed were some kind of electromagnets. The device had been found in the rubble of the Javits basement.

"I'm pleased to say that here we've already had some breakthroughs," Grobbs said, his words tinged with guarded excitement. "Based on preliminary analysis of the device, we've isolated and identified aspects of its circuitry, which represent a degree of miniaturization on a scale well beyond our present capabilities. Some researchers believe that if we can emulate the technology, we'll usher in a whole new era of civilian and military applications."

That sounded promising to Audacia and could serve as a good fit for her own agenda. She planned to make a run at the Presidency someday. Not in the immediate future, of course. She didn't want to get entangled in Van Zeeland's mess, a political vortex likely to suck in all who ventured too close.

Before Audacia made a serious run at the White

House, she needed to elevate her political standing. One method would be to hitch her star to any technological breakthroughs that Blackjack made down here. It would be a tricky stunt to pull off, considering that the work of her committee was highly classified. Still, as chairperson, there might be a way to make it happen.

"How long before any of these applications are marketable?" she asked.

"At least seven to ten years," Grobbs said. "That presumes current funding levels."

The general's unspoken message was clear. Funnel more money to Blackjack and increase the payout. That was doable, Audacia thought. Her committee exercised defacto control over a serious percentage of the black-ops budget. And having the wily Grobbs as a political ally couldn't hurt her Presidential aspirations.

She strolled to the final window. "And what do we have behind door number three?"

Bander altered the glass. The last chamber was far larger. It reminded her of one of those authentic jungle habitats employed by modern zoos. High grass and dense foliage covered the floor. Dozens of trees and bushes from a variety of species extended their branches to the arched ceiling. A pond thick with surface algae featured a sandy rock-strewn beach. The air within the chamber bore a faint violet tinge.

"The neuropox?" Audacia asked.

Grobbs nodded. "The containment atmosphere is saturated with it. What you're looking at is an ecological microcosm of what our world would have become had Spartan's plan succeeded. Using robotic technology and a series of one-way airlocks, we've introduced the flora, as well as fauna in the form of mice and other small mammals, to study the effects of the neuropox upon different lifeforms. So far, however, the vapor has had no discernible effect on any of them. It targets only Homo sapiens."

The bushes rustled. A naked man lunged out into the open on all fours, startling Audacia and eliciting a frightened gasp from Conchita. Covered in facial hair and wearing the tattered remnants of a filthy undershirt, the man looked more animal than human.

"Meet Colonel Robert Mavenhall," Grobbs said. "What's left of him."

Audacia stared in fascination at the wild-eyed figure.

"I only wish we could acknowledge the colonel's heroism to the world," Bander said. "The life he lived and the sacrifice he made deserves to be honored."

That wasn't likely to happen, Audacia knew. Although Van Zeeland in his tell-all speech had revealed the outlines of what had occurred at the Javits on that fateful Sunday, the Pentagon had managed to convince him to keep many details classified. The official reports released to the press indicated that Col. Mavenhall had been one of those killed in the battle with Spartan and that his body had been immediately cremated to stave off the possibility of contamination.

If the real story of Mavenhall's selfless bravery at the Javits were ever revealed, his fame would rival the greatest heroes in world history. But then the media would dig into every aspect of his life. Under such microscopic examination, there was always the chance of some reporter learning the truth, that the colonel was alive. Audacia didn't even want to think about the public outrage should the electorate find out that an American hero was being kept in a cage, no matter what the reasons for his confinement.

Mavenhall crawled over to a stunted maple tree, raised his leg and urinated on the trunk. He scurried to the pond, bent his head to one of the few spots not caked in algae, flicked out his tongue and slurped at the liquid. The chamber was outfitted with hidden microphones. Audacia could hear the sounds of him lapping the water.

"Is the glass two-way?" she asked. "Is he aware of us?"

Before the officers could respond, Mavenhall provided the answer. Finishing up at the watering hole, he raised his head to focus intently on Audacia and Conchita. A crude smile rippled across his face as he gazed back and forth between them. He opened his mouth and seemed on the verge of speaking. But instead of words, a series of deep-throated grunts emerged.

He trotted around the edge of the pond, came closer to the window. Sitting down, he raised his arms like a dog lifting its front paws. Arching his head back, he spat toward the glass, spraying it with a fine mist of saliva.

"Strange and fascinating," Audacia murmured.

"Creepy and gross," Conchita added.

"It's something he does with the female researchers on occasion," Bander explained. "Our anthropology and zoology experts believe he's signaling a desire to mate. They would love to insert a female into the habitat to see what happens. But as yet, we've found no volunteers willing to spend the rest of their lives in there with him."

The colonel's black humor brought home to Audacia the reality of Mavenhall's existence. He would never leave the containment. He would grow old and die inside these walls.

Mavenhall grunted and scampered back into the bushes.

"Hard to imagine someone living like that," Conchita

said, shaking her head. "It's so sad, so tragic."

"Indeed," Grobbs said. "Yet the colonel's sacrifice also provides us a golden opportunity to study the effects of the neuropox in a controlled setting. Although it's doubtful we'll ever develop an antidote that could reverse the vapor's effects, some researchers believe a vaccine might be possible. If so, it could ensure that our species is never again threatened by such a plague."

"You're doing excellent work here, General," Audacia said. "The committee will be so informed."

She wasn't just spouting political rhetoric. The efforts being undertaken here at Blackjack represented solid baby steps toward advancing American technology to undreamt heights.

Still, Audacia couldn't help but recall part of the classified report based from the confrontation at the convention center. According to that young psychic, Spartan had warned that intelligent species become addicted to technology, and that such societies ultimately degenerate into ever more violent wars.

Nevertheless, the fact that such technology existed out among the stars represented a long-term threat. Ultimately, human civilization would need to surpass the accomplishments of the Consortium. That was the only way to guarantee that Earth remained independent and free to choose its own future.

Made in the USA
Charleston, SC
03 November 2012